An INHERITANCE *of* LIES

An INHERITANCE *of* LIES

REBECCA A. CARTER

This is a work of fiction. Names, characters, organizations, places, events, and incidents are either products of the author's imagination or are used fictitiously. Otherwise, any resemblance to actual persons, living or dead, is purely coincidental.

Published by Lake Union Publishing, Seattle

www.apub.com

Amazon, the Amazon logo, and Lake Union Publishing are trademarks of Amazon.com, Inc., or its affiliates.

EU product safety contact:
Amazon Media EU S. à r.l.
38, avenue John F. Kennedy, L-1855 Luxembourg
amazonpublishing-gpsr@amazon.com

ISBN-13: 9781662534706 (paperback)
ISBN-13: 9781662534690 (digital)

Cover design by Faceout Studio, Spencer Fuller
Cover image: © Abigail Miles / ArcAngel Images; © fotoak, © mykhailo pavlenko, © Everett Collection, © Leonid Andronov, © spaxiax / Shutterstock

Printed in the United States of America

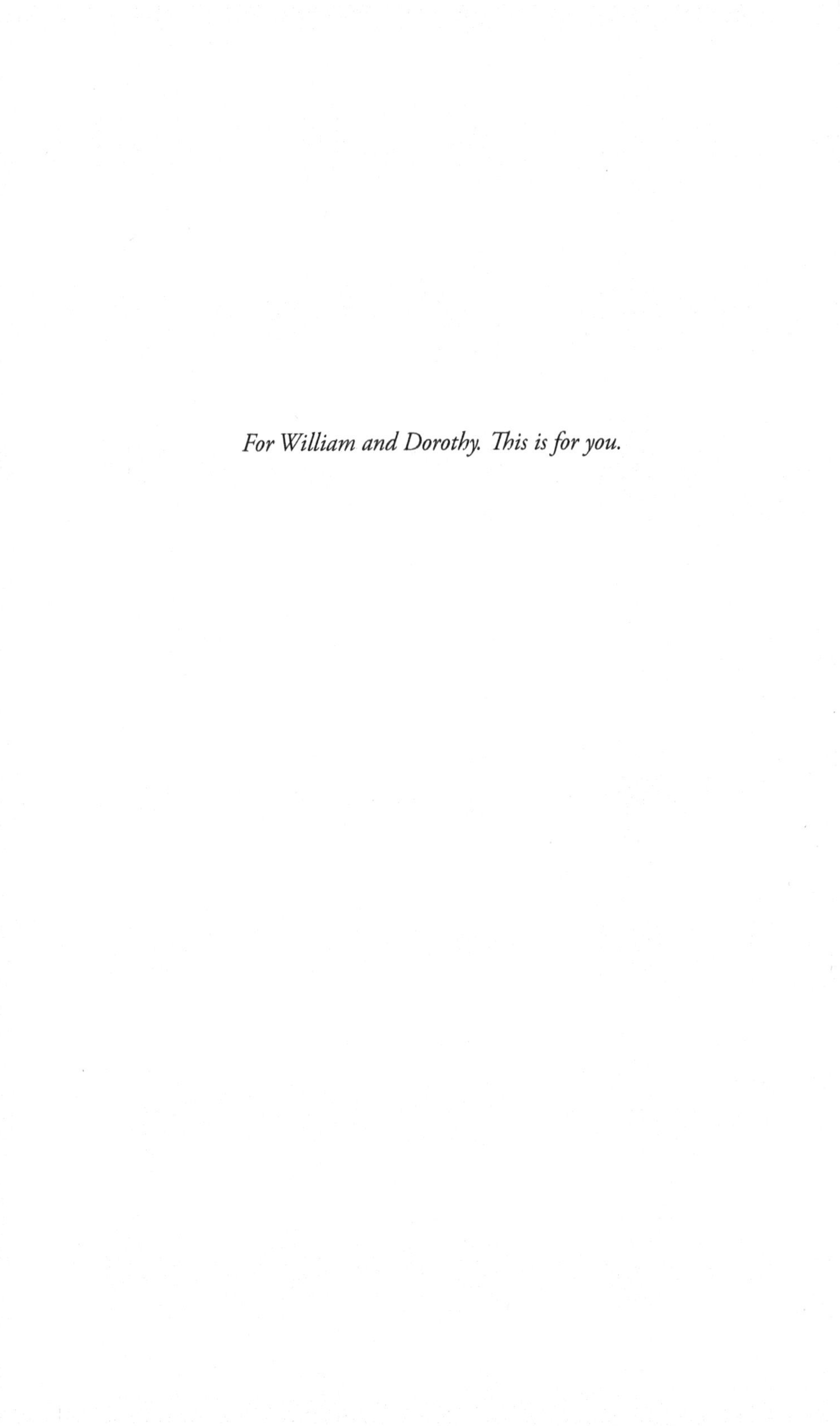

For William and Dorothy. This is for you.

Chapter One

March 21, 1915
The Bowery, Manhattan

If my parents were alive, I'd shame them and taint their reputation.

The thought strikes me as I saunter into the tavern at the Bowery. I'm not sure what raises eyebrows, quirks smiles, or creates a whiz of amused whispers in my wake. In horse race fashion, I'm betting on the fact I'm committing social suicide. Women aren't expected in taverns, especially not after sundown.

But none of this matters. These men won't remember me come tomorrow, and whose life am I about to ruin?

Not my parents'.

I'm ruining *my* life. My one and only.

Because I want to. Because I can. Because I'm desperate.

Squaring my shoulders, I plop my purse and my hat on the counter. The men next to me snatch their whiskey glasses and scurry away with bemused grins as if I were coughing up a bloody lung.

I take a deep breath to ground myself, but I grimace as cigar stench sneaks into my chest.

A part of me begs to return to Elijah and Lindsay. I can only imagine my friends' faces, going taut with shock if they learned what I am doing, and derision pushes a snicker out of me. It's strange what grief does to a person. Ten minutes ago, I was sobbing on a dark street corner a few paces from drunken sailors, and now here I am, *tittering* to myself, as if I were entertaining the lulls of a ghost.

"What may I serve you?"

A bartender stands opposite me. Blinking, in a moment of baffled thoughts, all I can utter is "What?"

He sighs and steals a worn dishcloth from his shoulder. Under his deadbeat eyes, bags are bulging. He looks old and, mostly, I can't help but notice, tired. As if he's been working for too long, which considering the time of the day, is most likely. "Do your young ears not work properly? What can I serve you?"

"But . . . I'm a . . . *young* woman." *I was kicked out of a tavern down the street ten minutes ago* is what I want to say, which triggered my sobbing episode on a corner, but I know better than tempting my luck more than I'm doing at the moment. I should stop.

"And I'm a barkeeper," he says in a huff. His forehead creases with his rising gray eyebrows, and he leans over the counter, as if to share a secret. "Can you pay your way?"

How dare he? I'm not wearing this beautiful attire, *my mother's finest*, for this man to believe I'm an urchin. My mouth hangs open, a deep furrow growing between my brows. Stepping back, I point at my garments. "Of course I can."

"Then it's none of my concern. What will you drink?"

"Oh." I shuffle through the glinting bottles on the shelves behind the barkeeper as I tug off my gloves. Most spirits make me easily tipsy, and I need to retain some veneer of clarity if I want to return in one piece to the Plaza. I just need *enough*. Enough to forget. Be someone else for a night. Be far away from my own world. "Red wine."

I shrug off my coat, casting a glance for the coat clerk. The men's jackets are piled on a stand by the entrance or slung over the back of their chairs. *Huh*, no clerk. Delightful. The site has a shine, with the green brocade paper on the walls and the low brass lamps. They could do with a little upgrade.

With a sigh, I set my coat down with my gloves. When I have my glass of wine and my coins are in the old barkeeper's hand, he shakes his head and vanishes at the back of the tavern. A younger bartender takes his place. He peers at me but says nothing.

The ambiance of the tavern settles into a background rumble, but the stares from the newcomers and the departing patrons burn on my back, some sharing whispered jests and loud guffaws. My mother's favorite silk blouse quickly turns damp with sweat.

As I pivot to the room, curling my fingers around my second wineglass, heads turn away, the tone in conversations over glasses of brandy shifts to sports and gambling, and men hide behind newspapers at their mahogany tables. I freeze. I'm like a caged tiger. An exotic bird. An attraction and an aberration.

My cheeks heat, and I manage to pass a dry gulp, as if instead of wine I were drinking sand. This is the last place I would've wound up, if my parents were still here. They taught me better than this.

What they didn't do was raise a timorous lady.

As an act of defiance, I keep my chin up and take a long draft of wine, but for all I know, I might as well be drinking the sting of my tears. Does it matter? What these rogues think of me? Tomorrow is my father's testament reading. If I ruin my reputation, from tomorrow onward I can retire into the countryside and become a lonely madwoman yelling at children from my derelict manor. Or I can head to the West Coast until gossip dies down in New York. I've heard Los Angeles is pretty this time of the year. Perhaps a bit too sprawling and prone to flooding for my taste, but neat and tidy, a bit rustic but just bustling enough. I've heard about its idyllic coastline and that it's filled with artists. It has much more sunshine than New York, and women sound freer there, which is always a perk.

If no one gets word of this, I'll return to NYU law school next week, the world moving on.

My father's fortune is now mine. I'm no different from a widow in front of the law, just turned twenty. I can do anything I want, unafraid of the consequences. The worst thing about having your wings cut is that in the freefall you realize there is nothing else to be afraid of.

I can look for a cure to my sorrows at the bottom of a bottle.

I can kiss a stranger.

I can dance on the street—lift my skirts and show my legs.

Or perhaps, even pose naked for a bohemian artist.

The possibilities are endless. All my own choosing, damn the consequences.

And all because my parents' car drove off a hill.

I tilt my head back to down the wine. The sweet warmth spreads its final notes in my chest, but sadness still presses on my soul like an anchor.

When I plop the empty glass on the counter, someone stations himself next to me. His blond hair is slicked back, and his smile goes up at the right angle. He sports fine tailored clothes. Almost in trend, there are no mends or tears. His shirt has a white collar, and a vibrant red tie is neatly loose around his neck, but the vest doesn't match the rest of his attire, as if it's the only good one he owns. Not upper class, but close. As close enough as he can get, I'm sure, which is never enough.

He clucks his tongue in teasing disapproval. "A lady shouldn't drink alone at a bar."

"And the duty of a proper man should be to leave the lady alone," I clip.

A smile. As untroubled as the man himself. "Touché."

My heart gallops. The sensible part of me asks to leave, but the part that begs to forget my life for a night keeps my calf-length boots on the spot.

"My, what do I have on my hands? A devil of the night or a proper man, Mister . . . ?"

"Jacobson," he says. "And you can bet on the former. Let me invite you to another glass of wine."

The third glass of wine and half of the fourth taste better than the first ones. The buzz finally sneaks into my head, making it easier to lose myself in this charade. Not the poor orphan, Alix. The sophisticated and mysterious lady, drinking the sorrows of her heart with a casual tête-à-tête under soft lights. It turns out Mr. Jacobson is a good talker. I don't have to put in a great effort to make him interested. He seems to love hearing himself speak just so. Low effort is what I need.

"What's your occupation, Mr. Jacobson?" I ask.

His laughter is husky. "Heard of the first transcontinental phone service in the United States that happened between Alexander Graham Bell and Thomas Watson a couple of months ago?"

"I did," I simply say. All the way from New York to San Francisco, the two men were able to speak as I'm now doing with Mr. Jacobson.

"I was part of the team that made it possible," he says with a proud smirk, caressing my wrist with his pinkie.

"Do you work for Mr. Bell?" I switch my glass to escape his fondling.

"I work for the company that erected the poles here in New York," he says, still proud as a peacock.

A silly laugh escapes my lips, but thankfully, Mr. Jacobson surely confuses my scorn with complacency as he catches my waist, pulling me close to him. He's all kinds of unscrupulous trouble disguised behind a pretty face, but as he gives a playful tap on the tip of my nose and his knuckles trail down my jawline, twitches of anxiety grip my chest.

I slap off his attempt to push a strand of hair behind my ear.

"Whoa." He furrows his brow. "What's the matter, sweetheart?"

"You won't stop *touching* me," I bite, shaking off his grip. Good Lord, what am I doing?

He takes a long draft of his whiskey and licks his lips, his sudden silence heavy in the air. "What am I supposed to do? Isn't that the reason why you're here?"

I step back. "Pardon me?"

"Come now, dear. A woman doesn't walk into a tavern alone if she's not seeking male company."

He thinks I'm a *trollop*.

I stutter, words sputtering out unintelligibly. Cold panic settles in my bones, and my pulse races in my head. The hums, the sconces, the alcohol, the glints in the glasses, everything muddles.

I rub my temple. This isn't how I thought this night would go. I turn on my heel to leave, but Mr. Jacobson snags at my arm and reels me back to him.

"Where are you going? We were having so much fun."

"I think there's been a misunderstanding. I'm not a lady of the night."

He looks at the dark outside the wood-framed windows as if mocking my statement, and my eyes sweep frantically across the busy tavern, flying over the conscious effort of every man not to raise his head in our direction.

The bartender is away, engaged serving glasses. My throat dries like old paper. As of right now, I've offered the duty of my well-being—or lack thereof—to this man. The patrons' refusal to look up is this entire tavern's silent acknowledgment that I deserve whatever happens to me out of my foolishness.

"And what kind of lady are you, huh?" Mr. Jacobson hisses so close to me the acidic stench of alcohol caresses my nostrils. "Every woman who deems herself respectable is long tucked in at home with their loving families. But you're here. Unchaperoned. Drinking with a stranger."

I pull my arm free and pick up my belongings. "Then good night to you."

I turn to sprint out the door, but Mr. Jacobson pinches at my sleeve. Slinging my arm back, I'm ready to punch him square in the jaw, but as my fist takes a swing, a hand captures it in a tight squeeze. "Finally! Here you are!"

Beside me stands a man with ocean-blue eyes. He must be a newcomer, since I don't remember him among the patrons.

"What?"

He frowns in picture-perfect innocence. "Oh, dear. Are you inebriated?"

"No."

He smiles at Mr. Jacobson. "Forgive my Addie. She loves being a social butterfly, you see."

Addie. I almost leap, my heart stirring from its hazy slumber. The name my parents nearly chose for me before they went for Alexandra. My fake childhood name. What are the odds this man would call me Addie out of all the random names that could've occurred to him?

"But I told you to wait for me, love." He scolds me so sweetly I almost believe we know each other. Do we? I might indeed be drunk.

Mr. Jacobson squints. "Is she with you?"

"My lovely fiancée." This stranger's smile is so pure it's contagious, but at once its edges acquire a dangerous sharpness. "Something the matter here? It seemed she was trying to leave and you were stopping her."

Mr. Jacobson retreats. "Not at all."

I huff. *Of course.* He backpedals now when another man is claiming me.

"Yes, something is the matter here," I chime. "But it's none of your concern."

With a pivot of my heel, I leave that stupid tavern.

"Come now, my dear dove, you misheard me," the man singsongs as he trails me outside. "I told you I'd be in the tavern *down* the street."

The frigid air hits my face, and tears, either of embarrassment or anger, prick at the corners of my eyes. I step under the streetlamps and tick them away with numb fingers, hoping everything falls away and I wake up in my warm bed with the scent of baked scones. I've never yearned for home so wildly, and the feeling slaps me in the face.

The man shoves his hands into his pockets. "That was a close call. Are you well?"

I sigh and slide into my coat. "I'm fine. I don't know why you had to step in. I had it under control."

His eyes widen. "Ah, had you? Because that man? He looked pretty convinced you were his plaything."

I raise my chin out of pure stubbornness and shove my hat on. I'm done. I should return before either Uncle Nigel, his shady assistant, or my nosy new maid realizes I'm turning in later than I should. And tomorrow, I need to keep a sound mind. This was a poor choice.

"I need no saving," I mutter.

"Liar," he says with so much nonchalance I whip my head at him.

"I beg your pardon?"

He shrugs. "You seemed pretty much in trouble."

Now, at a safe distance from the tavern, I can study him properly. His ocean-blue eyes accompany sideswept light-brown hair and a chiseled jaw. He's wearing a tweed jacket; underneath, a black waistcoat and a flimsy white shirt with a thin collar. I squint at his lack of headwear. From his wrist dangles a leather case. My chest stirs alive, as if it were trying to tell me something, but I ignore it because, for the love of God, I won't admit how handsome he is. "My name isn't Addie."

"I supposed."

I roll my eyes and start down the wet street.

"Hold up," he says. "It's not safe to walk down these streets without a companion."

I chuckle. "Mind your business."

"I'm not going to get into why you were in that tavern, you know, but I saved you back there. The least you could say is thank you."

I turn around. He's so close behind me, he almost collides with me. Thankfully for both of us, my hands land on his chest and stop him dead. I clear my throat, my palms retreating slowly, almost as if it hurt to let go. "I don't need a man's protection, thank you very much. Good Lord, why won't you all leave me alone?"

The arc lights cast shadows on him but cannot hide the recognition and tenderness quietly washing across his features, as if my body were made of glass and he could see the pain in my soul. Ramrod straight, all I can do is pray the darkness conceals the heat in my cheeks.

"And alone I shall leave you, but let me escort you home."

He's too poised for a man that must not be much older than I am.

I curl my fingers until my nails sink into my palms. I'm like a thunderous summer storm, while he's a gentle sun beaming through leaves and morning dew.

He must take my refusal to answer as silent permission, because his footsteps tap next to me. To an outward eye, I'm chaperoned, protected, but he leaves me alone just like a guardian—felt but not seen.

The Bowery, where train lines meet and classes overlap, seemed perfect to forget my pain. But I won't find what I'm looking for here. Clopping hooves and rumbling vehicles rolling past me, I leave behind the grimy streets, barging between loud drunkards, strolling couples, and sailors, and walk northward as fast as I can amid a growing damp fog.

"We could've taken the subway," my companion says.

"I'd like to walk," I chirp back.

Echoes of bells from a nearby church run through the streets nine times. When I reach the manicured sidewalks of Gramercy Park, the first needles stab at my feet, thanks to my unsuitable shoes. A bead of sweat threatens to break under my fur-collared coat, and my tongue is parched. I ventured too far south. It'll take me an hour to reach the Plaza Hotel by foot. My spirits falter. All that wine was a serious mistake. The twinkles in the buildings blur as an acute pressure builds in my head, my chest heaving up and down. I'm homeless. Parentless. Alone. *Directionless.* It's one of the first times I'm fully aware of the dimension of my situation, and this crushing grief can't come at a worse time.

I turn left and right, unsure what to do. I don't want to scream or sob in the middle of the street.

"Are you lost?" he asks me.

"No," I mutter, hiding under the brim of my small hat, and veer around the corner.

On Third Avenue, I mercifully find a taxicab trudging up the railway-lined street. I raise an arm, plunging forward onto the road while a train rattles overhead.

In normal circumstances, I wouldn't dream of using a car, but right now, it's a haven. I take a seat in the inviting velvety cabin behind the driver.

"A chilly night, huh?" my companion says to the man, sliding in after me.

His citrusy aftershave and scent of leather and flowers make my stomach flutter. I roll my eyes. Here I am, pining after a man when I have much more pressing matters at hand.

"You don't have to come," I say as coldly as I can manage.

"I said I'd escort you home, and I'll keep my word."

I sigh, and the address of my old house rolls out of my inebriated lips before I can stop myself. Chugging down a flare of fresh tears, I focus on the hazy streets, on empty lots, several fields with vegetable patches, and surging new buildings sited next to pretty townhouses.

Manhattan never looks the same, always morphing, evolving, towers aiming for the skies. Every day, I find a new landmark where there was simple air, bridges built across shores, roads rerouted, and railways gliding north and southward, east, and westward in more complicated grids than before.

The driver stops in front of my home. Is it *home* anymore? I don't have the time or energy for this. It's no longer mine, no, but this will be reversed tomorrow, when I have my parents' fortune.

I glance at the man by my side. He was downtown, while now we're almost uptown. God knows where he lives. Given his lack of headwear and his flimsy clothes, it seems he can't afford the ride back without sacrificing sustenance for a week.

"The gentleman will return home now," I tell the driver, giving him a dollar through the open pane.

My knight in shining armor opens his mouth, "There's no need for—"

I roll my eyes and unlock the door. He can spare me his humility.

When I've stepped out, I push the door shut, but he stops it and follows me outside. About to say something, he squints at the townhouse instead. "Are you sure this is your house?"

"Are you implying I don't know where my home is?"

He purses his lips. "It looks quite dark in there."

"My family is full of early risers."

"All right then." He cocks his head. He doesn't believe me. It's obvious. Warm light spills onto the street through the neighboring windows, and Mrs. Callahan's winter flowers sway in the crisp night air. In the meantime, my parents' townhouse, with splotches of muck staining the stoops and windows devoid of drapes, casts off shadows and death.

"I thank you for escorting me back," I say.

"Who says I didn't need your company? It's dangerous out there."

My lips quiver before I can stop them. I put my gloved hand against them, but I can't cover my smile fast enough.

His face lights up with a sudden smirk. A playful sparkle touches his eyes. And that warmth stirring in my chest messes with my senses again, as if my world curled on the edges. My heart keeps asking me to follow its lead, but my head is too heavy, dragging through the day, these months, my loss.

"Well, I thank you for the free ride," he says. "Have a good night, Fake Addie. Don't run into more trouble."

He turns around, but a part of me is overcome with guilt for having treated him so poorly. I cannot agree he's "saved" me, but he's indeed helped me. "Please, wait."

He looks at me over his shoulder. "Yes?"

"What's your name?"

He chuckles. "Since you're not volunteering your own, let's leave it under the veil of mystery. But if you'd like to introduce yourself, you can find me this week at the Children's Home Industrial School in Brooklyn."

He slips into the taxicab, his sharp, lean angles catching flickers of streetlamps as he settles in the seat. A small smile flitters over my mouth at the challenge, at his charm.

The taxicab wheels away then and turns the corner, disappearing into lazy late-night traffic.

I heave a sigh, starting down the sidewalk. My plan to forget has been an utter failure. I remember, more brightly than ever. A raging fire burns in my mind.

The Plaza sits in a drowsy mist down the block. I stop my conflicted emotions before they can take over me. Tomorrow, I'll rise to fight. But all I need now is to take a bath, then plop onto my bed and forget the world exists.

Chapter Two

March 22, 1915

Slanted, watery morning light sifts into my suite through a curtain gap, casting a glow on the photographs in my hands. Ignoring the dull headache in my forehead, I strain my gaze into my parents' faces, but they stare back at me from the past with nothing but silence.

How is it possible they didn't sense death lurking behind the next turn of the road? There they stood, in their last portrait ever, young and fair, unaware they would be below ground in a year's time.

Flames crackle in the hearth, giving me some warmth, but still, I shiver and drop the photograph on the pools of my black wool skirt. This must be a sinister jest of some kind.

I mute a broken sob, tears welling up.

Someone knocks on my door.

"You may come in," I croak, resigned to the fact I'll never be left alone for long again.

Emily, my new maid, walks in. "Mr. Benson is waiting for you downstairs and is wondering when you'll join him. The car is ready."

I turn away, pretending I'm straightening my back, though my sniffle reveals I'm crying. I miss Mia. She helped raise me for the last ten years, but that's another thing Uncle Nigel has done away with. The family's servants. My every waking moment since February has been shared with strangers. Stuck in a hotel, just a few blocks from home.

"We're still on time. Let my uncle know I'll join him in a couple of minutes," I mutter as I pick up all the photographs and bind them with cord, attaching two dry lavender sprigs my mother used to place under my pillow to help me with good dreams.

"Let me retrieve those things for you, Miss Benson," Emily says.

"That won't be necessary." I tuck a candle, my parents' monogrammed kerchiefs, and some jewelry into an oak chest. My parents' lives, reduced to a box. "I'll be there in a minute."

Emily bows her head. "As you wish, Miss."

She leaves me alone, closing the door with an intentional click. I stall on the first of the photographs in the stack, brushing aside the sprigs with a thumb. My parents stood behind me and my childhood friends, Lindsay and Elijah. I crane my neck toward the table next to the suite's entrance, where the bouquet of fresh tulips they sent me yesterday enlivens the sober decoration of the hotel.

Both wished me strength and good luck for today's reading.

The black-and-white photograph doesn't do justice to the depths of Elijah's brown eyes. He's been so attentive through this entire ordeal. Lindsay and Elijah lost their grandmother a year ago. He was so close to his nana. It took him months to begin anew without her and breathe again. I understand him all too well now.

He's always taken care of me. He's been my greatest friend. Even my lover. He and I ran in secret through Central Park to hug and kiss under a tree, several years ago, once we realized we weren't children anymore.

I shake my head. Those perfect days of sunshine and innocent love are way behind us. I can't dwell on memories—or I might as well drown.

With a deep breath, I tuck the portraits and the box inside my trunk and scramble to my feet. In my en suite bathroom, I splash cold water on my face and place a wet lock behind my ear before heading downstairs.

The testament reading and the rest of my life are waiting for me.

Outside, the morning is as bleak as my heart; rain pitter-patters on the windows of the glossy black 1915 Brewster Town Landaulet, which Uncle Nigel has requested from the Plaza to drive us down to Manhattan's busy financial district. My feet fidget inside my pointy boots as my nebulous gaze wanders over the passersby on the streets, people who scatter away from the unexpected rain, while others continue their stroll unbothered.

The dull buzz in my forehead has grown into a pointed headache, branching out to my temples. Every turn and every halt roils the bile in my stomach, so much that it keeps at bay the apprehension of being inside a car in a sober state of mind.

My uncle murmurs something as I step out on the street, tiny freezing specks of water melting on my black velvet coat.

He snaps two fingers in front of me.

"Yes?" I look up, running into the lapels of my uncle's pine-colored coat.

His eyes are a shade of dark gray under the brim of his hat, so unlike the icy blue of the rest of us, Bensons, including myself.

"I was asking if you're ready for the reading," he says with a polished Received Pronunciation.

"I . . ." My words die out, my thoughts trapped in a cloak of haze. I can't wash it off; I can't escape from it. Alcohol or grief, it's there at every turn.

My uncle sighs and seizes my arm with stiff fingers. He steers me into the offices of Mr. Miller, Son, and Associates, lest the people crowding the sidewalk sweep me away in the short space between the car and the building. The slick ground under my heeled boots gives way to manicured, shiny tiles, yet my uncle doesn't let go of my arm.

Is he afraid I might run?

He might be. Up until now my uncle has been overly comfortable with selling my parents' belongings. *My* house, my entire life, has been scattered for the vultures to feast on. I chew on my lower lip, wondering if I'll have to bargain, implore, or threaten to purchase it all back.

"Benson," Uncle Nigel says to the brunette woman working the reception desk. "Mr. Miller awaits us."

With a nod, the woman walks down a hallway in her sober panama skirt and white blouse, her heels clacking and fading.

My uncle loosens his grip around my arm.

"Thank you for returning my arm," I grumble.

Uncle Nigel turns his head, eyebrows raised and a flash of surprise running through his eyes. "*Pardon* me?"

"I said I hope they make haste," I say louder.

He rolls his shoulders. "It's an important day."

An important day, uttered with a voice so low and sharp one might think he's bitter about this reading. His countenance is stern, without any trace of crying or wakefulness. I've not caught a glimpse of sorrow for the month he's been with me. I don't expect him to ask me how I'm feeling, yet sometimes I so wish to ask him if he's sad over losing his brother, if he even *cares*.

I squeeze my eyes shut and walk away, giving little tugs at my bun, which seems to tighten with each passing hour. "Quiet down," I hush to myself. I can't let emotions overcome me here. Not right now. Not in front of my uncle.

Muffled trolley chimes and voices drift inside the hall.

Young and fair, Mr. Crossley, my uncle's personal assistant, stands next to the main entrance, a bored expression fixed forward, green eyes blank. Is he counting dust motes, or does he hate being here as much as I do?

I sigh as I slow to a stop. Perhaps I'm being unreasonable. Perhaps my uncle is mourning in private or putting on a brave face to ease me through this ordeal. It's most likely my uncle can see I refuse to accept my parents are no longer with me. That this is real. That nothing will fill the void they've left. That I am in fact not ready for this testament reading and I might as well flee or faint. No matter the riches that will come into my pocket, I am untethered from any love or normalcy, in every possible way, and the thought rattles me from the inside out.

I yank my hat off, a pin flinging up in the air. It clatters on the floor, and my uncle and Mr. Crossley turn to peer at me as if I had set something on fire.

"I'm sorry for the delay," the secretary says, saving me from having to explain myself as I bend to grab the pin. "Mr. Tannenbaum will see you now in Mr. Miller's office. Please, follow me."

Uncle Nigel strides into the corridor, stalking the woman. "Mr. Tannenbaum?"

"He's Mr. Miller's associate—"

"I know *who* he is," Uncle Nigel says. "I thought we were to meet my late brother's lawyer."

"Mr. Tannenbaum will provide all the necessary explanations, sir," the woman retorts.

The ghost of a smile trembles on my lips, but it quickly falls away. I'm not supposed to laugh.

At the office door, Mr. Tannenbaum reaches out to greet my uncle. "Mr. Benson, my condolences. Welcome to Mr. Miller, Son, and Associates. Miss Benson," he says, facing me. He grabs my cold hand and cocoons it with his own. "I'm so sorry for your loss."

Grief spears me, but I manage to keep my tears at bay. "Thank you, Mr. Tannenbaum."

"Where's Mr. Miller?" Uncle Nigel asks as I take a seat in one of the ornate chairs opposite the desk. Behind it, a sumptuous bookcase lodges law books, the gilded letters on the spines glimmering in the gray light seeping through the windows.

"Ah, yes," Mr. Tannenbaum replies, taking command of the desk with a handful of documents. "Apologies for Mr. Miller's absence. A most inconvenient affair. He's been off sick for a couple of weeks."

"Blimey. I hope nothing too bad," Uncle Nigel says, gripping the head of his walking stick.

By the door, my uncle's assistant takes notes on a notepad. His pencil scratches the paper like scribbles on sandpaper. I take a deep breath, closing my eyes for a split second.

"He's come down with something, I'm afraid," Mr. Tannenbaum says. "A stubborn stomach bug of some sort. He's on the mend, thankfully, but still regaining his strength, so he was unable to come in today. He sends his regards and condolences."

Condolences . . . such a simple thing to say, but the meaning behind it makes me want to scream. I sink my nails into my skirt, my headache drilling a hole into my forehead.

Silence fills the room for a long while, letting the far-off medley of clopping and hums in.

Uncle Nigel clears his throat. "Shall we begin?"

"Of course," Mr. Tannenbaum says. "Without further ado, as the late Mr. Benson's solicitors, we certify the veracity of this testament, composed by the late Liam Benson in this office."

I swallow a bitter lump, my mouth dry. Did my father ever sit in the armchairs next to the windows as someone scribbled? My father seems to come alive when Mr. Tannenbaum turns the first page and reads. "'I, Liam Benson, being of sound body and mind, decree that my worldly possessions, including all my monetary and physical assets, be disposed of as follows.

"'Should my beloved wife, Isabella Benson, outlive me, she shall inherit the entirety of my worldly possessions, monetary and physical assets, save for the following.

"'To my brother, Nigel Benson, I leave a sum of $15,000.

"'To my butler, Mr. Johnson; the family cook, Mrs. Thomson; the coachman, Mr. Brown; and our two maids, Mrs. Bowman and Miss Morris, I leave $1,000 each.

"'Lastly, should my wife be deceased, to my beloved daughter, Alexandra.'"

I startle at my own name. *Beloved Alexandra . . . my beloved daughter* . . . my father's supple voice wavers in my memories, fresh and recent, and I shake with fear of the day its sound might decay and disappear.

Mr. Tannenbaum turns to the next page. "'I leave all my properties and worldly possessions, including all my monetary and physical assets, save for the aforementioned, totaling $2.5 million, which will remain in the Benson trust fund and released, provided she secures a marriage. Until she marries, or should she fail to marry, all money and assets will be managed by my brother, Nigel Benson.'"

The word *marriage* jolts me out of my daze, cobwebs blown with a gust—claws, prying me away from my childhood.

I lean forward, gaping at Mr. Tannenbaum. "I b-b-beg your pardon?"

"Anything the matter, Alexandra?" my uncle asks.

The room tilts, my pulse thrumming in my temples. No . . . he always said marriage could and *would* wait. I was supposed to inherit my father's money. I heard him say it loud and clear last summer, when I snooped on a conversation between Mother and Father. They spoke about what would become of me if they died. It struck me as the kind of discussion parents usually have, but for them, their comments carried an eerie certainty, as if instead of wondering, they were *planning*.

"Alexandra will have our fortune, no doubt," my father said to my mother. "It's in my will. Fear not, dear. She'll make of her life what she may—and a great life at that. Alix is a brave young lady. She can overcome anything."

Can I, Father?

Can I, when you've set me up to fail from the depths of your very grave?

"That's impossible," I mutter.

"And what might that be?" Uncle Nigel presses, his knuckles whitening on the cane head.

I scramble upward, my hat sliding off my lap. It lands on the rug with a soft thud. "My father . . . he didn't . . . I was supposed to inherit—without the marriage part . . ."

"Of course, you should marry first." Uncle Nigel chuckles, as if there were no other possible arrangement he could conceive of. "You'll come to Liverpool and marry a good suitor. I shall have some promising prospects lined up in the coming days."

The words come like a punch to the stomach. I force myself to move, shift my posture on my numb legs, but it takes me a few seconds to regain my wits, a dull heartbeat thumping against my ribcage. "Would you repeat that again?"

My uncle presses his lips in a tight line. "I think you've heard me."

I open my mouth, but only air eddies out as sheer panic washes through me. Not only does he want to take me to England. In *wartime*. He's planning on marrying me off to God knows who.

A high-pitched whistle fills my ears, the room going hazy at the edges of my vision.

"It's a very sensible arrangement, Miss Benson," Mr. Tannenbaum chips in. "I've seen countless women lose everything in favor of the men in the family. Now, you'll get a happy marriage and your father's inheritance. And oh, good old England. A handsome country if I ever saw one. My, my, you should count yourself lucky."

He smiles beneath the fringe of his white mustache, and his eyes—they carry a paternal authority as they watch me over the brim of his wire-rimmed glasses. His condescension makes my stomach churn.

I reach out. "May I see the testament?"

"Goodness gracious, Alexandra." My uncle pinches the bridge of his nose.

Mr. Tannenbaum passes the documents to me regardless.

I ignore Uncle Nigel's and Mr. Tannenbaum's stares on my back and sit in the armchair by the window.

For a long while, I gape at the documents on the polished wooden table. This is the last time Father would speak to me, through the ink on these pages, and why would he choose to betray me like this instead? This was his last gift, in death. My freedom and his trust. His blessings for my own life, lived on my own terms. Why would my father do this to me? He was the one who most fervently supported my decision to study law. My parents were funding my university degree. And now . . . the only condition on inheritance is that . . . I should *marry*? It doesn't make sense. This doesn't sound like my father at all.

While my uncle and the solicitor mumble about the weather, I close my eyes and take a deep breath. Ever since I was a child, no matter if I came home crying from school or I fell and hurt my knee, my father's words remained the same: seek outside perspective, be rational, and remember to breathe.

"'Every maze has an entrance and an exit,'" I whisper, quoting him. It's ironic—it's as if deep inside he would've always been training me to face this very moment. The moment he would betray me.

I begin with what is known. I've already studied the law of succession. Picking up the testament with trembling hands, I push the rest of my problems aside to work out later.

This was scribbled by someone else—but the signatures on the pages are all even, my father's. I shake my head. Documents are usually jotted down by an appointed representative or attorney, not the decedent himself. A stranger's scrawls mean nothing, yet that stranger transcribed my father's decrees, and each one of them is a stab to my chest.

"But I don't understand," I hiss under my breath, my fingertips frantically spreading over the page.

I read the curly writing, browsing for a change in style, but it seems even.

There must be a loophole somewhere, anything omitted, yet the sentences spoken match the ones on the page. There's no clause to save my parents' fortune from my uncle's hands. No clause to save me from marriage and leaving New York. What will happen to law school now?

Behind me, the dry conversation has died out and an uncomfortable silence has settled.

"May I bring coffee, Mr. Benson?" Mr. Tannenbaum asks. "While we wait."

"Most obliged," Uncle Nigel says.

I raise the second page and caress the paper. The first pages are older, yellowy, a bit brittle, as paper ages through the years, while the last page is newer, whiter, the edges less thumbed. That's the one where the marriage clause is mentioned.

And it strikes me . . . this is not the original page. It's a revised will.

He changed it.

My father changed the testament.

I slump in the chair, as if I've been shoved. Desperation rushes through my veins, reaching every corner of me. At once, I desire to shout and find a way to voluntarily swoon. But some tickling inside me won't let me drown.

I must dig myself out from this grave. I can't let this bury me alongside my parents, even if I've been left to die.

I frown, allowing the inkling inside me to come undone like a yarn ball. One tug at the right thread.

Why did my uncle sell my parents' townhouse? The summer lake house I understand, and the boat I might understand too. The testament mentions the assets that could be first disposed of. But why sell the house where my parents and I lived? That isn't in the will. Why has he done away with our staff and brought in his own from England? In hindsight, it's like he was uprooting me, as if stealing me away overseas was his goal all along. Only my inheritance would've prevented this.

But he was acting as if he knew I wouldn't have it.

Did my uncle . . . *know* what was in the testament?

The acrid scent of warm coffee fills the room, making my head spin with nausea and a raging headache.

In all appearance, my father changed his testament, but any change needs to be dated. There is no date in any part of the will. My father swore to my mother last summer I would have their fortune if anything happened to them.

Wariness shoots through my chest. Either my father didn't respect me enough and changed the testament behind my back, or something more turbulent is happening. But someone is lying here.

The question is who?

A loud clank of a cup against a saucer brings me back from my reveries.

"If you're finished, Alexandra, we should get this over with," Uncle Nigel says.

My legs shake as I scramble to my feet, the papers rattling in my hand. *Be rational; remember to breathe.* I can solve mysteries later. For now, I need to find the way out of the maze.

Licking my lips, I turn to the desk. My uncle, Mr. Crossley, and Mr. Tannenbaum are all looking at me. What's the next problem to solve? It's not the marriage; it's not the fortune. The problem to solve right now is how I can get away from my uncle's grasp. As long as I'm an unmarried woman, my uncle can do whatever he pleases—force me to quit university, haul me to England, marry me off to a stranger . . . as long as it's in the testament, it's his power to do so.

The easiest way to solve this next problem is to steal his power over me.

I . . . should get married first. On my own terms.

"Yes, I am finished," I say, tottering over a wild idea. "But see, Uncle, the arrangement you're planning won't be possible."

My uncle leans in, a shadow crossing his face. I have his attention. "For what reason?"

I set down the papers on the table. "Because I already have a fiancé."

Chapter Three

March 23, 1915

The New York Law School rises to the sky next to Saint Paul's Chapel. Pacing the street in front of the entrance, I count bell tolls as clouds gather overhead, slanted golden light sifting through the dimming morning.

Elijah should be here today. On Tuesdays, he always comes early with some of his classmates to have coffee before class.

My breath fogs in the air, and I burrow in my coat with a shiver. Trolleys clang and carriages rattle up and down Broadway. I can't stand thinking I might be gone before summer has its chance to bloom. My place is in Manhattan.

Elijah turns the corner, bundled in a red scarf and a long black coat, his locks hidden under a bowler hat. He's holding several books, chirpily chatting with another man.

I stiffen as he spots me by the curb. He raises his eyebrows, hands his books to his classmate, and rushes to me with a bright smile.

I've tossed and turned all night, my mind spinning around cobwebs, endlessly trapped in this twisted game of ink and paper. But as I woke up, my suspicions about Uncle Nigel have not dwindled: They're raging.

Yesterday, I pretended I was sick after the testament reading, and no one inquired about my fiancé. But today, Uncle Nigel expects me to sit for breakfast at nine thirty with him, and no doubt, he will have questions. I need a fake husband. It makes sense to ask my friend Elijah.

We've loved each other before. And last I knew, the door was never completely closed.

"Alix, hello." He gives me a quick hug. "What are you doing here? Anything the matter?"

"I need to discuss something with you," I say, pulling away. "Do you have a few moments?"

"And more. I know a café around here. We can go."

I shake my head. "I don't want to take much time from you. I also need to return to the Plaza soon. Can we just head down to the park?"

"Of course. If memory serves me, a park always helps you think." He nudges my shoulder with his arm.

My smile curls up. I meet his gaze, his brown eyes filled with complicity. He makes me feel safe. "You know me well."

Casting a sad smile, I start toward Broadway next to him. What I'm about to ask of him is selfish. First, I'll ask for his opinion on the testament, and if there is nothing to do, I'll propose my plan. What else can I do? Most of the other men I know won't settle for lies and can't be bought by money. An orphan myself, I've got nothing to offer but a trousseau and broken kin. But Elijah might find the freedom I can offer tempting.

"How can I help you? How was the testament reading?"

"A disaster," I say.

"I'm sorry to hear. What happened?"

I dive into a detailed explanation of what happened in Mr. Tannenbaum's office while we walk past Astor House and venture behind the postal office and into City Hall Park. As we come to a stop under the blossoming shadow of a maple tree on one of the manicured pathways in the park, my spirits settle, as if what I'm telling him happened years ago instead of yesterday, but heaviness has clouded Elijah's face, as if it reflected the day above us.

He takes off his hat and presses it to his chest. "I'm . . . most sorry, Alix. I'm bewildered."

"Is there nothing that can be done about the testament?"

A shadow crosses over Elijah's features. A blond lock falls over his forehead, and I itch to push it back.

"It's difficult without seeing the testament, but from what you've told me, it'd be complicated to challenge it."

"I suspect it was changed."

Elijah frowns, putting his hat back on. "Was there a codicil? A note of the change? A supplementary document that amends a certain part of the will?"

"No," I say. "But the page wasn't as old as the other ones. And there was no date. And most importantly, you and I knew my father; he would've never done such a thing to me."

Elijah crosses his arms and gives his chin little taps with his knuckle. "It can still be the original. A reviewed testament must have a date in a codicil. But an original will doesn't require a date for it to be legit and legal. It just needs to be signed."

My shoulders sag. "What should I do, then? Should I accept my father didn't respect me enough? I know what I heard him say. My father was going to let me inherit as a feme sole. It's been changed."

And my uncle is hiding something—but this, I can't share just yet without sounding like a madwoman. If Elijah isn't seeing anything wrong with that last part of the will, I can't count on him to make sense of my worries.

I cross my arms, shivering.

Elijah gives my shoulder a gentle squeeze. "Your father loved you with all his soul, Alix. I'm not saying I don't believe you, but I'd need to see the testament. I can review it with my professor if you can give it to me."

I shake my head. "I couldn't snatch that testament even if my life depended on it. This is why I came up with another solution. And I might need your help for it."

He opens his arms, a little smile playing on his lips. "I'm all ears."

I square my shoulders, gulping. I'm placing years of friendship and love on the edge of a knife. "I need a fake husband. I need to marry you."

Surprise wipes the sadness and conflict away from Elijah's face. Raising his eyebrows, he leans on the trunk of the maple tree and blows his cheeks. "Alix . . . I . . ."

"I know what I'm asking of you is outrageous." I rest a hand on his arm. "But if you would please listen to me. You're no longer sixteen, and I no longer am fourteen. We love and respect each other. We've been friends for so long . . . it only makes sense I'd ask you this. You're the only person I can trust. If you marry me, my uncle won't be able to take me to England, and I'll have my inheritance. We can get a divorce in a year's time, and in the meantime, you will be able to live your life freely as long as whatever you do, you do discreetly."

Sadness so intense grips his face, his jaw trembles. "I . . . can't, Alix."

I step away as if I've been slapped. "Why?"

He leaves the support of the tree, straightening. Still, he looks down, not meeting my gaze. "Why did we break our courting? Because we—*you*, especially—didn't want our marriage to be settled at such a young age. Because you didn't want to cause strife between our families. I still remember our words: 'Let our lives be more interesting than marriage.' Do you feel differently now?"

I huff. "No, Elijah. I'm not ready to marry. But need I remind you I am being *forced* to wed? Forced to leave my home? My *country*? My friends? And trust that whoever my uncle chooses to marry me off to will not frown upon my going to law school? I must fool my uncle, recover my parents' fortune, and escape England. It is much to grapple. I can't let love meddle when I have so much at stake. God knows I love you, but I need focus. I thought . . . I thought you were my friend."

I lower my gaze, burning with the sting of tears. There's no one else I can turn to. What should I do now? Admit to Uncle Nigel I've lied?

"Alix . . . I am so sorry. I am your friend. My love for you is dear. I wish I could oblige . . . but I met . . . someone."

I jerk my head up. "Excuse me?"

"I met her early in the year, through an acquaintance of Lindsay's."

My skin tingles, as if it were about to crawl. "Are you planning to *marry*?"

A smile moves on his mouth but doesn't light up his face. "We're just merely starting to court. I already talked to her father about it, and he agreed to wait to make things formal until I graduate and start working as a lawyer and I can provide for her. But . . . yes, we're courting with the intention to marry one day."

A slow sigh comes out of me, my mind numb as if I lost connection to reality. "I'm . . . happy for you, Elijah."

I really am. I'm happy life has brought someone who wants to wait for him. Elijah deserves all the love in this world. The love I denied him when I was too young to understand what it was. But the ground opens underneath my feet now, sweeping me away, losing the only hand to keep me on the surface just when I thought I would have it.

I take a step back.

"Alix, if you would've said something sooner . . . I would've . . . I could've . . . if you were ready to—"

"Yes," I clip through my tight throat, "it was so inconvenient my parents died when they did and not when you were free to save me."

"Alix, that's not what I mean," he says, voice low and cracking.

I don't look up at him. "I . . . will appreciate it if you keep this conversation a secret. I'll let Lindsay know in due time that I am leaving New York."

"Of course. My lips are sealed. But please, let me take you for lunch later, eh? We can think up a plan."

"I can't ask you for more. I'll come up with another solution. Don't fret for me. Thank you, Elijah."

I turn on my heel and run. And even when Elijah calls out my name, I don't look back.

❧

Sitting on the corner of Fifty-Eighth Street and Fifth Avenue, the Plaza restaurant is alive with pleasant conversations, waiters slithering around the room, and piano music, the large windows embellished by heavy shafts of drapery.

I walk in, following a host, cold air clinging to my clothes, weak legs and low spirits. The last thing I want is to sit for breakfast with my shady uncle after what happened with Elijah. I have no plan. Nothing to support my lies.

"So good to see you joining breakfast, Niece," Uncle Nigel says. Then, to Mr. Crossley, sitting next to him, "We'll resume our conversation later. Go fetch me those documents."

Mr. Crossley stands, regarding me with so much coldness in those green eyes that I flinch as I sit in front of my uncle.

"Apologies, Uncle; I was having some morning air near the park and lost track of time."

Lounging in his chair, he grimaces at the tea bag in his cup, pinching it up with two fingers. He lets out a noisy sigh and summons a waiter.

"May I be of assistance, sir?" the man asks, clasping his white-gloved hands behind him.

"Will you please take this and bring real tea?"

"Of course, sir." The waiter picks up the cup and scratches his head, sidling away between the tables.

"Americans," my uncle grumbles, spreading the *New York Tribune* open in front of him.

My lethargic gaze roams across the crowded restaurant. A wave of nausea swirls through me. I settle it with the warmth of tea, which I don't find as offensive as Uncle Nigel.

"How much did you know about your parents, Niece?"

I look up, blinking. Today's headline about the Great War is displayed in bold on one side of the front page.

Germans Begin Aero Attacks on All Ships—Even Flag of International Relief Commission Not Respected—Steamer Escapes by Zig-Zag Course

"I beg your pardon?" I ask, spreading butter on a slice of toasted bread.

Uncle Nigel draws aside his newspaper and leans forward. "I was wondering if there were more people I should inform about your parents' passing. Did your parents have friends other than those in the address book I found?"

I frown, taken aback. "No, I don't think so. Why do you ask, Uncle?"

He sighs. "Now that this ordeal is almost behind our backs, it's important to keep others in mind. I would loathe leaving anyone uninformed before we depart. Were there any missing guests during the burial? Or acquaintances who shared correspondence with your parents?"

My eyes narrow, my mind traveling back and forth through these months, wondering if I missed someone. All my parents' friends and acquaintances were present during the burial.

Except one.

My father used to have an assistant. Although I didn't know his name, my gaze was always drawn to him. He didn't look much older than me. This mysterious boy worked for my father for several years. He used to stride in, talk to my father in his office, and slip out like a ghost, usually with papers and manila folders in his hands. Always silent, he moved like a cat in the shadows of my parents' townhouse. My parents never allowed me to get close to him for some reason. And he probably never cared that I existed, but in spite of our distance, I did care about him.

He seemed lonely. Sad. Haunted eyes a shade of dark in the distance.

Or maybe he was just busy.

I shiver, my heart stirring like last night. Wrenching, as if it were still trying to tell me something. But I roll my shoulders, easing the pressure of that inkling.

He had no reason to be at my parents' burial. He left one day and never came back. Just as though he'd never been there. And if he forsook my family—and me—he's as dead as my parents.

"No," I tell my uncle. "Every person of contact should be in their address book."

"Fine." He purses his lips, sitting back again. "I thank you for your cooperation. I know this has been a challenging time for you."

I scoop strawberry jam from a crystal bowl and spread it on my toast. The buttery scent rises in the air, but my appetite is gone.

"I'm afraid that's an understatement," I retort, my voice thinned down to a fragile thread. "I take it you're aware there's a war going on in Europe at the moment."

Uncle Nigel harrumphs, subtly hinting he's the one to command the conversation. "Quite. But England isn't Europe. It is safe."

"They're sinking ships," I argue, pointing at his newspaper with a chin jerk. "It's making headlines."

"While a dozen other ships sail safely every day," Uncle Nigel counters, his aloof gaze trained on me like a challenge. It's like punching a brick wall. He won't allow me to stir any war paranoia in him.

"I'm studying law at NYU," I grumble, desperation crawling into me.

He clears his throat. "Yes, about that . . . you may resume your studies when we return to England. If your husband approves of it, that is. Speaking of which, who is this fiancé of yours? When are we going to get acquainted?"

"There's no returning when I've never set foot on the island to begin with," I clip instead, my blood sizzling with anger.

"Call it as you may," he says, "but you need to come to Liverpool with me. I've already purchased the crossing. We'll set sail on the first of May, on the *Lusitania*. Will your beau accompany us?"

My knife slices into the bread and sinks so deep it nicks my fingertip on the other end. We're leaving in less than five weeks. That wouldn't have been enough time for a wedding, not even for one with Elijah.

Uncle Nigel regards me in silence while the waiter sets down a teapot. It gives me enough time to sort through my panicked mind.

He seems interested in taking me to England. Does he even want my father's fortune? He's putting on a perfect innocent display, but I still find it hard to believe that this uprooting is coincidental.

"Answer something first, Uncle, if you'll be so kind."

He dismisses the waiter with a flourish before he can pour tea into his cup. "So rich of you, when you've not even answered my questions."

"Yes, my beau will accompany us," I utter through clenched teeth. "Please, make sure you purchase an additional ticket for the crossing. Which begs the question, Uncle. Why do you want to take me to England?"

Uncle Nigel crafts a dry, tight smile. "I have a job and estates to keep. I can hardly continue working from America for long. It's outrageously expensive and inconvenient. Your remaining family is from England. It was your parents' home country after all. It's only fair."

"I'm set to marry," I say coldly, even if my blood is running hotter in my veins.

He tames down a new smile. "Is there a near wedding date that I should be aware of?"

The silver knife is weighty and cold against my palm, and I consider hurling it at my uncle. It'd be easy. My father taught me how to throw knives, a childhood pastime of his. "No. But you're forgetting I'm twenty years old. Almost twenty-one. I can perfectly manage on my own here until I get married in a couple of months."

He shrugs. "Your age is a trifling point. You're under my care until I hand you over to your future husband, as avowed in your father's testament. And that'll happen once you're in England. End of discussion."

I put down the knife with a loud clatter against the porcelain dish and take a big bite of my bread, savoring nothing. But I need to gain some precious seconds to tame my emotions and think.

I survey the content faces around me, the mouthfuls of coffee and baked goods, the merry pianist at the other end of the room, how the world revolves around this table as if I didn't exist. I want to scream for help, but I have no one to save me but myself.

It's so obscene that my uncle waited until we were in the restaurant or in Mr. Miller's office to make his intentions clear. One at a time. He's been nothing but methodical in *how* and *when* he delivered news. He knew I wouldn't cause a stir, among all these people, imprisoned by the golden cage of polite society.

I take a mouthful of tea. "Everything is so clear to you, yet your reasoning doesn't quite add up to me, Uncle."

My uncle's mustache flicks over twisting lips. With a quick flip, he folds the newspaper and puts it down on the table with unmeasured force. If we weren't at the Plaza, I might've thought he was crushing a bug. "I'm not sure why exactly you're so surprised about this arrangement, Alexandra. I suppose you want to inherit your father's wealth as soon as possible, hmm?"

His accent sounds overdone now. I'm sure he's stressing it just to vex me, as if—*God forbid*—I'd happen to forget my fate.

Tea churns in my stomach, and bile somehow finds a way to my mouth. "What wealth? The money that you now control? Or the things you've sold?"

"You're being a brat, Alexandra," he mutters, grabbing the teapot. "You'll retain your money, need I remind you, as any other British lady. But your father set aside some assets, such as the family's real estate, in case a calamity like this ensued, as I'm positive you noticed in a clause in the testament."

"So, you knew what was in the testament beforehand, Uncle? Is that why you sold everything?"

Because I saw a clause in the testament—they would've needed my consent. And I didn't get asked. The trickle of steamy tea cuts short, a single drip spilling into the cup. A few seconds lapse until Uncle Nigel puts down the pot. "Of course not. I acted so, advised by your lawyers. And in any case, your father and I kept correspondence, as you might know."

I don't. My eyes narrow at him. My family's history is bumpy and obscure. When Nigel arrived at my townhouse without a forewarning letter and introduced himself to my then-staff as my uncle, having been notified of my parents' deaths by my family's lawyers, I didn't even recognize him as my uncle, considering I only had an old photograph of him and my father from the time they were teenagers, way before my parents relocated to America. Is he telling the truth? I might never know, and I can't fight or rebuke the unknown.

"Now, enough with this poppycock," he says. "Tell me when we're meeting your beau, right this very moment."

His eyes slide to me, dark and cold like iron. Cornered, I reel away from him. My heart drums through my body, with fear and anger alike. If only Elijah would've said yes. Where is the exit out of this maze?

"He's not here," I say. "He's on a business trip."

He chuckles. "Well, that is convenient. When will he return?"

Clearing my throat, I scramble to my feet, hiding my shaking hands behind myself. "Sometime during the first week of April. If you'll excuse me, I must go write him a letter now and break the news."

With a wry smile, he waves me off, a humorous flourish. My blood runs cold in my veins, all my anger wiped out. He doesn't believe me. His disbelief is so obvious it's almost making him laugh.

I keep my chin high and calmly stride across the restaurant, but when I disappear around the corner, I run to my room.

Chapter Four

March 24, 1915

The clock in my suite ticks barely past seven before I close the door. The hotel is still asleep, the stained glass fixtures on the walls giving a dull glow.

I pad along the floral rug on the corridor, tying the sash of my silky robe, and stop before my uncle's suite, one fist about to knock, and flash a smile at a housekeeper. The woman gazes at me curiously, then goes round the corner, leaving me alone.

I take a deep breath, hoping it gives me strength and confidence, only to find neither. I barely slept a wink and rose from my bed in low spirits, a weight of defeat nestled in my chest. At least I have remains of ink on my hands, from trying to work out a plan—not from penning letters. This last part, no one has to know, though.

I press my ear to the door. Inside, my uncle mutters. He's talking with someone—Mr. Crossley, it seems. I frown. I don't understand what they're saying, as if they spoke a different language, and the whispers are too low to make anything of them anyway.

I sigh. Have I come to accept defeat? Or am I here to make up a bigger lie and beg for more time?

I was reckless and selfish to assume I'd have Elijah at my beck and call, ready to accept a shallow offer and condemn years of his life for naught. No matter what lively teenage love we shared. The same circumstances that drew us apart would make us suffer. And I can't ask him to leave his beloved now, no matter how strange the thought of Elijah being in love still sits in my mind.

No. Asking Elijah was a mistake. If I'm not ready to marry anyone for love, I'll need a stranger. Someone I can keep my distance from, our affairs detached and cold. This needs to resemble a business transaction. A sum of my inheritance will buy any man in need of it. I need an unscrupulous con artist; the problem is, can I control a crook before said crook ruins me? And where should I find such a man? Back in a tavern? Mr. Jacobson would've been one perfect candidate, should the swine have known manners.

Fake Addie . . . I stop my hand before my knuckles rap on my uncle's door. The memory of the blue-eyed knight in shining armor sends a flutter of hope down my stomach. Fate sounds ridiculous, but could this be a sign? I don't want to indulge in the thought of heavenly intervention, yet . . . I'll take what I can get. I might not be able to save myself from going to England. But at least I can save my fortune and my career. My life. No matter where I settle.

I step away from the door and run back to my room, my footsteps muffled on the rug.

The man who helped me at the tavern didn't say what time I could find him at the school. To distract myself, I send an apology note to Elijah and think about how much money I will offer my false beau and what we can say to fool Uncle Nigel, but the waiting for a decent hour to head down to Brooklyn is torture, pretending I'm indifferent while a swarm of housekeepers and Emily flitter around me.

I lie to my uncle to get him to request a drive from the Plaza. New garments at Macy's. No need for Emily, as Lindsay will be there with her maid. My excuse is sound, and Lindsay will lie to protect me if anyone asks her of my whereabouts. The driver has the address and the order to pick me up in two hours, but as soon as I climb into the stocky yet elegant red Landaulet and the chauffeur sets course through the busy streets of Manhattan, I ask him to stop.

"Sir, I know it was asked of you to drive me down to Macy's, but do you know where in Brooklyn the Children's Home Industrial School is?"

He turns. "Why, yes. It's on Butler Street, Miss Benson."

"Take me to the Brooklyn Bridge and wait for me there until I return," I say, giving him a five. "And I'd thank you for your discretion."

The man's brow furrows under the brim of his hat. "Miss Benson, Brooklyn is an impecunious town."

His breath fogs, and I can't help but feel sorry for him having to drive all day. But one thing he can spare me is the deprecation. He won't make me change my mind.

"May I ask, where do you live?"

The driver tilts his head. "Well, Miss, Brooklyn, actually."

"A word of advice. The rich fellows in the hotel can afford self-deprecation, but it comes off cheap in you. I know Brooklyn. Take me to the bridge, please."

❧

Off the Brooklyn Bridge, I find a carriage for hire to take me to Butler Street. Brick apartment buildings and bustling stores frame the streets of Brooklyn. Middle-class and lower-class workers live here for quick access to the city. I only remember Brooklyn from years ago, but the area doesn't strike me as impecunious, like the Plaza driver said.

The Children's Home Industrial School is a massive three-story Victorian building with steep roofs. A pointed wrought iron fence wraps the school's three wings. Patches dot the front yard, and small twigs, no doubt ripped from the trees on one of these windy days, lie around unattended. Although the structure is as sumptuous as an elitist boarding school, a hint of misery tinges the air. This is a place for destitute children, no matter how beautiful it looks.

I go up the cracked steps in my charcoal gray suit-dress and my feathered hat and stop dead past the threshold as several boys dash outside, the front door groaning shut behind me. I catch my reflection in a faded grandfather clock and wince. Compared to the children in mismatched and oversize clothes and the adults in outdated fashion, I'm terribly overdressed to be here. Emily chose this ensemble. If I had spoken against it, I would have probably made her suspicious. Still, shame flares through me.

"May I help you, Miss?" a woman asks me from the front desk.

"Yes, I'm searching for"—I remember now I don't know his name—"a young gentleman? With sideswept light-brown hair, tall, bright-blue eyes, sharp angles?"

The woman seems deep in thought for a couple of seconds. "Young gentleman must be Mr. Asher. You'll find him down that corridor. The last classroom to the right."

"Thank you," I say.

I'm not escorted, not announced, so I head down that corridor with plenty of chances to hesitate, unsure how to approach this situation. If asking Elijah was difficult enough . . . How do you announce to a stranger that you need to marry him? Will he even say yes? I have so little time I can waste in this search.

My fingers wriggle my bag's handle, anticipation frothing in the pit of my stomach.

The classroom is small, and tiny desks cram the sidelines. A coat of old grime covers the peeled wallpaper. Dust dances in front of my nose, and the weathered floorboards creak under my shoes. This place needs funds. Urgently.

Mr. Asher sits behind a nicked wooden desk, and light pours over the piled tomes around him. He doesn't hear me cracking the door open. All his focus is on the paper he's reading, a deep furrow over his eyes. A pencil is dancing on his fingers.

"Mr. Asher," I say, closing the door.

He startles in his chair and looks up at me, as if I had awakened him from a slumber.

"That must be quite an interesting read," I say.

He sets down the paper. "Quite, Miss Benson."

I leap backward, ramming into the door. "Pardon me?"

"Miss Benson, isn't that your name?"

"How—how do you know my last name?" I need water. I need air. I need to fling myself into the river.

"The other night, I couldn't stop thinking you looked familiar. And when I was leaving in the taxicab, it dawned on me. You and I happened to be at the same gathering early this year."

I remain, to my shame, gaping for what feels like a long time, reminiscing on the few parties I attended in January. When I regain some composure, I close my mouth and square my shoulders. "Which one?"

"Miss Ellis's townhouse in Bloomingdale."

Lindsay. She threw a get-together in January with childhood friends and several acquaintances, some days before my parents' accident. But in between so many copies of men carrying themselves with the same demeanor, Mr. Asher would've stood out. "I don't remember you being there."

"I didn't count on that. I had to rush out of the party before we could be introduced."

That's why he felt so familiar. I must've caught a glimpse of him. "How do you know Lindsay?"

He sighs and puts down his pencil. "I'm not acquainted with Miss Ellis. One of my friends is acquainted with her family. Sean Cooper?"

I'm not familiar with the name. I frown. "Are you rich?"

"God forbid, no."

"You're a social climber," I say.

His brow furrows, but a smile spreads across his face as he leans back in his chair. He lets out laughter that is neither a chuckle nor a snicker. "Such a cynical way to see friendship."

"I'd call it realistic."

"I have no interest in becoming rich. I'm happy in the in-between, Miss Benson, but why conform to what society tells me to do? Should I just mingle with my impure, underprivileged kind?"

A part of me resents him for being so calm in front of my unmannered digs. It seems he's too high above me to be bothered.

"I must be obtuse this morning. But how come you know one of Lindsay's friends to begin with?"

His expression turns somber, all light dropping from him. "One of the children I tutor was very ill. Someone suggested we take him to the New York Cancer Hospital."

"Lindsay's father is the administrator of that hospital." My cheeks grow hot. "I'm sorry about your student."

"Don't be. He's in good health now. But during our visits I became good friends with one of the physicians who works closely with Dr. Ellis."

"And that'll be Dr. Sean Cooper." I contemplate hiding under a desk. What a cynical fool I am. Underneath the tailored clothes and veneer of good behavior, all I have become since my parents died is a wild animal. Mr. Asher makes me feel *unworthy*. But he seems sharp, unafraid, and witty. And he called me Addie. I recklessly want to hold onto him as a heaven-guided solution. Perhaps I'm a desperate lunatic, but I'll play along. Our paths seemed destined to cross at some point.

I set down my purse on his desk. "So, you're a teacher."

He opens his arms, encompassing the room. "That I am. I'm employed here and at Walden School, but I spend most of my time here. These kids need more care."

"What do you teach?"

He shrugs. "A bit of everything. Math, music, gymnastics. Why so many questions, Fake Addie?"

This job must not pay well at all. But it's obvious Mr. Asher is here because he wants to make a difference in the world. I'm measuring what the odds are that he accepts my proposal, and they're not in my favor. Accepting my proposal would entail pretending to be my fiancé, boarding an ocean liner, and beginning anew in England, and what for? Money? That's all I can offer him. He seems proud of who he is, of what he does. He certainly cannot have use for my plot. I need him, but despite all my money, he doesn't need *me*.

And this would be the second man who refused to help me in the short span of a day.

With a flicker of powerlessness, I turn on my heel and dash to the door, but Mr. Asher appears, skidding to a stop in front of me.

I recoil a step in dead silence.

"What are you doing here, Miss Benson?" His voice is a low baritone, my last name a clipped roll from his lips. His eyes lock with mine, a glint of puzzlement and intrigue, and it's as if I could see myself reflected in that abyss of teals.

Warmth moves through me, like a river of fire. I let out the air I've been holding. "You called me Addie."

"Yes, I'm aware."

"My father wanted to call me Adeline, until my mother asked him to name me after Princess Alix of Hesse and by Rhine."

"Alexandra Feodorovna, empress of Russia," Mr. Asher says. "You certainly embody the personality of an empress, but I'm still unsure why you're here."

"My parents are dead."

He nods just once. "I'm sorry."

Still, the question lingers between us, but he seems too polite to ask it—why would that concern him?

"I thought that you calling me Addie was a sign from them, if there's something after death, mind you. It was silly."

He frowns. "I don't think that's silly."

Hope blossoms in my chest. Instead of laughing and waving me off, he believes in something greater than himself. Perhaps, he might be the one I'm looking for. "What's your biggest dream, Mr. Asher?"

He seems to smile at the candor of the word. *Dream.* He's like a content cat licking his mouth. "Fake Addie, not many people have the privilege of dreams and idleness."

"Then call it goals. Semantics."

"I believe you're asking the wrong person, because I have very little I want."

In layman's terms, he can't be bought. I respect that. But that makes him useless to me. I'm wasting my time and his. "I understand. Thank you for your time, Mr. Asher."

I take one step toward the door and brush the knob.

"Cameron," he blurts out, stopping me with the dashed vulnerability in his voice. "My name is Cameron."

There's something alluring about his name. As if he were meant for stardom. Cameron Asher. It's a name for motion picture stars and socialites, the likes of William S. Hart and Douglas Fairbanks. A name you wouldn't find out of place if its owner was rubbing shoulders with young Vanderbilts and Rockefellers. I realize, with a pang of sadness, he's perfect for me—for *my* plan. Put him in tailcoats and he could pass for new money.

I clear my throat and subtly wipe my sweaty hands on my skirt. "Now that my parents are dead, my life has simply been obliterated. I can't remain unmarried for too long, or my uncle will manage my fortune. He's forcing me to drop out of NYU. And he plans to take me to England and marry me off to a stranger . . . I need a fake husband, Mr. Asher."

He chuckles, and with a deadpan tone, as the implications seem to dawn on him, he simply says, "No. Outlandish."

It's as though he believes me childish and small—it makes me feel like a piece of rotten meat spewed onto the ground.

"Of course. You're clearly content, and asking you to leave it all behind for me is nothing but inane. Thank you, Mr. Asher."

I throw the door open as if I could run away from myself.

"Wait," he says.

I halt at the threshold and wonder if I should ignore him and run for the hills. One more blow and I might turn to dust.

When I swivel, he beckons with a finger and sits on a school desk. "Have you heard the expression 'Shoot yourself in the foot'?"

I raise my eyebrows, pondering the phrase. "I don't think I have."

"It originated a few months ago in the European trenches. Soldiers shoot themselves in the foot so they don't have to go to the front line."

"What does it have to do with our conversation?"

"You're shooting yourself in the foot so you don't hear what I have to say."

I'm about to make a face, but I refrain. "You said no and proceeded to call me outlandish. Did I mishear?"

"I doubt you understood the context."

I clench my jaw. "Enlighten me, then."

"Instead, indulge me by answering something, please. You're unwilling to fight, and that baffles me. Why give up so soon?"

"I am more willing to fight than you imagine. But I won't tolerate being vexed."

"Fair. Tell me about your plan."

I raise a shoulder. "Why? So you can say no once more?"

A smile plays on his lips. Good Lord, he's such a tease. "Maybe. What does it entail?"

"You must pretend to be the middle son of a wealthy family from the West, come with me to England when we sail on May first, and"—I clear my throat—"marry me."

"Whom should we fool?"

"My uncle."

He nods and stares into space, as if he's assessing the scale of the charade. "What makes you think we'll fool him?"

"My uncle comes from England, and it's unlikely he'll know the grounds of our relationship are a farce or if your background is real."

He purses his lips. "Why not marry immediately? Is there a real need to go to England?"

"That's what I'm trying to figure out. My uncle won't hear a word about it. And I doubt he'll support a sudden wedding now. He wants it to be in England."

He clears his throat. "I see. And . . . *officially* speaking, are you happy with going to England?"

I try to keep an even tone, "No. He knows I am not happy."

"And should *I* be approving of going there?"

"Yes, you should. I've thought about it. Your fake family is stranded in the old continent due to war. That will prevent any attempt from my uncle to meet your folks and give you a reason to support his cause. He won't oppose our marriage if he sees you're on his side."

"You forgot to mention I will also have to pretend to be smitten with you."

I huff. "I thought that was implied. But you will owe me nothing, and I'll owe you everything. My only requisite is that you don't interfere in how I live my life or spend my money, but I'll reciprocate and not interfere in how you live yours, as long as it doesn't harm our charade."

"Where's the catch?"

"No catch. We don't even have to be friends."

He crosses his arms. Am I losing him?

"How long?"

"Two years, no more. Perhaps one. Once it's reasonable enough for your fake family to find safe exit to any other European country, you'll tell my uncle you want to return to America. You'll be my husband; he'll have no choice but to accept it. You can go about your life once we've returned."

He sighs. "I would be gone for too long, too soon."

Away from his school, his life, his family.

"That's why I knew you'd say no."

I take a step back, about to break into a run. Thankfully, Mr. Asher ignores me as he pushes himself off the desk. "What would be in it for me?"

"Money. Real estate. Connections."

He inhales and exhales through his nose with a pensive face. For the way his cheeks go hollow, I'm sure he's biting the sides of his mouth, which I shouldn't find so endearing, but I do.

A long silence follows, and with each second, the air becomes heavier.

"How much money are we talking about?"

"Two hundred grand. Plus real estate."

He coughs in what I assume is a way to conceal his surprise. With that money, Mr. Asher could buy mansions, horses, schools for the children he tutors, cars, housekeepers, and not work a single day of his life.

"That's quite a considerable sum we're talking about."

You must really be a wretched little thing is what he's not saying. I freeze, trying to rebut it, but he's dissolved my wit as if I were sugar in coffee. I'm only left with cheap self-deprecation. "I'm desperate."

"I want some of that money in advance."

I roll my eyes. "I supposed you would. My uncle will release some money from my trust, especially if he believes it's for our wedding. What do you need it for, may I ask?"

"If I'm to leave, I want to make sure the kids are all right."

He's so selfless I want to vomit. It puts a mirror in front of my own selfishness and desperation, and I don't like it. But—"Are you accepting my proposal?"

"Why, Miss Benson, no marriage proposal?"

"Don't be an idiot."

His laugh is like crystalline waters, but when it dies down, we're again engulfed by silence, my question unanswered. I chew on my inner lip and wriggle my bag handle.

He sighs. "May I think it over?"

I attempt to keep my tone cool, though my heart just dropped to the floorboards. "Of course, Mr. Asher."

"Why aren't you calling me Cameron?"

"I'd rather keep things formal."

"Detached."

"Semantics," I say. "I'd appreciate it if you gave me plenty of time to come up with a new course of action should your answer remain no."

"I'll have an answer for you as soon as Sunday."

In four days. I swallow a beat of defeat. It's time I'm in no position to waste, but I have no other recourse but to compromise. "I'm staying at the Plaza. Come look for me when you've made up your mind."

I don't wait to hear anything else. I speed out of the classroom, then out of the building, and climb back into the carriage, and while I'm cruising along the Brooklyn Bridge, I close my eyes to the obsidian river.

Chapter Five

March 28, 1915

Sunday. It's the deadline Cameron—*Mr. Asher*—gave me. I lower my eyes from my reflection over the vanity mirror to my writhing thumbs on my lap. I should've asked him the time I should expect his visit. Now all I can do is wait for the rest of the day, restlessly pacing my suite.

Emily tugs at my hair, pulling my head back.

"Ouch."

"I apologize, Miss Benson. Your hair is in knots."

The result of my tossing and turning. My rumpled sheets remain as witness, waiting for the housekeepers to set down fresh linens.

"Your uncle has been aggravated by your continuous absence from Sunday mass," she says.

My brow furrows. Why does she sound as if she were angry? God has taken my parents away from me. I don't owe *Him* anything. Yet Emily continues before I can retort anything, "But would you like to spend just another day in your room? It's a sunny morning. We could have a walk down the park. Perhaps we might run into your lovely beloved there? Unless you decide being a recluse is more entertaining."

"Mr. Asher isn't even in New York yet." I take a sip of my minty tea, poison glinting in my eyes over the rim of my cup in the mirror's reflection. I hate the silly little smile of hers, always trembling at a corner of her thin lips. Who the devil does she think she is? I'm day by day ditching the black in an attempt to move forward, as my parents didn't want me to mourn them the old way, yet I should still be mourning them regardless.

With a jerk of the brush, she untangles a lock of my hair, sending my cup out of my lips. Warm rivulets trickle down my neck. Thankfully, I've avoided spilling most of my tea, but that doesn't stop me from setting down the cup on the saucer with a loud clank and turning with daggers in my eyes.

Emily's are so wide they might fall from their sockets.

"I'm ignoring your careless tone this morning, but could you watch what you're doing, Emily?"

"I'm so sorry, Miss Benson." Yet she sounds shallow, as if she were repressing a fit of laughter that, far from good-humored, is as scornful as her attitude.

I leap to my feet. No, she's not *sorry*. She's a useless maid who carries herself as if she were wearing a crown.

"You're sorry," I say, wiping the tea off my neck. The anger of these weeks bursts inside me. "I don't think so. You're—"

Three musical knocks come from the door, stopping the ugly things on the tip of my tongue.

"What now?" I bark, shooting a glare at the entrance.

A man from the front desk slides into my room, clearing his throat. Evidently, he's heard my shouting. "I am sorry to interrupt, Miss Benson. There's a very obstinate gentleman at the lobby requesting your presence. He said you were awaiting a response from him."

Cameron.

"Oh—of course." My throat has thinned to a thread. What awful timing, with Emily right in front of me. "My friend Elijah, Lindsay's brother," I lie on the go, hoping my voice doesn't sound too high pitched or strained. "I wanted to know if they'd join me for dinner tonight."

I rush toward the door.

"Miss Benson, you're in your housedress and your hair is undone," Emily yelps.

I halt on my tiptoes and look down at the navy chiffon waving at my shins and my brown leather boots. My hair is halfway up, halfway down, as Emily was putting it up. But the receptionist is waiting, and so is *Cam*—Mr. Asher, with his answer.

In two leaps, I yank my coat and my hat off a hanger and run out the door, making sure with a glimpse over my shoulder that the man is behind me and not dallying with Emily.

Mr. Asher stands near the bronze main doors in the slanted morning sun, tall and lithe in a dark suit, his hair pomaded and perfectly dirty blond in the light. He passes for a Plaza dweller, but I'm afraid Emily or Uncle Nigel's assistant might spot us. The last thing I want is them asking inconvenient questions.

"Good m—" I grab Mr. Asher by the highfalutin vest that peeks over his jacket and drag him out. "All right then, out it is."

A chilly breeze rustles the early leaves on the park trees. Gray clouds are rolling eastward. Staying in playing card games seems like a good idea. If I could only shove Emily's words down her gullet.

Running across the street in front of a chiming trolley, I steer Mr. Asher into the cover of Central Park. Behind us, the hotel doors are clear of prying eyes, only doormen and coachmen strolling under the porch, but still I shove Cameron behind a robust tree.

"I didn't think my best suit would horrify you to such great lengths as to hide me from the wealthy sharks in there, Miss Benson," Mr. Asher says.

"Excuse me?" I frown. "No. That's not the reason. I didn't want my new maid following me." I huff. "You believe you're too good for rich people, don't you?"

He smirks. "Not at all. But I love to tease you. You should've seen your face."

"You puzzle me, Mr. Asher."

He takes off his hat. "You could call my father Mr. Asher. I'm Cameron."

"You're the only Mr. Asher I know."

"Does that mean you want to meet my parents?"

I huff again, but this time only to disguise my chuckle. He's making me laugh. How dare he? "I believe you've come with an answer."

"I have," he says. With a slight tip of his head, his azure eyes take me in from head to toe, and a soft smile moves at the corner of his mouth. To my great shame, he sets my skin aflame and treasonous pleasure swirls in my stomach. He cannot be any more irritating than this, can he?

"And what is it going to be?" I utter through a clenched jaw. I hate that my fate is hanging from his fingers, just like the threads of a marionette. I press my teeth harder as truth sinks into my very depth—my fate is indeed in the hands of everyone else but me.

He looks up at the swaying trees. "You lied to me."

I blink. "What do you mean I lied to you? I did not."

"You're staying in the hotel. You asked the taxicab to drive us up to that house. Did you think me so little honorable?"

It's so hard to know when he's teasing me or when he's serious.

"I owe no one my real address, neither you nor the Queen of England, should she have any interest in knowing. It's not about you, Mr. Asher."

He smiles. "Technically, the ruler of England is now a man."

I grunt in a very unladylike manner and swivel on my feet, striding away from him. "You're an exasperating know-it-all."

I sigh to the undulating charcoal pond. Winter paints New York in shades of gray and onyx and navy. I've heard spring is wetter and darker in England. I flinch. One thing my parents and I have in common, the fact none of us will experience a spring in this city ever again.

"I came to say I accept your proposal," Mr. Asher says.

My eyes go wide, prickles running down my legs. Afraid I've not heard him well, I turn to him very slowly. "You're accepting?"

He nods. "That's what I said."

A problem has lifted off my shoulders, but instead of lightness, the pressure of what I can only call fear flares through me. Is this what they mean when they say "Careful what you wish for"? Step after step, I close the distance between us. "Why are you accepting?"

"Because I can't sit back when I see injustice. Call me a rebel, a misfit."

I cross my arms, not believing a thing he says. "Some might argue a woman's marriage isn't an injustice but a fair ancestral practice."

He shrugs, all nonchalance. "And I would say to hell with ancestral practices. No one should ever be married against their will."

"I'd say the money is also a good incentive."

"I won't lie. The money made all the difference."

It sounds like a good enough reason for me. He's talking riches, and that I understand.

"It might be dangerous." I step closer, as if I were sharing a secret. "Europe is at war."

"Maybe I like the prospects of traveling and living an adventure." One of his eyes squints, almost a wink if I didn't know any better. "Are you trying to make me change my mind?"

"Perhaps."

He puts his hat on, adjusting it at the right angle. "So, Miss Benson, no marriage proposal after all?"

I chuckle, trembling with useless pleasure. "No. Don't be ridiculous."

"Of course, this should be my move."

Before I realize it, he's on a knee on the ground.

"What are you doing?" I hiss. "Stand *ri*—"

He shushes, then grabs my hands, warm fingers forcing my fists open.

"Oh, George, look," says an elderly woman. Next to her, there's a man with white hair, all-black attire, and a high topper.

Mr. Asher cranes his neck in their direction. "I love her so much I want the entire world to know."

"What are you doing?" I repeat in a tight hiss as more people gather around us.

He winks. This time, the twitch on full display. "Playing my part as best I can. Now, Alexandra Benson, it'll be my privilege to serve you as your fake husband. Please say yes for our audience."

A flash of amusement glints in the blue of his eyes. He's so delightfully naughty and loving every second of my torment.

I force my lips into a smile and say yes.

Mr. Asher stands and presses a light kiss on my forehead.

Loud claps block the trolley clangs, the murmurs, and the clopping hooves.

I close my eyes, lost in the feeling of his lips against my skin. For the first time, it feels as though things will work out, and hope shines its way through into me.

And wouldn't it be pleasant if this were real? If this man were truly in love with me and tendering the promise of marriage to me? I never figured myself as a bride. In fact, not even when Elijah courted me did it feel as though one day I'd walk down the aisle wearing a beautiful white dress, holding my father's arm.

But now I imagine Mr. Asher and my father side by side, the way he would've asked my father for his blessings and the manner in which my father would've accepted, with his gentle smile. Mr. Asher and my father would've liked each other. There is something about Mr. Asher's lightheartedness that would've meshed so well with my father's sense of humor.

Men hoot behind me. My eyes blink open, stopping my daydreaming in its tracks. I never figured myself a bride because I never wanted to be one. Where has this delusion come from?

"Ah, man, kiss the bride proper!" one of the men shouts, and the others howl in laughter.

I whip around, mouth hanging open, but Cameron swings me back into his arms, stopping me with a thump against his chest. He trails the side of my head and my loose curls, cutting my breath short. My eyes drag up to his face and those mischievous blue eyes.

"For our audience, Fake Addie? Imagine a Plaza guest is seeing this. We don't want any crack in our lie."

My heart pounds in my head, heat pooling in my cheeks. I remember Elijah's kisses—how much I missed that sort of brush on my lips. Will a kiss be as electrifying with Mr. Asher?

Lost in a forbidden thrill, lost in the lie, my fingers close around his forearm.

"Just a peck," I utter through clenched teeth. Because he's right—and I hate that he *is* right. I have nowhere to hide, and I was the one who sought a fake fiancé. The one who accepted every consequence in this game. He's just playing by my rules, pretending he's smitten with me. He's a good liar. Perfect for *me*—my scheme. If we were a real couple, we'd kiss. I don't want to risk a second of our ruse, but I hate him for using all my weaknesses. Are they *that* out in the open?

He finds my mouth. Closing my lips between his own, he drags the kiss long as his hand cups my nape. Molten fire streams through my veins; my heart goes wild and feral against my ribcage. This is not a peck, but it's not a full kiss either. It hangs in between, and it stirs hunger awake, a hunger that I never knew when Elijah kissed me, a hunger that screams for more when Mr. Asher's lips retreat from mine.

What happened? My problems have billowed away, and there's only fire, blazing alive within me.

While my world stops spinning, Mr. Asher loops my arm in his and ushers me away.

"My father would've smacked you if he had seen what you just made me do," I grunt, ignoring my shame and the headiness.

"I have no doubt," he mutters. "If it makes you feel better, you may slap me on your father's behalf. Go on, don't shy away." He offers his open cheek with a beckon.

Repressing a snort, I shove his face away. "I'll let you live. This one time. Just don't do that again."

"Why, Miss Benson? Did you like it?" He smiles endearingly but straightens and stops in the middle of Gapstow Bridge. And right there I fear I might've made a mistake by involving myself with a man who can look so guiltless after setting my whole world on fire with just one fake kiss.

I wave him off. "Consider yourself lucky we're in public, more like. My mother used to say casual murder was reserved for the privacy of our home." I won't let him see through me.

The Plaza juts over treetops, the sky overcast with purple colors, breeze turned into wind, lifting swirls of dust.

With a sigh, Mr. Asher looks upward. "Do you think that's an ominous sign?"

"It's just weather." But what if he's right? My breath catches, or perhaps it's been that way for a long time. I grab his sleeve. "Do you think you should've asked my uncle for his blessing first? One word from him and he can call the betrothal off."

Cameron's cheeks go hollow. I'm starting to notice he bites the insides of his cheeks when he's pondering. He taps my cold fingers in a reassuring way and lingers on them for a brief moment. "I don't think so. Most likely, your father's memory will be enough to deter a refusal. If he's your uncle, he won't deny one of his brother's last wills."

"That's true. He didn't seem to oppose it. And I don't think he will now, especially as you won't pose a problem to his plans. But this is overly messy . . . I haven't thought this through."

"Let's start with the basics. Does your uncle know about the betrothal?"

"He does, but I could see he was not convinced. It's a good thing he was too stunned to question me. I managed to tell him that we've already had my father's blessings since New Year's Eve, and that you were away, on a business trip, returning early April. But he'll ask more questions. You weren't here through my parents' deaths. He's definitely going to ask me about that."

"The foundation of our lie is that my family is from the West. We're wealthy. What are we doing?"

"Doing?"

"What is the source of my family's fortune?"

I'd not thought about that detail. It says enough of the faith I had in Mr. Asher being mad enough to get on board with this. I raise an eyebrow. "Steel? Common enough."

He nods. "Then we have a business. If they're stranded in Europe, we could say the reason I had to leave on an urgent trip was to tend to the family business before your tragedy struck and that I couldn't come back until I had sorted it out."

I tame down a smile. I have no option but to admit it. "That's brilliant."

He smiles. "Of course it is."

"You clearly don't know humility."

"The pot called the kettle black."

I slap at his lapel, trying not to laugh. Having Cameron with me lifts the anchor etched in my chest, allowing fresh air to reach my lungs. With him, it's easy to forget the darkness in my life, and it shouldn't be that way. It's not fair to my parents' memory. "You're in need of suits if we're to make my uncle believe you're a rich man. Did you have any commitments for today?"

He shrugs. "Not many."

"Let's visit a tailor, then."

"It's their day off."

"Not if you have the money. We have a week to make you ready."

Chapter Six

April 3, 1915

"The *Lusitania* is one of the most beautiful liners; at least you'll travel comfortably," Lindsay says wistfully. Beside her, Elijah flashes me a sympathetic smile and inhales deeply. I love Lindsay because she means well, but she always misses context by a mile.

She hugs me. My best friend has always smelled of lilies, and I'm determined to ingrain her scent in my memories.

"I'll miss you so much, Alix."

"You've only said that for the millionth time today," I tease her with a shake in my voice, giving her one last squeeze before pulling away.

She slides her fingers along her blond plait. "But it's the truth."

"You're just complicating things, Sister," Elijah says as his strong arms go around me.

They've been having luncheon with me, and ever since I broke the news about the result of the reading and my uncle's plans to Lindsay, the shadow of my parting has hovered over us like the clouds covering Manhattan.

"I'll miss you too," Elijah whispers.

"Me too," I say in his ear.

"Is your uncle keeping you so busy?" Lindsay asks me as I escort them to the lobby doors. Elijah beckons at his driver to ready the car.

"I'm afraid, yes," I lie. My uncle is busy arranging our move overseas. I was busy with Cameron, building the fabric of our lie, teaching him the ways of the upper-class men. I kept my friends away from my plans the moment I decided I needed a stranger, but I wasn't ready for the separation to be a hurdle this big.

"I understand," Lindsay says, shadows in her eyes. She reaches for a box in the big pocket of her fluffy beige coat and hands it to me. "We bought this for you."

"With my money," Elijah says, as I inspect the little box wrapped in a red ribbon.

"I contributed by teaching piano to some children."

Elijah coughs. "Two lessons."

She elbows his ribs. "More than enough."

"You didn't have to buy me anything," I say.

"Open it, silly," Elijah says.

I smile and untie the ribbon with impatient tugs. Inside the box lies a thick floral-embossed locket. Gaping, I grab it with trembling fingers and spring it open, expecting it empty. Instead, the image inside pushes an instant yelp out of my lips. A picture of my parents, smiling in one second locked into eternity.

"We had a couple of old photographs of your parents at home," Lindsay says.

Elijah points at a hidden clasp. "And if you open that, you'll find another surprise."

The locket is so thick because it spreads open to house three photographs. My parents' photo is in the middle. On the left side stands a grainy picture of Elijah, Lindsay, and me when we were children. The third one remains empty. "Thank you." My voice is tiny with emotion as I pull both in for a new hug.

"Please, come visit if you feel sad," she says. "I wish we could help."

"There's nothing to do, Linds. But I love you both so much."

"Miss Ellis," the driver says, handing Lindsay a folded piece of paper. "Your mother has sent this note while you were at the luncheon."

"Thank you, Jones," she says. Lindsay squeezes my shoulder. "I'll see what my mother wants, but please, spend some more time with us before you leave."

Elijah and I stay back, and we share a side-eyed glance, our smiles pressed tight. We've not spoken since I left him under the maple tree, and even when we've been keeping our composure with Lindsay, we've not been comfortable, words left unsaid between each other.

I clear my throat. "I thank you for keeping quiet until I was ready to tell her."

"It's the least I could do," he says. "I wanted to apologize for the manner in which I refused . . . I should've explained myself better."

I shrug. "You didn't have to. I selfishly believed you were going to be there forever. What I asked of you wasn't right. I'm sorry."

"I still want to help you come up with another plan. Or are you relenting to your uncle? That's what you told Lindsay, but I don't believe a thing."

I chuckle, my fingers coiling around the locket. "The two of us know I won't go down without a fight. Don't worry about me, Elijah. I have it sorted."

"You found someone?"

"Yes," I whisper. "But please, keep it to yourself. No one can know about this. There is no need to overcomplicate things more than they already are."

"Your secret is safe with me. I'm happy that you found someone to help you, but I'm still so worried about you, Alix. And so sad that it couldn't be me. I would've helped you, but—"

"Yes, you have a darling now." I slip the locket in my pocket. "I know."

"May I be honest with you for a moment? Only if you look up at me."

Reluctantly, I lift my face. His brown eyes are like liquid, milk chocolate, deliciously warm. A thrill of expectation rushes through my stomach. "If you must."

He grabs one of my hands, brushing his thumb over my fist. "What you didn't let me say that day was that, should you have told me you were ready to marry me for love, I would've dropped my word and my engagement and married you in a heartbeat. No matter what a crook that makes of me."

My breath hitches. "Elijah."

I had it so close . . . I just had to pick up on what he wasn't saying out loud. I would've taken him gladly. I love him. I always will. And I would've fallen back in love with him, I'm sure. But how could I do such a thing? I'm not ready to marry. Elijah deserves better than a lie. Love is all a big distant dream.

Sadness grips me from the inside, darkening my heart. He deserves much more. He deserves to be happy *now*. I can't leave the door open.

"You deserve much better than me. Please, be happy. Either with . . . What's her name?"

"Anne," he says.

"Be happy, either with Miss Anne or by yourself or with someone else. I'll be gone for too long." Despite his warm fingers wrapped around mine, they grow cold. "Don't worry for me. I know what I must do, and I already have a plan in motion. It'll work out. I'll return before you know it. Let's just . . . not allow this to break our friendship, please?"

He smiles, but the grin's tilt is tainted. "Never, Alix. Just know that it was not my intention to leave you alone when you needed me the most."

"It was fair that you said no. You deserve a marriage where you're loved from the beginning. I was being selfish. I love you, Elijah."

"Me too." He takes my hand to his mouth and kisses its back.

"I'll write you from England and let you know how boring my life is."

"Fine, but I want you to find things to be happy about, even there."

I smile. "I'll do my best."

We hug one last time, and I stay under the chandeliers in the lobby, watching after his retreating back. Lindsay's billowing dress peeks below her coat, and Elijah covers his curling golden locks with his hat as they walk out.

Long after their car has merged with the traffic, the world keeps moving around me, hotel guests checking in and out, bellboys gliding their carts to the elevators.

I grasp a fistful of my skirt. They're gone, and the sting of grief tears through me. I am empty without them. And Elijah . . . we could've been so much more. But I'm trying to grab something that is coming undone, like that time I went to the beach with Lindsay and Elijah when we were children. We built a beautiful sandcastle. It took us all day, and we were so proud. But the tides started licking at the shore, and I rushed to save our creation. It looked so steady I thought I could transport it somewhere else, but all I held was pastry sand.

Our castle melted before I could blink.

I rush upstairs and storm into my parlor. The fireplaces have been lit. Flickering shadows dance along the room, firelight titillating on the mint-and-pink wallpaper.

I click my chamber's door shut and switch my desk lamp on. It's next to one of the windows overlooking Central Park. Low, bone-tinted clouds pack the sky, as if they were waiting to shed either snow or rain.

Rage snakes through me as I sit in the upholstered chair. This hotel is just around the corner from home, allowing a perpetual sight of places I walked past with my parents. We could've been at a very different hotel, but my uncle booked these suites as though he was reminding me I have no control or power over what is coming undone before me.

Just one more thing I didn't see coming, even if it was in plain sight.

I still can't believe he wants to take me to war-torn Europe, where they draft boys my age to kill each other in trenches. Why does it feel as though I'll never see my friends again? I promised I'll return, but how much damage will distance do to our bond? I'll come back a stranger, no matter the letters. Elijah will forget me and be married. And so will Lindsay. Our lives will have changed. And it'll never be the same.

This is what finitude feels like, an abyss. A wave wipes out whatever remains of us. When I was eleven, I had the chance to dismantle that castle before the tides dissolved it. Life has shown me it will take away from me the things I hold most dear. But this time I won't stand still and simply watch it disappear.

I put paper and a pen out.

Dear Lindsay, dear Elijah, I write with a shaking hand. I take a deep breath. *Today's luncheon has been the most pleasant event in the last months. You're the siblings I never had and I will always cherish the thought of you.*

Remember that sandcastle we built on the beach?

My pen shakes again, leaving a splotch of ink at the question dot. I sigh, closing my eyes. Is cutting ties the only way forward? My law books pile on a dresser, forgotten, and my heart is hurting with all the things I already lost, strewn on the floor like invisible breadcrumbs. I already gave my notice to NYU this week. This, in addition, is rubbing salt into the wound.

I stand, dropping my pen as if the entire desk would've gone up in flames. "No. I can't do this."

I take my coat, stealing glances over my shoulder at the stationery. I throw the door open, then slam it shut. The April edition of my *Harper's Bazar* subscription is neatly laid on a table by the main entrance. I whisk it away and storm to the hallway, shutting another door just as loud as I can.

"Mind you, Miss Benson, the doors are not to blame for your problems. The Plaza has a strong policy on noise."

Mr. Crossley stands at his threshold, three rooms from mine. His blond hair is slicked back, his stance straight and proud. His eyes are foxy, icy, and unwavering. One of his steep cheeks tugs up in a side smile. I shiver. I've never seen him smile before.

"I've been residing here for a month. I know," I grunt, walking toward him. Alas, I have to pass by his door to reach the elevators.

"*Harper's Bazar*, huh?"

I clutch the magazine against my chest. "Yes. Any problem?" Doesn't he have any more interesting matters to focus on? That is what I want to ask, but I bite my tongue.

He shrugs. "I've heard things about it."

I stop, fighting the temptation to make a face. "Such as?"

"About its frivolous ideas and subtle liberalism, besides the latest Parisian fashion trends."

I don't bother holding back my smile of disdain. "I see. What kind of reading material do you prefer, Mr. Crossley?"

He leans on the doorjamb. "Newspapers."

I huff. "Of course."

He raises an eyebrow. "Any problem?"

"I've heard things about newspapers, is all."

He flashes a coy smile, as if I've greatly amused him. "Such as?"

"Their stale ideas, besides the latest flag-waving partisanship think pieces. Things men discuss ever so fervently over brandy and cigars."

"Do you find patriotism a bad thing?"

"There are always two sides for every story."

Mr. Crossley chuckles. "Are you sympathizing with the Germans?"

I flinch. A part of me can't help but feel he's either assessing me or playing with me.

"That's ridiculous. I hardly entertain thoughts of politics and war. As we were discussing, all I care about is the latest Parisian fashion trends, which for your information, now thanks to the war, are starting to be New York's. If you excuse me, I'll go find a suitable spot to read my frivolous magazine."

I walk toward the elevators and don't deign to look back.

Downstairs, I flick the pages of *Harper's Bazar* in a corner of the tearoom, sipping hot lemon water.

The dark day seeps through the stained glass skylight overhead, tinting the stone walls and the floors with faint rainbow patterns. Physically, I'm surrounded by the exotic palm trees in the veranda, but my mind is faraway, as if the mirrors under the arches in the westernmost wall and the caryatids guarding them held the pathways to different worlds. As I close the last page of the magazine for a second time, I take the pendant out of the pocket of my black dress and caress it with my thumb.

My new life is calling me—nay, dragging me away—while the old one keeps demanding my attention. What's the worst that could happen if I let the two worlds converge? The complications have deterred me from introducing Cameron to my friends. I can't make them carry the fib on their shoulders. Besides, Cameron has connections within my outermost acquaintance circle. His friend, Dr. Cooper. People owe me no loyalty. Someone would speak. The secret would be out, my plans ruined.

Holding on to my old life might destroy me, but I can't let go of it. I don't have the *strength*. Maybe if we could just lie a little bit more . . . if he could lie to his friend . . .

I need to see Cameron.

Chapter Seven

It starts snowing as I head to Cameron's apartment in Greenwich Village. The brown-brick building rises four stories before me in the quiet afternoon. The watery cobblestones mirror the smoke waltzing off the rooftops. Far off, the barks of a dog echo in the eddy of small streets.

I pace back and forth by the entrance, frosty flakes dusting my hair and shoulders. Perhaps he's not even in yet. I'm not sure if Cameron wants me to be here or if we even have the kind of closeness that would deem my visit a pleasant surprise instead of turning me into an uncomfortable guest. I've known him for a *week and a half.* Not to mention this must be inappropriate, showing up at his quarters without a chaperone or a foreword. The idea that briefly flitted through me at the hotel seems silly, but it's all I have left to avoid saying goodbye to my life. And he, once again, is the key to the lock.

I might also have grown used to his presence, the soft sound of his voice always carrying gentle jauntiness, how steady the ground feels when I'm around him. When I'm on my own, loneliness is too loud, and the world spins too quickly. But this, I'll never admit out loud.

A carriage trots up the street. The man and woman in the forward seat cut a suspicious glare at me. Skidding to a stop, I bite my lip to pretend I'm not acting like a lunatic.

I've sent my driver to drink a warm beverage while he waits for me. He's mentioned a tavern three streets from here. If I told him I'd reconsidered, he'd drive me back, no questions asked.

"No, you're here now," I whisper, storming inside. Cameron's apartment is down an aged yet clean corridor on the fourth floor. The sconces cast a gleam on the white linoleum with black lines running along the sides.

I knock on Cameron's door and wait for a full minute. Nothing. Shivering, I regret staying in the cold for that long. My toes are numbing inside my boots, chill seeping through the soles. Pulling my wool jacket tightly around me, I strain my ears in the hope I can hear something. Through the walls, I catch a child's laughter, a conversation growing a bit louder—yet nothing from Cameron's place.

I bang my fist repeatedly until Cameron's voice booms on the other side. "Fuck. Stop. I'm home." He swings the door open, leaning on the jamb. "No need to be a goddamn ass—Alexandra."

"I love it when men talk dirty," I say. "You need to lie to your friend."

He rubs his forehead. "Excuse me?"

"Sean, was it?" I duck under his arm and walk into his apartment.

"Do you wish to enter my humble abode?"

"I was freezing in that hallway," I say over my shoulder, heading toward the far end of the corridor. Light spills through a quartet of big windows in the open kitchen and the living room. The flurry flakes are piling on the windowsills now, snow plunging hard. In the sitting room, a hearth is lit. Rounding an open trunk, I skitter to the roaring flames, reaching out to them.

"Thank God," I mutter as soon as heat warms me.

"There's something called coats—you should try one."

"I left the hotel in a rush. I didn't think it'd be this cold." Not to mention, I could've run into someone if I had gone to retrieve my coat. As things are, I can barely sneak out undetected, and when I go out alone, I always get away with it because I'm supposed to meet my friends—thus, chaperoning in my destination. But my constant outings will end up raising a red flag at some point. That is, if Uncle Nigel cares. So far, he hasn't shown any concern or interest in what I do with my time. That, in itself, only feeds my doubts.

Cameron stacks several books, sheets of paper pressed in between, and plops them onto the kitchen counter.

"You don't have to tidy up just because I'm here," I say.

"Would you like some tea?"

"Please."

"I only have black tea." He rubs his nape. His eyes are bloodshot. It's the first time I've seen him so . . . discomposed.

"That will suffice. What were you doing?"

"Taking a nap." He puts a kettle on the stove.

"Long day?"

He looks over his shoulder, lifting a quizzical eyebrow. "Why so many questions?"

I raise one of my eyebrows. "Why are you avoiding *my* questions?"

"You don't usually ask me about, well, anything. You could say I'm . . . taken aback."

Heat pools in my cheeks. Have I not taken an interest in him? I browse through rushed memories of us, engulfed by our ruse, Manhattan society, or by me teaching him how to use all the silverware set for dinners and luncheons, but among those memories, I barely recall a time I asked him about himself beyond brief questions here and there. The character he's playing has taken over him. There's not much room for Cameron.

A slash of guilt pushes a huff out of me.

"I thought we'd meet tomorrow for the luncheon with your uncle," he says. "What brought you here?"

I look down at the rolled magazine sticking out of my big pocket. Perhaps he's had a rough day. While my troubles are bad, he reminds me that there are people out there living far worse lives than mine. What has truly made him consider I'm worth helping?

No, it's not that he thinks me worthy. It's been the money. He sees profit. Deep inside, I like that our grounds are so clear, our relationship so transparent—something I wouldn't have with Elijah. Money was all I could offer, and I happened to get lucky in hitting Cameron's weakness.

"I'm sorry for invading your home like this," I say.

Silence fills the space between us. In the mirror over the fireplace, I watch as he sets two cups on the kitchen table.

"You said I need to lie to Sean, I think."

"Forget it."

"Look, I told you where my apartment was in case you wanted to visit me. I'm still half asleep, so why don't you sit here"—he taps the back of one of the chairs—"and explain yourself?"

"Fine." I leave the magazine atop a low table and sit in the spot he's offered.

The whistle from the kettle draws his attention. While he's busy, I peek at the room. Black brocade covers the walls. In front of the hearth sit a jade camelback sofa and an armchair. Clothes are folded on the sofa's seat, and stacks of books pile up around the place like small towers. He's packing his trunk, deciding what he'll bring to England, and making room in his apartment for his new, fake life. In the kitchen, the cabinets are white, in contrast with the black stove. More books sit precariously balanced on top of each other on the counter. Between them, the sheets of paper stick out like children thrusting out their tongues, languidly bending downward. My eyes follow the lines until the very end, where my name, in neatly typewritten letters over the sand-colored page of a telegram, catches my attention. "Is that my name?"

"Hmm?" Cameron asks, turning sharply. "Oh, yes, right." He retrieves the books, stacks them farther from me, and clears his throat. "It is. It's a telegram for one of my students at Walden. Her parents are traveling and wanted to know how well she's doing with math."

I raise an eyebrow, but I press no further. "Is this apartment yours?"

"Rent." Cameron throws tea bags into our cups and pours steaming water. "All right, what've you been thinking about?"

"I'm having a hard time breaking up with my old life," I say as he sits across from me.

He takes his cup to his mouth. "Why would you need to do that yet?"

"I can't make my friends carry the burden of our lie." It's such a relief, being with him where no one else will eavesdrop. Libraries, parks, museums, or cafés, none have felt safe enough. I'm probably becoming paranoid, but I always have the feeling someone is watching us. "And, should our relationship go public before we're away, our mutual acquaintances could tell my uncle you're not who we say you are."

His eyes light up with realization. "I see."

I take a sip of tea, hoping the warmth comforts me. Outside, snow keeps fluttering to the ground. "This is why you need to lie to your friend."

He stands. "I had my last suit delivered yesterday. I was to try it on. Would you like to see how I look in it?"

"Cameron," I groan.

Licking his lips, he sets down his cup on the counter. "Ah, yes. I am going to try it on."

My mouth falls open while I stare at him strolling around the corner, grabbing the telegram and a book at the last second. I finish my tea in one gulp and puff through my nose. He's a simpleton if he thinks we're done.

I sink into his armchair. From my spot, I can see down the corridor. Cameron's bedroom is on the left by the entrance. White daylight spills inside through his open door. It flickers with the shadow of his bare torso, clearly defined along the floor as he dons a shirt. I cut my gaze away, a nervous heat condensing in my cheeks, and pry my mind away from his kiss in Central Park, still kindling back to life from time to time.

The apartment is warm and filled with the scent and crackle of fire-licked wood. The soft sounds lull me. Creaks on floorboards, drawers rolling shut, clacks of footsteps—it's a melody, so easy, weightless. I could close my eyes and listen forever.

I startle just as my head nods. With wide eyes, I confirm Cameron is still in his room.

"Not possible," I utter, picking up my *Harper's Bazar*, convincing myself I've not nearly dozed off in Cameron's apartment. For a long while, I browse through the magazine. Now that I'm paying attention to its contents, I clench my jaw at the flick of every page—stories on English manors, the latest trends for wedding frocks, a Cunard advertisement—as if the editors were mocking me.

"You're taking longer than a woman on her wedding day," I say to Cameron, shoving the magazine shut.

His steps immediately follow. "I'm ready. I couldn't find the cuff links."

When he comes into sight, my breath catches and tides of pleasure and comfort move in my stomach. Not yet ready for polite society, Cameron's waistcoat and jacket are unbuttoned, his tie dangles around his neck, and he's fastening his cuffs, and still, he's one of the most attractive men I've seen.

He looks up and stops at the threshold, his messy hair shining faintly under the pool of a wall fixture. "What do you think?"

I hold his gaze for a second too long, the ghostly feeling of his kiss snaking through me once again.

"Finish dressing," I say, turning a page of my magazine to pretend I'm not bedazzled. In all fairness, I chose him well. Only a man aware he's in control can make me feel this way. And Cameron is.

"Nervous about the luncheon tomorrow?" he asks, unfurling his jacket sleeves over his cuffs.

"No," I say. "You've been a brilliant student. Are you worried?"

"No." He rolls his shoulders, as if adjusting his jacket. "I'm ready."

I narrow my eyes. "There's only one fork that goes on the right side—which one is it?"

"Seafood," he shoots without hesitation. "Followed by two spoons—dinner and soup, then come the knives."

"Good. You're offered sweet sherry before the meal, which glass are you choosing?"

He smiles, turning to peer at me. "None. Sherry is a digestif. It should be offered after the courses."

"You'll do well." A smile feathers on my face. "I've been wondering. How much does your friend know about your real life?"

Standing in front of his full-body mirror near the corner, Cameron tugs at his sleeves. "Enough to know I am not born into wealth."

I sigh. "Then you'll have to tell him you've lied to him."

He lets out a noisier sigh. "I won't, under any circumstances, lie to my friend."

I sit up in his armchair. "We can't allow anyone to learn about our ploy. All it takes is one person saying the wrong thing, and they'll ruin everything."

He casts me a dead look in the mirror. "Remind me why I am doing this?"

I drop the *Harper's Bazar* edition on the table. A dark-haired lady is on the cover under a cherry tree, and her puffy coat and long pleated skirt billow in the wind. She seems happier than I'd ever be if a gust would blow my hat away. "Money?"

He lowers his eyes, and his fingers struggle to knot his tie. I get up and approach him, afraid he has second thoughts about us—our *plan*. He might, and it'd be fair. Asking him for more sacrifices might be crossing a line. I asked him to leave everything behind to marry me, a complete stranger, and he's stoically putting up with me.

And I happen to know why. His weakness isn't parties and a lavish life. "No, not money," I whisper. "The children."

A muscle twitches in his jaw, as if he's not sure whether he's disappointed or surprised or sad. "I've been drafting my resignation letters." He tries to mask his sadness, but I hear it, drenching vowels and consonants.

Shame presses my tongue. While I've been locked in my ivory tower, Cameron has been facing losing his life.

"I'm sorry," I reply. "I'm being insufferable, but you'll learn to like me."

He chuckles. "I thought we didn't have to be friends."

"I guess we don't have to be." I gesture at his tie. "Let me?"

He shrugs. "It's all yours."

Careful to avoid his chest, I pick the skewed knot and loosen it. Even if I intently focus on the black silk, Cameron's gaze roves my face, setting my skin aflame from the tip of my nose to the shape of my cheekbones.

"How did you learn to tie a tie?" His breath caresses my forehead.

I hold back a sigh. "My many lovers, of course."

Cameron's shoulders stiffen.

When I look up at his face, I can't help but laugh at his wary eyes. "I'm jesting. What does it feel like to have humble pie, Mr. Asher?"

He laughs, his frame loosening. "You have teeth, Miss Benson. I love it."

"I actually tied my father's ties since I was a child. It was a game." Cross the wide end over the narrow one, wide end goes through the loop, and down it goes; the silky knot slides up, closing in on Cameron's neck.

With my handiwork already finished, one of my hands falls to my side, yet the other flicks and rests on his chest over his soft shirt. Cameron doesn't back away, his heartbeats strong and fast against my palm.

"May I ask you, when did your parents die?"

"This January, on the evening of the twenty-eighth. They were coming back home from a trip upstate. They drove off a cliff.

"The car was a hodgepodge of metal and broken glass, and their bodies were so damaged I could only identify them by their personal effects." A lump lodges in my throat, sharpening every word to glass. "The police hinted they'd committed suicide, but they could never do—it."

Tears hold onto my eyelids, my soul screeching a cry in the dark. They never could've done such a thing. It's impossible. They were happy, in love. They were adventurous and loved life. One of my last memories of them was on Christmas, merrily dancing before the fireplace. To even think they could veer their car off a road on purpose would add insult to injury.

He sighs. "I shouldn't have asked."

I crack a watery smile. "You need to know this information to fool my uncle. No matter how hurtful it is to me."

Cameron presses his lips in a tight line, shadows dancing in his blue eyes. "There's something you should be aware of."

"What is it?" I ask, my brows knitting.

The air around us drops like an anchor, his face filling with a pressing darkness. My body knots, expecting the worst. Is he going to tell me he's abandoning me?

He whips his head to the mirror and lets out a dour chuckle. "Nothing. The pain will fade—in due time."

Was that everything he wanted to tell me? "You sound like you speak from experience?"

He clears his throat, turning full body from me to tie his vest. "I do." His voice is airy, with an edge of tension.

I gulp. Not a good idea to press in that direction. Whoever he lost, it still hurts, no matter what he said. "Well, there is something you should be aware of too."

"What is it?"

I lick my lips. Should I even share my doubts about Uncle Nigel? "I'm not even sure if this is relevant, but I have grounds to believe something happened with my father's will."

He squints. "Such as?"

"I believe it was changed. Either by my father at the last minute or—"

"Or by your uncle?"

I frown. "Yes. How did you know I was going to mention my uncle?"

He shrugs, buttoning his jacket. "You made it clear that your uncle is the testament's beneficiary, and you're trying to get married as soon as possible to inherit. I put two and two together."

I wait for him to dismiss my idea like Elijah. But the dismissal never comes. "So, you believe me?"

"Why would I not believe you?"

I open my mouth, ready to explain myself, but the words weigh on me, so I shake my head and simply smile. "Thank you, I guess."

"Ah, she finally says the two magic words." He turns his head to me and winks. "You're welcome."

He steals the voice from my throat, the ideas from my mind. Pleasant warmth spreads through me. "Either way, I don't think it's relevant anymore. Just be aware that my uncle might try to trick you. He didn't believe me when I told him I was already engaged."

He tsks. "You don't have to worry. I'll have him charmed before you can say Jack Robinson."

A snicker flies out of my lips. Stepping away from him, I graze the open lid of a trunk. "Are you already choosing what will come with you?"

"Yes, but I'm traveling light. My brother will send the rest when I've settled," he says absentmindedly, clasping the last button on his jacket.

I press my lips into a tight line, my fingers itching to do that for him. "What did you say to your family?"

"Only that I was hired to help someone in Europe with school matters."

"It must be great to be a man." He doesn't have to justify his every move and will never be frowned upon anywhere he goes. The world lies at his feet.

"I can't complain," he says. "But make no mistake, freedom like ours, it always comes at a price."

"Nobody cares how you feel," I say. A man could never dream of the emotional support and leeway I have for being a woman. "At least nobody says you're a hysterical brat."

"Believe it or not, I was called a brat once."

Although he's trying to hide it, there's an air of sadness about him. It's his duty as a man to remain cold and in control, yet it's not fair he can't show his emotions. Since I've dragged him into this, all I can do is show him I care for him. "Forget what I said about your friend."

"You might think I don't want to let Sean know because he'll be mad, but there's more to it than just treating my student. Sean wouldn't let me pay for the treatment, checkups, or medicines. If now all I can come up with is I'm rich, not only do I risk losing a good friend, but—"

"Looking like a grifter." He could be jailed. I could be ruined. We're, in fact, in so much danger. One wrong move, one poor word choice, and it'll be our end. I nod. "I understand."

His brow furrows. "Maybe there's a way to fix this. Maybe I can let Sean in on what we're doing with the testament—"

I shake my head no. "It's too dangerous. And you're already giving up too much. It's my turn. My separation from my friends is inevitable either way."

He can't save me from everything.

Again, his gaze burns me. Only this time I get lost in it for several seconds. Our eyes swim with emotions. A whirl takes over my senses, threatening to push me into his arms.

I swerve my face, and Cameron clears his throat, turning toward the mirror. "How do I look?"

"Dashing," I say, and I'm not lying.

"Why thank you, Miss Benson." He tightens his tie around his collar. "Great knot, by the way."

"I take it you know how to knot your ties, so don't get used to it."

"What if I don't and I had to resort to paying visits to the brothel down the street to get it knotted?"

I stiffen, holding my breath, but as a smirk tugs at his cheek, I grunt and walk away. "You're silly. We know your tie would be flung away instead of tightened."

"Is that your way of saying you find me attractive?"

"Please, stay silent. You're giving me a pointed headache. Here." I tap at my temple.

He chuckles, sliding off his jacket. "Remind me again what time I should be at the Plaza tomorrow?"

He doffs his vest. I'm enthralled by his suspenders, crossing over his back and latched onto the back of his trousers. They curve over his shoulders, running along his back, and the sharp V lines of his torso. His white shirt is fitted, and his muscles move underneath as he works on his tie.

I blink. Oh, God. Why is he undressing? Why do I keep staring? Why am I even in his apartment? This is . . . so indecorous. I'm lucky he's not taken my visit the wrong way.

"That reminds me, I must leave. But tomorrow, at one. I'll go back to the hotel now so you can keep undressing, you scoundrel."

I dash toward the door, his guffaw loud at my back. "You forgot your magazine."

"Keep it. It might serve you well!"

Chapter Eight

April 4, 1915

The residents' Plaza restaurant is packed to the brim; building conversations and laughter mix with beams of watery sunshine on the glittering chandeliers. I conceal my trembling hands by pressing my fingers onto the porcelain cup. The blazing maroon liquid sloshes against my lips. With regret, I put the cup down.

"Why so nervous, Miss Benson?" Mr. Crossley asks, sticking an olive pit out of his mouth. He drops it on a plate. My uncle's assistant has been chewing on the same olive for five minutes, slouched and untroubled in his chair in a way I could only dream of. Our permanent table near the corner has expanded to house four guests. The only empty spot is Cameron's.

"It's not every day that I introduce my beloved to my family." I lightly tap my napkin to my lips, refusing to peek at the entrance. Cameron is late. I'm going to kill him. "Which begs the question, what are you still doing here?"

"Where does he come from again?" Mr. Crossley asks, ignoring me.

"Denver."

"And who did you say his family is?" my uncle asks.

I have the feeling they're questioning me in case I contradict myself. I know I can't. I've rehearsed this information with Cameron so much I am sick of his fake family. "The Ashers."

"Never heard of them," Nigel says.

"You don't have to. His family invested in steel and helped set up the railroad in Denver. He's new money. Not a Vanderbilt."

I nod toward Alfred Vanderbilt, who currently sits five tables from ours, engrossed in conversation with a friend. From time to time, their laughter reaches us.

The good thing about Cameron's story is that it's believable, yet it doesn't compromise much. Digging out the truth would take my uncle too much precious time and resources.

"But he's a teacher?" Mr. Crossley wonders.

I cast a sharp look at him. "Yes."

"It's fine, Mr. Crossley," my uncle clips. "I must admit, my niece is right. I allowed your presence at the table, but don't overstep. I'm sure Mr. Asher will answer all our questions. Should he ever attend our luncheon."

I clench my teeth. "I'm sure an urgent issue held him up. Perhaps the snow is at fault."

"I don't understand why you didn't bring him up sooner," Uncle Nigel presses. "Purchasing a ticket to the *Lusitania* is proving a nightmare now."

Pretending I'm hurt, I lower my head and clutch the napkin to my chest. "Cameron had to leave shortly after he proposed to tend to family business, and I was too miserable to discuss romantic matters with a practical stranger. I feared he would never come back. I was angry and ashamed I might not be appealing anymore now that I was an orphan. What was I supposed to do, Uncle?"

Considering he met a girl who didn't want to leave her bed, it is believable.

"Yet I never saw his letters. How did he communicate with you?"

He's behaving the way I expected, all defenses up to attack. I lean forward, a picture of perfect innocence widening my eyes. "My maid Mia picked up the letters and gave them to me. That is, before you fired her. In his last letter, Cameron said he was returning. Besides, you read his telegram, isn't that right? He just arrived in Manhattan this Friday. Do you think I'm lying, Uncle?"

Uncle Nigel sighs and straightens in his chair. "Nothing of the sort. I only hope this is not a way for you to thwart our plans to leave for England. It's the most convenient arrangement for you right now."

"I am in no way trying to go against your wishes, Uncle. Besides, Cameron is happy with going to England. His family is stranded in Europe."

"If you think about it, Mr. Benson," Mr. Crossley chimes in. "It's all the better for her and you. That tanned skin would've never married well in England."

I whip my head toward him. "Pardon me?"

"I'm just saying, you're not blond and fair skinned, and those are the most desired traits for a good English wife."

My mouth hangs open. What exactly do they mean? They're but a tone or two lighter than me. My skin is sandy and my hair is a shade of walnut, yet my eyes are ice blue. My parents were English. I'm as English as the next English rose; only, I come with American hardware. And what if my skin were darker? Or if my eyes were a rich honey hue? Would they treat me differently? They definitely would. Would I be stripped of my money and thrust into servitude? Would I be disowned?

"True," my uncle says. "You can thank that Spanish mother of yours, Alexandra."

"Valeria." Mr. Crossley rounds every letter of the name on his tongue.

"What did you just call her?" I retort.

"Isabella," my uncle corrects, his expression a thunder of fire on his assistant. Isabella, in honor of my mother's Italian grandmother.

Silence, as thick as smoke, surrounds the table. Mr. Crossley and Nigel share a visceral stare.

Mr. Crossley pulls a face and immediately produces a smile. "Right. My mistake." He tilts his cup. "This coffee was heavily leaning into the Irish side."

I stand. "It's then very convenient that my having a suitor will save you all that hassle with my inconvenient skin tone."

"Now, missy, you know it was an observation without malice."

How dare he? It was such an indecorous remark. So out of line. Cameron walking into the restaurant saves me from chucking my lukewarm tea at Mr. Crossley's face. He's tall and lean in his fitted navy blue suit with a cream tie, his jaw and shoulders are sculpted in sharp angles. He looks like a man made for business and high-class parties as he tilts on his left side to talk to the host.

"Excuse me," I tell my uncle and his assistant, skirting the chair, and dash to Cameron, slithering around the busy tables.

"You're late," I whisper, unmoved by the comfort he makes me feel.

He smiles at the host. "She'll show me to my table. Thank you."

"You are late," I repeat, stressing every letter.

"I overslept. I was working late last night on my notices to hand in tomorrow to the schools."

His eyes lose their natural glint. A storm of shame breaks loose inside me. His new leather shoes are still wet with snow, and I can only imagine him rushing through the ice-filled streets to arrive on time while dealing with his broken heart. Even if he's late, I'm happy he's finally here. Safe. All *mine*. This possessiveness and protection shrink my lungs with surprise. Where these feelings come from, I don't know, but when I speak next, they infuse my voice with a sweeter tone. "You're here now. Are you ready?"

With a quick glance, he takes in the entire restaurant. "As ready as I can be."

I was awed when I first explored the corners of this hotel, by the chandeliers, the softness of every fabric, the gold accents. Cameron must be impressed, but he does little to show it. I can distinguish a flash of curiosity in his eyes only because I'm inches away from him, but he remains solemn and focused.

I turn to our table, and Cameron laces our hands with a warm squeeze and stamps a quick unscripted kiss on my forehead, making me trip on a chair. My arching eyebrows must give my surprise away. "Remember we're young and in love, dove."

Not many people can catch me off guard like he does. This, of course, I'll take to my grave.

"Good afternoon, gentlemen," Cameron says with an unwavering tone. He's turned on a switch, as if swooping in with a new personality were *that* easy. "I'm deeply sorry for having made you wait, but crossing uptown through the fresh snow has proven a challenge."

"You're forgiven, Mr. Asher. Thank you for joining us." My uncle signals at the chairs. Our cue to sit down, as though we were trained elephants.

Cameron places a hand on the small of my back and ushers me to my seat. He waits until I'm seated to scoot me closer to the table, then takes the chair next to mine.

Pleasure cruises through me as my uncle's expression fills with wary respect. But soon enough, his respect fades into blood thirst. "I've heard you're a teacher, Mr. Asher."

Straight for the jugular, I see.

"That I am, sir," he says, then proceeds to talk about his schools. Brooklyn raises the eyebrows of my uncle and his assistant, but Walden School . . . that one perks them up.

"I've heard of that school. Quite popular among the Manhattan socialites," my uncle says. "What do you like so much about teaching there? What makes it so popular?"

"The progressiveness, sir. Faculty is addressed by first name. It's hands-on learning and oriented toward the future and critical thinking. We educate skilled, aware citizens. In our school, learning takes root. We don't introduce our pupils to mere superficial knowledge. It's all about heart over brain, idealism and passion over realism."

I gape. With every brush of his real personality, I'm reminded I barely know Cameron at all. All I cared about was his fake persona rather than his true self.

Playing my part, I give him a reassuring squeeze on the shoulder. "Isn't he brilliant?" I ask. Yet on the inside, cracks run all through me. He burns so bright when he speaks about teaching.

"Why is American society so invested in progressive thinking?" Nigel wonders aloud.

"Why not? The world evolves and won't stop evolving."

"In my opinion, it's more cycle than evolution," Mr. Crossley chimes in.

"I agree. But each cycle takes on a new shape regardless."

He pops a piece of bread into his mouth. *"Touché."*

A waiter appears to take our orders.

"Swiftness, please; we're starving," my uncle says, no doubt as a dig at Cameron. The waiter nods, and once he leaves, Nigel refines his interrogation, "Teaching at Walden School, it strikes me you'd even consider a position at a school for destitute children."

"It helps me to keep myself in check, to work directly with those who need help. Those kids aren't responsible for their circumstances. I'm far more privileged than them, so I believe it's my duty, in order to help create a lawful society, to invest my time in the less favored."

My uncle nods, and I crack a small smile as Cameron turns his head in my direction. Another battle he has sorted without a scratch.

"Not that invested in the family business, then?" Mr. Crossley says.

"Not that much, no. Being a middle son, I have more leeway to pursue my truest aspirations."

These days, I've learned that Cameron is actually the younger sibling. His older brother is a doctor, and his parents are a saleswoman and a retired policeman turned private investigator. I make a mental note to ask him why neither of the siblings followed in their father's footsteps.

Uncle Nigel laces his hands on the table. "It's obvious you love teaching. Won't you miss it? You're losing many opportunities to follow my niece to England. It feels subpar."

A gasp passes my lips, too late for me to repress it.

"Why would you call your family subpar, Mr. Benson?" Cameron asks with an edge. Mimicking my uncle's stance, he laces his fingers on the table.

"A poor word choice on my end. What I mean is you obviously have stronger callings; in comparison, joining hunting parties on the English moorlands and drinking fine brandy by the fireplaces while you discuss politics and the latest news from the Great War *do* seem subpar."

I shoot a poisonous stare at my uncle, but he's too fixated on Cameron to notice me.

"Certainly. But see, Mr. Benson, it turns out I quite enjoy the idea of England. There are people in need on the island as well. Orphans due to war or poverty. I can resume my labor in England, I assure you."

I draw circles over Cameron's jacket, on his lower back. The only one to catch a sight of it is Mr. Crossley, who crafts a shaky smile but says nothing.

"Then, of course," Cameron continues, "my family, including my parents and sister, are stranded on European soil as we speak. I'm deadly worried about them, and I would like to be closer to them.

"And last but not least, however, the most important detail is I do love Alexandra. I would follow her to the very heart of the war if need be."

With those lethal blue eyes, stern face, and passionate discourse, Cameron could fool the devil himself. I slowly stop tracing circles on his back. I don't need to pretend a blush. A flare of heat invades me head to toe. He's so brilliant I ache—pleasure, safety, and unease running at once inside me.

My uncle seems reluctant to give up yet, though. "We're at war, Mr. Asher, and it's a complicated one at that. I don't know if you're aware of it."

"Oh, I am perfectly aware of it, Mr. Benson. Are you, though?"

Cameron, single-handedly, has managed to throw a punch without a fist. My uncle smiles, but if he's about to counter, the waiter stops him. The man in the brass-buttoned jacket sets down soup dishes. Delicious warm scents swirl to my nose: peas, onion, mushroom, and tomato. In the middle of each plate, they've placed a triangle of toasted bread.

I lean over the table, clutching my napkin on my chest. "I trust that you won't deny my father one of his last wishes, which was seeing his loving daughter happily married to a man she loves, Uncle. I hope that in your heart, you want that too."

My uncle's smile is so tight I'm afraid it will tear like paper. A couple of seconds pass, but to me it's as if the clock had stopped ticking altogether.

"Of course, my dear. All we want is a proper life for you. Mr. Asher seems quite the gentleman, and I want to respect my brother's wish. You have my blessings. So, Mr. Asher, welcome to the family. Now, let's eat before our meals go cold."

Mr. Crossley unfurls a napkin with a jerk of his wrist. "Bon appétit," he says in perfect French.

Chapter Nine

April 23, 1915

Our car tootles through packed traffic, following the throng of vehicles verging into Fifth Avenue.

"I hate Friday-afternoon traffic," I say.

Wriggling my hands on my lap, I force my head to empty so my imagination doesn't run wild with visions of my parents' car tumbling down a hill.

The last weeks' snow has downsized to icy water by the sidewalk. If not for the heavy rain drumming against the windows, blurring the dim daylight outside like smudged paint, I wouldn't mind the twenty-minute walk between the small Princess Theatre and the Plaza. At least we'd get some distance between Mr. Crossley and us. Boxed up with the driver at the front of the car, he can surely hear everything we're saying through the thin glass.

"It doesn't seem like a normal traffic jam," Cameron says.

I'd thought him absorbed by the city.

"Did you enjoy *Nobody Home*?" I ask. It opened three days ago, a two-act play about the complications of courtship.

He smiles. "I found it endearing."

"Endearing," I repeat, the word strange on my tongue.

He chuckles. "Anything wrong with endearing?"

"It sounds a bit . . . condescending, Mr. Asher," I say with a quick bat of my eyelashes.

The car hits the brakes, jolting us forward. I stop myself from hitting the wall, landing flat on my palms, my wrists taking the brunt of the thump.

The driver punches the horn and screams at a car, an arm swinging out the window. A faint Italian accent slips in his voice.

Cameron whistles, a leg stretched out against the front wall.

I gasp, then stutter, words lost in my throat. In my mind, my parents' car topples over and over down a slope in the night, glass shattering, steel buckling, wheels still spinning without a road underneath, and my parents inside, tumbling like ragdolls, their bodies breaking, bleeding.

Cameron places his hand on my arm. "Alexandra. Are you all right?"

With his help, I slip back onto the seat. My heart thrums so loudly the noise around me becomes muffled. "I am."

He caresses my cheek, and either his fingers are too warm or I am too cold. "Are you sure? Are you hurt?"

I nod. "I'm fine. You?"

"I'm good."

Mr. Crossley has not so much as blinked or uttered a single thing. He's observing the situation straight-faced. Is he even human?

"My apologies," the driver tells us.

"It's fine, Mr. Bianchi," Cameron says.

"I'll take a small detour and hopefully avoid the jam at Fifth Avenue."

Mr. Crossley, although nobody has consulted him, nods and gives directions to the driver, as if he'd known the city for far longer than a handful of weeks.

"I was thinking next time we can go see *The Tramp*," Cameron says, calm settling again inside the Landaulet. And if I didn't know him any better, I would say he wanted to distract me.

"A Chaplin fan," I say. "Do you think it's already released in England?"

He gives me a playful tap on the chin. "We still have a week left."

A week. The time frame lingers in the air. With the whirlwind of events, I've not stopped to consider how close the date of our departure is. And now . . . it's nearly here. My gloved thumbs fumble against each other. My world has been spinning out of control for too long. This theater run with Cameron feels like a miracle, an echo from a time that no longer felt within reach.

"I wanted to ask you something," I say, watching the seats forward. Ahead, Madison Avenue is emptier, the car now advancing at a higher speed. Mr. Crossley's head is cocked left. It's not the best time to ask Cameron about his family, but I found the question slipping from me. Choosing my vocabulary with care, I ask, "How come you didn't follow your father's steps? How did he take you . . . not becoming a businessman like him?"

Cameron's side smile quirks with a tremble. "It was his idea, in fact. He asked me to follow my aspirations. I think . . . he realized life is short and my life is mine to live. Which reminds me of something." Lifting a finger, he bends and fumbles underneath the seat.

"What are you doing?"

He fishes out a brown bag. "Look what our driver has obtained for us while we were at the theater." Cameron slides out a bottle of champagne and two flutes.

"What are we celebrating?" I ask, while Cameron pops the cork open with a flourish.

"Do you know why I almost arrived late for the play?"

He pours the sizzling gold into my flute, his warm fingers closing softly over my hand to steady it from the jostle of the car.

"I didn't have a chance to ask you before the lights went down."

"Mr. Bianchi, would you like some champagne?" he asks the driver. Cameron moved into the Plaza less than a week ago, and he already knows the drivers, waiters, bellboys, and the rest of the staff, while I haven't bothered to speak with them in nearly two months. While I take pride in being courteous to the people serving me, in my daze and grief after losing my parents, I forgot to make others feel human.

"No, thank you, sir, I can't drink at work, and I'm headed straight home after I drop you at the Plaza. I have a small bambino to greet in sound mind."

Cameron smiles. "A very good reason."

Fifty-First Street glides past, allowing sight of Fifth Avenue. Cars and carriages pour into the boulevard, slowing us down.

"Mr. Crossley?" Cameron asks.

My uncle's assistant waves him off.

"And that good news is?" I ask as Cameron helps himself to a glass of champagne.

"Walden School called me in for a meeting today. They've offered to hold my position at the school."

He clinks his glass against mine.

"Cameron?" I say, my voice high with joy. "For how long?"

A question aimed at Mr. Crossley and not him. My uncle cannot know Cameron plans to return to America.

"For as long as it takes, that's what they said. In the meantime, the founder is giving me recommendation letters to bring to England."

"I'm so happy for you." Careful not to spill the champagne, I throw my arms around him, pulling him so we are chest to chest. His new scent of citrus and cedar clings to me. I freeze mid-hug, my eyes wide. This time, I've crossed the physical boundaries of our relationship.

Pressed to me, Cameron is also still, his breath tickling my hair.

The car slows down as I pull away. In the rearview mirror, Mr. Crossley has, of course, witnessed everything.

"Congratulations," I whisper.

Cameron smiles and raises his glass.

I down the flute in one sitting while the tune of "Cupid at the Plaza," one of the songs from *Nobody Home*, plays from afar in my memory, as if it were mocking me. I cannot stress enough the irony of it. Cupid, the god of love, at the Plaza, while we're pretending we're a married-to-be couple.

Since Mr. Bianchi has taken another detour, we round onto East Sixty-Third Street to avoid the traffic jam and reach the Plaza from the north.

The street where I grew up. I'm not ready to see my parents' home again, not when I'm so close to leaving Manhattan. Holding my breath, I count the seconds until it rolls by, rows of dark brown. Thanks to the vines that wreathe up the neighbor's facade, my gaze falls on my parents'.

Thankfully, we leave it behind quickly, but my neck cranes, following the brownstones until the row blends away with the street.

I sigh, turning.

"Everything fine?" asks Cameron.

I flash a tight smile. "Yes."

The Plaza juts out on the corner near Central Park, cream colors against dark skies, guests walking in and out of the hotel. Rain has subsided to a drizzle when we step out of the car.

Cameron rushes to grab my hand. "Do you know if your parents' home sold?"

The question is as abrupt as if he'd pulled a rug from beneath my feet. I look to the hotel entrance, but Mr. Crossley is already walking in. No doubt to report to my uncle.

The tip of my shoe steps on a shallow puddle, the light layers of tulle in my petticoat underneath my red coat dampening. I sigh. "It did, shortly after it was put up for sale."

Cameron nudges me away from the puddle, closer to him. "Has anyone moved in?"

I blink. "I'm not sure."

He leans toward me, a smirk curling a corner of his mouth. "It's not far from here. Would you like to investigate?"

"Excuse me?" I let out an incredulous chuckle.

His thumb traces an arc on my wrist. "There won't be a better time for it. We've been safely driven back to the hotel. They won't even think about us now."

"You can't be serious."

"No, I am very serious indeed. I saw the way you looked at it. It's the last time you'll have with your family's townhouse, at least until you can recover it from whoever bought it. We set sail in eight days. Up to you."

"You're making me regret telling you about that house." I can't hide anything from him, can I? Not even my heart's deepest desires, it seems. I purse my lips, trying not to smile, but soon enough a smirk spreads on my face from cheek to cheek. "But . . . if you insist."

Chapter Ten

Half an hour later, after having changed clothes and paced my suite back and forth, I slip out of my room. The corridor is so silent I flinch at the thumps of my muffled footsteps on the rug.

Tiptoeing down the hotel's marble staircase, not daring with the elevator attendant, I sneak into the main corridor of the hotel on the ground floor.

"I thought you would change into more-comfortable attire," Cameron whispers as I wind around a corner.

I gasp, whirling on my heel. Cameron is leaning on the wall, his navy blue suit changed for dark trousers, waistcoat, a white shirt, and jacket.

I glare at him, grabbing my chiffon skirt beneath my coat. "It's a tea dress. It's the most comfortable thing I own. Unless you'd like to lend me some of your clothes?"

"The goal is not to draw attention."

I cross my arms over my chest. "Exactly."

Chuckling, he pulls himself off the wall. "Are you ready?"

"As ready as I will ever be."

Cameron and I follow down the corridor, past the tearoom. Chatter eddies from the busy room, but neither my uncle nor Mr. Crossley is there. But as we're about to round into the main lobby, Uncle Nigel strides out of the Oak Room down the marbled corridor. My breath catching, I grab Cameron's jacket and swing us behind a luggage cart.

The bellboy is about to ask something, but Cameron hands him a folded banknote and winks. The boy, I'd say no older than sixteen, winks back and keeps pushing the cart.

"What was that?" Cameron whispers.

"I spotted Uncle Nigel," I mutter, sidling like a wisp in the air, still clutching Cameron's lapel.

Cameron straightens to peek over the stacked trunks and suitcases. "Golly, true. He's walking to the elevators. Quick, come."

I stiffen as Cameron grabs my arm and rushes us out the revolving doors with a little help from the bellboy, who covers our exit by stopping the cart a moment, blocking the view from the bronze bank of elevators. Despite the tension building in my stomach, I can't help a titter as Cameron and I edge Central Park, a three-block trot up Fifth Avenue.

Panting more out of excitement than exertion, Cameron and I rush around East Sixty-Third Street and turn to skulk on the edge of the corner. The Plaza peeks through the trees, glimpses of white as the sun dips behind the skyline.

"All right, that was more fun than I expected," I breathe, straightening. "Do you think he noticed?"

Voices drift from the park and the streets, busier now that the rain has given in to clear skies at last, but none shouts our names. The damp day makes my skin clammy, and I wipe my hand's perspiration on my coat.

"I don't think he did. But next time, I'll release a gaggle of geese as a distraction. Will work like magic." He playfully nudges me with his shoulder.

An image of geese on the loose across the Plaza's lobby, the panicked guests, and flittering feathers runs through my mind. I wrestle a smile. "Why are we even doing this?"

He smiles up at me, shrugging. "Call me sentimental."

I shake my head, but a smirk tugs at my cheeks. "And reckless at that."

"Come now, you must admit you adore me." Cameron straightens, encompassing the street with the open arc of an arm. "You may lead the way."

Past Madison Avenue, four stories, three windows wide, my parents' sleek townhouse sits sandwiched between two others. It remains still and silent, the world behind the shut windows a dark void. No delicate curtains sway in the breeze; no flowers grow in pots on the sills; no sounds or laughter drift from the interior.

"Now what?" I ask.

With a mystifying smile, Cameron rushes up the stoops two steps at a time and plainly knocks on the door.

I cover my mouth. "What are you doing?"

"Hello?" He places his ear to the black-painted wood and grabs the silver knocker, now sullied and dull; he clacks it a few times. "Hello? May we speak of our lord and savior Gasoline Gus?"

I mute a snort. "Now they won't open up, you lunatic."

Cameron tries the doorknob, and I widen my eyes.

When the thing doesn't cooperate, he glides down the stairs with a sufficient smile. "The house is as silent as a cemetery."

"That's strange," I admit. "At least a couple of servants stay back even when the masters are away."

"Is there a way for us to sneak into the house?"

I cross my arms. Admitting I know ways to go in and out undetected might prompt questions I wouldn't like to answer.

Cameron waits, relaxed, all nonchalance, with a tiny smirk, as if he is sure my confirmation is about to burst out of me. How he can read me so well, I don't know.

"No."

Cameron nudges my shoulder with his arm. "You tell me you never snuck out?"

"They're probably closed off by now," I offer.

He taps his nose. "It doesn't hurt trying."

"Fine," I say, rolling my eyes. "Follow me."

Down the street, there's an entryway to the back alley. The houses look so sad and discolored from here. My townhouse looks more deserted, rivulets of grime running down the faded walls. When

Cameron and I open the fence delimiting the back patio, memories flash through my mind, filled with the scrape of wicker chairs on the now-dusty terra-cotta floor and the scent of lavender and parsley my mother used to grow in the now-empty pots.

"Nobody's lived here for a while," Cameron mutters, looking in through the kitchen doors. "Where's the way into the house?"

"Right here," I say. The pantry window is on the left, an added extension meant to work as a servant's room that my parents used as a cold room given the little sunlight it received. The window lock was broken, and I trust it's still that way. Dust and rain have coated the glass. By pressing my fingertips on both lower ends of the frame, the window ratchets up. The weather has battered the unattended wood, but once I move it several inches, Cameron helps me pry it all the way up.

"Ladies usually go first, but let me go in advance," he says. "I'll assist you with climbing inside."

"I need no assistance."

He puts a crate at my feet. "How will you explain any tears on your clothes made by shards or splinters?"

I survey the alley and the adjacent townhouses, in search of prying neighbors. The last thing I'd like is having Uncle Nigel come retrieve me from the police headquarters, yet thankfully, no shadows flicker behind the curtains.

Sitting up on the windowsill, Cameron swings one leg in, then the other and gracefully lands inside the pantry. I use the crate to repeat his steps. Once I jump inside, I totter on my unsuitable pumps.

With a quick motion, Cameron holds me and steadies me.

"Thank you," I whisper. But he says nothing. Our eyes meet and pause. With a tender touch, he drags his thumb slowly over my knuckles, a small smirk dancing about him. The afternoon sun draws the lines of his high cheeks.

I ignite with fire. If I stepped any closer, I would have no other choice but to kiss him.

Cameron lets go with a caress and breaks the spell. I blink, craning my neck to observe the pantry—if only to kill the little twitch of pleasure in my stomach. A layer of dust cloaks the empty shelves. There are no jars, no canned food, no bottles of wine, no dried meat hanging from the ceiling.

"Did your uncle really sell this?" Cameron whispers.

"That's what he said."

He cracks the door open, the hinges whining like a cry in the silent house. He looks left and right, but his expression reveals little to nothing when he turns to me. "It's empty."

We venture into the dark winding passageway the staff used to access the dining room from the kitchen. The enameled white sink has grayed up, but its edges still shine under the afternoon sunlight, and dust whitens the dark floorboards. I wipe away tears that have shown up without proper notice.

In the parlor, the ghosts of my father, reading his newspaper, and my mother, knitting on the divan before the fireplace, waver—the scents of fire-licked wood and rainy days clinging to the air. Now the curtains are half shut and the fireplace dead, the room devoid of furniture.

Nothing would've prepared me for this sight. *Nothing.* It catches my breath in a knot, as though I were walking thanks to the aid of strings, my body no longer mine.

In the foyer, there are no candles lit, no mirror where to take one last glimpse, and no sunflowers in a crystal vase. The curtains in the dining room are open, the warm dusk setting the marble fireplace alit in orange light.

"I don't understand this," I mutter.

"Almost two months is enough time to move." Cameron's voice is jarring in the silence, in this house, where my parents are still alive through my memories. The thought that they'll never get to know me in this new version of myself, that they'll never get to meet Cameron, again pushes tears to my eyes.

"Last time I saw this house, I was walking out in late February. Now, I'm here once more, but everything has changed." I cover my face. "Not even I am the same person. The girl my parents knew, she doesn't exist anymore."

"You might not be, but I know they'd love the lady you're becoming."

As I lower my hands, Cameron smiles at me, though the gesture is tainted by an emotion I can't pinpoint. Empathy, perhaps? I wouldn't like to think it's pity.

"Tell me, what were your parents like?"

"Oh, they loved to be productive," I say. "They always seemed a bit martial in their ways, waking up so early, and in the way they conducted themselves, with hustle and bustle. They didn't know what relaxation was. They were also highly perceptive—they always sensed me, even when I tried to become invisible. They were also overachievers, like me, and independent thinkers, and always straightforward. They raised me to be opinionated and strong. When I think of it, that clause in my father's testament makes even less sense. They never would've hidden anything from me. They never could've betrayed me like that."

The static of Harry Macdonough's voice creeps through the dining room wall. I grew up with his tunes played on my neighbors' phonograph—the fact they're still big enthusiasts of his music brings me comfort, like a distant warm embrace. At least, one thing remains the same.

Cameron takes off his jacket, sets it down on the windowsill, and reaches out to me with a flourish. "Shall we dance?"

"What for?"

"We're supposed to dance together at some point. Wedding? Parties?"

"True," I concede, sliding off my coat.

Cameron sets it down with his jacket on the windowsill and pulls me closer to him, his fingers stretching across my back.

"I can't believe we've just run away from the hotel. Something tells me I'm never going to get bored with you," I say while he sways us to the cheery faint music.

He dips me to the floor, making me gasp. When I crack an eye open, Cameron's smiley face hovers over me. "Never bored, dear."

Heat pours through my body. Warm and fluttery, coursing through my veins. He's doing this for his students. Not for me. He's doing this because the perks outweighed the cons. There's nothing romantic about this. *Nothing.*

He straightens me and sends me into a spin, and when I slide back into his arms, he takes us in a trot forward. We set off in circles, the motion making me dizzy and high with glee. As I float guiltless in his arms, laughter bursts out of me.

Harry stops singing, and the tune changes to a ballad. Cameron and I slow to a sway.

I tame down my smile with a bite of my lip and focus on the collar of his shirt. The first button is open, one thing I did not notice until now. His warm cedarwood scent inebriates me, and my head tilts greedily, my nose inching closer.

"What do you think the situation is like in Europe?" I ask.

"I've heard it's ugly, I won't lie."

"Are you not worried?"

"I'm not."

I frown. "Why?"

He breathes in, his chest hardening against mine. "England isn't at war."

"England *is* at war."

"The war is not on its shorelines is what I meant."

"What if it reaches its shorelines? What if Germany sends soldiers? They're already sending U-boats to the coast."

"You'll be safe no matter what." His hum is so convincing, a steady affirmation on highly unsteady ground.

"How can you be so sure?" I steal a glance at the worry washing through his features. His eyes fill with urgency, and he takes a sharp breath, as if he were about to say something—but nothing comes out.

There is darkness to him, clinging on the edge of his silence. No, that emotion coursing through him is not worry. It's not pity. Is it guilt?

"I just am," he simply says, and a pointed smile pushes all the darkness away from his face.

"You're still in time, you know," I say and bite my lip.

His hand twitches in mine. "In time for what?"

I can't believe what I'm about to say, but I hope it soothes my remorse for ripping him away from his life and putting him in danger if I give him a way out while he still can. "You can say no to coming with me and call off . . . the engagement. I'd pay you a percentage of the agreed money for your troubles."

Cameron lets out half a chuckle, half a sigh. "I can't. And I wouldn't, even if I could."

My brows crease. "Why? I'm offering you money still."

"Sometimes, there are more reasons than money."

My furrow deepens. "Such as?"

"May I ask you something?"

I nod, holding his gaze like a challenge. He's changing the subject, but I'm too unsettled to ask what all those charged silences mean—if they mean anything at all.

"What did you have to hide from your parents when you snuck out of the house through that window?"

My mouth hangs open. I knew he'd ask. "I did not hide anything."

He smiles. "You see, it would've been more convincing if you had said you knew the window's lock was broken. Now I'm sure you hid something from your parents."

Heat pools in my cheeks, and Cameron lights up with a proud smile. "Ah, the lady is blushing. It must be a good story."

I stop myself from sticking my tongue out at him. I can't lie, and before he wheedles that information from me with irritating questions, I volunteer it. "Elijah and I courted when I was fourteen and he sixteen. We kept it a secret, even from Lindsay. I snuck out to meet him at the park at midnight after our servants turned in."

Cameron's touch inches upward, cupping more of my back. "How long did it last?"

"Seven months."

One of his eyes squints. His hand tightens a hair's breadth. "Did he kiss you?"

His questions are soft, not demanding, yet I can't escape the hypnotizing blue infinity in his eyes. Even when I gulp, the truth flows out of me. "Yes, he did."

Cameron says nothing for what feels like an eternity, but a muscle in his cheek twitches up. "Why did it end?"

"We didn't want anyone to decide our lives for us. If his parents had known, they would've tried to get us betrothed, and mine would've pushed back. We would've lost our friendship in a pointless family quarrel. Eventually, people started noticing our attraction, and since I couldn't meet what was expected of us, we decided our friendship and our lives were more important."

His hand frees mine, only to lower to my wrist. Cameron gives me the silkiest of brushes on the soft part there, where my veins flow green.

My thoughts melt like butter. I hold my breath, praying he doesn't notice my pulse pounding like a drum.

"Do you still have feelings for him?"

"Why are you asking?"

"Do you?" One of his eyebrows rises slightly.

"I did," I say. "Until not too long ago. I don't have romantic feelings for him anymore, but I still love him. He's my friend."

"Why didn't you ask him for help?"

"I did ask him. But he's spoken for. Are you done with the questions?"

He's not blinked yet. "I have one more. Why do you always wear your hair up? Have you always sported it like that?"

I frown. "No. I've done it since my parents died. Don't you like it?"

He lowers his head, and I flinch just a second, thinking he's going to kiss me, but he presses his lips to my ear, soft like a feather. I don't know what's worse, the release of a kiss or the torture of anticipation.

"I prefer it when you wear it down," he says, caressing between his fingers a curl that's escaped from my low bun.

My blood threatens to explode.

Fighting a moan, I crane my neck, and our lips align an inch away. I trail his sleeve, every inch of me knotting. My eyes close at the same time he cocks his head, the tip of his nose slightly brushing mine.

A loud knock from upstairs whips our heads upward. The sun has sunk behind the buildings, and shadows are eating away at the walls.

"That's come from inside this house," Cameron mutters, closing his arms on me.

Tiny goosebumps break on my skin. I pay attention to the sounds in the house, blocking out the phonograph playing next door. When I was little I feared ghosts were hiding behind swaying curtains. I'm not a child anymore, but I snatch Cameron's shirt.

He waves me off, as if asking me quietly to stay back.

I shake my head no. "I think we should leave," I whisper.

"It's a little late for that," he says, releasing me. He walks to the fireplace and grabs the fire poker, offering the second one to me. "You stay here."

"No," I mutter a bit too loud. I don't know why we're whispering. Whoever is here already knows about us.

"Fine, stay behind me."

Not minding his request, I start to the foyer. The track of our steps runs on the dusty floorboards, but there's the print of another person's footsteps, heading upstairs. Someone snuck in while we were dancing and stood only several feet away from us. A shiver prickles over my skin.

I crane my neck to the top landing. The slanted sunlight flickers on the wall, catching my breath.

I look at Cameron, as if I were asking *Did you see that?*

And as if he were a mind reader, he nods.

My senses heighten, and a buzz skitters under my skin.

A bang follows from the second floor. And by the sound alone, they're opening a window. My eyes widen. Whoever our lurker is, they're trying to escape.

"The next door's vine," I mutter.

Cameron and I rush upstairs and storm into the deserted hallway. A breeze carries faraway city sounds—clopping hooves and conversational voices from the street. No steps resound from inside the house.

The window in the room that used to lodge my father's office is thrown open. Cameron runs there while I circle around, the poker held high, lest this was not the only intruder in the house.

"Hey, you, don't run," Cameron yells. "It's a guy. He's running away."

Cameron storms past me, and at the last second I stretch out my arm and snag at his sleeve, stopping him. "Are you following him?"

"I can still catch him."

"Let him go."

"He's broken into your house."

"It's not *my* house," I say with a bitter lilt, "and technically, we've trespassed too."

He lowers his poker. "Do you think he was stealing anything?"

I shrug and turn around. The only thing left from my father's office is a stove in the corner. "I don't think there's much to steal."

"Then something has brought him in. Wait here. I'll verify he was alone."

Cameron jogs toward the back, opening all the doors, then dashes upstairs, jumping the steps two at a time. Swiveling slowly on a heel, I browse for anything out of the ordinary, the hairs on my nape standing on end.

"What were you looking for?" I whisper. Besides my father's office, this floor housed a small nook next to the front windows where we had a small fireplace and two settees, a bathroom, and bedrooms for the servants. I wander out of my father's office, perusing the bare walls, the sconces without light bulbs, the faint spiderwebs undulating in the corners, the dark hearth. Above my head, Cameron keeps opening and closing doors, the floors creaking under his footsteps.

There's something out of place; I can feel it.

My gaze roams through every threadbare detail as I walk across the entire floor, and I stop in front of the fireplace, staring straight at a white envelope propped on the mantel. It's folded, my name stamped in neat typewriter lettering.

My heart flips. Was that person trying to give me this or retrieve it?

"Everything is clear upstairs," Cameron announces.

My muscles have frozen. Craning my neck toward him feels like a titanic effort. "I don't think he wanted to steal anything."

Cameron stations himself next to me, frowning at the envelope. "What's that?"

"I think this is what he was doing." With cold fingers despite the warm evening, I slip two papers out. The first one has a message. I don't recognize the handwriting, but it reads, clear as day, *Nigel is lying.*

The second sheet is a dark photograph of two documents on a table. The grainy image seems well lit, but the edges of the scribbles blur. It's strange because, as a rule, documents aren't portrayed. They're mimeographed if there's a need for a copy, or handwritten.

Straining my eyes, I read the paragraphs. Paragraphs way too known in my heart. It's my father's will.

"'Lastly, should my wife be deceased, to my beloved daughter, Alexandra, I leave all my properties and worldly possessions, including all my monetary and physical assets, save for the aforementioned, totaling $2.5 million, which will remain in the Benson trust fund until she turns of age. Should we die before she is an adult, she will become the ward of my brother, Nigel Benson, until she turns eighteen. On her eighteenth birthday, my providers at Mr. Miller, Son, and Associates will funnel all remaining assets to Alexandra's name, making her the sole heir to my inheritance, save for the aforementioned bequests.'" The last line congeals the blood in my veins. No marriage clause to be seen, unlike the one I read weeks ago. I remember Mr. Tannenbaum turned the page right before he mentioned the marriage clause; how conveniently the sentences sat through the document, making it just too easy for anyone to switch a new page for the old one. I remember the quality of the paper, the previous worn out and only one brand new.

This document was dated in January 1914, just over the signatures, while the one they read was drawn up without a date. Just like I knew and Elijah pointed out, legit reviewed wills have codicils. A note, amending a clause. An addition, stating it's been revised on a certain date. The one read in March had none.

"I knew it," I whisper, new goosebumps running through my skin.

It was swapped.

Nigel is lying.

"It's a photograph of my father's true will," I say.

Chapter Eleven

May 1, 1915—Day 1 of 7

NOTICE!

> TRAVELLERS intending to embark on the Atlantic voyage are reminded that a state of war exists between Germany and her allies and Great Britain and her allies; that the zone of war includes the waters adjacent to the British Isles; that, in accordance with formal notice given by the Imperial German Government, vessels flying the flag of Great Britain, or any of her allies, are liable to destruction in those waters and that travellers sailing in the war zone on ships of Great Britain or her allies do so at their own risk.
> IMPERIAL GERMAN EMBASSY.

Cameron glowers at *The Sun*. The German embassy's warning stands next to the *Lusitania*'s advertisement. Outside our car, Cunard Pier 54, along with the rest of Chelsea Piers, is bustling with shouts, car honks, and lousy pressmen flitting among passengers. The day has dawned with dark clouds crying a drizzle that patters incessantly on the car windows. New York seems like it's weeping.

"They'll try to sink the ship," I say, feeling the brim of my hat with clammy fingers. The *Lusitania* sails under the British flag. This crossing couldn't come at a worse time.

Cameron wrinkles the newspaper shut. "We'll see."

Someone knocks on the window, making me jump in my seat. Uncle Nigel is outside, the handle of his cane still on the glass, his face somber under his hat.

I lock dead eyes with him. *Nigel is lying.* If I said these days have worsened our relationship to a gelid tension, I'd be falling short. Whoever put that note in my parents' townhouse wanted me to know. But now, instead of feeling rightfully vindicated, many questions disturb my sleep, and all I want is to find a way to put my uncle in jail for it.

I suspected Cameron settled the whole charade in my old house. He drove me right into it. Yet I met Cameron by absolute chance before the testament reading. It's impossible he's involved.

But if not him, who was it? Who might have such dark motives to play this game? Is it even someone I know? How did they know I was in the house, that I'd find the note?

My uncle clacks his cane on the window once more with rhythmical taps. This time, Cameron and I slide out into the chilly day. Around me, life moves at a high speed, as if I were numbly witnessing my life snatched from me. The day of our sailing cannot possibly be here already.

"Have you seen this?" Cameron voices to my uncle, striding around the vehicle, the newspaper held high.

My uncle barely deigns to glimpse at him. "I have, Mr. Asher. It's all German buffoonery."

Mr. Crossley places a suitcase on one of the stacks of trunks. "Twenty-five knots, that's the *Lusitania*'s speed. No ship has ever been torpedoed over fourteen knots."

"Very true, Mr. Crossley. Besides, the British Admiralty will escort us once we reach English waters. Now let's get to the pier. I want to board with enough time to spare."

"What if they end up sinking the ship?" Cameron asks.

"And what if they play Alpenländische Volksmusik instead, Mr. Asher?" Nigel sneers.

"They won't attack first," Mr. Crossley chimes in. "Cruiser rules. The Germans abide by them. Nobody sinks a ship without inspection."

"Why don't we push back the date until war tensions deescalate?" I offer.

Nigel sighs. "Alexandra, do not be difficult."

"Would you risk your niece's life?" Cameron asks. "We have a chance to stay safe, here in the US, Mr. Benson."

Nigel chuckles. "Interesting train of thought, since part of your family is in Europe."

"I can only do so much for my family, but if I can keep Alexandra safe, I will. That should be your priority as well."

"The more we wait, the more dangerous a crossing will become. War doesn't seem to have a fast ending. We're boarding the *Lusitania.* That's final."

Photographers take pictures of a girl, who hastens inside the Cunard building.

"What about we sail on the *New York*?" I propose. "An American flag is safer. Cameron and I heard yesterday they're sailing not long after us. We'll arrive in England a day later than scheduled."

Uncle Nigel turns to a porter, vaguely waving toward the trunks. "Those to the Parlor Suites B-67 and B-70, and that one to B-61. Only that one to the storeroom. Maid's and assistant's there go in B-71 and B-72."

The porter frowns at the trunks and scribbles the cabin numbers in chalk on the lids. A chilly breeze sweeps through the street, crawling under my dress.

Drizzle is like little diamonds on Cameron's hair. "Mr. Benson, you need to consider—"

My uncle turns. "Mr. Asher. Perhaps I mightn't have spoken clearly. As much as I respect my brother's blessing upon your . . . peculiar betrothal, Alexandra is still my ward until you take her in marriage.

If you're afraid of a little German U-boat, you might as well stay back because you're not cut out for the Benson family."

Disbelief shoots through my veins.

"Uncle," I bark. How dare he speak to him like that?

"I won't listen to more foolishness," he says, lifting a finger. With a whirl, he marches through the open gates of the building.

Cameron sighs, putting his hat on. "God knows I've tried."

"There's nothing we can do," I tell him, looping my arm with his. At least, he's with me, in this sea of liars and danger.

The gray light plays with the pink granite walling the piers. At the entrance, a hive of people and reporters furiously buzzes around a tall man, whose head is only visible above the hats surrounding him.

As we come closer to the ship in a clerk's wake, his words blend with the background noise inside the industrial terminal, among loud conversations, carts, and conveyor belts.

A man complains in passing to a Cunard clerk about the lack of luggage inspection. Not too far, I find Alfred Vanderbilt, cheerful countenance under his hat despite the tension running through the terminal. He waves at me and shows some documents to a clerk, missing my greeting in return.

By the quay, the *Lusitania* rises in nautical glory. Four black smokestacks jut from a stacked white superstructure. Known for her luxury, a match only for the White Star Line ships, the *Lusitania* is one of the few liners that haven't been drafted for the war. A gold band runs along the base of the superstructure, giving the ship a dignified look. Her name and port of registry are painted in black, but a string of maritime signal flags crosses bow to stern, billowing in the morning breeze.

The gangplank is sturdy yet wet, stretched out several feet in the air, and it moves to the idle wobble of the *Lusitania*. The hatchway on the dark hull is wide open for us, the white interior suspiciously homey. My steps waver on the slick wood. I want to swivel on my heel and run with the money I've slipped into my pockets this morning and any more clothes other than the blue dress, boots, and cream-colored coat on my back.

With a clench of my jaw, I enter the *Lusitania*'s hall on E-Deck. The floors outstretch in a composition of diamond-shaped black-and-white linoleum. In the middle of the hall, two gilded elevators manned by attendants work at the heart of the grand staircase. While we stand in line for one of them, I let out a shaky breath. I've avoided thinking of the moment my feet would no longer be touching American soil. A moment buried now under the distress of our departing, being ushered back and forth, and commanded under wet hair and clothes.

The elevator takes us to B-Deck. The circular purser's office takes the post opposite the elevators, framed by two white Ionic columns. The clerk leads us into a corridor behind the staircase.

"Alexandra," my uncle says. "Your parlor suite is B-67. I'll be in B-70 across the passageway. Mr. Asher will stay in B-61, first corner down the corridor to the left."

I turn to my uncle. "Left? Interior cabin?"

"Count yourself lucky I was able to purchase a ticket for your groom-to-be."

"I thought Cameron would stay with me."

Uncle Nigel pinches the bridge of his nose. "Good Lord, Alexandra."

"Leave something for the honeymoon, darling," Cameron says.

"Cameron, that's not what I meant!" I yelp, wanting to throw a shoe at his head.

"I don't mind," he reassures me. "And I will concede, this time he's right. We'll sleep in different rooms until we're married."

I don't know if he wants to get in my uncle's good graces, but it seems unfair that he has to be in a claustrophobic cabin while I have too much room to spare. "But . . ."

Cameron smiles. "I'm happy to have my own cabin. I thank you, Mr. Benson. I'll be right around the corner."

Nigel is lying. What if I'm just afraid Nigel will find out I know he swapped the testament? Staring at my uncle is like staring in a mirror at night with only the candlelight creating shifting shadows in the room behind you.

"I will leave you to settle." My uncle bows and turns the corner of a passageway connecting starboard to port.

I sigh toward one of the fixtures on the coffered ceiling, as if it had answers to my questions. As I give up and open the door to the parlor, a clerk appears to bring my trunk in.

"Where should I leave it, Miss?"

"Oh," I say, glancing at the room. "By the bed, thank you."

He tips his hat and wheels the cart inside, minding the low table in the middle of the parlor. The clerk deposits the trunk next to one of the two narrow metal beds.

"Thank you," I say, taking off my hat.

"Have a great day, Miss."

I sit on the damask couch and unbutton my coat, sliding it off my shoulders. What to do now? My heart is pounding too fast, as if by racing, it could stop my life from plunging forward.

Leaving my coat a mangle on the couch, I leap to my feet. I must get busy. Chores will keep me from thinking too much about what I can't control.

My suite has two rooms with two different entrances, one connected to the parlor and one leading to a lavatory. Inside, I find an enameled bathtub and a sink with an adjoined room for the toilet. Beyond the cabin windows framed by blue drapes, the promenade stretches out, passengers already walking up and down its length and admiring the views. One of the windows is open, letting in the port scents of coal and seaweed. Plasterwork runs along the ceiling. In my bedroom, a white built-in wardrobe and chest of drawers stand in front of the beds.

I should leave sorting through my trunk for Emily, but I don't like her sifting through my belongings. I kneel on the dotted carpet and unlatch the trunk's lid, swinging it up with a swift motion, and frown, taken aback by the stacks of books, folders, and dark clothes, while I expected dresses and toiletries and photo albums.

I shuffle through the contents and pull out some folders to access the ties that have slipped underneath. The smell of peppermint wafting from them belongs to my uncle.

I groan. "I can't believe it. They've brought in the wrong one."

This is so inconvenient. As I throw the folders inside the trunk, a few papers escape, landing at my knees. Sighing, I collect them, my gaze halting on messy handwriting. There's no doubt this almost illegible flourish is my uncle's. I sit on the floor, thumbing through the pages. Numbers and so much foreign gibberish. These look like the reports I saw on my father's desk when I helped him with some administrative tasks when his mysterious little helper quit the job overnight. My father never explained what these documents were for, but they're the same, without a doubt.

Only these are . . . in German.

My uncle's voice booms down the corridor. My body jolts, and I gasp. Pushing the papers into their folders, praying I haven't disarrayed them, I then shove them into the trunk, which I clank shut. He cannot know I found this.

I dash toward the desk in the parlor and plop into the chair with my purse, pulling out my silver compact. I pretend I'm applying powder with little taps on my nose. In the reflection, the parlor door swings open after a dry knock.

I turn, gaping, as if I didn't hear my uncle's screams.

"What's this fuss?"

Uncle Nigel enters, scolding a clerk. The man is as red as a beetroot. "You hear me out, I made my instructions clear enough as to which cabin my trunk should go to. Someone chalked it wrongly."

"My apologies, sir. I'll make sure the trunks are delivered correctly." Another clerk skitters into my cabin with a whiny cart, hunching as if he wanted to go unnoticed.

"You, incompetent failures," Uncle Nigel spits.

"Uncle Nigel." I bolt upward. "Apologize immediately!"

My uncle takes a look at me as if I were an insect that had just crawled into his house. In the silence, Emily slips past the threshold. But I keep my eyes on my uncle, challenging him.

"I beg your pardon, Alexandra?" he hisses.

"Apologize immediately to these men," I grit through my teeth.

"You better stay silent," he says, poking a finger into my shoulder. "You'll never understand how businesses operate. Our trunks were unlocked for convenience. Imagine if they'd ended up at a stranger's cabin."

"Then take better care of them next time. I saw you pointing very vaguely at the trunks. Don't blame others for your lack of direction and care."

He raises his eyebrows and takes another look at me from boots to hair. The clerks have sped out of the room, and they can't hear whether Uncle Nigel will apologize or not, but I can't tolerate the way he's treated these two men when it was clearly his fault.

His hand flies to me. Before I can deflect it, a raging blow hits me square on my cheek, sending me two steps back.

I blink, fire filling my skull. Cupping my left cheek, I glower back. The edges of his tall frame blur. "Did you slap me?" A stupid question, it's obvious he did, but stupor doesn't let me think straight.

Behind him, Emily covers her mouth, her brown eyes wide.

"Learn to respect me, Alexandra; or next time I won't be as soft," he hisses, coming close.

I lunge forward.

Cameron stops me, appearing like a shadow, and gently yet firmly pulls me back. "What happened here?"

"My niece must learn manners, Mr. Asher." My uncle straightens his jacket. "Women must be tamed before they get ruined. I don't know what my brother was thinking. She's a disappointment."

I gape. I don't care much about my uncle's opinion, but he's implying my father failed as a parent, that he didn't raise me well enough.

"Excuse me, may you repeat?" Cameron pokes a finger inside his ear. "See, sometimes I go a bit deaf when I listen to absurdity."

"You've heard me," Nigel says.

Cameron lurches toward my uncle, but I grapple a handful of his jacket, halting him.

Mr. Crossley dashes into the cabin and throws an arm over my uncle's shoulders, pulling him away. "Let's all calm down, shall we?"

"Do *not* slap Alexandra again, Mr. Benson," Cameron growls, stepping in front of me. "Or you'll have to answer to me."

My uncle lashes out, but his assistant squeezes him away with a jerk. "Aren't we all a bit tense this drizzly morning, huh? War tensions, luggage misunderstandings, delays, right? He'll meet you again for dinner. How does that sound?"

"Like an awful idea," I whisper.

My uncle glowers as Mr. Crossley drags him outside, white knuckles wrinkling his jacket.

"Leave, Miss Atkinson," Cameron says. It's neither threat nor demand, but his low-pitched snarl is enough to raise the little hairs on the back of my head.

Bowing her head, Emily closes the door with a click.

Cameron turns, one thumb trailing down my cheek. The sting sears under my skin, but I don't want to push Cameron's caress away. "Are you well?"

I sigh. "As good as I can be. My pride has taken the brunt of it."

"Would you like to take one last look at New York with me?"

Come this moment, I could stay cloistered in my cabin, lamenting the unfairness of my fate; dwelling on what's coming undone one piece at a time, my uncle's slap, how much I'll miss my friends, how much my parents make me ache with memories, but none will grant me peace. If I don't stay with New York for as long as I can, I'll regret it.

With a quick nod, I grab my coat and hat and go with Cameron one deck up through the main staircase. Outside, lifeboats ring the Boat Deck across the entire superstructure. The floor remains wet from the rain, yet fierce sunshine streams through the thinning clouds. Crowds gather on the quayside, waving hats and handkerchiefs. Somewhere, an orchestra is playing "It's a Long Way to Tipperary."

"A war song, how apt," I mutter.

A couple casually strolling aft brushes past me. "We were supposed to leave at ten in the morning, but here we are, long after twelve, still in New York," the man says to the woman. "I'm sure the delay was Turner's fault."

"He might've lost his nerve," the woman replies. "I can't blame him."

"Do you think an experienced captain would panic?" I ask Cameron.

The turbines come alive underneath our feet, their thrum reverberating through the floor.

"Apparently, they can," Cameron says. "I've been told our captain should've been Daniel Dow, but on one of the last crossings, he alleged stress and left the ship to Captain Turner."

Deafening blasts from the *Lusitania*'s horn block the music and cheers. Covering my ears, I find an empty spot between lifeboats 12 and 14. Portside is quieter, all the bustle and chaos coming from starboard, where most people wave goodbye to their loved ones.

Cameron and I gaze out to the city's pointy skyscrapers. With a jerk, the *Lusitania* draws back into the Hudson River, three little tugs helping her out of the Cunard mooring. Water laps and churns right beneath us, brown and frothy. It's not a long way until the ship angles back and her bow aims southward. On the piers, throngs of people still wave white handkerchiefs under the open city. I clutch the cool railing, a lump rising within me. With its towers grazing the sky, New York starts gliding away, inch by inch, and a part of me breaks in two, like metal crumbling under rot and decay.

Cameron caresses my back. "We'll return soon."

No . . . I don't believe it. There go my parents buried in the soil of this country, my city, my university, my friends, my memories, and the girl I used to be. All of it will stay in its busy streets and quiet parks, in the hush of lapping water near the shores, in the screech of the seagulls, the trolley chimes. My hectic haven.

I dab at my eyes, wrestling down my emotions, and I cup my cheek, biting hard into my lip until I taste copper. "These weeks have gone in the blink of an eye."

And I was trapped while everything moved against my will, exactly as the ship is moving and tearing me away from New York. Pain and desperation stir in my chest, as if I were being ripped away. What would happen if I jumped off the ship and swam ashore?

"What happened with your uncle?" Cameron asks, drawing me back onto the liner.

Looking at the bubbly water, I tell him about the porters chalking up the trunks wrongly, his insults, my demanding he apologize.

Cameron squeezes my shoulder. "He surely has a short fuse."

"I don't think it's a short fuse, Cameron. I believe he thought he'd lost what was in his trunk and that tipped him over the edge. I opened it by mistake and found . . . something."

"What, exactly? Cheeky photographs of women in their underthings?"

"Ew." I grimace, chuckling. "No. Actually, I found reports. My father also worked with them, but I don't know what these said." I look around, making sure nobody can eavesdrop on our conversation. "They were in German."

Cameron frowns. "That's—"

"Unsettling?" I finish his sentence.

"Did you keep any of them?"

"I couldn't. He might miss them."

He squints at the skyscrapers as we slither past lower Manhattan, air ruffling his hair.

I tip down my head. I can't stand seeing the city grow smaller. Beyond the quirks and turns of the river awaits the immensity of the ocean. And farther away, the unknown. An unknown life, in an unknown country. Far from home. And my only confidant—this man—standing next to me. My chest feels as though it's been hollowed out, but at least, Cameron is a light filling that echoing space.

"I have a hunch your uncle will be a frequent patron at the Smoking Room." Cameron winks. "Do you know what that means?"

A small smile pierces my dry lips. "That, once again, we'll have the chance to break the law?"

He smirks. "That's my girl."

Chapter Twelve

"Are we still going into my uncle's suite tonight?" I ask Cameron in a whisper. We were among the first passengers to come into the Dining Saloon and be ushered to one of the twelve-seat tables. We're alone, yet patrons are starting to fill the empty spots around us. I won't have another chance to rehearse details with Cameron for the rest of the evening.

Cameron nods. "We'll allege we want to take a stroll as soon as your uncle says he's headed to the Smoking Room." He takes a swig of wine. "You look lovely tonight."

"Why, thank you," I say with a shy chuckle. Layers of pink drape around me; from an empire waist, an overskirt with leaf designs and an exquisite chiffon petticoat cascade below my knees. With a flip, I move one of the wispy wings of pink tulle attached to my straps for modesty. My hair is up in a complicated style that's taken Emily about thirty minutes and many, many pins that bite into my scalp. "You look rather dashing yourself."

"I appreciate it but no need for the compliment. I'm only wearing a suit." He's being too modest. He's in full dress—a black tailcoat with matching trousers and a cream waistcoat, a silky vanilla tie around his neck. On his cuffs shine two moonstones. His hair is swept to the side, and he smells of a new soap—tangerines.

And his gaze . . . it sends tingles down my legs.

"I had no idea this room sat on two tiers." I shift in my damask-upholstered chair.

The vast dining room spans starboard to port. It's covered in white panels, and halos of fixtures cast a glister on the gold accents. In the hub of the two rooms, a dome caps the well, with a central chandelier and divided segments of paintings, and plasterwork medallions.

Cameron chuckles.

"What's so amusing?" I wonder aloud.

Throwing etiquette out the nearest porthole, Cameron props his elbows on the table. "I'm laughing at the randomness of life. A month ago, I was teaching destitute children, and now, I'm on an extraordinarily luxurious ocean liner on my way to England, a whole new life ahead of me." He chuckles again, setting the glass on the table. "It's one of those things that catch you off guard."

I envy how aloof he is about the idea of starting anew, as if changing continents were as easy as moving from room to room. A rush of apprehension washes through me. I gave him the chance to quit the charade in time, and he refused. Our affair is nothing but a transaction, but I can't resist surveying his thoughts.

I tilt forward, yet I would not, for the life of me, put my elbows on the table. "Would you consider this an upgrade from your previous life?"

Cameron opens his mouth but immediately snaps it shut, his attention landing over my right side. My uncle, dark in a tailcoat, takes up the spot next to me.

"Good evening," Uncle Nigel says.

"Good evening," I reply, stiffening. The ghost of this morning's slap burns. Emily has applied powder and blush to conceal the slight bruise on my cheek, but the area still stings when I touch it.

Silence settles while around us voices grow louder, fancily dressed guests walking into the saloon.

My uncle sighs. "I must apologize for this morning's behavior, Alexandra. I realized how unfortunate my . . . reaction was. For that, I am sorry."

I repress a disdainful chuckle and turn my head ever so slightly toward my uncle, a side glance enough to take in his edges.

"I accept your apology," I concede without much enthusiasm.

Soon, other passengers join our table. Our nearest diners are two British couples: Mr. and Mrs. Bartlett, who I later learn was a Rothschild before marrying Mr. Bartlett, and Mr. and Mrs. Learoyd, though the latter have a marked Australian accent.

Next to Cameron is Professor Brodrick, a young man from Massachusetts. From the moment they shake hands, seeing the two bonding becomes my entertainment for the evening. I stir the asparagus and artichokes on my plate while Cameron's eyes brighten and his cheeks go up, happy wrinkles appearing where I've never seen them before.

"I'm working for a mining corps in Russia," Professor Brodrick explains. "In fact, some of my friends and colleagues are aboard too."

"Why aren't they sitting with us?" asks Cameron, browsing the room with his gaze.

"We just found out we're all here. They're on the C-Deck tier, somewhere? It's not of worry. It's happened before. It's not our first time traveling on this ship. We've made arrangements to dine together for the rest of the crossing. You should join us in the Smoking Room."

Cameron looks at me. "I would love to, but I had plans for a night stroll with my fiancée."

"Oh." My cheeks flush hot, having the sudden attention from the two men.

Professor Brodrick reaches out over the wineglasses. "My apologies. It wasn't my intention to steal your fiancé from you, Miss . . ."

I greet him with a firm shake. "Benson. It's a pleasure to make your acquaintance, Professor. I don't mind if he joins you in the Smoking Room. I'm glad to see Cameron making new friends. Please, go."

Cameron frowns at me, but Professor Brodrick smiles. "The offer is open for the entire crossing, of course."

"I can't let down my future wife like that," Cameron says. "She was eager to stroll under the moonlight before the weather cools down."

Heat fills my every inch.

"Wise man," Mr. Bartlett chimes in. "It's better to keep the ladies happy."

Histrionic laughter rises from our table.

"Miss Benson, I'm so sorry about your parents' passing," Mrs. Bartlett says, to which I nod, fighting the sudden knot in my chest. "What a lovely family you were. I'm so happy your dear uncle was here when tragedy struck."

I lean back, frowning. "My uncle wasn't—"

"I wasn't in New York yet, Mrs. Bartlett," Uncle Nigel retorts. His gaze targets her with such malice it reverberates through me like thunder. "You must be mistaken."

In front of me, Cameron's jaw twitches.

"Oh." Mrs. Bartlett's smile trembles. "My apologies, Mr. Benson. I thought I saw you in Manhattan. But my memory must be at fault here. What about you, Mr. Asher? Where are you from?"

My mind spins. Why has my uncle reacted so viscerally to a simple mistake?

"I'm from Denver," Cameron says, flashing a wide smile—back in character.

"Really?" Mr. Learoyd interjects. "I was in Denver on a business trip last year, and I thought I knew all the tycoons in the city."

I down my entire glass of water, my fingers faint. Next to me, Uncle Nigel is trained on the conversation, a hungry glint of curiosity in his dark-gray eyes as he raises his glass to his mouth.

"My family is in the steel business, but you wouldn't have met them. They've been stranded for a long year in southern Germany due to the war," Cameron explains, as if mustering ice-cold blood were as easy as breathing. "I wish that my being in Europe will help me find a safe passage for them to Switzerland."

"Fair enough. I'm with Learoyd and Boggio in Sydney, you see. I'm but a wool merchant, so steel, sadly, is a bit out of my scope." Mr. Learoyd nods. "I'm sorry about your situation, Mr. Asher. I hope your family can exit Germany safely."

My muscles loosen.

"Speaking of Germans," Mrs. Bartlett chimes in, "have you heard they found three German stowaways this afternoon?"

"German stowaways?" Nigel asks.

"Hiding in a pantry, of all places," Mrs. Bartlett says. "Rumor has it they're not stowaways but German spies."

My uncle waves this off. "My, that sounds like claptrap."

"The rumors seem legit," Mr. Barlett chimes in. "Detective Pierpoint, a Liverpool inspector aboard, has been questioning them all day long."

Mr. Learoyd nods. "I've heard rumors the ship is carrying large amounts of ammunition."

Uncle Nigel sets down his knife with a clank. "All twaddling, no doubt." His remark sounds dismissive, but he's taut. I keep a blank expression, but I pass an empty gulp down my throat. In front of me, Cameron is silent, an aloof air masking the darkness in his eyes.

"That might be the reason why Captain Turner got the jitters," Mr. Learoyd jests, raising pleasant laughter across the table.

"Sadly, reality is more boring than rumors," Mr. Bartlett interjects. "A seaman informed me that our two-hour morning delay was due to the Admiralty's requisition of the *Cameronia*. We had to wait until the passengers and crew were transferred. With that said, who's ready for the Smoking Room, gentlemen? Mr. Benson, would you join us?"

"It'd be an honor," Uncle Nigel says.

I stand. "Cameron, I believe I'm ready for that stroll."

He smiles with a nod, pushing himself up. "Good night, ladies and gentlemen."

When I've intertwined my arm with Cameron's, my uncle gestures, summoning his assistant out of thin air. Does this man ever eat? Sleep?

Have time to read one of his newspapers? He's like a genie, bound to my uncle's every whim.

I stoop to Nigel. "Now that my betrothal to Cameron is official, I think we can be spared the chaperone."

"My house, my rules, Niece."

"We're on a ship," I point out.

He takes a sip of his sherry. "Mr. Crossley will accompany you, and that's final."

Making a face, Cameron ushers me out of the Dining Saloon before I can sputter a profanity. After a quick stop on B-Deck to gather our coats and hats, we go one deck up in dead silence to Boat Deck. Crosswinds welcome us on the promenade, chill stabbing at my cheeks left and right. Flinching, I wrap my fur collar around my neck.

"Come into my arms," says Cameron. He looks back at Mr. Crossley. "If that's fine by our chaperone."

A hard cold smile. It's like witnessing a statue move. "Hands where I can see them."

With deliberate slowness, Cameron grazes my shoulder and tucks me in against his chest.

"My," I jest. "It seems like he's growing fond of us."

Cameron chuckles, starting down the empty promenade. Dinner is over, but guests shilly-shally in the warmth indoors. I can't blame them. The *Lusitania* is sailing toward a pitch-dark sky. The waning moon eastward casts a silvery rippling path on the inky waves. The smokestacks rise in the night, black columns lit by the deck floodlights. Steam is invisible, but its constant whiz signals we're marching at full speed toward the Atlantic Ocean.

Behind my back lie New York and Lindsay and Elijah, who must be about to sit to dine, and me, already a ghost of times past, just like my parents are to me.

"Have you seen how my uncle reacted?" I whisper.

"Let's hold our conversation until we're out of earshot," Cameron replies through gritted teeth. "The dinner was fantastic, wouldn't you say?"

"Delicious," I reply.

Cameron glimpses over his shoulder. "Did you have the chance to dine, Mr. Crossley? I hope you did."

Taking the hint, our chaperone halts to give us some privacy. Some of the rectangular portholes across the Boat Deck are lit; the medallions atop the frames elongate upward like screeching ghosts. Once we've crossed under the wing of the officers' bridge, Mr. Crossley resumes his walk behind us.

On the forefront of the promenade, the dark ocean opens ahead and sways of cold wind creep under my clothes through the gaps of my layers. A shiver skitters through me.

Cameron sweeps me closer under the guise of playfully sidestepping around the promenade corner.

The sea's salty scent carries a sharp tang of distant ice and rain. We're chasing the front that rained on Manhattan this morning, but I don't know why it smells of snow.

"Have you ever crossed the ocean?" I ask Cameron.

"I haven't, but I know people who have. Why?"

"The air smells like ice."

"We're headed toward the ice fields, where the *Titanic* sank. That's what you smell."

"It's May," I refute, wrinkling my nose.

"Yet out here, it's as cold as the dead of winter," Cameron says. "It's never fully spring in the North Atlantic."

"Is he out of earshot now?" I mumble.

"I think he is," Cameron whispers. His nose is red, and gusts make his coat billow. I love to see him wearing it. A new design—a cinched elegant cut, fastened by a row of buttons—it hints at his lithe body underneath.

I tear my gaze away.

"You also saw that, did you not? I don't believe Mrs. Bartlett was mistaken. And the way he reacted when they said there were German-speaking stowaways aboard? He's hiding something. We need to do away with the assistant."

"Let's walk him around, and I'll leave you by your door. We'll wait thirty minutes."

Round we go down the entire length of the deserted superstructure, only crossing several officers in their long dark coats and peaked caps. Astern, two walkways connect the superstructure to the second-class deck-island. Likewise, their promenade is empty, save for a man taking puffs of his cigarette, smoke swirling away in the night. In the first-class Verandah Café, two women remain at the tables.

I wonder if this trip will allow for some relaxation. Right now, if Cameron made a sudden move, he'd break my shoulders like a twig. I wish I wouldn't have dined, for fear coils in my guts.

Mr. Crossley approaches us again as we come into the deckhouse.

"I saw many books in your apartment," I tell Cameron. "Which one would you recommend?"

"What would you like to read?"

"I'm open to many genres."

He seems to think as we go down the carpeted grand staircase. "Did you read *The Secret Garden*? It's a children's book, but I think you may identify with the main character. She's an orphan, and she's taken to England to live with her uncle. But in the manor, she discovers many secrets, like a strange rose garden."

"It sounds intriguing."

"I brought it with me. I can drop it by."

"Would you not miss it? I can borrow it from the ship's library."

He smirks, taking off his hat. "Why, I bought it for you."

I stop walking, my mouth hanging open. "You did?" A genuine smile creeps onto my lips. Where does this lie end? It's all pretend, but I can't stop wild thoughts—wild thoughts about the possibility that Cameron cares about me. If anything, these two years will be a pleasant affair. I foresee myself investigating the moors and having picnics with him under a tree; Liverpool visits on the weekends in our best clothes; foggy evenings spent in theaters, cafeterias, and bookshops, or seeing the autumnal raindrops from a couch in front of a crackling fireplace; and suddenly England doesn't seem so grim and unwelcoming. I chose very well. I was very fortunate to find him. And I have nothing but gratitude for him.

"You should go to the Smoking Room with Professor Brodrick and his friends," I propose off the cuff. I want him to have a good time.

Cameron's brow furrows. He cranes his neck backward, toward Mr. Crossley, who, without any trace of doubt, has heard me.

"I'm tired this evening. Perhaps tomorrow."

He mouths to me *What are you doing?*

I bite my lip to repress my smile, and Cameron's scowl deepens, his gaze roving over me. His confusion sends tingling ripples under my skin.

He stops walking. "Wait here. I'll bring you your book."

We arrive at my cabin way too soon. Our mission has lost my interest for a long minute.

Cameron struts down the corridor, leaving me with Mr. Crossley. He remains a few feet away from me, next to the grand staircase.

I flash him a tight smile and unbutton my coat. I have the inkling he's been commanded not only to perform chaperone duties but also to prove or disprove if Cameron and I are really in love.

Cameron reappears with the book and offers it to me. The cover is green with golden ornamented letters and a girl in profile kneeling on grass. "Here you go."

"When were you going to give this to me?"

"On our wedding night," he whispers. "To remind you that even unfavorable circumstances hold opportunities and beauty."

Cameron was shopping around Manhattan at some point, thinking of our . . . wedding night, out of all nights. I should at best articulate my gratitude, but I can't find the proper words to convey the wild emotions raging in my chest.

Cameron kisses my forehead with soft lips—for charade purposes—yet my insides turn into melted butter. My fingers fail to grasp the lapels of his coat as he walks away, leaving his pristine scent of soapy tangerines with me.

"That'll be all, Mr. Crossley." I hug the book, heat blinding my senses, and tumble into my cabin. I can't make sense of my emotions—my thoughts are cluttered, strewn all over.

I slide off my coat, which is too woolly and too weighty, when two minutes ago it was not. "All right, focus," I command myself. Emily isn't here. She must be dining wherever maids dine aboard.

Peeling off my dress is a bit of a fiddly activity, but I manage just fine after a few tries. One hook after another, adding the right pressure on the side of the bodice, and I'm freed.

I'm clasping the last hook on my tea dress when someone knocks on my door.

"Who's this?" I say into the air.

"Cam. Are you ready?" Cameron asks on the other side.

I poke my head out of the cabin.

"I am," I say, although I certainly am not. Not for what I might find inside Nigel's trunk. My body trembles with each step I take.

"Do you think he's allied with Germany?" I dare voice the question I've not even allowed to ask myself, running my nails along the ruffles of my dress. The faintest orchestral music waltzes from belowdecks, swirling through the empty corridors.

"Hard to say before seeing those documents," Cameron says.

"How would you know what those documents are either way?"

He chews on his inner cheeks, hollowing them. "It was enough to spark your suspicion. I assume they're different from your ordinary business paperwork."

Cameron knocks on my uncle's cabin door and waits with his hands in his pockets. He's in shirtsleeves, his suspenders hanging at his sides. "Mr. Benson?" He listens in, leaning forward. "It seems he's away yet." He turns the knob and, with a low whine, the door creeps open to a pitch-dark room. "Lucky it's open."

Of course, Nigel wouldn't look for the section steward or even use his own set of keys. It tells a lot of his arrogance.

But this might be silly. His cabin is wide open to anyone who might wish to wander inside. It might not be exactly arrogance, yet he's clearly not worried. For all I know, those documents could be harmless business procedures or just a fancy lamp prototype. Uncle Nigel might be a crazy inventor by night, German just being an academic pursuit. Or we might be arriving too late, and he could've already hidden the papers under lock and key at the purser's office.

I glance over my shoulder. No stewards will see us sneaking into the parlor. "What if he's sleeping?"

"He would've locked his door from the inside if that was the case. Getting cold feet?"

I am, but I'll be caught dead before I show it. I square my shoulders and enter first, following the trail of light spilling from the corridor. I have to be careful with the table in the middle of the room; it's bolted, and its edges are sharp. I learned this in the afternoon the hard way. By tomorrow, a bruise will have sprouted on my knee.

Cameron shuts us in, and in the beat of a heart we're engulfed in total darkness. Though, in the same beat, lifetimes can pass through and through, and I do my best not to picture him closer, his breath inches from my lips.

I shake my head, startling myself. What a fool I am, daydreaming of his kisses when he'd probably laugh at my ridiculous thoughts. What is even happening to me? *He doesn't feel that way about you, stop it.*

"Where would my uncle hide those documents?" I ask, being more practical.

Cameron clicks the lights on, blinding me. "You start searching the parlor. I'll go for the bedroom."

Good. I don't want to delve into my uncle's drawers.

Cameron heads to the next room with long strides. Not missing a second, he flings a drawer open. This suite is a twin of my own, only inverted, same damask settees and mahogany furbishing.

The low table has a drawer; a bare breath of wood and old cigar waft to my nose as I roll it open, but it's empty. From the other room comes the shrill of metal hangers being pushed on the wardrobe bars.

In the desk drawer, there's stationery, his cabin and trunk keys, a fountain pen, and a Bible, but no folders. Next, I kneel on the floor and peek under the couch and under the tables, but there's nothing strapped below.

Standing in the middle of the parlor, I spin on my heel. Am I missing a spot? My uncle didn't bring many items with him, two trunks and two suitcases. Those documents are either in the trunks or in the purser's office.

Cameron has already searched Nigel's suitcases, both open on the bed, long gutted of clothes, which are already collected in the wardrobe. I close them with a thud, leather and peppermint snuffing out with the motion.

"The parlor is empty," I tell Cameron and sit on the edge of the bed, the weight of these hours suddenly heavy on my shoulders.

Cameron looks around the room. "Nothing in his wardrobe or chest of drawers."

"They're valuables. They're probably with the pursers now. Why else would he have his cabin doors unlocked?"

Cameron lifts a finger, one of his eyes twitching in an involuntary squint. "If those papers are confidential or endangering, I doubt he's left them under the care of someone else. No. They are here."

"The trunk?"

He sighs and returns the suitcases to the top of the wardrobe. "It's empty."

Giving up hope on the parlor, I switch off the lights and shut the door to the bedroom. "Where would you hide such documents?"

"Close to me."

I tilt my head, pondering where that might be. In my memories, my mother smiles tenderly and sneaks a lavender sprig under my pillow.

The same sprigs I collected inside that box weeks ago. *To aid you with sweet dreams, keep these close to you,* she used to say. Close to me . . .

Just like in my suite, two beds stand on opposite sides of the room. With a jerk, I snatch the pillow of the one to my right, but there's nothing underneath.

"Help me lift these mattresses," I tell Cameron. With his assistance, we hoist the first one up. But there's nothing attached to the mattress or on the wiry base. "Perhaps this is the one in which he'll sleep," I muse. "Perhaps, the housekeepers won't even touch the linens on the second bed if nobody is sleeping in it."

Cameron and I lift the other mattress and, tucked by the bedstead, I spot the dull carton covers.

"You genius," Cameron mutters, a side smirk tugging at his cheek. "How did you guess it?"

I tell him about my mother and her lavender under my pillow. "I don't know why it occurred to me."

Cameron puts down the mattress as we lock eyes. He huffs, as if he was speechless, marveled by something he's seeing in me. Some seconds slip by, a growing need to come closer to him thrumming in the very air, until a thump outside snaps us back into reality. As efficiently as I can, I tuck the bedding while Cameron pages through the documents.

"What do you think?"

"I barely know German," he admits. "But I know something—this isn't your normal business paperwork. These numbers . . . I swear it looks like . . . What was the name? A numbers station."

"What is that?"

A shadow crosses Cameron. "In short, encrypted messages transmitted in number sequences. Intelligence officers use them."

Encrypted messages, intelligence . . . the words ring through me, like cues of some knowledge hidden in a dark corner.

"Intelligence officers, meaning"—I struggle to rescue the things I learned from adventure books—"*spies*?"

Cameron fixes me with a gaze over the papers. "In short? Yes. That's a possibility."

My thoughts collide against each other, the mangle lashing out and swerving in a thousand directions. My body doesn't feel solid, as if I were about to turn to sand and fall apart. "How do you even know what a numbers station is?"

"My father," he answers absentmindedly, turning another page. "He's well versed in intelligence work. Policemen affairs, I guess."

I find it strange that a mere policeman would be well versed in intelligence work, but I nod regardless and nibble at my lip. Those documents . . . I remember them well, filled with endless numbers. My father could've padded his office with those papers. He kept them neatly piled inside a drawer he always shut with a key. "What if he's a spy?"

Do I mean my father, my uncle, both?

"Those imbeciles, Adam!" my uncle shouts from the outer corridor.

Cameron and I freeze, staring at each other with the pale shade of terror washing across us. The parlor door cries as it's pried open an inch. My uncle's growl is audible yet unintelligible.

Cameron and I push the folder back under the mattress and turn the lights off.

"They'll keep their mouths shut," Mr. Crossley says, whose Christian name is, apparently, Adam. The parlor door whines open now.

"I agree," Emily says. "They're well trained."

"Well trained? I told them to wait in America, and what do those nincompoops do? They follow me aboard."

"I could go down and make sure they're silent," Mr. Crossley says. "We could extract them when we arrive in—"

"No extraction," Nigel says. "They're on their own now."

"On their own?" Emily yelps.

"You heard me, Ilse. And they better keep those traps shut or else *I'll* go down to E-Deck and kill them with my bare hands. Ich schwöre bei Gott."

I repress a gasp, clamping a palm onto my mouth. For a moment, they fall silent, and my cold muscles go taut like violin strings. Have they heard me? Nausea swirls in my stomach.

Cameron grazes my arm, making me jump.

"Come with me."

With a touch as light as a feather, he ushers me through the dark room. As soon as he opens the bedroom door, we tumble to the corridor. Beads of sweat cover my back.

Uncle Nigel's voice echoes outside, too loud for indoor conversation. My breath wheezes in and out as I press my fingertips on my temples. Spies? Killing? Ilse? My maid's using a false name. And they're all in on it. My uncle, Mr. Crossley, and her.

"This is impossible." I run from port to starboard and storm into my parlor. "This can't be happening."

"Alexandra, I need you to calm down," Cameron hushes.

"*Nigel is lying.* Now it makes sense." Tears suddenly fall from my eyes, my chest heaving up and down. "Who put that in my old house? Cameron, this cannot be happening."

Cameron pulls me in for a hug. He's steady while I'm crumbling to pieces. His arms are warm and make me feel safe, but deep inside I have never felt as scared and alone as I do right now. I grip a handful at the back of his shirt, while I sink my teeth into my bottom lip to stifle a sob.

Cameron doesn't say anything but holds me for as long as I cry.

Chapter Thirteen

May 2, 1915—Day 2 of 7

The first morning light crawls into the cabin, dulling the ornate electrical candles over my bed. I raise my head to the coffered white ceiling and sigh. I stayed up all night, reading the book Cameron gave me, and I tried not to think about what I now know. Of course, I failed miserably. My eyes were following Mary Lennox on her adventures in England, but my mind swirled far away.

I never imagined I'd see Nigel so angry. Why would my boring, pompous Uncle Nigel otherwise want to kill innocent stowaways with his bare hands, if he were not a spy? Why would my uncle speak perfect German? Why would we have found intelligence documents in his trunk, written in German? At the very least, Nigel is affiliated with the German government.

And so are Mr. Crossley and Emily—*Ilse.*

All the clues are there, like a breadcrumb trail. But if my uncle is a spy, where does that leave my parents? My father worked with the same documents. But it doesn't make sense. My parents rubbed shoulders with the rich and famous, yet they were boringly ordinary. Tea by five, modest social outings on weekend nights; Dad worked at the British consulate and oftentimes from his desk. Mom was a housewife.

I knew what my mother's favorite fragrance was and Dad's favorite restaurant down the block, but I never wondered where my father's immense fortune came from. I always assumed my grandfather bequeathed him millions. At home, there were barely any photographs of my family. Nobody ever visited on Christmas, not even Uncle Nigel. My grandparents died during my childhood. When I asked about England, or when I expressed curiosity about traveling there, my parents never acknowledged me. They never talked about the way they met or their lives prior to moving to America.

Did I even know my parents at all?

In whose hands am I? In those of liars and murderers? Uncle Nigel—if he's my family at all—is taking me to England for a reason. And the reason might have nothing to do with lodging me in a big estate and letting me roam the moors in pretty dresses.

It might not be about the money at all either.

Where is the exit to this maze? What does this maze look like from above? What am I not seeing?

I shove the book shut and scramble out of bed. Daylight glimmers on the paneled walls of my cabin. Unsure of the time, I draw myself a hot bath and select my clothes for today. I'm about to choose a black mourning ensemble, but I'm in the mood to wear a beautiful dark mauve if only to lift my spirits.

By the time I slip into my dress and spritz perfume on my neck, I'm ready to begin my day, and my maid hasn't yet come into my room to wake me up. I huff. Well, as it turns out, I don't even need her. Here, I've done all the things I delegate to her every morning. In hindsight, her snootiness has never been normal.

I glare at the cabin. All around me, as if creeping in the walls, eyes and ears follow my every move. I'm never alone. Whom can I openly trust? Only Cameron, and still . . . not completely. All those things he seems not to dare say waltz through me every now and then, setting a tangle in my throat that refuses to go.

I make a beeline to my uncle's cabin, walking past passengers who seem headed to the dining room or to the upper decks. It's not as early as it seemed. Breaking the news I don't want Emily anymore will anger my uncle; he might give a hint of the dark truth lurking behind his phlegmatic behavior, but is that what I want? Or do I want to keep living a lie?

Halting, I unravel my fingers from my skirt and rap my knuckles on the door. Uncle Nigel speaks softly, but I don't hear muffled steps toward me. Is he talking to himself? I don't think he's heard me. Well, since he's awake, I might announce myself. I turn the knob and walk into the parlor. Uncle Nigel stands at the threshold of his bedroom, Emily holding onto his lapels. Standing on her tiptoes, she tilts her head and . . . kisses him.

Oh, my God.

I skid to a stop, then trip on my shoes as I throw myself to the exit.

"Alexandra, don't you know manners?" Nigel scolds me.

My back hardens as I stop. So, this was why Emily—*Ilse*—was late. She was *kissing* Nigel. And I say kissing, because if anything else has happened, I don't want to know.

Raising my chin, I turn to them. My uncle is awaiting my reply, buttoning his jacket. Emily's head is high, her nose wrinkled in that snobby way of women thirty years her senior, as if she were the mistress and I the servant.

"Emily was late," I say, taming the rage in my tone.

"You woke early," Emily retorts. "Would you like my help to finish dressing?"

Did she insult me? I look sensibly dressed. I stop my arms from crossing over my chest. Instead, I raise my chin higher. "I finished dressing without your help."

"And your hair?"

"It's down, where it will stay moving forward," I reply coolly.

"It'll look unkempt in the wind."

My hands give a shake. I ball my fists. "That's what pinned hats are for."

My uncle clears his throat. "You both can leave the footle for later. What made you think you'd find Emily here, Alexandra?"

Emily. Her Christian name. Not addressed as Miss Atkinson as a master does with servants.

I fight the muscles tugging at my eyebrow, but it rises regardless. "Did I not find her?"

The comment grants me a glare from my uncle, but a repressed smirk pulls at Emily's cheek.

"However, having run into her here was not my intention. I was coming to tell you, Uncle, that I won't require any more of Emily's assistance, unless specifically requested."

Nigel takes a step back. "Alexandra, you can't do without a maid."

"Well, look at me," I say, treading with care. I can't make mistakes now. "Emily, you're dismissed for now with one task. Please tell Mr. Asher he can wash in my lavatory from now on if he wishes to. Also inform him I'll be waiting for him at the Verandah Café. Go enjoy the ship afterward."

With that, I walk out of the suite and let my hands shake again.

"I must say"—Cameron slides into the wicker chair next to me—"a terrified Miss Atkinson has knocked on my cabin to let me know Miss Benson was offering her lavatory for my daily ablutions." He chuckles. "What did you do to her?"

"I stood up for myself," I clip. "And we both know that's not her real name."

"Let's keep their false names for simplicity." A waiter appears next to Cameron to take his order. "Black coffee. No cream. No sugar."

The Verandah Café is a breezy space with ivy climbing around columns and walls. This morning, streaks of raindrops splash the skylight above us, sun seeping through gaps in the overcast sky. The big glass in the back wall could open to the promenade if the weather were warmer, but I don't expect to see it happening during this crossing.

"So, you're a black coffee drinker?" I muse.

"Helps me wake up." Cameron eyes the cup in front of me and the half-eaten cookies on their saucer. With a blasé motion he leans back, propping his head on his hand with his pinkie tucked between chin and lower lip, and those teal eyes glide across me with a slow swing. "Tea drinker only?"

"Mostly," I say, and I'm proud my voice doesn't waver, even though I dig my nails into the napkin on my lap. "Have you accepted my offer to use my bathroom?"

"Gladly." He steals one of the cookies and studies it as if it were a strange mechanism. "Not very hungry this morning?"

"Not after what I've seen." My stomach churns. I wonder if I look as sick as I feel or if that was a subtle way of asking how I am after last night.

Cameron pops the cookie into his mouth. "What have you seen?" he harrumphs, sweeping the coconut flakes off the table.

"My uncle and Emily are having a dalliance. I caught them kissing."

Cameron coughs. Putting a fist to his mouth, his wide gaze remains on the windows. "Golly," he finally says, his voice strangled from the cookie crumbs. "Mixing business with pleasure."

In addition to Cameron and me, a couple occupies a table on the opposite end of the veranda. When I'm sure they've resumed their yak, I lean closer to Cameron. "Do you think my uncle is really a spy? Why do you not seem worried about last night?"

Cameron sighs. "Because I think it's early to tell—"

"What's so early to tell? You were there with me last night, he spoke German, and he has intelligence documents. And now we know the will has been switched up. Cameron, were my parents also spies?"

Cameron lowers his head and presses his lips into a thin line, making me reel back in my seat with a strange feeling simmering in my chest. "I don't know."

"Humor me," I whisper. "For the sake of conversation, if he's a spy, what would Nigel want with my family?"

The waiter places Cameron's coffee in front of him. He waits until we're alone again to reply, "Money?"

"That could be one thing but why me? Why my parents?"

Cameron takes a sip of his cup. "To gain access to England? What makes you think they were spies?"

"My father worked for the British consulate, and I saw documents on his desk that were similar to the ones we found yesterday. What if Nigel . . . *killed* them?"

The thought alone makes my skin crawl.

Cameron heaves a deep sigh and slips his coat off his shoulders. "I wish I could give you an answer."

"No, you can't, but I know who can. The stowaways."

Cameron sets his jaw forward and chuckles. "You know I've been the mastermind behind several trespassing offenses, but those stowaways are under custody belowdecks."

"I need to try." My voice dithers.

Cameron rubs his face and whispers, "All right, what do you want to do?"

"He said they were on E-Deck. My uncle wouldn't have suggested going to a crew area belowdecks. That means they must be in a third-class cabin. That saves us much time."

A smile tugs at Cameron's mouth. "That's very bright thinking. And since you're on a roll, dear, let me ask you: How do we access third class?" Cameron leans so close I can see a playful wink even if he wants to put on the show of contradicting me. "I remind you there are railings delimiting the spaces on the promenade."

"Do you see that couple over there? Before you arrived, they were saying how lovely the C-Deck à la carte restaurant is but how unfortunate it was seeing steerage passengers peeking in through the promenade windows. They're not surveilled, as it's obvious some have jumped over. But . . . I was thinking someone might be able to help us."

"Who?"

"We met someone who's been here before."

Chapter Fourteen

"Ask Professor Brodrick for help," Cameron says. "You're off your trolley."

"He mentioned he's traveled on this ship before," I say, shrugging. "Have a little faith."

"He was pleasant company, but we barely know the fellow."

I wave him off, my gaze searching among the few passengers on deck. Clouds are thinning above us, but the day remains gusty. After searching two full decks, my gaze finally falls on Professor Brodrick. He's on a deck chair, a drawing pad on his lap, tracing charcoal lines on an almost-blank page.

Before Cameron can stop me, I step forward. "Professor Brodrick! Such a pleasure to find you here. Do you draw?"

He lifts his head and smiles. "Miss Benson, Mr. Asher. What a surprise. I do draw indeed. A little activity when I'm not busy with rocks. How was the rest of your evening last night?"

"Uneventful," Cameron says as Professor Brodrick stands, tucking his paper-wrapped charcoal stick into a pocket in his oilskin pad, which he closes with a flip.

I elbow Cameron in the ribs. "I told you. You should've gone to the Smoking Room with him." I turn to Professor Brodrick. "Forgive him. My fiancé is stubborn."

Cameron slings an arm around my shoulders. "Look who's talking, Fiancée."

Professor Brodrick chuckles. "Would you two join me for a warm beverage?"

"We'd love to, but we might need your help for something else first." I ignore the way Cameron's arm tightens around me.

"My pleasure. How may I help?"

"How well do you know this ship?"

He smiles, a sweet tilt on his face. I've not noticed before, but he must not be much older than Cameron.

"Quite well. Ask me anything."

"Let's see . . ." Professor Brodrick unfolds a deck-plan brochure, provided by Cunard, and spreads it out on a table in a corner of the Lounge. "There should be a couple of ways into third class."

Cameron and I lean forward, following the traces of the professor's fingers on the map. "The Shelter Deck is the most obvious. The railings aren't surveilled all day."

"I was thinking of something perhaps more . . . private," I say.

Next to me, Cameron sighs.

Professor Brodrick scratches his forehead and flips the map around. "You like a challenge, I see. Excluding areas with too many officers, your best chance would be . . ." He taps the map. "Here. Enter the Children's Room, across the stewardesses' quarters, and into third class. I heard their cabins are connected by doors."

I gasp. "That's brilliant."

"I don't mean to throw a wet blanket on this," Cameron says.

"Oh, but you will," I grumble.

"What if the doors are locked?"

I cross my arms. "If the stewards had to carry keys to every door, they'd be a walking orchestra."

A dry smirk slips on his mouth. "Skeleton keys exist."

"You're ruffling my feathers today," I say, not letting Cameron's comment deter me. It's a perfectly sensible plan.

Cameron looks at Professor Brodrick and nudges his chin my way. "I can't win this argument, can I?"

I roll my eyes.

"I'd say the lady looks quite determined. She reminds me of my sister. Odds aren't good, Mr. Asher." Professor Brodrick laughs. "Do I want to know why you need to go into third class?"

"Better not to ask," Cameron says.

"Then I'll wish you good luck."

"Thank you so much, Professor Brodrick," I say.

"Lord. Just call me Carlton. We're past pleasantries."

We spend a few hours in the Lounge with our new friend, warming ourselves up with tea, coffee, and cookies, sharing stories about his well-paid job in Russia, his sketches, and his family. The treats at the Lounge are all I manage to digest the closer dinnertime creeps. As I pull my dress on in my room with shaking hands, my stomach shrinks, my chest hollows. But by the time I join Cameron at the landing of the grand staircase on C-Deck, I muster my best smile.

"So, tell me, wise one," Cameron says as a way of greeting. "We know about the doors, but how are we going to get into the stewardesses' rooms without said stewardesses' notice?"

"Leave that to me," I say, glimpsing around. The grand staircase is bustling with people and elevators are trudging up and down, and I prefer this conversation to stay private. This is one of the busiest times on the ship, before dinnertime. With the clock about to strike seven, children are not yet ready to be put to bed, but the parents and their staff are busy.

"Why are you carrying a box?"

I frown at the package in my hands. Does he think me daft? "It's chocolate cake. I need something to bribe the stowaways with."

As if it were not obvious I'd need a reward for the information. What better than cake? They won't have the chance to taste chocolate in prison.

He scratches his neck over his collar. "They'll know we're first-class passengers, Alexandra; we won't fool anyone."

He's right. My short-sleeved dress is the color of mandarins, its draped skirt reaching under my knees. It closes around my waist with a big bow. Cameron sports a fitted brown suit, all the rage right now, unlike third-class men who at best are wearing sack suits. The lower classes are always behind in fashion.

I shrug. "We need to look like we belong in first. I don't want to be detained next to our German fellows."

Cameron chuckles, a smidgen of relent flittering in his voice. "And you assume that slinking across corridors will be less flashy than jumping over the fences?"

I sigh. "Obviously, if we're caught trespassing, we can't allege we're lost, can we? But if they catch us wandering about a corridor, they'll believe it."

Cameron's smile becomes tainted with an emotion I can't decipher. I'd say sadness, but he loses it so fast I might've imagined it.

"Why trust the stowaways?"

"Why not?"

"Why not report your uncle to the officers?"

People trickle into the room to leave their children under the care of the stewardesses, and my breath quickens the more I wait idly conversing about the pros and cons with Cameron. This morning seems too far away in time, though not even twelve hours have slipped from me. "Because that way I won't have answers."

He sighs, throwing his hands in the air. "Need I remind you I am your fiancé?"

"Need I remind you that you accepted my conditions, which included *Don't interfere*?"

"Even if I believe you're doing something very, very stupid?"

"I'm going to do this with or without you. So, stay silent and follow me into that room or please stop delaying me."

He points in the direction of the Children's Room. "God knows I've tried. Ladies first."

With a straight back and my chin held high, I cross to port side. The deafening clamor of childish laughter, singsong, and shrieks seeps from the room as Cameron and I stand last in the line.

"That box won't pass for a child," Cameron says.

"Why are you being so tedious?" I growl.

He clasps his fingers around my arm. "I'm trying to avoid you the—"

"Good evening," a stewardess says. "How may I help you?"

"Good evening." I flash a bright smile. "My fiancé and I are here to pick up my sister's little princess. She's two years old. Name Beatrice."

"I'm sorry, Miss. I have no clue. When did you drop her off?"

My smile is so tight my cheeks hurt. "My sister said earlier today."

"I'll go see if it's one of the toddlers in our cabin."

The woman rushes toward one of the doors in the room. While one of the stewardesses is gone, the other remains busy trying to feed a cranky toddler in a chair.

I keep my ridiculous smile in place as I venture into the room.

"What are you doing?" Cameron asks me.

"Pick up that ball," I say through gritted teeth.

With a quick stoop, Cameron takes the brown sphere.

A long-clothed table is ringed by a cozy corner and bolted chairs, pushing all the children to the end of the room. In the corner, two boys hoop roll next to boys playing with toy soldiers and girls playing with dolls and toy blocks. They're too close, calling for disaster.

"Hold my box for me?" I ask Cameron. "Give me the ball."

What I'm about to do is cruel, but I have no other option. I ensure with a glance nobody's attention is on me and hurl the ball at the children. The sphere plows through the room, flinging the toys away, and collides with the hoops, sending them to the wall with a violent jerk.

A silence as dark as the calm before a storm sets in the room; then the first shriek breaks out, and sobs follow. The single stewardess in the room bolts to her feet, dashing to calm them.

I cover a snort against my forearm.

"Good God," Cameron says. "Why are you laughing? This room has shifted into a hell realm."

I snort again, the piercing wails ringing in my ears. It's not funny, but my hysteria looks strikingly similar to amusement.

The second stewardess runs into the room, little fake Beatrice surely long gone from her mind.

I grab Cameron's arm and rush into the narrow corridor. The stewardesses in charge of the Children's Room share a cabin crammed with bunks, thin mattresses covered by woolly blankets, a sturdy wardrobe, and a mahogany washbasin with a mirror. I swing the far-end door open, holding my breath, and run into darkness. The slit of light pouring from the room behind me outlines bars of metal bunks and an enameled washbasin, the brass on a nearby door shining faintly.

I blink, eyes adjusting to the dark corridor, searching for light from portholes, but there are none.

Cameron nudges me forward.

"How did they shove a cabin into a *thoroughfare*?" I hiss, stumbling into the room.

Cameron shuts the door, muting the cries and commotion from the Children's Room. "Welcome to the life of stewards. If you think this is infuriating, you should see how firemen or trimmers live."

I try the doorknob, which mercifully gives and clicks the door open. I sigh as the third-class hall appears in front of us. My legs wobble, and my dress weighs down on me as I step out of the cabin, sweat dampening my back.

"We need to continue," Cameron says.

Steerage passengers stop to glare at us. Taking the staircase downward, I flash a grateful smile at them for not making a scene. Should they cross to first class, the passengers would do much worse than gape.

Echoing stairs bereft of any intricacy lead us down, round and round onto a secluded hall. The deck name shines in stately brass letters over a set of benches pushed against the walls.

"E-deck," I whisper, though I'm not sure if Cameron has heard me over the ship's engines.

Goosebumps rise all over my exposed clammy skin. White always makes everything aseptically cold, like recent snow on a silent night. My heels clack against the floor. Wincing, I unlatch my shoes and leave them under a bench while Cameron sets down the box on the seat and scuttles through the closest passageways.

"What are you doing?" I hiss.

"Wherever those stowaways are, they must be guarded."

I sit on the bench with a strange pressure building in my chest. Maybe this is as inane as Cameron says.

"I didn't think about that."

"You didn't, but I did." Cameron sways slightly on the balls of his feet, tilting left and right to peek at the corridors, like a bloodhound scenting the air. "From here, we shall be careful—the officers must be somewhere. We need a plan. Ideas on next steps?"

"I didn't think of what to do or say to be allowed in and talk to them." I feel utterly ridiculous. "How many officers are we talking about?"

Cameron squints away, across the corridors. "Probably one, at the door. At most, two."

"They won't let me walk into the cabin."

"But I can," he mumbles. "I can let you in."

"You aren't going to knock the officers out, are you?"

He laughs darkly. "No. I'll distract them."

While I'm a rumble of apprehension, Cameron is almost visibly tingling with anticipation. A nudge of suspicion washes across me like trickles of dark water.

I stand, picking up the cake box. My sitting concedes too much power to him. "Who are you, Cameron?"

His head whips down at me with a scowl. "Who am I?"

"You're not even shedding a drop of sweat."

"Fake Addie," he says, and his voice turns sweetly spurious, which disturbs me more than his excitement. "When you're not born in wealth, you might face situations in which—"

"What are you on about?" I cut him off. "You're middle class, went to normal school, and could afford living in Manhattan. Stop talking as if you're too poor and life was complicated."

That trickle of suspicion grows, and doubt tears my chest. Cameron is good at lying, that I knew. His knack for breaking the law might've been a surprise, but not as much as his cool and nonchalance in such a situation. Nigel is already lying. Is Cameron lying as well? I couldn't stand it—*tolerate* it—if that were the case.

Everything spins, tingles filling my palms.

"There is something else," I whisper.

A shadow shifts in Cameron's eyes. "We need to find those stowaways."

I blink, my spiraling halting. The floor is solid again under my feet. He's right, and he's making himself useful by helping me, but he's a fool if he believes I'm sweeping my distrust under a rug.

Together, we cover the first section. Save for some befuddled passengers, the corridors remain empty. We're lucky the cabins on the *Lusitania* run in rows, straight vision aligning port and starboard, the space solely divided by funnel casings.

At once, Cameron and I turn to the open watertight door by the stairs. Cold numbing my stocking-covered toes, we skulk across eerily silent corridors. The quiet hangs low and tense like an invisible cloud, as though someone were following us; something felt but unseen prickles along my spine. The little hairs on my arms rise. This can't be a usual quiet—it belongs in places in which something is afoot behind the scenes.

Cameron taps my shoulder and signals to the end of the section. With a firm nod, I advance down the corridor, then peek around the corner, catching a dark uniform in front of one of the middle cabins. I leap back, bumping into Cameron's chest.

"I think I found them," I whisper.

Cameron frowns, as if he were trying to organize his thoughts or situate his position in this maze. He's cold like the ocean, scheming and in control rather than nervous and floppy, which is perfect given the situation—and yet . . .

"I'm going to the other corridor to distract him. This can be dangerous—be careful and scream if you're in danger."

I nod. "I will."

He puts a finger under my chin and lifts my head. "Before we part ways, I need you to plan what you're going to do in that cabin. Think up your questions. They need to be quick and to the point. If they catch us, we could go to prison for espionage. Understood?"

He cuts a dark glare my way, and he catches me off guard.

I push down a lump in my throat. "Understood. How will I know when to go to the door?"

"You'll hear. Use your time wisely. I don't know for how long I'll hold him." With the ghost of a caress on my cheek, he goes the other way.

I wait for a minute, my body as tense as one of those wires securing the funnels while I assort my questions. Besides, going to *jail*? That is something I didn't consider beforehand—an oversight, given I'm a law student. He's right. I'm blinded by my need to know. This isn't the good idea I thought it was. What am I getting us into?

I rush to follow him and stop our inane plan, but a commotion of limbs tumbling down on metal resounds through the passageway, halting me. Metal? What's that sound? I tiptoe back, finding the stairs leading up and down to the next decks, their iron a bit rusty and flaky at some parts near the landing. My eyes widen. The stairs . . . Has Cameron thrown himself down the *stairs* on purpose?

When I poke my head around the corner, the dark uniform is running portside. That was my cue! Was this Cameron's plan all along? Does he even know how to throw himself down a flight of steps without breaking a bone or his very head?

My feet hesitate at the corner, but at once the reason why we're doing this returns to me, and with that, my senses. I race to the door. No time to back down. Cameron drawls from afar as I turn the knob, but it doesn't give.

"Shit," I whisper and tiptoe to the corner. Cameron sits on the floor. Since the officer is bending toward him, a silvery key ring peeks from under his jacket, attached no doubt to his belt. Cameron lifts his head, eyelashes casting shadows on his cheeks.

The door is locked, I mouth, signaling at my hip.

"I need assistance," Cameron mumbles.

"Of course, sir," the man says, reaching out to Cameron.

Cameron slips on the linoleum and splays himself in the arms of the officer. Light as the touch of a spider, he fumbles on the officer's belt while he purposefully sways and trips.

I remain petrified, clutching the box, watching how he unlatches the key ring and throws it at my feet.

To distract the officer, Cameron tackles him to the floor with a comical jerk. "I deeply apologize, sir."

Laughter tickles in my throat, but I down it with stubborn determination. Fast as lightning, I leave the hall, unlock the door, and storm into the cabin, halting dead at the sight of the stowaways.

I've not thought this plan through. The men sit on their bunk beds, handcuffed to the frames and ladders, but what if they had not been chained? After the first seconds of surprise wear off, they smile and chatter in German. I don't know the language, but the tone alone makes the hairs on my nape stand.

"I don't have much time. I know you speak English," I say. "Does the name Nigel Benson ring a bell to you?"

Silence. They look at each other. Smiles.

"I heard him talking about you," I insist.

One of them, the first one to my right, a man with green eyes, scratches his chin. "You shouldn't be on this ship."

"As it turns out, you shouldn't either. He's angry. I'm sure you're hungry, so here." I give the cake box to the man with green eyes. He takes it with a hesitant tremble.

"Did he send you?" A small yet meaningful give.

A tremor snakes down my legs, but I keep my focus.

"We have no idea what you're talking about," the one to my left adds through the muffle of his broken nose. Blood stains his knitted sweater.

"We wanted back to Germany," says the third in broken English. "We poor."

"My parents are dead, and I suspect it's because of my uncle," I mutter. "I fear for my life. You're the only ones who can help me understand, please."

I wince. Self-deprecation sickens me.

They glance at each other, talking in their language.

"Do *not* speak German," I hiss. "Answer me."

They chuckle; then I catch my name in their quick whispered tittle-tattle. They know who I am.

"My uncle won't intercede or extract you once we reach England," I prod to make them speak. "He'll get off this ship and forget you exist. You'll go to jail. You owe him nothing. In fact, he was threatening to come belowdecks and kill you."

"We're expecting someone to kill us before we can speak," the first man mumbles. "If not him, then others."

Cameron's voice echoes down the corridor. He and the officer must've approached the cabin.

"Then help me."

"You shouldn't be on this ship," the green-eyed man repeats.

I turn all my attention to him, for he seems the most sympathetic. "But I am."

"You must leave."

"Considering we're in the middle of the ocean—"

"No, I mean you must leave this cabin, then *him*."

"Is Nigel a spy?" I ask under my breath, stepping too close for comfort to the man. If he wanted, he could stand and snatch at my skirt.

"Yes," he says, turning the blood in my veins to jelly.

"Sag ihr nichts!" the one who has a broken nose snaps.

I grip the cabin key close to my chest, its cold seeping into my fingers. "Is he dangerous? Did he want my parents dead?"

"He's dangerous, he'll kill if needed or given the chance, and yes, he was after your parents. Don't ask us the reason—we don't know. We weren't involved in the car crash."

"Halt die Klappe, du Idiot," the spy with the broken nose barks.

The car crash . . . I didn't mention *any* car crash. Slowly, I retreat until my back touches the door. The cabin tilts, and all I see is my parents' car flying off a cliff, the bright glow of the flames in the nearby trees, while Nigel drove away, relishing his victory, the wheels whirling slowly on the road, round and round they went—while my parents died in the fire. This is worse than a greedy uncle. Than a testament swap. Nigel is lying. My very life—and Cameron's—is at stake.

I must look ashen, for the one who spoke broken English studies me with a frown.

"Sie ist nur ein kleines Mädchen," he tells the one with the broken nose.

The green-eyed spy lowers his head and looks as though he gulps. "Und sie hat recht."

"Why did he kill my parents?" I press. "Why does he want to take me to England?"

"We don't know. But leave him as soon as you step on land. Now, get away from here."

Chapter Fifteen

Warm tears come to my eyes. Was coming here worth it? What should I do with this information? Panic swims through me like the trickles of a creek, branching in different directions. I'm unable to stop it from fully taking control of me. With a jerk, I pivot to the door at the same time it swings open, making me shriek.

Cameron's hard expression lands on me, and he puts a finger to his lips. He gives the three men a dirty look. "Time's up."

I'm too light-headed to remember what to do, so Cameron grabs the key from my numb hands, dashes to the place where he was with the officer, and drops the ring on the floor, the silver shining faintly against the linoleum under the pool of a fixture.

Holding my wrist, he ushers me in the opposite direction. "I asked him for a glass of water, but I couldn't hold him back anymore. He was becoming suspicious."

The world becomes a smudge of similar white passageways, but Cameron seems to remember the way back. He scoops my shoes from beneath the bench, and we run up the stairs until we're out on C-Deck. The sea gusts gasping into the long promenade manage to slap me out of my daze.

My breath comes in and out, a quickened panting. Elbowing a steerage couple strolling up their deck, we reach the railings. Cameron assists me in climbing over. Stunned faces gape from both sides of the promenade. Couples and families whisper in our wake, yet I don't look back. A shaky sigh passes my lips as soon as I enter the first-class hall and I'm engulfed in conversations, warmth, and music.

"Did they hurt you?" Cameron asks, steering me down the grand staircase.

"No, they were handcuffed," I whisper.

"What did they tell you?"

I blink, coming back to my senses as we enter my cabin. Am I more shocked by what I've heard the spies say or by Cameron's behavior and mastery at deception?

"No, Cameron," I say.

"No, what?"

I jerk my arm free from his grip. "No, let's talk about who you are. Why are you able to unlatch a key ring from an officer's belt without his notice?"

"Is that what you want to talk about?"

If it's self-preservation while I assimilate the stowaways' confession or true suspicion about Cameron, I don't want to know. I want answers, no matter how far-fetched my reasoning might be. "Yes."

With a sigh, he leaves my pumps on the floor, stows his hands in his pockets, and ambles a couple of measured steps away, one pointed shoe in front of the other. "I already told you I didn't have an easy life."

"Yes, you're so fast to remark I've had it easier than you. But that's not an excuse. You weren't born in a slum. You were born to a middle-class family."

He sits on the couch. "What makes you think I didn't have a complicated life just because my family wasn't poor?"

Closing my arms over my chest, I make a face. "You tell me."

"My father was forced to retire young. What my mother made at the store didn't support us through the month. At ten years old, I was forced to work until my father got back on his feet." He licks his lips and sighs, a speck of hesitancy flickering through his aloof demeanor. "But I was a child and I didn't want to work, so . . . I took the easy path. I pilfered from houses, I pickpocketed, I swindled travelers and gullible people with sad stories. I stole food from stores. My parents believed I was cleaning chimneys and selling newspapers, and while I did that sometimes, the pay wasn't enough. I became a clever liar and a good thief.

"The streets aren't easy. They're dangerous and rough. As the son of a police officer, I was not proud. I'm still not."

I plop into the desk chair, empty of emotions, save for simple relief. "That's why you want to help destitute children."

Cameron nods. "I swore to myself I wouldn't let others go astray like me."

His reason, after all, wasn't as dark as I feared. "I'm sorry."

"I should've told you sooner."

I remain in the seat, trying to swallow a lump. "The stowaways know Nigel. One of them confirmed he's a spy."

"Simply confirmed it? As easy as that? What else did they say?"

"They said I must leave him as soon as I arrive on land." And that they want to go to Germany. A crack of sympathy runs through me. Aren't we all yearning for home? They didn't even look dangerous, just resigned to the fact they'd rot in an English prison—or get killed.

"Have you thought they might be lying to you?"

"Why would they lie?"

Cameron shrugs. "Bored men having a share of fun after being locked up for hours on end?"

Anger sparks to life behind my ears, making them hot. "You weren't there. They mentioned the car crash. It's impossible they knew. I didn't say anything about it."

He studies me for a long while, mouth pressed, as if something brimmed on the tip of his tongue. I long to ask him what he wants to say. But I keep it to myself.

With a quick motion, he rakes through his pomaded hair, creating grooves through it. "All right," he says. "So, you got your answers. Now what?"

Why is he so aloof? This is a serious matter, and he still acts as if the news weren't an earth-shattering event. Does he even *believe* me?

"I don't know what to do."

Cameron looks at me again with a silence so dark it might be the last straw, pushing my distrust to newer heights. He wipes the side of his mouth with a thumb, hunching forward. "Truth is you don't have to do anything."

"Of course," I say, jolting to my feet. "But you didn't hear them saying Nigel is dangerous and that he'll kill if given the chance. You didn't hear them admitting that he indeed killed my parents. Should I just allow Nigel to murder me? Murder you?"

He stands. "That's not what I said."

Then what is it that you're saying? I want to yell. Pacing my suite, I clasp my mouth shut. I can't let Cameron hear all these ugly profanities brimming on the tip of my tongue. Keeping my anger in is like grasping a blade, cutting me through skin, muscle, and meeting steel on bone.

The note—*Nigel is lying*—only piles up over the spies admitting to Nigel's crimes. I don't want to believe Cameron is also hiding something from me. But if the unwilling cooperation and skepticism he's displaying are due to that everlasting carefree attitude in him, he's going too far. He doesn't believe me—or doesn't care what Nigel can do.

My parents, this crossing, Cameron, suspicion—they all revolt in the depths of me. I come to a sudden halt, too tired to even produce new words, new *thoughts*. I can't bear the thought of trifling with him any longer.

"I need to sleep," I say, striding to the bedroom. "Good night, Cameron."

I slam the door shut to the parlor and turn the lock, not minding if he stands in the middle of the room until dawn.

I drop on the bed and count the seconds to lose consciousness.

Chapter Sixteen

May 3, 1915—Day 3 of 7

The cards in my hands don't look promising. I flick a jack of clubs out of my deck and lay it on the table.

"Your turn," I tell Cameron over the happy melody playing at the Lounge.

Cameron takes a sip from his coffee, glancing at the piano over the rim of the cup. I'm not sure if what flashes in his expression is approval or dissatisfaction. High above us, bright daylight seeps through the stained glass of the skylight.

With a quick flip, Cameron puts a king of clubs on top of my jack, winning the trick.

I raise an eyebrow, thinking of my next move. We're in a tie, and this is the last trick in the game. I suspect Cameron retains a king somewhere, but I have only so many options. Sighing, I pull out the two of spades.

Cameron turns in his king of spades. "I win," he says, taking the cards.

I munch at the tip of one of our cucumber sandwiches so I don't make a face. "Then you lead the next game. Are you trying to make me complain and break the rules of whist?"

"After last night, Fake Addie, it seems breaking rules is your specialty. Not mine."

Silence cuts through the table as Cameron and I glare at each other.

I woke up this morning, tired to the bone and dry eyed, with streaks of black mascara on my cheeks. Cameron was asleep on the couch. Neither of us has spoken about last night. I'm beyond thankful my uncle is still sulking about the stowaways, and out of the way.

However, I can't avoid his assistant.

Mr. Crossley stops by our table. "Are you familiar with the expression 'Cut the tension with a knife'? This table is the living illustration of that."

"Why would we not be familiar with the expression, Mr. Crossley?" Cameron asks. "My books say it's been in use for a century."

Mr. Crossley grabs his hands at his back. "I'm sure Mr. Benson would like to know why."

"Cameron and I had a misunderstanding last night, is all," I say, resentment bitter like lemon on my tongue.

"Did he try to pressure you to bed?"

I gasp. "Absolutely not. Good Lord, Mr. Crossley. In what world—?"

"Who do you think I am, hmm?" Cameron asks with a bored, monotonous voice, sifting through his cards. His shiny laced boot sways in the air, one leg crossed over his knee. There it is, the aloofness again.

I swallow a ball of bread and cucumber with a tight throat.

"My fault," Mr. Crossley says.

"A thief believes everyone steals, perhaps?" I say. "Have you ever pressured a fiancée of yours? Are you married, Mr. Crossley?"

He raises his eyebrows, a big smile curling up on his face. "Aren't we inquisitive this morning?"

"I'd like to know you better, Mr. Crossley. After all, it seems like we'll share a lot of time together, with you being my uncle's assistant." I flash him a smile, yet my blood sizzles just like the seltzer water in my glass. No matter how upset I am with Cameron, I know him. Unlike these people.

"Well, to answer the latter, no. Not married. Not betrothed. And then, no, I've never needed to force myself on a woman. They always willingly go to bed with me."

Cameron huffs, and I roll my eyes. "Do you have a sweetheart at home?"

"I'm as free as the wind, Miss Benson." He smirks, running his fingers through his blond hair. "Duty calls. However, you should try a game of shuffleboard. Up the stakes."

I watch him go, frowning at his back.

"You should be more careful with that man," Cameron mutters.

"So I should behave differently and show I suspect them?" I grumble. "I'd call that a good way to get us murdered."

He shuffles the cards in his hand. "All I'm saying is you must keep your composure."

I lower my head to the dark-green carpet and track Cameron's profile from his shiny boots to his swept-aside hair. The tone under our shoes complements his camel suit.

I narrow my eyes. "Keep my composure like you? Mr. Crossley has insulted your honor, and you've not so much as batted an eyelid."

"Becoming defensive would've made me look guilty of something I've not even done."

"What am I supposed to do?" I hiss. There he is, again the calm pond while I'm a raging fire.

He tsks, setting down the cards on the table. "Fine. You know? I must admit he was right. If we play shuffleboard and you win, perhaps you'll stop brooding."

I grunt and peel myself off my comfortable seat, snatching my black coat from the armrest. It's not a long walk—the Boat Deck surrounds the Lounge on both the left and the right—but the mere thought of sunlight and physical movement makes me pout. "I'm not brooding. And I'm not playing."

He stands and lifts a finger in front of my face. "I have a challenge for you."

I grimace. "A challenge?"

He straightens the big black bow that keeps half my hair up. "I want you to take a day off from your worries."

"May I know why?"

He shrugs. "A restful mind finds answers and solves problems. So, since we're in the middle of the Atlantic Ocean and the weather is lovely, I challenge you to act as if everything were completely normal. If you fail, I'll request something from you."

I squint. "What kind of request?"

"Nothing nefarious, I promise."

I cross my arms. "And what if I succeed?"

"Then you'll be welcome to request anything you want from me."

A treacherous smile tugs at the corners of my lips. "Even if it's a nefarious request?"

"Even so." He winks and extends his hand. "Are we game?"

"I also have a challenge for you before I accept."

He doesn't lower his hand. "Go ahead."

"You must show the real you."

He smiles, and a slight twitch of his shoulders catches my attention as he tilts toward me. "Care to elaborate the terms?"

"Show me the real Cameron, not the aloof man I've met these weeks."

"Deal. The terms remain." He sways his hand, still up between us. "Are we game, then?"

I shake his hand. "We are."

⁂

I raise my cue in the air. "Victory! Seventy-five points!"

The audience gathered around us claps. A thin cover of clouds blocks out enough sunlight to relieve the ocean's glare on the eyes, but the day is bright, and the breeze, though chilly, is gentle.

"Ah, no," Cameron counters, checking the chalked lines on the deck. "You're cheating. This isn't over. It's on the line."

"Lies," I say, walking to him. The disk is less than an inch away from the grainy white line. "It's not touching it!"

Cameron points down. "Yes, it is."

I lower my head. I hate to admit it, but as I was gliding these disks on the wooden boards, the sunshine warm on my face and the salty wafts cleansing me from the inside out, all my troubles fell behind me. No fake marriages, no spies, no testament mystery, no lies.

"You sound like a really bad loser," I rebut.

"Let's settle this," Cameron says, looking at the passengers around us. Among them, he points at a random man. "You, good sir."

The man replies, "Me?"

"Yes. Will you kindly serve as an impartial referee?"

As I turn, I lock eyes with Alfred Vanderbilt, who's fancily decked with a derby hat and a long coat. Most people would cower in front of his family, but Mr. Vanderbilt is a free-spirited man. Showing his lighthearted attitude, he steps forward with a little spring. "My pleasure."

He approaches and studies the lines, bowing a bit for a better angle. "The disk is not touching the line."

"I win," I chirp.

Cameron grunts, leaning on his stick. "Settled. Alexandra wins."

"I must admit, I'm not the best referee." Mr. Vanderbilt pushes the brim of his hat upward with a poke of his walking cane. "I was hoping for Miss Benson to win."

"Thank you, Mr. Vanderbilt," I say.

He nods with a sweet smile and disappears into the corridor of the Smoking Room.

"Did I just ask Alfred Vanderbilt to umpire our game?" Cameron whispers, amusement flittering across his face.

"I guess you did. I didn't know you were so competitive when you lost." To make a point, I swing my cue to my left. A yank knocks it away, and a childish yelp shrieks in the air. Out of the corner of my eye, the shadow of a young boy flings forward.

I cover my mouth. Cameron, moving like a whip, drops his stick and reaches down, catching the boy before he can kiss the floor. With a playful roar, he hauls the kid up and spins on his heel, making the child fly around. The boy's shriek becomes a lighthearted giggle.

My heart starts beating again, and I lower my hands, huffing.

"This is why you shouldn't be running close to where there's a shuffleboard game in the works." Cameron sets him on his feet. Lowering to a crouch, he snatches the boy's flat cap from the deck and plops it onto his blond head. "Are you all right, friend?"

"Yes, sir. Thank you, sir."

Cameron smiles. "Glad to hear. Now go play and be careful."

The child runs off into the thinning crowd.

"That was impressive," I admit with a smile of disbelief. More than impressive. A flutter is running down my belly.

"Ah, children. You develop fast reflexes while working with them," Cameron explains, returning our cues to the steward in charge of the shuffleboard equipment.

"You'll be a wonderful father." I blink. My comment is so ill timed. "Oh. I didn't mean with me, of course."

Cameron chuckles and walks aft by my side. The idea takes rotten roots in my most hideous feelings. What a lovely father he'll be, with his will to change the world, his broad-minded views, and his adventurous approach. Ugly feelings well in the pit of my stomach with a harrowing jolt, resenting whatever girl he chooses to marry once he gets rid of me.

"Have you ever thought about it? For when you're done with our arrangement?" I press, the sentence sour on my tongue.

"No, I haven't, to be honest," he says.

"But have you ever wished to?"

He squints at the ocean. "Of course. Of course one day, I'd like to settle down and have a family."

"Did you leave a sweetheart in Manhattan?"

He chuckles. "What kind of man do you think I am? No."

"You sound as if you had someone in mind."

He glances at me with a passing smile. "I was thinking about being a teacher. Those kids . . . I was already performing fatherly duties. Is it me or did you sound a . . . bit jealous, Fake Addie?"

"That's ridiculous," I say. "I was wondering if you were giving thoughts to your future life, that's all."

One in which you'll not have room for me. Despite the cool breeze, my cheeks are ablaze, and I hope Cameron thinks it's the result of exertion and not shame.

"All we have is the now," Cameron says. "I wouldn't like to miss out on the many wondrous things the world has to offer because my head is up in the clouds." He grips the handrail and props a boot on the lower rail, lifting himself. "Like those porpoises over there. Look."

But it's not the porpoises I'm interested in watching. Desire burns in me to admire him while he admires the ocean, right in this moment, forevermore, and engrave him in the depths of me.

Cameron wraps an arm around a shroud, light sparkling in his blue eyes. His stare is a sea filled with wonder and fulfillment, hair ruffling in the breeze and coat billowing behind him.

Despite his aloofness, his mysterious silences, the secrets and surprises, Cameron is one of the few good things I have in my life; this thoughtful, stubborn, charismatic man, who dropped everything on a moment's notice to follow me into the unknown, and the prospect of not having him sets a whirl of terror inside me. Between death and loss, between my old life on the East Coast and my new one in the English countryside, and the mystery and danger bridging both shores, Cameron is my only safe haven.

My heart soars, wings taking me high. I'm weightless, and it's all because of Cameron.

My eyelids fall shut, truth coming at me from all sides. Like a speeding tornado on even ground, it can't be escaped.

I'm falling in love with him.

Right when I didn't want to. Right when I was most resisting the idea. But he's taking over my feelings so greedily, a nearly lustful sensation courses in my blood. I don't want to resist. Perhaps it's why I keep resorting to ways to overlook everything that doesn't add up with him. He's a mystery, but a mystery I *chose.* I shouldn't feel the way I feel about him. After all, I've known him for a month and a half. Yet is it so terrible I'm developing feelings for a man with whom I'll spend two years side by side? A man whom I'll call husband? A man who no doubt will respect me? A man who would support my goals and my dreams, even if this marriage were real? He's giving me more than I care to admit, and I have something better than money: my love, if he wants it. He might leave, but living with a cold heart is worse than living with a stolen heart.

I want to berate myself for being so absurd. We might not have that time. And he'll leave once our time is up. Is that maybe what he wants to tell me? Has he noticed I'm falling in love and is trying to turn me down? Why would he nearly kiss me, then, when no one else was around? I'd understand the first kiss, in Central Park, but what about that moment in my parents' townhouse?

"Caught you," Cameron says, jumping from the railings onto the deck. "It looks like I won our challenge. I thought you'd pose a bit more of a problem." He tsks. "Disappointed."

I purse my lips. I'd rather drink salt water than admit to going through a qualm about my feelings for him. I clasp my hands together behind me, rocking on the balls of my feet. "It looks like you won. What will you request from me?"

I perk with anticipation, wrestling down a smile.

He lifts a finger. "I need to think about it."

"My, my, what will cross your mind? I'm terrified." No, the prospect makes my stomach flutter. "I hope you're not going to make me shine your boots."

Cameron chuckles. "There's a good boot shiner aboard."

"No laundry either."

"Cannot a man think in peace?"

I make a face. "All right. I'll let the man think."

He gives me a devious smirk. "You're blushing, Miss Benson."

"I happen to get red cheeks when men exasperate me."

"No, you don't, but your left eye twitches a little," he says.

My mouth hangs open, but before I can retort, he continues, "I've been thinking of our wedding."

"You think a lot about it for"—I lower my voice—"a fake relationship."

"I'd say I'm thinking ahead."

"At this point I'm not sure we'll even have a wedding, but fine, what have you been thinking about?"

He wraps me in his arms and glides me in a circle, making me catch my breath. The notes of the orchestra spin in the sky. He must've heard it playing before I did. He's so suave, I have to admit.

"I suppose this solves it," I say. My heart drums as he moves us, left to right, right to left, onward and backward, as if with a new step he'd challenge me to follow along.

"We need to look like a convincing couple during our wedding," he says. "So it's important we dance often beforehand."

"How do you do it so well?"

"I took lessons," he replies.

I chuckle. "You know what I mean. Evading the problems hanging over our heads like a sword."

"It's what I tried to show you this morning." He approaches my ear. His breath caresses my hair. "Maybe your uncle is an impersonator, maybe he's your real uncle, maybe we have to pretend we're playing along to save our lives—the thing is, letting the circumstances control you is a perfect way to lose your sanity."

"It's not as easy as you paint it to be."

He pulls away, enough to look at me, yet his breath still grazes the tip of my nose. "It really is. But I'll manage to show you."

Chapter Seventeen

May 4, 1915—Day 4 of 7

I close my eyes to the windows, failing to pin my hair with a barrette for the tenth time. This was far easier with Emily, and I'm exhausted. I haven't slept well for months, and not even early nights like yesterday restore my sleep pattern.

"I might be able to help," Emily says, as if summoned.

My heart flips. I whirl around in the chair. My maid—Ilse—stands under the threshold between the parlor and the bedroom. I stop my tongue before I call her by her real name. "Emily. How did you enter?"

She retrieves the key from a front pocket of her navy blue dress. "I've still got this. I came to return it."

I gulp, my mouth drying. I don't know why, but I don't believe her. "Then please, leave it."

"Would you mind some help?"

I sigh, turning. Truth is, I was close to giving up. But . . . What if she does something to me? What if they suspect me? I have only a few options, but it stands to reason that if they wanted me dead, I would be.

"Just this one time."

In the quiet, the key clangs against the wood when Emily sets it down. "What were you trying to do?"

My heart thuds on my temples. "A simple half up, half down, but I can't manage my hair today."

"I see the bruise on your cheek has almost healed."

I harrumph.

With quick fingers, she starts threading a strand of hair from each side of my head. "I also lost my parents when I was young. Sometimes . . . I see some of me in you."

I bite my tongue, refusing to let her soften me. As if she didn't have anything to do with my parents' deaths. She's dangerous. She'll hurt me if given the chance. But showing compassion might soften *her*. "I'm sorry. When did you start working with my uncle?"

"I was sixteen. It's been ten long years."

"So, he's known you since you were nearly a girl, and you're having a dalliance regardless."

Emily clasps the barrette onto my hair with a loud click. "Yes."

"He's using you."

"I'd say what an awful opinion you have of your uncle." She chuckles, patting my shoulders. "But who says I'm not using him as well?"

I turn slowly, my whole frame stiff. "Pardon me?"

She smiles. "Call for me if you need anything."

With that, Ilse leaves, shutting the door with a click. The key shines faintly on the desk.

I frown, confusion washing through me. Then I shake my head, pushing her out of my mind. She must be playing with me.

"Time to work," I mutter as I pull paper and pen out from a drawer.

I'm not relaxed by any means, but let's put Cameron's hypothesis to the test. Yesterday, I gave him my undivided attention. After listening to piano serenades, having silly conversations, eating tea and cake, and taking endless strolls on deck, by nightfall his voice had engraved in me, every inflection, how it raised when he became excited and how it lowered when his mood decayed.

My fingers curl around the fountain pen, my emotions a muddled conflict I can't control. I've not inked the first word when a knock startles me in my chair.

"You may come in," I say, opening *The Secret Garden* at a random page and sticking it up to my nose.

"You're awake, Miss Benson?" Mr. Crossley pokes his head into my room.

"I don't sleepwalk as far as I know."

He stays at the threshold. "Really? I would question that given your book is upside down."

I look down, running into sentences in reverse. With a sigh, I rise and set the book on the desk. "I was too distracted looking out the window. What do you want?"

He leans on the jamb, and his gaze roams lazily along my buckled pumps, my white stockings, my fitted dark-green velvet dress, and my waves cruising down my back. I fight to keep my eyes on him with a raised eyebrow and not look away in shame upon such an outrageous study.

"You've changed," he says, the corner of his lips twisting up.

"What do you mean?"

"When I first saw you I couldn't tell if you were twenty or forty, with your dark outfits and your hair always tight in that matronly bun and the little light you had in your eyes."

"I was mourning." I bite at every word.

"There's light in your eyes now."

"Why does it sound so bad when you say it?"

He shrugs. "Such verbal violence this morning. You're one of the wild ones, Alexandra."

"I wasn't aware we're on Christian-name terms." I cock my head, frowning. "And was that an insult or a compliment?"

He smirks. "A compliment. I reckon your parents would be proud of you."

I flinch, my muscles curling. How dare he mention my parents? Having an opinion on their behalf, no matter how flattering it might be? "What is your name, Mr. Crossley?" I growl, finally understanding he's only probing for a crack in my lies. First, Ilse. Now, him. They must've teamed up.

"Adam," he says.

"And what are you doing knocking on my door on this fine morning, Adam?"

"Duty. Mr. Benson invites you to breakfast in his parlor."

"Oh, is he even alive?" I wonder.

"Apparently he is."

"What does he want?"

"He wants to mend fences with you, I suppose."

"Let him know I'm grateful for his courtesy, but I'll be having breakfast in the Lounge."

"It's not an invitation, I'm afraid. When he requests your presence, he's demanding you obey."

I huff. "You must be jesting."

His features are set, no life to them save for the patent lack of humor. "Do I look like I'm jesting?"

I grunt and turn to the desk to pen a quick note to Cameron. "All right, I'm going."

Mr. Crossley clears the door. "Wise girl."

"Are you also going to escort me to the other side of the corridor?"

"Of course."

I flash a pointed look at him and cover the twenty steps between starboard and portside.

Mr. Crossley raps his knuckles on my uncle's door and swings it open. "Here she is."

"Ah, thank you, Mr. Crossley." My uncle stands next to a chair in his parlor. "Niece, please, sit down."

On the table between my uncle's chair and mine lies a coffee jug, a teapot, and an assortment of cheese, bread, fruit, and croissants.

I gulp a dry lump and waver, shifting my weight from one leg to the other. Three days ago Cameron and I were shuffling through my uncle's belongings. It feels impossible he hasn't somehow smelled the wakes of fear we left behind us.

"Thank you for joining me this morning," Nigel says.

The spies' confession rushes through me. His words in this cabin several nights ago rattle me. It's impossible not to imagine him driving away while the fire caught and killed my parents, a smug smirk plastered on his features. In my veins, my blood sizzles. "I don't think I was left much room to decline your . . . invitation."

"Don't mind Mr. Crossley. He's always taking things out of context."

We both remain in our posts on opposite sides of the parlor.

"To what do I owe this breakfast in the intimacy of your cabin?" I ask, eyeing the threshold, where the ghosts of him and Ilse still kiss. A shiver runs down my spine.

"I wanted to maintain a civil conversation with you."

"Is that the reason for our new seating arrangement in the Dining Saloon?" Yesterday, a steward sat Cameron and me at a four-seat table, far from the one we'd been occupying to date. "To maintain civil conversations?"

"I appreciate the intimacy of a family table rather than being sat with strangers," Nigel explains, sitting. Out of courtesy, I set myself down in the chair across from him.

"And why exactly? Socializing is good."

"You can thank your scene on Shelter Deck the other night."

My eyes widen, no answer coming out of my stuttering lips.

"Did you think I'd not find out about your little escapade? What was your business with third class, may I ask?" He pours himself a cup of steamy coffee as if *he* didn't have any business in third. Soon, the scent fills the air of the cabin, masking the peppermint.

I stiffen in my chair and pretend I'm wiping a hair out of the braid trimmings on my dress. No, that's not the real reason for us to be seated somewhere else during our dinners. Chitchat might lead to traps, conflicting narratives. Like Mrs. Bartlett, when she said she'd seen my uncle before my parents' passing. But our adventure has given my uncle the perfect excuse to take the focus off himself and make us the scapegoats.

"Cameron and I took a couple of wrong turns when inspecting the ship," I say.

"Well, don't take wrong turns again," Nigel says. "We don't want these people to spew lies about indecorous behavior."

"We're to be married soon. What indecorous things could you be so worried about, Uncle?"

"That's not an appropriate subject to tackle."

"You seem worried enough to broach it." I stand. "Let me stress this: Cameron and I are *betrothed*. We're not doing anything indecorous, but if we were, you wouldn't be able to stop it. You wouldn't even know."

Nigel's expression flares, breaking his facade of serenity. "Alexandra. Sit. Down."

I plop down into the chair with a loud sigh.

Picking up a dark pipe, he takes some seconds to light it up with the touch of a match. "I'm concerned about your state. Ever since this trip began, you've been more insolent and uneasy, and I was wondering if your fiancé is treating you well."

If I'd been drinking, I would've spit the liquid. "Why would Cameron not be treating me well?"

"Mr. Crossley reported some tension." Nigel shrugs. "And as I've said, you've been more uneasy and insolent—"

"Since this trip began, I heard you the first time." And of course, that trickster of his assistant would tell on us.

He gestures toward me. "Case in point."

"You call it insolence, Uncle, but I'd call it temper. So much pain, it must build some after all."

He twists his lips, swaying the pipe. "Temper rarely suits a woman."

"I see. You would prefer I be silent and compliant in a corner, seen but not heard."

"Is this the way it's going to be with you moving forward?"

"Didn't my father tell you I wasn't an easy child growing up?" It's a ruse, me leading him into a trap. If anything, my father actually made me who I am. My uncle should know about my childhood. A brother would complain of uncooperative children, seek advice in letters. If Nigel isn't my uncle, this is where he'll run into a contradiction.

Outward, I keep a tight uncompromising smile and pray he doesn't notice the way my nails sink into the flesh of my palms.

"I'm honestly baffled." He takes a sip of his coffee. "That man isn't good for you. I can tell he has you on pins and needles."

A gasp is about to hiss out of me, but I clamp it in. Of course he'd deflect.

"Cameron treats me with the respect I deserve, so you can forget about your concerns."

"You're my ward until you become someone's wife. The fact you're engaged to this boy means nothing yet."

A ring whistles in my ears, blood sizzling like pressure in a kettle. He's trying to get rid of Cameron. "It must be hard for you that you won't benefit from my money anymore."

He freezes, astonishment straightening his features. It'd be comical if it weren't dangerous. "What are you implying?"

I lean forward. "I'm implying that the mere reason you've never liked Cameron is because you want my inheritance money for yourself."

"I beg your pardon? From the very beginning I encouraged you to marry. I want you well married and happy, Alexandra. I won't tolerate this slander against me."

I stand. "Happy, you say? You're dragging me to Europe and demanding I stay silent and obedient while you pretend I'm a puppet you can move on strings. I won't be told what to do. In June, Cameron and I will be husband and wife. And there's nothing you can do to stop it."

I stalk toward the door with long strides and storm out of the cabin.

"Alexandra, return at once," Nigel barks.

I dash across the passageway as if the devil were after me, then shut myself in my parlor with a loud slam. With a breath heavy and sharp, I plonk my head against the door and feel the pearls around my neck.

He'll kill if needed or given the chance, the spy said. Not content with having killed my parents, now Nigel wants to pave the road to get rid of Cameron.

And it'd be my fault. Cameron is a victim of my absurd plan. Here he is, in a ploy of espionage on a ship threatened by Germany. If not for me, he'd be among textbooks and his pupils, blissfully unaware of this perfect storm circling above my head. This isn't *his* battle. In my ambition to outsmart my uncle, I dragged an innocent person into a hell from which I don't see a safe exit.

"Cameron," I whisper, then yell, "Cameron."

A distant rumbling talks back—engines and promenade conversations beyond my portholes. The pearl necklace feels like a noose around my neck. With a yank, I fling it overhead and onto the couch.

"Cameron." I run to the bathroom. When I barge into it, the chamber is dark, but the humid scent of soap wafts to me. Where is he? I need to find him, see that he's fine.

I race down the corridor and knock on Cameron's cabin.

"Yes?" The lock gives with a click.

"Thank God," I mutter.

I turn the knob and storm inside, closing the door right behind me. Cameron's arm is yet outstretched toward the entrance. He's holding a comb in his free hand. He looks recently bathed, his hair wet.

"Alexandra," he says. "What are you doing here?"

My body breaks in shudders. He drops his comb in the washstand and grazes my cheek, making me jump. "What happened? You're trembling."

He's fine. He's unharmed. But for how long? With stutters, I tell him what happened in my uncle's cabin.

"My uncle wants to get rid of you." Tears blur the walls and Cameron's frame, my chest rattling up and down. "What if he wants to kill you? Or what if he wants to kill us both? What if that's been his plan all along? Kill me to have my inheritance? If you think about it, it would've been very difficult for him to do it in New York. But nobody knows us in England. It'd be easy, Cameron, and I am so sorry."

Cameron cups my cheeks and presses his lips on my forehead. "I won't let him touch you. Or me."

"I'm so sorry," I repeat in a sob. "Be it not for me, you'd be safe and sound. I can't believe I've done this to you."

Cameron pulls me in, his arms closing in on me, until my tears dampen his woolly gray waistcoat. "I won't let it happen, Alexandra. Don't fret for me or your well-being."

"It's my fault," I say.

"It's not your fault," he whispers. "Look at me, hear me speak, I am here for you. I won't let him hurt you. Or me."

I close my eyes and focus on the hypnotizing way he speaks, like an ebb and flow, like the waves on the beach, and slowly, my breathing subdues to the rhythm of his voice.

Chapter Eighteen

The ship rolls up and down, sending breaths of spritz over the railings. Big round clouds band together on the horizon, yet the sun gleams over the Atlantic waves. It must be one of those perfect nautical days regular cruisers mention when they waltz onto dry land with a healthy sunglow.

"If we're to accuse Nigel, I must find my father's true will," I say. "That's the only thing that authorities will believe."

Cameron has convinced me to bask on the teak promenade chairs. Underneath my problems, hours later his embrace is still warm around me, my blood carrying chaos and heat and sparks in little prickles.

"Where can he be hiding it?" Cameron ruminates. His shiny boots are crossed at his ankles, resting on the end of the chair.

"You're not countering or offering another alternative?" I ask. "No attempt to stop me?"

He shrugs. I focus more intently on the glinting rippling surface beyond the railings until my eyes water.

"When it comes to you, dear, there's no stopping you from getting what you want, so why stand in your path?"

I raise my chin, fighting the flutter in my chest. "Don't call me dear."

"Why? Do you prefer I use love?" His voice is smiling. "Quite British. I like it."

"No." I turn my head, a bitter churn sprinkling to life at his razorblade smirk. He's acting as though he's not taken over my very thoughts. How dare he steal my heart? I have problems to think about, yet here I am pining over him, worrying about his well-being while he's as cool as a cucumber. Or at least he likes to pretend he is, yet the way his fingers curl around the armrests of the teak chair might tell another story.

His eyes rove over my face for what feels like a lifetime. "I decided what I want."

"Pardon me?" I ask.

Simply Cameron, always taking me through sweeping, twisty roads. I never know where the next turn will come from.

"The challenge you lost."

I sigh. "Cameron, this isn't a good time."

He chuckles. "Who's the bad loser now?"

"I'd thank you if you shut up."

He raises his hands. "I won the challenge, and I want to collect."

"What do you want?"

"Another kiss."

My muscles contract as if I were to leap overboard. "Another *what*?" My voice rises an octave. He surely must be jesting.

"Another kiss." His tone, though, is as flat as if he were asking me to pass the salt.

"Are you listening to me? My uncle probably wants you and me dead. We should focus on finding out where he's hiding the will, if he's hiding it at all. For all I know, he might've burned it to ashes. And you're thinking of kisses and fooling around like we're honeymooners without a care in the world. Could you please stop playing with me? We're not having a wedding, Cameron; Nigel has tricked me."

Cameron grunts, plopping his head against the headrest. "Say what you may, but your uncle is playing a game with you. A game you're losing without any of his effort."

I lean toward his chair. "And what do you suggest? That I dance with you, that I celebrate my demise, that I paper over the cracks, and that I go about kissing you, future husband?"

Cameron leans on the armrest. Our faces are too close for comfort. "You're giving up. It's not a total surrender, I reckon. But slowly and surely, I see you conceding. You knew he was leading you on from minute one. You came to my class because you knew something wasn't right. What I'm proposing is you grow bigger than your circumstances. You're smarter than him. Act as such."

His brashness freezes me to the spot. Cameron is always soft with me. But . . . What if he's right? I've fought too hard to allow Nigel to blow it all away. I need to stop giving him ammunition to use on Cameron and me.

I sigh.

"Go ahead and claim your prize, then," I challenge him, though a part of me sizzles with anticipation.

His harrumph caresses the tip of my nose. "If it's like this, with you feeling as if you were on a firing line, I don't want it." He stamps a peck on my cheek and gets up. The ghost of his kiss lingers on my skin, elation blending with my confusion as I watch his retreating back, sidling away between the passengers on the promenade.

"Where are you going?" I jump to my feet and run between the same passengers until I grab his arm. "Hold up, Cameron. I only want to know one thing—"

He whips around and opens his mouth, as if he's about to say something, but his eyes widen at something beyond me. "Fuck. Not now."

"What are you—?" My question dies as I whirl. My uncle's assistant is walking up the Boat Deck, scanning the occupied teak chairs. "My uncle must've sent him after me again."

Cameron takes the narrow wooden staircase on the side of the deckhouse. The Navigation Deck isn't closed to passengers, but it's rare for anyone to climb on here. Housing the quartet of black smokestacks, the deck's floorboards have lost some shine over the crossings, and the wind cuts fiercely around the base of the funnels. Come every nightfall, officers are stationed behind the railings, surveilling the horizon among the vents, their uniformed silhouettes eerily cut in the brightness seeping from the skylights.

Cameron trots, looking back, and dodges a shrouded wire.

"Did he see us?" I whisper.

Circling around the Saloon's dome, Cameron and I drop to a crouch.

"I think he did."

It might be the situation or the strange blend of emotions, but a giggle escapes me. Cameron puts a finger to his lips but smiles, and for a moment I forget we're under the hiss of the steam and the hum of vents and the ring of voices from the deck below. I can't help but look at his mouth, so close yet so far from me. He had to be teasing to lift my spirits—or annoy me—but I want him to claim his kiss again, so I can give it to him.

"Miss Benson," Mr. Crossley singsongs. "I saw you coming up here with Mr. Asher. Come out. Your uncle is calling for you."

Cameron and I slink round the second smokestack to portside while Mr. Crossley nears the third one on starboard. Cameron's cheeks go hollow, as if he were planning something.

"Should we run back to the stairs when he turns?" I propose.

"To starboard? No, he's too close. There's a ladder portside. I'll go first; then I'll help you get down."

Peeping around the smokestack, Cameron moves his lips as if he is counting under his breath. On three, we storm out from behind the funnel and come into full view, but as I'm gathering my strength to confront Mr. Crossley, nothing but vents welcome my bravado. He must be rounding the fourth smokestack.

With a fast swing, Cameron pulls the railing gate open and jumps off the deckhouse, his frame gliding down the narrow ladder and landing on his feet with a thud on deck.

"How did you do that?" I yelp.

"It's not that high, Miss Benson." He stretches out his arms upward and beckons with his fingers.

Just as my shoe touches the first rung, Mr. Crossley walks around the funnel. "Miss Benson."

"Oh, Lord," I utter, trampling down the rungs two at a time. The tip of my pump slips on one, and my entire body gives way. I shriek, feeling the floor coming at me, but instead I crash on Cameron's chest with a thud, sending him backward.

"I have you," he mutters in my ear, pulling me in tightly.

I chuckle, my fingers spreading over his arms laced around my waist.

Just as Mr. Crossley reaches the ladder, Cameron sets me down, and we bolt down the promenade among gasping passengers, who step aside for us and close again in our wake.

With a glimpse over my shoulder, I confirm Mr. Crossley is not following us. He's smiling subtly from atop the ladder but fades from my view as Cameron steers me away. "This way," he says, stalking inside the deckhouse, yet as soon as we're in the corridor of the Smoking Room, he halts, and I hit his back.

"Carlton," he says. "Sorry."

I step aside from behind Cameron to find Professor Brodrick.

"If you're running away from the lifeboat drills, I completely understand."

"I'm afraid not," I say, breaking into a run with Cameron down the passageway.

Professor Brodrick keeps up with us. "Why are we running?"

"Long story," I say.

"Need somewhere to hide?"

"Any idea where?" Cameron asks.

"Follow me." He jogs inside the Smoking Room. Across revolving doors, I encounter first a long corridor, filled with red settees and round low tables to host private meetings. The Smoking Room opens up just behind the wall. A fireplace crowns the aft wall, and chandelier sconces cast soft pools of light on the walnut paneling.

"I can't be here," I whisper, padding the red carpet delimiting the cherry-colored settees.

"I dare anyone to say anything," Cameron growls.

"If there's a detour no one thinks you'll take, it's this one," Professor Brodrick says. "It doesn't matter—it's early yet."

He's right. Men don't feel like making deals in the morning; they're more prone to do so under cigar smoke and brandy and full bellies than with puffy eyes and hangovers. Only a couple of old men lounge at the tables. One of them is reading the *Cunard Daily Bulletin*. In passing, I read a headline about a Seamen's Charities Concert on the evening of May 6.

The Smoking Room connects with the Verandah Café through a hidden corridor. I'm about to counter this isn't a very good place to hide when Professor Brodrick slides one door open and we're out again on the promenade, overlooking second class on the other deck-island.

Professor Brodrick crosses the walkway.

"Is he taking us to second class?" I wonder aloud.

"It seems so." Cameron looks around.

With a shiver, I loop my arm around his and watch out for my uncle's assistant.

Cameron's friend raises his head.

"Hey, Professor Holbourn," Professor Brodrick calls out, drawing the attention of a man ambling around our promenade with a girl with a big bow and a brown coat. "Having your daily stroll with Miss Avis, huh?"

The man, Professor Holbourn, walks to us with a big smile. Under his arm, he carries several sheets of paper that ruffle in the wind. "We're going to see if we can spot porpoises."

Professor Brodrick motions at the gate. "Any chance you can remind me how to open this?"

"Of course. Here, I'll show you."

Professor Holbourn passes the papers to Cameron, scribbled copies of how to put on life jackets, accompanied by simple sketches. Leaning over the gate, the man fumbles on the other side's lock. "They usually close this in the night, but they don't seem to care much about second class coming in and out of first on this crossing. We're invited to the concert on the sixth." With a yank, he opens the gate. "There you go."

"Thank you so much," Cameron says, giving him the papers back and then running across the walkway with me. "And nice to meet you."

"I appreciate your help," Professor Brodrick says; then, he turns to us. "What are the odds someone looks for you in second class?"

Chapter Nineteen

The answer is none. With lemonade and sandwiches in the second-class Lounge, Cameron, Professor Brodrick, and I are practically invisible. The Lounge is atop the deck-island, surrounded by the promenade; at its heart, a skylight governs the central staircase.

"Beautiful for second class, isn't it?" Professor Brodrick draws my attention back.

"The carpet is an exquisite piece," I say, admiring how well the pink suits the mahogany furbishing. My eyes linger on the passengers pouring in and out of the staircase. Although hidden at first glance in one of the corners of the room, I shrink every time any man raises his voice.

"Nobody seems to care about our presence here," Cameron says, addressing my silent concern.

With stiff shoulders, I force my body to turn to the table and grab my damp lemonade glass with clawlike fingers.

"You heard Professor Holbourn. On this crossing, the lines between Saloon and second class are very relaxed," Professor Brodrick says.

"Is he giving those pamphlets out to the passengers?" Cameron asks.

"Oh, no doubt. He's insisting on life jacket awareness and those farcical lifeboat drills. I helped him with the sketches."

They chuckle, while the memory of the lifeboat drills makes me wince. The effort put into the drills was nothing but laughable, and considering the state of war, the way the crew climbed up the davits into the boat, sat idly for a full minute, and jumped back on deck inspired anything but trust.

"Yet I understand his concerns," Professor Brodrick adds. "I share them, to some extent. We're not making as many miles a day as we should. Rumor has it Captain Turner hasn't lit up all the boilers. Many fear this will make us an easier target."

"My uncle insists the Royal Navy will escort us into Liverpool," I say.

"I'm sure they will, Miss Benson," Professor Brodrick says. "I didn't want to worry you."

"You didn't," I say.

"She's more worried about a challenge I won," Cameron says, before taking his lemonade glass to his lips.

I kick his shin under the table, making him choke on the liquid.

"Speaking of challenges," Professor Brodrick tells Cameron with a coy smile, as if he is pretending not to have noticed my kick. "We're going to host a gambling gathering after the seamen's concert in our cabin; if you want to join, you're free to."

"Is gambling allowed?" I ask.

"It is if you don't get caught," Professor Brodrick replies, making Cameron and me laugh.

"Then I guess Cameron has no other choice but to join," I say. "He has a knack for the forbidden."

Professor Brodrick turns to Cameron with quizzical eyes. "Do we have an interesting story behind that?"

"If only I could talk," I say.

"You two are out to get me," Cameron says. "Nice."

Hours blend into each other in our little corner, and the spies, the testament, and all the scary things around me fall away until the sun dies outside the portholes, red bleeding into sparkling gold, just like blood pouring into champagne.

And I wonder if that's only a promise of what's to come.

Mr. Crossley retrieves me from my suite for dinnertime with a dark look, still sulking about this morning, no doubt. Looming like an ivory tower, he stays two steps behind me, yet his glare burns on my nape.

"I can find the dining room on my own," I say.

"You think you can fool me."

I stop and frown, shock hitting me like a splash of cold water. But when I turn, I've composed a perfect facade of innocence. "I'm not sure I understand."

He cracks a sardonic smile on that innocent-looking face. "I'd appreciate it if you didn't take me for an imbecile, Miss Benson. Did you think those little outings during the past month would go undetected? I'm always watching."

I shake, but I won't let my arms cross over my chest. I can't get defensive. Cameron said there's no reason for it if you have nothing to hide. While I do have things to hide, I must keep my cool. "What outings, Mr. Crossley?"

"When you met Mr. Asher in that tavern in the Bowery. The school. How you visited the tailor with him. How there was not the slightest sign of courting between you until a couple of weeks ago. The times you visited him in his apartment. Does any of this sound familiar, Miss Benson?"

A histrionic laugh drifts out of my lips. He followed me, every time. How did I not catch him, not even once, lurking in the shadows? I shouldn't blame myself for something I couldn't control. How can you outsmart anyone if they're always ten steps ahead? The fact I'm unscathed as yet is surprising.

"I don't know what you think you saw."

He lowers his head, his green-eyed stare deepening. "I know what I saw."

Fear runs wild, tainting my thoughts. I take a deep breath and hold it in so my voice doesn't waver. "It's what happens to eavesdroppers and snoops—they always lack context. This is none of your business, but when Cameron and I were in that tavern, it was hardly the first time we saw each other; otherwise I wouldn't have let him escort me back home."

"See, the dates there don't add up, Miss Benson. He wasn't supposed to be in the city."

"Fine. You caught us," I say, sarcasm heavy in my tone. "I lied so I could have some time with my betrothed before strangers would have an opinion on our relationship. As you can understand, I was mad and needed to sort out some matters with him. And we went to a tailor?" I push a theatrical gasp out of my lips. "Cannot a man have new clothes?"

He lets out a dry chuckle. "Again, you're taking me for an imbecile. I made diggings into the Ashers in Denver."

I take a step back, my fingers sinking into my evening gown. "And what did you unearth? Worms and seeds?"

"Yet to be discovered from the source I sent to Denver. Will get my information as soon as we dock."

"Cameron is no liar," I spit through my teeth. "Is this fun to you?"

"I'm doing my job."

I chuckle, but Mr. Crossley ends my laughter. "*And* if your fiancé is a liar, wouldn't you like to be aware of it before he runs with your fortune? Unless . . . you're involved in the scheme, which sounds plausible."

"I beg your pardon? Once you receive your confirmation, I hope you come with an apology. Not to me, but to my fiancé. Now why in the world are you not ushering me into the dining room if that's your insignificant task for the night?"

I huff and take a sharp turn to the staircase. I remain a statue of indifference even though shivers run down my spine. The clack of my heels drowns in the rugs, so I walk with long strides, pretending I'm not about to turn into a puddle.

"Good evening, love," Cameron says at the dining room entrance, flashing a smile; then he directs eyes alit with rage to Mr. Crossley. "Sweet of you to escort my future wife."

"Mr. Crossley wanted to make sure I'd not get lost," I say dryly. "What are you doing here?"

"I've booked a table for two on the upper tier."

"Mr. Benson expects her at his table," Mr. Crossley says warily.

Cameron extends his arm toward the door. "You're welcome to confirm it with him."

When Mr. Crossley stalks into the dining room, Cameron entwines our fingers. "What happened? Are you all right?"

"I think we're in trouble," I say, then quote Mr. Crossley. This information would rattle many men, but Cameron remains calm.

"He's sworn he'll get the information as soon as we're in England." My throat tightens.

"It won't matter," Cameron mutters. I'm sure he meant it to be a murmur and go unheard in the noisy evening. A dark feeling creeps into my chest as I stare at his lost expression, the muscle twitching in his jaw.

Once Mr. Crossley returns with a confirmation, we're free to go one deck up. The restaurant upstairs is more intimate, the tables destined for up to four diners. On our table by the well, two lit candles wait for us.

"You don't have to worry." Cameron offers me a seat. They're bolted to the floor in case of rough seas, but I appreciate the gesture. Below us, at the table edging the confines of the well, Nigel glances upward.

"Do you think he can read lips?" I ask while Cameron moves over to his chair.

"He probably can. But he has no equipment, and we're too far from him."

My shoulders lose some of their stiffness. "Why did you not choose one of the more secluded tables?"

"Do you think Nigel would've allowed you to dine with me if he couldn't see us?"

"No," I admit. Falling into silence, I allow my thoughts to revolve around the dark feeling in my chest. "You keep asking me not to worry about you. Why?"

Cameron encloses my hand on the table. It twitches under his touch, enough of a shift for him to notice as I understand the dark feeling in my chest is sharp, plain distrust. What is not adding up with Cameron? I go back to all those strange silences and half-finished sentences . . .

Cameron's hand retreats to his end of the table. "I know everything will go just fine."

I lean over. "How can you be so sure they won't kill us?"

"Of that, I can't be sure."

"Then how can you be so poised all the time? What do you know that I don't?"

It's exactly that, isn't it? He knows something, and one day I won't be able to turn a blind eye.

Cameron sighs as a waiter appears to take our orders. I sit back, ordering with a dry voice, feeling I might start shouting any moment now. If the spy plot weren't enough, the distrust that fills me sometimes when I look at my fake fiancé sickens me.

And still, he's all I have. I hate that I have no choice but to live with it.

Cameron strokes my cheek. I catch him midway to slap his caress away, but glances from below the well stop me. I can't afford for Uncle Nigel to catch a sign of commotion. With a flick of my head, I press Cameron's caress onto my face. This is for show, not for us.

"I can't sit back and let things unfold, as laudable as that ability is in you. I need whatever sliver of control I can have. I've tried doing it your way, and I can't."

Against all odds, Cameron cracks a faint smile. "And I love that about you, as much as it drives me mad." With a thoughtful expression, he picks up the fork and taps the tines on the table. "Would you be comfortable with running away and leaving everything behind should the worst happen?"

"I would," I reply without a second thought. "But how about we alert the authorities first?"

"We'll need proof of the scheme, the spying, and—"

"—and my father's real testament. No way to know if there's still a will at all, though."

"It must be somewhere. The photograph in your house shows someone still has it."

The waiter sets dishes with consommé and croquettes between Cameron and me and serves us red wine. Alone again, Cameron looks around. The nearby diners are too engrossed in their conversations to mind us.

"This is all I know," I whisper. "Those men confirmed he's a dangerous, lethal spy, and that he was behind my parents' car crash. They didn't know the reason why. And I don't know if he's my real uncle or why he's so invested in taking me to England. All are loose threads. I must connect them all."

"We've searched his cabin thoroughly," Cameron whispers. "Whatever your uncle is hiding, it's not there."

I look down, a slight pout on my lips. Where could he be hiding the testament? The folders, he needs them. The will is an important face on this dice of lies, but Nigel mightn't need easy access to it, only to keep it safe.

"His other trunk went into the baggage hold," I say. "All we need is the key. It was in his drawer in the parlor."

Cameron nods. "Then that's where we'll go tomorrow."

Chapter Twenty

May 5, 1915—Day 5 of 7

My two photo albums are buried underneath a jewelry box in my trunk. I ruffle the pages of one, across my own memories and my parents'. Memories of what I love and I've lost, save for the last one. It was the only photograph I allowed of Cameron and me.

I purse my lips. Cameron has a perfectly elegant expression, casually serious, but I looked so sour. My brow wrinkled, my jaw set downward, gaze clouded. My appearance makes it easier to ruin the portrait. I press the locket onto the black-and-white paper and cut around Cameron's face with the tip of a letter opener with an embossed Cunard insignia, leaving my bitter self alone in the photograph.

In my locket, the third wing remained empty. Now, Cameron sits in that one, next to the wings that hold my friends and my parents. This isn't me pining over Cameron but a sensible decision given my uncle's suspicions. As I click the locket shut, doubts gnaw at me. Love, tainted as it is by distrust, is an inane thought, yet I can't deny the molten metal flowing through me when I think of Cameron.

I slip my locket around my neck without giving it another thought.

The door opens with a whine. Cameron, with fresh clothes under his arm, stops and takes me in. I didn't expect him so early.

I step in front of the album, fiddling with my locket. "Do you know how to knock?"

He shrugs. "You've always been away when I've come to make use of your bathroom."

"This suite has two doors."

"I use both alternatively." Cameron walks by on his way to the bathroom. "What were you doing?"

I move to hide the album from his angle. "Nothing."

He slows down, an eyebrow arching slightly. My knees wobble as the *Lusitania* rises over a wave and crashes down. Cameron grabs the doorframe and I the desk, but we don't move, sharing a long look. An awkward silence fills the room.

"Were you not going to shower?" I ask.

He smiles and comes achingly close to me instead. He stares down, his intense gaze cutting to my lips.

My heart races as I think he's going to kiss me. My insides coil, anticipation stabbing me with licks of pleasure.

With a quick slip, Cameron whips the album from the desk.

"Hey," I bite, running after him.

He sidles away, prying it open enough to peek at the page. "Oh? Here's a cut photograph?" he gloats, almost as if he was too pleased with himself.

"Hand it back," I hiss.

Stretching his arm up to keep the album as far away as possible, he offers me a mischievous wink. "Are you carrying me in your locket? My, my, Miss Benson, one might think you're developing feelings for me."

"That's the purpose." I defend myself. "My uncle needs to believe it."

He harrumphs and grabs my locket from my chest. An uncontrolled gasp sneaks past my lips.

"Hard for your uncle to see through this embossed locket, isn't it?" he wonders aloud, his stare gliding up to me, blue as a torrent of cold ice.

"Give me the album." I lunge at him, but he skitters around the table and bumps into the desk, rattling it in its bolted spot. Cameron perches on it, almost as if he were lounging.

"You'll have to pry it from my hands," he says, raising his arm. His clothes fall, sprawling on the desk. His nonchalance makes my blood sizzle.

I stand on my tiptoes, but the album is completely out of my reach.

No, he's not getting away with this. Ramming into his side, I leap, and my fingertips slap the edge of the cover. The album whirls away and flops open onto the carpeted floor with a soft thud, photographs flying away from between the pages.

Cameron's smile fades as he takes in the image atop. My mother's.

With a grunt, I lower to a crouch and collect the photographs and the album. "Are you done fooling around?"

"You look like your mother," he says. "I hadn't—I hadn't thought of that before."

"So I've been told." I straighten, not daring to look at him. "The skin, the full lips, the snub nose, all hers."

"As beautiful as it gets," he whispers.

I shuffle through the rest of the photographs so I can return them to their spots. But my fingers freeze, my eyes catching on the names and numbers scribbled on the back of many portraits.

"What's the matter?" Cameron looks over my shoulder.

I turn to him, frowning at the images. "These are my parents' acquaintances. Each photograph has something scribbled behind. But their names . . . they're different from the ones in my parents' address book."

Who I thought was Mary Baker is called Anna Clark. Who I thought was Arthur Brook is Joseph Wright, and just like that, I have over twenty strangers in my hands. Politicians, embassy workers, lawyers, bankers . . . people I've known all my life, that I've seen coming and going, are only a lie. Just like my parents. Just like my life.

Cameron reaches out. "Mind if I take a look?"

Heart thumping, I pass the photographs to him.

Cameron shuffles through them, stares at the portraits, reads the scribbles, and sudden realization flashes through his eyes.

"What is it?"

"I know . . ." He shakes his head. "These are coordinates, the numbers. I'll see if the library has a cartography book I can use to determine the locations. Would you mind if I kept these photographs with me?"

"No. But what are those photographs, Cameron? My parents were spies, were they not? Who are these people in reality?"

"I need to check the coordinates first, before I can . . . say. I believe these people might've been . . . people who were important to your parents." A muscle twitches in his jaw.

"But how can you know? All of this?" I wonder aloud, a sour lump crawling up my throat. My limbs tremble with watery jitters as all the suspicion I've been harboring stirs alive once again. "Coordinates, how do you know how to read coordinates? Did you also learn that on the streets?"

His face is solemn, apparently unfazed by my sarcasm, but something dark wanders through his eyes, slowly and methodically, as if his thoughts were shifting in front of me. "I'm a teacher. I'm supposed to know."

I whip my head away and sigh. As a teacher, he should know coordinates. It makes sense. But the suspicion doesn't leave me. I don't know what I'm resisting, what I am *failing*, to see.

"Let's focus on our mission today, which is the trunk," Cameron says. "I'll go snatch the keys now."

"I'll go with you."

He stows the photographs inside the album. "It'll be a quick entry and exit. It's better if I go on my own."

"Fine." I pass the sour lump down my throat. "I woke up in the mood to write a letter to Lindsay and Elijah. Meet me at the Writing Room when you're ready."

The Writing Room is located forward the grand staircase on Boat Deck. The room stretches out, supported on intricate pilasters, the walls framed in silk panels. Desks run along starboard and portside on a pink carpet, while in the middle of the room, a seating area cozies up to a fireplace underneath a dome. Behind, a sumptuous dark library holds books to lend to the passengers.

At this time, only Mrs. Bartlett is at the port side, reading by the hearth with tea and an olive shawl around her shoulders. I've not had the chance to approach her these days. I want to ask her when she saw my uncle in New York and where, but she seems so enthralled by the novel I prefer not to disturb her yet. I select a pen and papers from a stack for the passengers and sit on the starboard side.

Writing to Lindsay and Elijah has always been as effortless as breathing, but I stop after the introduction. My pen shakes in my grasp as it dawns on me. I want to tell them everything.

I'll address the letter to Elijah and ask him to deliver the news to Lindsay. Learning about this all through a letter might come as a shock to my friends, but I believe Cameron and I have only a slim chance of survival. Someone has to know the truth. Cameron offered for us to run away because, no matter how nonchalant he looks on the outside, he must also believe we have little chance of making it out alive. Even at this very second, Nigel could be plotting our demise one deck below.

As the sentences pour onto the page, my thoughts follow. Our scandalous behavior has made us gain relevance and, thus, safety, and as long as I'm useful to them, I'm out of harm's way. Yet the outcome seems set in stone. Only one destination, the grave. The ways I can expect death, multiple.

They might say Cameron killed me and then died by suicide, or that I killed my fiancé and now I'm locked in an asylum—the tragic ending, the tear-inducing tale.

They might say Cameron and I eloped because they opposed our wedding—the happy, complacent lie. They might say we're living on a tropical island while our corpses rot in cold dirt.

I tell my friends everything, from the day my parents died, my initial suspicions about the will, how the idea of a fake marriage came to be, about Cameron, and how I discovered the spying plot. The air is oppressive, like a whalebone corset that's been tightened too far. I close my eyes, my head heavy.

"In one or two days," I write, "we'll arrive in Liverpool, and I'm terrified for my life, but more terrified of seeing Cameron die. I regret dragging him into this deadly game. He didn't deserve it."

Love has humbled me. Death and my upbringing built walls of arrogance and defensiveness around me, but Cameron has melted them away. And I stand as if naked and vulnerable, trying to cover myself. "I hate that I'm powerless."

And I hate that I'm still seething with the need for justice. I hate that I'd risk our lives because of it. Am I really that selfish? The need to triumph over Nigel and see him jailed is stronger than my common sense. The need to see with my own eyes that I was right all along, that my father respected me and never would've betrayed me, and that there's a true testament blinds me. We'll see land in no time, and with that, I'll have to decide. If I were smart, I'd pretend everything was fine and arrange a suitcase in secret to run away with Cameron. But I'm not smart. The truth is my selfishness, no matter what I want to disguise it as, could be the end of us.

Behind me, a waft of Cameron's scent fills the air with a hint of the foam they use at the Barbershop. I raise my head to the windows. The day has opened. Hazy sunshine streams through the half-drawn silk curtains.

Cameron takes in my three-and-a-half written pages. Without saying anything, he picks up a couple of sheets of paper and sits on the desk opposite mine. Women raise their heads. My first thought is that Cameron is naturally stunning this morning in his black three-piece suit, but the reason is that this is a women's room, and Cameron seems unfazed.

"I'll finish in a minute," I mutter, scribbling as I try to keep my chain of reasoning.

"Take your time." He tugs the desk lamp on. "I was going to pen a letter to my family myself."

He makes my heart ache. No matter the distrust, or the secrets he seems to harbor, I feel at home, utterly at peace, completely safeguarded from my own insecurities and wrongdoings.

It takes a strong dose of willpower to tear my attention from the way he twirls the pen on his fingers and focus on the last part of my letter. Cameron and I write in silence, accompanied by the splash of the ocean, the whir of the engines, the muffled sounds of passengers returning books, and the soft scrawls of our pens over paper. My writing is loopy and takes some room, but at seven pages, this is by far the longest letter I've ever written. I fold it and stow it in a big envelope. As I'm writing down the address, Cameron flashes a gentle smile. "Are you ready?"

"I am."

Our next step, per our plan, is convincing a steward to take us into the cargo room. Skulking to crew areas on our own was out of the question. The ship isn't designed for easy access or class mingling; we'd need to break into heavily secured areas.

As we stand, Mrs. Bartlett stops next to our carrels. "Miss Benson, Mr. Asher. It's nice to see you again. We've been missing you at the table."

Cameron bows his head. "Likewise, Mrs. Bartlett."

I smile, my shoulders peaking. It seems like I'll have the chance to speak with her after all. "I also miss the table, Mrs. Bartlett. Alas, my uncle decided he wanted a more private placement. He's not a social fellow. How've you been?"

Beyond the pleasantries, I want to make sure Nigel hasn't been nagging her. But she smiles, not a shadow crossing her face.

"Oh, I'm doing well. I'm restless, though. Trying to pass the time until we arrive in Liverpool."

"I wanted to ask you, if you don't mind, when and where you think you saw my uncle before tragedy . . . struck."

She laughs. "Oh, Miss Benson. Forgive me for that mistake. I probably took someone else for him."

Cameron smiles. "Humor us if you'll be so kind, Mrs. Bartlett. It's not important if you mistook someone else for him."

She licks her lips. "If I must be honest, I think I saw him in the middle of January near your house. He was talking to that blond assistant of his."

I look up at Cameron. My wide eyes must say everything my words can't utter, because he shares a concerned look with me and nods.

"That's of great help," he says. "Thank you so much, Mrs. Bartlett."

After wishing her a good day, we set off for the Purser's Bureau, but my hands shake so much I hold one of Cameron's tightly.

"I believe her, Cameron. Nigel was in New York," I whisper, stomach churning. If I speak louder, I might puke. "Before my parents died. Do you remember when Mr. Crossley gave our driver directions? That day, I thought he was too familiar with the city."

"I believe her too," Cameron clips. "Do you remember what to say to the purser, or should I speak?"

"I do. I can talk."

The purser's office resembles a birdcage when it's closed. Right now, the white grills are open, passengers buzzing around the windows, inquiring about jewels, valuables, messages, and marconigrams. When I give our letters to the purser, my heartbeat is so faint I might collapse.

"I have another ordeal, and I'm not sure if you could help me," I say.

The man slips a wary glimpse at me, then at Cameron. "I'll try to help with anything I can, Miss."

"Before we took sail, I borrowed a valuable pen from my uncle, and I meant to place it in his trunk when I was done, but I placed it in mine by mistake."

"It's one of the first fountain pens ever made," Cameron chimes in.

"I'd like to return it to his trunk belowdecks without him knowing," I say.

The man twitches his lips. "I'm afraid I can't let you in the baggage hold, Miss Benson. Just explain the situation to your uncle, and I'm sure he'll understand."

"Mr. McCubbin," I say. "My uncle won't understand, and I won't have a chance to sneak it back before he realizes it's missing."

"In said case, I could arrange the trunk to be brought up to your cabin."

"Can you guarantee the trunk will be delivered to me and not to my uncle?"

Mr. McCubbin moves his head, frowning.

"And if he sees it's missing before I can explain, he might as well claim the crew stole the pen."

"You don't want that man to come here denouncing a theft," Cameron pushes.

I hold my breath, fearing he'll refuse again, but Mr. McCubbin raises a finger and stands from his chair. He exits his birdcage-like bureau and stops an officer on the staircase. By the loops on his cuffs, he must be a high-ranking officer.

Distrustful yet curious glances land on us. Instinctively, I step closer to Cameron, my shoulder brushing his chest.

He puts a hand on the small of my back. "Keep cool."

After a quick exchange, Mr. McCubbin comes back. "Mr. Lewis has approved of you going belowdecks. One of my assistants and a junior officer will accompany you. Please, understand this is the only time you'll be allowed into the baggage hold."

I hop on the balls of my feet. "I appreciate it. Thank you, Mr. McCubbin. Thank Mr. Lewis too."

One of the purser's assistants and a young officer lead Cameron and me to the crew quarters on C-Deck and downstairs to the bowels of the liner. The air turns damper and noisier, and my pulse spikes the lower we go.

The crew watches us warily as they cross our path. After several doors, an elevator, and narrow passageways, the officer greets the baggage master, who cracks a door open to a large room with bare lamps casting pools on netted stacks of trunks and crates. The wood floor, weathered down by a couple thousand crossings, creaks under my boots.

While the baggage master and the purser locate Nigel's trunk, the officer's silent scrutiny stiffens my shoulders. Shadowed under the brim of his cap, amused curiosity wavers in his expression. He mustn't be much older than me but holds an air of authority. Thankfully, he asks me no questions, probably because he understands I don't want my uncle to learn I've done something bad. I keep an uncompromising smile, the turmoil inside my chest pushed as far down as possible. By my side, Cameron remains silent as well, watching the officers walk away with an air of boredom.

The two men unfurl a net and lug a trunk into view. "This must be the one."

"Thank you, gentlemen," I say.

They step away yet stay with the officer where they can watch us, leaving Cameron and me to our devices. Clothes, books, and other valuables wait inside the packed trunk. Cameron and I ruffle through the items as fast as possible until our fingers brush carton folders. Cameron snatches them and slides them under his jacket. I comb for more folders, quickly scanning under the pool of light from the lamp overhead, but I don't find any more documents.

"Alexandra, look," Cameron says, showing me a book. I blink, mind blank until the white page in front of me takes shape. What I've mistaken for novels are three leather-bound diaries. Cameron's long index finger rests below a handwritten name on the first page. *Valeria Lavalle.*

Lavalle was my mother's maiden name, but I have no recollection of any Valeria. Is this related to my mother's family? My Italian grandmother was called Gabriella, and she married a Spanish man who was working in England. Besides my mother, Isabella, named after my great-grandmother, my grandparents had only one other child, a boy who died at ten of fever.

I stare blankly at the page until a thought strikes me—Mr. Crossley mistakenly calling my mother Valeria instead of Isabella.

Cameron and I look at each other; a feral recognition glints in his eyes, a weight sinking into my chest like a fist against soft muscle.

The officer's shadow appears behind Cameron. "Did you finish, Miss Benson?"

I stand as Cameron stows the diaries in his jacket. "I did."

Cameron closes the lid and straightens behind me. His fitted jacket is bulky with the diaries, yet he misses no step, trailing after me to hide the strange rectangular bulges.

Once they net the trunk into place, they usher us out of the room with almost aggressive efficiency, as if the crew feared getting caught doing something they shouldn't. An officer shuts a door, cutting a glare at us.

"Those bloody Germans, am I right?" a young sailor whispers to a crew member as they turn a corridor. "Can you believe, cake? Only crumbs when they found the box."

I startle at the mention, and the sailor falls silent, scratching his nose as they walk down the corridor.

"Why so many seamen in these corridors?" Cameron asks.

"Just ordinary duties, sir," the officer replies. "Nothing to worry about."

Pressure over the German threats or real danger, they'll never let us know. But—it's the Germans.

As soon as we arrive on B-Deck, I thank the purser and the officer and walk away with Cameron. My spirits are as low as they were belowdecks. What if the secret reaches Nigel's ears? Will this be what brings our demise, my selfishness finally catching up with me? In order to unearth secrets, it's necessary to get into dirty soil, but how far can you go until the earth has swallowed you and now you're six feet under?

Cameron lays out the folders and the books on the desk in my cabin. My fingers shyly curl into my fists. Nigel has my mother's diaries, but why? And why was my mother called Valeria? Was it a secret middle name, or did she also lie to me?

I should be digging with voracious hunger through the diaries, searching for clues and answers, but fear of what I'll find keeps me as still as though my feet had melted into the iron beams below the floor.

Cameron searches through the folders, and my hope dwindles like a suffocated flame with each one he shuts. He's not finding the testament, no clues, no answers. Midway through ruffles of pages, Cameron stops, lowering his head to inspect something.

"Alexandra," he says, lifting the folder. Attached to the page, a photograph stares back at me. My parents and I were at the beach. My father stood in a straw hat and a white sack suit, and my mother with a big hat and a white dress, both barefoot, sand and waves washing at their feet. I was in my father's arms, a toddler in a white dress, smiling at the sun.

Cameron is speaking, but I can't understand anything with the shrill in my ears. Unable to blink, I try to understand the gibberish underneath the photograph, although it's unlikely I'll recognize the language no matter how much effort I put in.

"Why is everything written in German?" I hiss, the room spinning. "Why is this man so obsessed with my parents?"

I moan and turn away, unable to make sense of myself. There's material to sort through, and I'm being mangled by my emotions and fear.

My forehead comes to a rest on the wall. "Control yourself."

"Alexandra," says Cameron.

The tips of my shoes swivel to meet him. "I'm sorry."

With a thumb, he wipes the wet trail my tears have left, and for a moment, I forget about my grief.

"You oughtn't to apologize." His blue stare undresses my soul.

My troubled emotions fall away, and all I want to do is grab his lapels, lose myself in him. Into all these things that might vanish if I don't stop this.

"This is too big for me, Cameron," I say. "Maybe that's why my parents never told me the truth, because they knew I couldn't stand it."

"Your parents . . . your parents raised a strong woman," he whispers, a dark emotion swimming across his features.

"My fate is in their hands."

"No, it's not," he barks. "You won't give up now. I won't let you."

Tears pour out of me, hot and salty, trickling down my cheeks and onto my lips. Quivers ripple through me, from head to toe. I've been so, *so* ridiculous.

"There's no testament." My lips tremble. "All this time, someone must've been playing with me. And if I can't prove he switched the testament, I'll lose it all. That is, if we survive, Cameron."

"We have enough documents to get him jailed and investigated for espionage. And the real testament exists. You saw it in the photograph."

I shake my head. The emotional weight of my father's betrayal clouds my mind. "You don't understand. I know the real testament exists. Or it *existed*. But even though I've seen the photograph, as long as I can't hold it in my hands, it won't feel real. I'll always be in doubt whether it ever happened or it was a joke. Since that testament reading, I've cried equally over my father's death as well as his possible betrayal. All I thought I knew of my parents, or even my own life, is a farce. They never trusted me with their secrets. I need the testament to verify that not all my father's words were a lie."

A shadow passes through Cameron's eyes, turning the ocean blue into a stormy sea. His mouth opens, but he shuts it again with a snap of his jaw. He straightens, determination hardening his features.

"Do you want that will? If those papers are on this ship, I'm going to give them to you."

Chapter Twenty-One

Cameron jerks the door open and heads down the corridor.

"Cameron?" I ask, skittering after him.

I poke my head around the corner. His determined strides and straight back turn toward portside.

My eyes widen. "Cameron?"

A strong rap of knuckles on wood. "Mr. Benson? Are you in?"

"God," I mutter, running across the passageway, my frantic gaze sweeping for Mr. Crossley, Ilse, or a steward. Thankfully, only one passenger is in the corridor, and he continues his walk without minding us.

"Cameron, lower your voice."

He barges into the cabin without minding my hushed warning.

"Cameron," I hiss, shutting us in. "Are you insane? He could come back any moment."

"Then we better rush," Cameron simply echoes from the bedroom, opening the wardrobe with a swift arc of his arms, as if he were ready to confront my uncle with the cold blood of a murderer.

"Let's return tonight."

"If I keep vanishing after dinner, we'll give him more reasons to suspect us. No, tonight he'll see me join Carlton in the Smoking Room, and you'll have a restful night knowing your father respected you."

"What if my uncle comes back?"

Cameron turns sharply to me and points at the portholes. "I'll smash his brains out and throw his body overboard at nightfall."

I draw back, little bumps breaking out across my skin. His words hang low over our heads. And Cameron's face . . . it's still . . . dangerously calm, as if he'd tamed all rage and only a collected resolve would have overtaken him. He would do it. He'd kill Nigel. Now I can only stand in his way or help him help me. I'm not going to make him waste more time.

I fling my uncle's trunk open and pull everything out. Clothes, books, a couple of bags and shoes, all spilled on the carpeted floor.

There's nothing new since last time. In fact, it seems Uncle Nigel has barely touched it at all. My fingers feel the inner walls. Solid wood, without any dents. No fake panel, no hidden sections. Perhaps mystery books weren't so right in the end. Perhaps I can't outsmart a spy. He'll always be one step ahead of me.

I sigh, defeat sinking claws into me, but Cameron's resolution, relentlessly slamming drawers shut, gives me another push. My fingers curl around the lid, ready to close it, but my thumb grazes the rough edge of cut-off velvet.

I blink, slowly understanding the lid is upholstered in navy blue, while the rest of the trunk is not.

"Cameron," I say, poking at the rectangular paper-shaped bump behind the cover.

He kneels beside me and feels the velvet. His lips mutter a profanity.

"Was this here the first time?" I wonder.

We share an incredulous look. The velvet panel is pinned by four thin metal tabs. Cameron and I turn them one at a time and peel off the cover. A stack of adjoined papers flops into the trunk.

Cameron and I lean in, peeking inside. Is this what I've been looking for? Finally within my reach? I let out a shaky breath and rescue the stack from the bottom of the trunk.

I gape at Cameron, hesitating, and slowly turn over the documents.

I stare at my father's testament for a couple of minutes, the world going numb behind me. I don't mind the clutter, the fact Cameron and I are kneeling on the floor of Nigel's cabin, or that he could return at any given moment. He didn't destroy the evidence. Perhaps all he wanted was a trophy. Perhaps we all are a little proud, starving for ego victories.

I thumb through the document as in a fever dream until I reach the newer, whiter part. This is the document they read, but at the end someone clipped two yellower, older pages, matching the rest of the document. My father's signature is very similar on both copies, but when faced, one is clearly signed by another person—the traces are less sharp, the slant less decisive.

Two similar copies of a testament, but a life-changing contrast between the two.

"'Lastly, should my wife be deceased, to my beloved daughter, Alexandra,'" I read with a dithering voice, "'I leave all my properties and worldly possessions, including all my monetary and physical assets, save for the aforementioned, totaling $2.5 million, which will remain in the Benson trust fund until she turns of age. Should we die before she is an adult, she will become the ward of my brother, Nigel Benson, until she turns eighteen. On her eighteenth birthday, my providers at Mr. Miller, Son, and Associates will funnel all remaining assets to Alexandra's name, making her the sole heir to my inheritance, save for the aforementioned bequests.'"

No marriage clause. I laugh, perhaps too loudly for where we are, but I couldn't care less. "It's here, Cameron. We found it!"

My arms go around him.

Cameron's cross behind me, pressing me against him.

"I can't believe it's been here all along," I mutter through a smile.

"Hiding in plain sight," he whispers.

I pull away and sigh, as though I'd been carrying the world on my shoulders. My fingers flitter over his neck. With a tilt of my head, my nose brushes Cameron's by accident. I inch away, but Cameron halts me and fondles the tip of my nose with his, his Cupid's bow skimming over my lips.

A feminine laugh in the corridor makes me jump.

"Goodness," I mutter, stiffening. "Help me arrange all this and let's run."

We gather Nigel's belongings and organize them inside the trunk as though nobody touched them. Lastly, the velvet cover goes into place. Once the cabin looks neat, Cameron returns Nigel's trunk keys; then we crack the door open and return to my suite with quick strides. Only God knows what would've happened should Nigel or Mr. Crossley have found us ruffling through the trunk. My blood rushes in my ears, but after I reach my suite, I drop onto the couch, hugging the testament.

My father loved me. Not all his words were a lie. Nobody can erase the crimes committed and nobody can turn back time, but with this, it's as if someone had snapped the chains that anchored me to the ground. Now I'm roaming free skyward like a feather trapped in a current of air.

Cameron sits next to me, opening the documents on the table and setting the diaries in a pile.

"I wish I would've studied German when my mother suggested it," Cameron says.

"You gave me my father's testament," I say.

Cameron turns and traps a lock of my hair between his fingers. He straightens it, though the strand bounces back into a curl.

"You found it yourself," he says.

"You didn't let me give up," I whisper.

This time, I'm the one who leans forward.

Cameron's sharp breath feathers on my nose.

He frames my cheeks as someone knocks on the door and opens it without waiting for a reply. "Miss Benson, it turns out I'm not only a newspaper kind of man."

Mr. Crossley.

Chapter Twenty-Two

Mr. Crossley halts at the threshold, looking at the open folders and diaries and Cameron and me on the couch, leaning into each other.

He's seen it. He's seen it all.

I leap to my feet and skitter around the table, hiding my father's will behind me. "You certainly don't know manners, Mr. Crossley."

He lowers his head, as if he could see through me. "You have the information."

Cameron stands and grabs Mr. Crossley's jacket, pushing him inside. He rams him into the wall with a dry thud.

Ilse slips into the cabin, pulling a small handgun from her pocket. "Unhand him at once." Her real accent shows through, cold and hard.

My breath hitches. When we boarded the *Lusitania*, a man was complaining that no one had questioned him about his baggage. And this was why. They've smuggled weapons aboard. The rumors about the cargo, the ammunition, what if it's all true? Will that grant Germany the right to sink the ship if we're inspected?

"Cameron."

But Cameron doesn't even flinch. He keeps Mr. Crossley against the wall.

"It's all right, Ilse," Mr. Crossley grunts. "They know. We know. Let's call a truce."

She lowers the gun. "But—"

"Let's call a truce."

She slams the door shut and leans against it, her gun still in her hand.

My legs shake.

"Unhand me now!" Mr. Crossley demands.

"Not until the lady gets rid of the gun."

"The gun is staying," Ilse grumbles.

"We're unarmed," I retort.

A dry smile moves on Ilse's lips, her fingers shifting over the gun's grip. "As if I don't recognize what your beau can do. The gun stays."

"Excuse me?"

But Ilse just keeps that dry smile and those challenging sharp eyes.

I turn my head to Cameron and Mr. Crossley. The silence rolls over the cabin, the thrumming of the ship loud. Cameron glimpses back, his eyes cold and dark, but draws his attention again onto Mr. Crossley.

"What did she mean?" I insist.

"I don't think now is the time," Mr. Crossley grumbles. He lifts his arms, a book still in his hand. "I could knock you out with this if I wanted, Asher, so you should take it as evidence of my good intentions."

"And I could break your head against the wall," Cameron hisses, snatching the book from Mr. Crossley and throwing it on the floor. Cutting a dark look toward Cameron, Mr. Crossley shoves him away, yet Cameron rams him into place again.

Mr. Crossley sighs. "All right, Ilse, pocket that damn gun."

With a louder sigh and an eye roll, she slips it into her pocket. "Are you happy now?"

"You better explain everything," Cameron grunts, easing the pressure on Mr. Crossley.

Drawing a short breath, I crouch to gather the book. *The Phantom of the Opera.* "What are you going to do to us?"

"Nothing," Ilse croons from the door. "If we get along."

Cameron spins Mr. Crossley and pats him along the waist and arms. After kicking his ankles apart, he bends and taps down his legs.

I frown. "What are you doing, Cameron?"

"He's checking that I don't carry weapons under my clothes," says Mr. Crossley. "A better question would be where did you learn to do this?"

"I was raised by a policeman."

"Well, that's interesting," Mr. Crossley says. "I thought you were a rich pal from Denver."

"Don't do anything you'll come to regret," Cameron spits, releasing him. With a warning look, he signals at the couch with a chin jerk.

Mr. Crossley smiles and sits down, propping a leg on his opposite knee as if he were about to sip on some sherry under the Spanish sun. A folder falls on the floor, which he disregards. "Ask away."

I shift my weight from one leg to the other and look around. Ilse remains at the door, and Cameron puts his back to the wall, facing the room.

"Don't think for a moment we're hostages," Cameron growls, crossing his arms.

Ilse shrugs. "We're all hostages in one way or another. But you won't leave this room until we've talked this through."

Cameron chuckles and shakes his head.

"Who are you?" I snap, my hands balling.

"Adam Becker. And that's Ilse Schulz over there."

Cameron crosses his arms. "No Crossley and Emily Atkinson, I see."

"These days, we're Adam Crossley—assistant to Nigel Benson, and Emily Atkinson—maid to Alexandra Benson. Tomorrow, who knows?"

I set the testament and his book on the desk and take a seat in the chair across from him. "Who is Nigel? Is he my real uncle?"

"Getting to the point, aren't we?" Mr. Becker props an elbow on the back of the couch. "He's not your uncle. His name is Jörg Müller."

The shiver that runs through my spine is as chill as a winter whisper.

"Where is my real uncle?"

"My information is he died months ago."

My heart hollows and drops, just as if the floor beneath my feet cracked open and I had fallen through. I'm all alone in the world. No parents. No family. No one to hold my hand once Cameron leaves me. If I survive, all I will have is my fortune.

The prospect feels emptier than a month and a half ago.

Maybe I was wrong. Maybe living with a cold heart is better than living with a stolen heart.

"What are you going to do to us?" I repeat.

Mr. Becker scoffs. "We're telling you: nothing. If we wanted you dead, you'd be."

"You'd have to take me down first," Cameron growls.

"Who says that can't be arranged, Mr. Asher?" With a glance, Mr. Becker seems to share an entire conversation with Cameron. Then, my fake uncle's assistant smirks—but keeps the fun to himself.

Behind me, Ilse is still against the door, her eyes trained on me, on Cameron. She might've stowed her gun, but I can't forget it's still there. It's as though it weighed in my own pocket.

I lean toward Mr. Crossley, my fingers squeezing the edge of the seat. "I don't trust you."

"Well, you should."

"Why should I?" I wonder aloud, with a bite in my tone. As if he hasn't been devious at best.

"Because Ilse and I are your only options to walk out of here alive. You need us as much as we need you."

"That's interesting," Cameron says. "Who says I can't do the job?"

Ilse chuckles. "One against three?"

Mr. Becker lifts an eyebrow. "You sure had a reckless or delusional mentor, Mr. Asher."

I frown. "Mentor?"

"Why do you need us?" Cameron fires back instead, his blank expression unreadable. His thumbs, though, move over his crossed arms to a tune only he can hear.

"Let's not reveal all our cards yet, shall we?"

The cabin frazzles before my eyes. What are they not telling me? What context am I missing? I shake my head, my thoughts spiraling, and I focus on the most pressing matter at hand. I can solve Cameron's mysteries later. But I can't keep playing cat and mouse with Mr. Becker or Ilse. They said they won't do anything to us—if we get along. I don't believe for one moment our lives aren't hanging in the balance.

And I need answers. Answers only *they* can provide.

"You killed my parents," I hiss.

"*I* didn't kill them," Mr. Becker says. "Neither did Ilse. Or the three men from our team detained belowdecks. Jörg did. He ran amok. Murder wasn't in our mission. Not yet. We were conducting surveillance."

I kick upward, my tight muscles straining with repressed shudders. "Not *yet*?" I want to murder him. I want to murder her. I want to murder Nigel—*Jörg*.

"Why did he go amok?" asks Cameron.

"Unclear," Ilse says.

"That's a load of bosh," Cameron retorts, leaning on the back of a chair.

"And still, it's the truth." Mr. Becker's brazen tone is like a sharp slap.

With a dark glare, I march left and right. "Did you know my parents? You called my mother by her real name."

"If you're asking if we knew them personally, the answer is no. We knew them as much as rival spies can know their enemies. My information was that she went by Valeria years ago, but it seems like she changed her name when she left England. Once we were here, we learned she was now Isabella."

So many questions brim on my tongue. Why did my parents leave England? Why did she change her name? Why did they die?

My fists curl. "What was your mission? What do you want from me, from my parents?"

He leans forward, propping his elbows on his knees. "We wanted information from your parents. The thing, Alexandra—may I call you Alexandra?—is that the United States doesn't have an elaborate espionage system, and the British Admiralty has been placing people of interest in positions of power on American soil to aid England against Germany. Your parents were the leaders of that team. Our mission was to get those names to prove America is helping Britain and involve the US in the war. But we've not found the list."

Cameron straightens, eyes flashing with what I'd only call realization. "And . . . What's the reason we're headed to England if your main mission is across the pond?"

A sardonic smile creeps onto Mr. Becker's lips. "For two reasons. Jörg has a small mission in England to cover for a few months. Given the strict measures the MI5 has placed on the English borders, a German spy needs a creative way to infiltrate England. And you, as the daughter of an Englishman, are still considered an English woman with full rights to enter England as you please. Marrying an American, though, will strip you of your right to British citizenship. Not that Jörg cared, unless you eloped before he could enter England."

I shake my head, force my throat into a dry gulp. Jörg's plan builds like a spiderweb. How silly I was, thinking I could outsmart him. There was a much larger game at play.

"But here's where we tell you we've got worse news for you," Ilse says.

I glare at her, stopping halfway in the middle of the cabin, and cross my arms. "What is it? Stop playing with me."

"Given we failed the main mission," Mr. Becker says, "Jörg is going to drag you all the way to Germany as a political prisoner."

I take a step back, eyes widening. "He wants to—what?"

"No," Cameron spits. "I won't allow that."

"That's why you need us," Mr. Becker says.

I press my palm to my mouth, in fear I might throw up. "But—" My lips stutter, my fingers go cold. "I didn't even know my parents. I know nothing."

"You're still the daughter of a spy. Given all this"—Mr. Becker's hand flitters over the table—"casual clutter, I believe you didn't know. But others might think you're lying."

I fall into my chair, swaying it on its hind legs. A lump rises in my throat, bitter like bile. Is it fear or sheer abomination? Possibly, both. I've been a tool, and only a few brushes of luck here and there have saved me from dying like my parents.

But my fate, perhaps, will make me wish I were dead like them.

"He won't get the chance," Cameron tells me. Then, eyes shining with murder, he turns to Mr. Becker. "I've got all the evidence I need to jail you, Miss Ilse, the fellows belowdecks, and blip off your big boss. I'll save Alexandra, and the king of England will probably name me a lord in gratitude for my services to the crown."

Ilse lets out a sigh.

"Yes, yes. Congratulations, big timer." Mr. Becker shrugs. "You'll paint a bull's-eye on your forehead. You might as well sit and wait to be killed by other German spies."

Jaw clenched, Cameron sticks his hands in his pockets. "We already have that bull's-eye on our foreheads, Becker."

My head turns left and right, going between Cameron and Mr. Becker, a nervous flutter running across me.

"You're not listening to me. That's where Ilse and I come in handy. Not even the Admiralty can sense the way we think, how we operate, where the danger can come from. We can help and provide the protection you need as long as this war lasts. It's really a generous offer."

"How nice of you." Cameron chuckles. "I take it that you don't want to know what we know?"

"Not in the slightest, no," Ilse says.

"The less we know, the better for all of us," Mr. Becker says.

Silence is deafening in the parlor for a split second. My mind spins with information, with all the ways this could go wrong. And still, my need to know outweighs it all.

"How did Jörg change the will?" My voice is still tiny, and I hate the glint of pity in Mr. Becker's eyes. But I'm too tired all of a sudden to make a move, pull a face.

"He paid Mr. Tannenbaum to swap the documents and to tamper with your father's signature. We slipped something into the coffee of your father's lawyer so he'd be indisposed the day of the reading."

Massaging my forehead, I lean on the armrest. They didn't leave any loose ends, did they? That's what they were doing in New York before killing my parents. Circling us all in. I cannot take any more of this poisoned truth, but I'll push forward. Nobody said the truth was beautiful. Truth is a thorned rose.

Cameron clears his throat, startling me. I can't fathom how he's not yelling—I certainly feel like it.

"So, tell us . . . Why are you here, *Adam*?" Cameron clips.

"See?" He smirks. "We're good friends now."

I harrumph. My words are mangled in my throat.

"Don't think I won't beat the information out of you," Cameron says. "What are you two doing here, betraying your kaiser?"

Mr. Becker shrugs. "A change, if you will. Ilse's story is her own to tell."

"And I won't disclose it *now*, thank you."

Mr. Becker chuckles. "I will share mine. The Admiralty might've been flirting with me for a while, for starters. With more money, safety, better conditions, *respect*. One day we'll talk of the spotless ten years of service to my empire and how none of my actions, my influence, or the times I risked my life applied when it came to saving my brother. How the kaiser shrugged me off like I was a nuisance. One day, Mr. Asher."

"Does it have to do with the stowaways?" I ask, pressing my legs together so my feet don't start bouncing.

Mr. Becker's smirk widens. "Aren't you a smart thing? You may say that was the last straw. I don't take kindly to feeling expendable or disrespected—or both. We have extraction plans in place. Jörg just decided to not act and forsake half his team. He also put our mission in danger when he killed your parents, and we had to cover for him under death threats. That made us see he'll always choose himself and his comfort. He has no honor. And see, Alexandra, I am a killer. Not a ragdoll. I'm tired of letting Jörg play with me. And I'm tired of this senseless war."

The way he pleasantly says *killer* sends churning nausea down my body. But by the way his eyebrows set over his lost gaze, I can believe he's tired and that something happened to him, that he's desperate enough to find a way out.

I cross my arms. "I don't believe you're doing this out of the kindness of your heart. What do you want in exchange?"

"You're right," he says. "Don't make the mistake of thinking I have a heart. It's easy. You give us Jörg's cut from your father's will and help Ilse and me start anew by pretending we're all a big, happy family. I'll procure false documentation from a collaborator in Liverpool."

I bolt upright. "You want to pass for a Benson?"

He lets out a small laugh. "Why, don't I pass for one? If Jörg fooled you, I surely can fool strangers. Ilse will be my dear betrothed. Even though she'd poke one of my eyes out if I dared look at her for too long. We might have to rethink our roles."

I steal my gaze from him. With the blond hair, the snarky attitude, the icy stare, and the pale sharp features, he could pass for a Benson man. But I won't admit it.

Cameron chuckles, moving around the chair with arms akimbo. "Hiding under a false name. I assume Germany will place a juicy dead-or-alive reward on your head. I'll concede, that's smart."

Mr. Becker shrugs. "And you'd benefit from being smart too. We're all in the same boat. Pun absolutely intended."

I swallow a dry lump. "I won't wait. I'll turn in all these documents to Captain Turner."

Ilse huffs. "Do you want to enrage a spy in a locked space such as this ship? Not wise."

"How can I be sure you're telling the truth?" I say.

"You can't," Mr. Becker replies. "But you don't have any other option but to trust us."

Cameron's glower deepens, casting a shadow over his eyes. "You're a bastard."

"I know," Mr. Becker says. "But we still need each other. What's it going to be? Do we have a deal? Or do I go tell my boss about all the documents you stole from him?"

My head turns left and right, going between Cameron and Mr. Becker. My fists ball. For a moment, I'm about to wipe that smile off Mr. Becker's face and kick him and Ilse out of this cabin myself. But I'm between a rock and a hard place. What are money and pretending they're family if they save not only my life but Cameron's and protect us from Germany? I'll have a safe way out with Cameron, but my body shakes.

I'm tied. No matter what I choose.

But after all, the ropes we choose are better than the ropes that catch us unaware.

Still, when I nod, I feel like I'm making a pact with the devil. "Deal."

Chapter Twenty-Three

I don't fully trust Mr. Becker or Ilse, so I leave the documents, including my father's will, inside my own trunk. Mr. Becker and Ilse leave my cabin, promising that they'll keep us informed on next steps and what Nigel—*Jörg*—is up to. But on our way to the purser's office, the world frays around the edges, the colors vanishing.

I stop walking, placing a hand on the cool wooden wall of the corridor, and close my eyes, hoping the dizziness doesn't accompany me in the darkness, but my head dances to the sway of the *Lusitania.*

"Are you all right?" Cameron reaches for my shoulder.

I don't move. Any sudden shift and I might fall apart. "Do you trust them?" I whisper.

"I don't think it matters," Cameron says. "They're right. We have no options."

"True." I force my eyes open, my lungs to take in air, my body to relax. If they were lying, they still need me to enter England. Yet I can't wash off the nagging thought I'm waltzing into a death trap.

At the purser's office, Cameron slips a piece of folded paper to Mr. McCubbin. "Please send this marconigram as soon as possible."

"It will be sent as soon as this evening, sir," the purser says. "That'll be a dollar or ten shillings."

"What are you sending?" I ask while he pays.

Cameron signals to the staircase and gently steers me away.

"It's a message to Liverpool," he whispers, entering the corridor with me. "As brief as possible, I'm letting it be known I request authorities to be present at port by the time the *Lusitania* docks."

My fake uncle, Jörg, turns the corner.

I stiffen, flashing a weak smile his way. "Uncle, I don't feel well today. I must be seasick. Don't expect me for dinner."

"Very well, Alexandra." He nods. "Rest. It'll help you."

I let out a shuddering breath; my body is in knots. In hindsight, everything makes sense. Jörg came into my life with the uncle scheme on full display, and the more confident he felt, the further his farce crumbled. He shouldn't have let me roam the streets of New York alone, as much as his assistant tailed me; he shouldn't have let me get rid of Ilse; and if he was truly concerned about what I did or didn't do with Cameron, he would've made sure I was chaperoned at all times. Do I go missing for most of the day? Nobody seeks me out. Apart from showing how little he cares about my safety or reputation, no matter my age, he is no longer trying to keep up the charade. Which can only mean the masks are slipping off. And our time is running out.

"My whole life has been a lie," I mutter. What I thought was light was only an ebbing star in a foggy winter sky.

"There's nothing you can do about it." Cameron squeezes my shoulder. "But your future? That, you can change."

"That feels so far away, Cameron. And even then, it's compromised."

"Come now, you've learned your father respected you. You have the testament. Even if Becker is lying, there will be officers ready to arrest Jörg. We have enough to dispute the will. You should be happy."

I fully catch the way he mentions disputing the will but not marrying me. And the subtle difference twists my guts. After all, I'll end up alone. With a lot of money. But he won't be there.

I shake my head. I don't want to listen to any more of this. "I want to get inebriated."

I don't know why I thought Cameron would say no, but he smiles and says, "That, I can give to you. Anything else?"

"Ice cream."

He squeezes my chin with two fingers. "Wait for me in your cabin." His husky tone makes the hair at the back of my head stand on point. It's so strange what he does to me, how mourning, distrust, loss, and love can coexist when it comes to Cameron.

He turns, but I snag at his sleeve. "I'll wait in *your* cabin."

He whips around with an amused expression.

My fingers twitch, a flutter of incandescent butterflies swarming inside me. I have no inkling as to why I said that, but I stand my ground, my chin tilting slightly higher.

"You know where to find it," Cameron says.

As soon as I step into his cabin, a new pang of indignation about how Nigel—*Jörg*—confined Cameron to such a tiny space stabs at my ribcage.

I take a seat on the edge of his bed, the mattress creaking underneath me. The cabin smells of Cameron and fresh linen.

Seconds tick by, slipping from my grip, and Cameron's impending arrival is weighing on me. I play with my thumbs on my lap, wondering why I'm here. This can only lead to trouble.

But again, does it even matter? To the world, he is my fiancé. And I have no family reputation to ruin. I'm right where it all began. Only now do I know my life is made of fake pieces.

Fake uncle, fake fiancé, fake parents . . . all lost or about to be lost.

I leap from the bed and roam about the tiny room. Cameron keeps this place organized. His pajamas lie folded on the convertible sofa by the wardrobe, next to a small pile of books and my photo album.

Dubliners by James Joyce sits atop the pile. It's thin. The book has only 152 pages. Passages have been underlined with a pencil, little annotations left on the margins. Before I can read them, the door groans open and Cameron slinks inside, closing it with a foot. In one of his hands, he holds a giant crystal bowl topped with melting scoops of chocolate ice cream. In his other hand, a big bottle and two glasses dangling from between his fingers.

He smiles, but in his eyes there's a flash of something small. Disappointment?

He signals at the book. "Do you like 'The Dead'?"

"Is it good?"

He sets the glasses down on the washstand table. "Very good. My favorite by Joyce."

"It might be a good change of pace after *The Secret Garden*."

He shows me the bottle. "Rum. It's spicy, but I find the mix with the sweetness of ice cream to be a remarkable combination."

I take the ice cream bowl from him. "I don't know who you must've bribed to get ahold of this entire bottle, so let's enjoy it to the fullest."

The cold numbs my skin almost immediately, so I have no option but to put the bowl down. I prop a knee on the mattress and slide onto the bed, sitting against the wall with my legs crossed toward the edge.

I'm on Cameron's bed.

Even my internal voice yelps.

Cameron, thankfully, doesn't mention anything. He approaches, pouring rum into one of the glasses. "Here you go."

Our fingers brush before I snatch the glass away, almost sloshing the alcohol all over my skirt. I down the rum in one swig.

"Easy there, Fake Addie," he says.

Bitterness travels down my throat, and as much as I fight my knee-jerk reaction, my nose and mouth wrinkle, making Cameron laugh.

The rum sets a lake of fire in my chest. I plonk my head against the wall, squeezing my eyes shut. I might pay dearly for this. Spirits go to my head easily—I should know better.

"Did you make any progress with the coordinates?" I ask.

"Yes, some progress, but I need to grab a better geography book at the ship's library. Did you . . . check the album out while I was gone?"

"Why would I do that?" I drawl to the setting warmth of the alcohol. It's already beginning to lull me into its drowsiness.

"Never mind. All right if I take off my jacket?" he asks me under the glugging of alcohol being poured into his glass.

"Since when do you ask for permission to take off your clothes in front of me, you rascal?" I wonder aloud, my little smirk kicking up. Memories from our time in his apartment wash through me like hot liquid, making me yearn for more time with him. This is our fifth day of sailing. Five out of seven. So little left.

A chuckle, the click of a glass being put down on the washstand table, the swish of a jacket's silk interior sliding against shirt sleeves, I could keep my eyes shut and just hear Cameron go about life. This time, I wouldn't fight the sleep.

I take one of the spoons and let the ice cream melt on my tongue, the icy chocolate sending a stale burn through my temples. I wince.

"Are you all right?" Cameron says.

"I've always been sensitive to frozen foods," I say as he settles down on the edge of his bed at a reasonable distance from me. Quite the gentleman—the problem is I don't want him to be a gentleman.

Leaving his spoon hanging from his mouth, Cameron rubs the space between my eyebrows with his thumbs, the rest of his fingers as delicate as clouds on my cheeks. It's the first time I've been touched like this, and the sheer pleasure traveling through my body makes the world tilt.

"Thank you," I say, grateful my whisper masks my stutter.

Cameron draws back, not without stroking my cheek first. When I open my eyes, he's tackling spoonfuls of ice cream as if nothing had happened.

"Have you ever had rum?" Cameron asks, scrambling to his feet. He takes his glass from the table. The butterscotch liquid gleams under the lights as he swings it to his mouth.

"I have, today," I admit. "It's . . . bitter."

The bowl on the bed is nearly empty, liquid chocolate pooling on the bottom. I give it to him, so he sets it on the table. But I do raise my glass from the bed.

With a side smirk, Cameron grabs the bottle and serves me some more. "Such inconsistency, one might say." He takes a thoughtful look at his glass. "It's made of fermented sugarcane; it should be sweet, but it's not."

"Everything fermented ends up with a sour tang." I let the aftertaste set in. A warm buzz slowly fills my chest, giving my thoughts a spring in their step. "But I like it."

Wincing, I reach out to Cameron for more.

He raises an eyebrow. "I think you've drunk enough."

"No. I haven't. I'm perfectly in my senses."

"Are you?" He sits on the edge of the bed. "I dare you to walk in a straight line from the washstand to the door."

"In this shoebox of a cabin? No problem."

I bounce out of Cameron's bed, and the floor that was steady half an hour ago now rolls up and down. The furniture frazzles, the corners of my vision darkening. I grab the sink behind me.

I can do this.

"Any problem?" Cameron seems amused, and I can't wait to make him lose that silly smile.

"The sea is rougher," I say.

"No, it's not. You're drunk, darling."

Darling goes straight to my legs. Now they're wobblier. "I am not, and don't call me that."

I take a deep breath to clear my head and, step by step, march to the door under his watchful gaze. My feet fumble on the up-and-down motion of the *Lusitania*, and my vision skews. It's too late to conceal my straying when I put my palms on the doorjamb and close my eyes, accepting defeat.

"That was surprisingly close," Cameron says.

I take a new deep breath and turn to the bed, the floor heaving up and down like a moving chest. I cling to the bedpost and sit next to Cameron.

"I'm drunk," I admit, collapsing next to him.

Cameron chuckles. "Feel better? Distracted?"

He leans down next to me. The bed is narrow, so his left leg presses against mine despite his right being out of bed, foot firmly planted on the floor.

I sigh. "I got what I wanted. Not bad for a change."

"May I ask you something?"

I blink my eyes shut. "Ah-hmm."

"Why don't you like it when I address you with endearments?"

Because it does things to my body I've never felt before.

"It reflects something we're not," I whisper.

He shifts. The mattress tightens under his weight and settles with a creak. "I guess I'll use Fake Addie."

Please don't use just that one, I think; call me love, call me dear, call me dove. But outside, I keep silent as a tomb, my lips shut tightly. The truth I'm swallowing seems to hang like a heavy presence over us.

Cameron sighs, letting his breath drift out, slowly, loudly.

I grow conscious of *me*, lying next to *him*. The way our clothes brush. The heat from his body. A small shift and I could touch him, caress him, hold him. *Kiss* him. It would be too easy.

"Thank you," I say, if only to burst the tension building up in the cabin.

Cameron turns his head, our blue-eyed stares meeting. He flashes a brief-yet-warm smile. "What for?"

I shrug. "For everything, I believe."

The fact he chuckles disappoints me. "You've drunk too much, Fake Addie."

I pretend a smile. "Perhaps."

"Or are we sharing secrets?" He might be a bit tipsy as well. Or just uncomfortable. I wish we'd had more time together so I could read him better. "Now that we might be being honest, I remember when you asked me what my dreams were."

"And you pointed out very coolly that you didn't have dreams." I look up at him. My eyes are welling, but I don't trouble myself with hiding it from him. He's probably going to attribute it to my being inebriated and nothing related to my feelings for him. But the truth is I yearn for Cameron as if I were already losing him, each second luring him further and further away. "It turns out I don't think I have dreams either."

He flashes a sad smile. "Well, it's a good time to create dreams. What would you like to do with your new life? When all of this is over?"

"You still think we're making it out alive."

"Humor me," he says. "Would you like to go back to law school? Take a break? Pivot to another career?"

I sigh. My eyelids are heavy. I don't resist. "This is most likely the alcohol putting words in my mouth, but I think I'd like to see what this fuss with England is."

Cameron chuckles. "You've come a long way."

The ghost of a smile fights to reach my lips, but the drone of the ship lulls me, and I fall into a light wavering sleep instead.

A while in, Cameron strokes my hair, fingers cruising through my locks.

"You're keeping one secret—you've not worn your hair up for a while now," he whispers, as soft as a spring breeze. "I'd like to believe it's because you decided giving life a chance is a worthwhile risk.

"I know I told you I didn't have dreams, but that was because I'd bet on the safe side for a long time. But you showed me the beauty of dreams. You entered my classroom, putting everything on the line, and proved it's not bad to take risks. It's a shame your beautiful, inquisitive mind wasn't curious today, of all days, because I wanted to tell you one of my secrets. If you'd only asked me what my dreams are, Alexandra, I would've told you I have so many now, and that you're in each one of them."

Chapter Twenty-Four

May 6, 1915—Day 6 of 7

Diary of Valeria Lavalle

28th of October, Kensington

Dear Diary,
Jörg has brought me flowers this morning after his daily training. Although he's the most delicate man, he enjoys portraying a tough character. He wants to make his father proud, become someone important. Honor is important to him. More, I fear, than I ever will be.

I drop the diary on my lap.

The world falls away, and thick silence dances in my cabin.

Only my heart reverberates in my chest.

My mother knew Jörg.

My mother wrote this in late 1889. When she was still living with my grandparents in a borough just outside the city of London. She was nineteen. Five years before she had me.

With shaking hands, I grab the diary and force myself to read.

> Yet I can see past the tough exterior, the tortured, artistic spirit living inside a boy forced to grow up too soon. I think he still feels guilty for his mother. His father has raised him with the notion he killed his mother at birth. I so wish to heal him, help him see his worth. But sometimes I ask myself how can I love someone who hates himself? It's a never-ending battle. It hurts too much.

"Who were you, Mom?" I thumb across the pages of the thick diary, through a recollection of Jörg's demons and how my mother wanted to scare them away, and how she lost time and time again. She swore she was happy when Jörg asked my grandfather for her hand in marriage, but she didn't sound happy. Later in March, she wrote next,

> Jörg is a righteous man. He steals kisses from me when the chaperones look away, but where's the spark? Mother tells me that I should put those delusions to rest. Marriage, she tells me, is a sacred union and that passion is an idealistic fib from the youth.
>
> But surely that must be untrue? A misconception? Passion must exist, but, as much as I know Jörg loves me, I can't help but feel I'm also the right thing to do, what's expected of him. He's ready to settle and I'm the best choice. It's a sensible type of love, but is it the kind of love I want?
>
> I dream of an otherworldly type of love, of reckless kisses in the rain, of overseas adventures. I want to be chosen because someone can't live without me, not because I'm the right choice at the right time.
>
> Is this really what I want?

I hope that wasn't what she wanted. Mother also wrote about abuse. During arguments, Jörg shouted; he broke a vase full of wildflowers; he ridiculed Mom by imitating her with a high-pitched tone; he refused to communicate. I can easily conjure Jörg acting that way.

Revolted, I shove the diary shut and open the next one. Even though I know how this ended, I'm cheering for Mom. I'm hoping she opens her eyes and chooses Dad.

One diary finished in April and the next one resumed in June 1891. In this one, Mother had already met Father.

> Dear Diary,
> The wedding day is nearing, and I can't forget about Liam. What's wrong with me? I'm spoken for. Liam is one of Jörg's friends. I shouldn't think of him this way. But Liam is wild and lighthearted. Mother dislikes him. She swears the boy is a daredevil, but we danced the other day at the Summer Ball, and I felt as if I floated. The fact I'm writing this is vile, but I can't help myself.
>
> He's offered to tutor me because, Lord knows how, he learned I want to study despite my parents' refusal. I might not be able to concentrate with those playful dimples and blue eyes, but I said yes. He's the first man who supports me in pursuing academic interests rather than finishing school.

She didn't write for a long while, but when she returned, she'd called off the wedding. Splotches of ink showed Mother was crying when she was penning those words.

> Dear Diary,
> I loathe myself for choosing Liam. I broke Jörg's heart, ruined my reputation, and hurt my parents. Jörg has

run to Germany, where his mother was originally from. And I can only wish him the best and hope he forgets me and meets someone who can give him all the beautiful things he deserves.

But for the first time . . . I'm happy. For the first time I feel as though I have any semblance of a life.

Liam has asked me about America. About us moving to the New World. He has not wasted a second in making my life an adventure.

"Oh, Mom."

How well I understand her.

She got her reckless, adventurous love.

A new family.

She also acquired an enemy.

And a turbulent life.

But in the end it was her own choosing.

She lived the way she wished.

"I just wish you hadn't dragged me into it," I mutter as I open the third diary. This one spanned from 1892 to 1893. She wrote about her life with Dad, their wedding, and their happiness. With a knot in my throat, I relish every word, engraving every detail in my mind.

Dear Diary,

I can't believe I'm saying this, but I'm with child! I keep dreaming about my baby, even in a wakeful state. I can't wait to hold her or him in my arms.

But we're both scared. I don't want our little one in the midst of Liam's world. Liam has presented his demission to the Admiralty. But his brother has warned us. No one ever abandons the Admiralty. Enemies don't forget, never rest. The past will always come knocking on our door. Liam wants to train me.

> But we're both firm in our decision that we want our child to grow up safe and sound. Thus, we're leaving for America before the year's end. Our child will never learn what transpired in England.

"This is why Jörg killed them." The past. The open wounds.

Heart pounding in my head, I clutch the lapels of my housedress, and the diary falls open on my lap again. I let out a hard huff, my eyes welling with tears.

My mother doesn't use the words, but my father was already a spy. And then, as I grew up, he trained her in secret to become a spy herself. My parents fled when they knew they were to have me. My parents didn't force me into a world of intelligence work, but it's clear they never broke ties with the Admiralty, or that he was contacted later with an offer to spy from America. That would explain the millions.

They lied to me, all because they wanted me safe.

I chew on my lower lip. Safe, but at what cost? My blissful ignorance could have cost me my life. This spring, I slept two rooms away from Jörg while he might've been reading this diary. Do those wounds still hurt him? Is he numb to them? Did he laugh these diaries off, knowing Mom was dead?

Outside my door, conversations rise with the hum prior to dinnertime. I sigh and leave the bed. I've been hiding today, claiming I had a headache and needed to rest. In my defense I'd say I needed it, but the reason was cowardice and not a real ailment.

My hair still smells of Cameron. He slept next to me, though by the time I woke up, he had already gone to the Barbershop. My mind spins around his confession. *If you'd only asked me what my dreams are, Alexandra, I would've told you I have so many now, and that you're in each one of them.*

Someone knocks on the door, drawing me back into my cabin.

"You may come in," I say, putting the diaries inside the trunk. Only one photo album remains outside, on my desk, but after searching most of its pages, I've not found any more scribbled names on the backs of the photographs.

Ilse walks in. "I wondered if you wanted help with your hair for the seamen's event."

I shrug. "We both know you're not my maid."

"But Jörg still believes it. I told him we're making amends. Let's find a dress first."

I sigh as she opens the wardrobe door. There's no stopping this woman, but . . . I understand why she sees a lot of herself in me. We're both stubborn women. I still shrink when I think she contributed to my parents' demise. We're enemies, collaborating due to our circumstances, out of our own interests, and yet, we're closer to seeing our humanity win over the hatred war tells us to have for one another.

And I still have to hear why she wants to desert her country. Mr. Becker said why, and with that information I can decide if I can trust him or not. But she didn't.

Once Ilse has helped me into a dress, the shock from my mother's diaries has slowly eased. I can focus on her.

"Why do you want to desert Germany?" I ask as she pins my hair up.

She smiles, a final pearled pin pressed between her lips. Ilse flicks it out and sticks it in my hair. The bite to my scalp makes me jump.

"I'm sorry. I'm afraid my maid's skills leave much to be desired." She sighs, turning my head. Her eyes roam over my high hairdo. "I won't bother you with the sad details, but I was an orphan at a young age. No family left behind. I was destitute before I turned six. Part of what proved you two aren't the simpletons I thought you were was seeing your fiancé actually cared for children that were exactly like me. Mr. Becker learned the money Jörg released from your fortune ended up at the school in Brooklyn. I saw that you two wouldn't ever take an innocent child and turn them into a tool. Before Jörg found me, I had to sell my body and steal. Then, clean. Endure the abuse of my masters."

I turn in my chair. "So, Jörg saved you?"

"No, Alexandra." Her face hardens; her gaze grows distant. "He just made me another kind of tool. A tool for his own benefit and the benefit of the Deutsches Reich."

"Is that why you're *using* him?" I'm about to say I can't fathom how any woman could stand Jörg. But my mother used to be engaged to him, and the price she paid was high.

"No, Fake Cousin-to-Be." She winks. "I'm doing it because men lose focus when they're physically entertained. And we need Jörg to lose as much focus as we can. Do we have a deal, after all?"

Ilse's words dizzy me. I hear a high-pitched whistle. I close my eyes just so the room stops spinning. My life is full of mischance, but I tend to forget that others' are as well. I won't lower my guard. I can't forget they might be lying—and that they have openly contributed to my parents' murder. But they're about to put their lives on the line. Not for me. But they're taking me along the way no matter the reason. They could just kill me, rob me, or both. They could rob Jörg.

But they decided I'm a worthwhile risk. Someone deserving of compassion and help.

Deep inside, my parents would respect Mr. Becker and Ilse. They'd tell me that they're a guide out of the maze. That sometimes, we have to make friends with the devil. And that I should take their help. My parents will always live through me. I'll never go astray if only I listen to their voices, whispering from the depths of my soul.

"We do."

Chapter Twenty-Five

Ilse is still on my mind as I'm about to enter one of the elevators by the grand staircase, but I stop short and whip my head upward. The beautiful wrought iron encloses the occupants in an iron trap in the middle of the staircase. These elevators are like a pair of pretty coffins.

"Miss?" the operator asks with a polite smile.

I teeter backward, casting a faint smile his way, and swerve to the staircase.

I'm so engrossed by my terrible inkling that I almost bump into Cameron's arm, held out for me.

"Feeling better this evening?"

Gooseflesh blooming under my gloves, I accept his arm. Has he always smelled this good? Has his hold always been as steady? "Much better."

"Have you slept all day?" His forehead wrinkles.

"Not all day." Heat blooms in my cheeks as I remember we slept together in the same bed. "I've been reading my mother's diaries."

"Anything interesting?"

"Would you like to sit?"

He smiles. "Is it that scandalous?"

"My mother knew Jörg."

His eyes widen, his face paling as if blood had drained under his skin. "Oh."

"Precisely." I tell him every detail in whispers. This afternoon, due to the Seamen's Charities Concert, two lines of people coil from the Lounge doors into the white hall. Ladies and children wait on the couches around the fireplace opposite the elevators. The place is alive with voices, but the smiles are void and the sound of laughter is arid.

"So Jörg deserted England for Germany," Cameron muses. "Does it mean that . . . ?"

"That Jörg deserted England because he was heartbroken?" I wonder aloud, tracing the beads on my dark-blue dress. "Probably. He was hurt, and so he wanted revenge. That's why he killed my parents."

He shakes his head. "Of course."

A man filches a paper from the wall right next to us and wags it in the air, stopping whatever I was about to ask.

"We're barely making any progress. And this is all they supply us with. A life jacket guide. Very useful for when a German torpedo dunks us into the ocean."

"Paul, watch your tone," a woman pleads, looking around with frantic eyes. "The Royal Navy will escort us into Liverpool."

From the Lounge escapes a murmur of clinks and chatter. I strain my ears to keep up with their conversation.

"Well, Gladys," he utters, "extinguishing the lights again tonight won't do much, I'm afraid. We need speed, not concealment."

"Are they turning off the lights?"

Even though it's a rhetorical question, Cameron nods. "All outboard lights. I saw it last night."

"Did you leave the cabin?" I try to soften the dip of my brow, but it's evident that disappointment is clawing its way through my face.

A caring tug claims one of the corners of Cameron's lips. "You seemed to be having a rough sleep; I wanted to let you rest."

Fine. I shouldn't care. My eyes flicker to the windows. Funny how things we take for granted evade our attention. These days sunshine has streamed into the hall through open curtains and large windows, brightening the breezy rooms of the *Lusitania*, but even though the sun is still setting, the heavy drapes are shut. The fire of the sunset should pour through the skylight over the staircase, but they've placed a cover upon it.

In the Lounge, chairs and tables have all been arranged to face astern, toward a central stage. The room is full to the brim with saloon and second-class passengers, heads and heads spanning portside to starboard. The windows and skylight have been covered here too.

Far away, I spot Professor Holbourn with his little companion, Miss Avis. With a brief wave, Cameron greets Professor Brodrick, who sits with several men at one of the starboard tables.

I locate Mr. Becker's blond hair among the guests before our steward shows us to our table.

Jörg turns to acknowledge our presence with a nod. The hairs on the back of my head stand on end as I take one of the chairs. I imagine him years ago, coldly and immaturely in love with my mother, hating himself for having a soft soul. A soul that, without a doubt, he has annihilated at this point.

Apparently, just like his honor. My mother said it was important to him, but Mr. Becker said he had no honor.

"So nice you finally joined us, Niece," Jörg says. "I thought you wouldn't."

"Why would I not join you?" I ask. "I slept aplenty."

On the two tables in front of us sit heaps of caviar and oysters placed on ice. I grimace and settle for the charcuterie and cheese from the plate next to me, my jeweled bracelets catching the shimmers of candles and low lights dancing through the room, but while people laugh and conversations float, the air is as thick as it was in the hall, if not worse. Shoulders are stiff, stares remain wary, and gestures guarded, and that apprehension also bathes those at our table. Two chairs from me, my fake uncle barely turns his head toward me and Cameron. Mr. Becker, in between us, sits pretending disinterest, but I feel him almost counting the breaths we take.

It's a game of nonchalance in which all participants sense all bets are off.

A white spotlight clicks awake over the stage. Mr. Harkness, one of the assistant pursers, steps into the halo of light, introduces himself as our host, and summons the first passenger onto the stage. Followed by a trail of claps, the man stands in front of the audience with a couple of sheets and begins "O Captain! My Captain!" by Walt Whitman.

Around me, the night slips forward. Several passengers and crew take up the stage to perform. The crowd sings "For He's a Jolly Good Fellow" to Staff Captain Anderson, and some passengers, among them Alfred Vanderbilt, dance to different songs, but the celebrations and entertainment can't divert my attention from Jörg. One piece of charcuterie and a sip of wine at a time, anger fills my rushing blood, flowing with alcohol right into my head. My fingers curl around the flute so tightly I fear I might shatter the glass in a hundred pieces.

My mother loved *him*, but no one could blame her for choosing my father. No one save for Jörg. Jörg could've been my father if things had been different. And I bet that's all he sees when he looks at me. The what-if.

I'm sure he always wanted to kill her. And he did. Now he sits next to me eating fine caviar, and my mother rots in a hole in the ground.

Emboldened, drunker, and angrier than before, I down my entire third glass of wine. I sigh, my mind swimming in a pleasing haze. At my side, Mr. Becker raises an eyebrow at me.

On stage, Parry Jones and his Welsh choir have finished their performance to a loud ovation. People stow money into baskets depending on how much they liked the performance. The choir has collected ten dollars.

"You all right?" whispers Cameron.

I entwine my hand in his and lean over, my shoulder brushing his. "No."

Cameron strokes my jaw with a thumb. Two chairs over, Jörg sighs and eyes our pressed bodies.

"Anything the matter, Mr. Benson?" asks Cameron, the slightest doubt cracking his voice.

"What indecorous behavior. God knows I'll put an end to this engagement if you don't start behaving properly. Move apart. Now."

I open my mouth and push myself upward, but Cameron puts a hand on my shoulder and pins me to the seat.

"Next on stage," Mr. Harkness announces with a cheerful voice. "Saloon passenger Mr. Cameron Asher will delight us with a piano performance. Chopin, opus 64, number 2."

I turn to Cameron. "Are you playing piano?"

Cameron smirks. "Try not to gouge his eyes out while I'm away."

"I make no promises," I whisper but flash a smile. This man will always catch me off guard.

With a wink, Cameron stands and sidles between the tables to the stage. The pianist gives up his bench to Cameron, who flips his tails up as he sits down, his back ramrod straight, and puts his fingers on the keys. The room hushes down, and the piano's first melancholic notes titillate in the air like soft rain on a pond.

Cameron's eyes fall shut, and his fingers leap over the keys. His head cocks left, and a small smile challenges the solemnity of his expression. I remember reading this was one of the last waltzes Chopin ever wrote. Cameron is able to express the melancholy of the song without a single note going amiss.

As if I'd been brought to my knees, reverence grips my chest—reverence for the sacredness and beauty of music and the sacredness of a man giving into passion. He keeps me on the edge of my seat, tiny bumps rising across my skin. The piece lasts less than five minutes, but when I move again it's as if I've been still for eons.

Cameron's last note fades in the night, and claps thunder across the room. With a shy smile, he nods at the audience. Around our table, people are stuffing wads of bills into the baskets. He collects fifteen dollars. At the back of the Lounge, Professor Brodrick stands, clapping wildly.

Cameron claims back his seat next to me with a sardonic smile. "Glad you kept that promise."

"That was extraordinarily beautiful, Cameron," I say.

I stare at my fake uncle as Mr. Becker and Cameron exchange a couple of pleasantries. Jörg's expression has a curious shadow as he strokes his chin. Mother described Jörg as an artistic spirit. I'd pay dearly to know what he's feeling. Is it envy? Is it admiration?

A hushed murmur cuts across the Lounge.

Captain Turner, in his dark uniform, walks toward the stage.

I hold my breath, expecting he'll reveal that a German submarine lurks in the vicinity.

"Good evening, ladies and gents. It is my hope that you're enjoying the Seamen's Charities," he says. "Let me begin by thanking the performers and the audience for your generous contributions. As you might know, we'll soon be entering the war zone. We've had reports of submarine activity near the coasts of Ireland and England."

An alarmed whisper rolls across the Lounge. Captain Turner raises his voice. "However, when we enter the war zone, we shall be under the protection of the Royal Navy."

"Are we in any danger, Captain?" asks a man.

"In wartime, there's always a factor of danger at play, but I must stress that there's no cause for alarm. Tomorrow, we'll steam at full speed to arrive in Liverpool in a timely manner and outrun any submarines. Before I leave you for the night, I would like to request your collaboration. You might have seen my crew extinguishing the ship's outboard lights, blacking out portholes, and blocking all skylights. I ask you to keep your curtains drawn, and to the gentlemen, please do not light cigarettes while out on deck. I bid you all good night."

The captain walks off the stage and out of the Lounge, leaving behind him a bustling medley of concern until the orchestra takes over and breaks the chords of a happy tune. Despite the music, panic skitters about, and thousands of gloomy remarks rise like a flock of angered birds.

"Excuse me," I say and head the same direction as the captain. If the life jacket notices were few on the white walls, now the sketches are everywhere, fireworks of ink reminding me of the danger.

I spin on my heel. All the doors are closed. The curtains are tightly drawn. Where to go? I can't escape.

"Alexandra," Cameron calls from the Lounge entrance.

I run out on the unlit deck. The cutting chill catches my breath as I dash amidships. The lifeboats are swung out, ropes groaning as their hulls swing merrily six stories over the sea. I grip the handrail with a shaky pulse and strain to see anything in the shadows. The wedge of the moon casts a silvery path on the rippling water. In the firmament, stars ebb behind ethereal clouds. It should be a beautiful night.

Something covers my shoulders. My numb fingers quickly grab Cameron's jacket. He stands next to me, gazing out at the ocean.

"You play piano," I mutter once the silence feels too heavy.

"My mother played at church." A cloud of vapor sifts out of his mouth. In response, a shiver runs through me.

Winds bluster across the deck, spraying cold sea mist on my face. "You didn't tell me you were going to play."

"It was a last-minute decision," he says. "I surprised you in the end, did I not?"

"It was a welcome distraction." What I won't admit is that he can soften me no matter how angry I am; it is such a great power to give to him freely. I imagine him in our house, in a knitted jumper, playing Christmas carols next to a frosted window. A smile trembles on my lips only to fall away. That house doesn't exist, and that life will never happen. I'm an heiress to an empty kingdom, a Miss Nothing with money and a death wish.

"Are you watching for Germans out here?" he asks me.

I glance behind us to make sure we're alone. "I'm not as afraid of those at sea as I am of those aboard."

"We're not at risk."

With a grunt, I spin on my heel. "I loathe that supreme optimism of yours." What is he not understanding? Or most likely, what is he not coming to terms with? Our possible demise? We'll arrive tomorrow in Liverpool. We've got no more time. It's gone. Invisible walls are squeezing us in. We might be saved—or we might not. His absolute unwillingness to accept we're in danger twists my guts.

If it's unwillingness at all—and not any lies shining between the lines.

"Alexa—" Cameron's voice fades behind the deck door I glide shut between us. I take the stairs, trotting down almost two steps at a time. A maid crosses my path, carrying pillows and blankets upstairs. Passengers mustn't feel safe sleeping near the waterline in case a torpedo strikes us in the dead of the night.

"Alexandra," Cameron says behind me. "Stop. There is something you need to know."

I don't look back, almost jumping off the last steps. What am I so afraid to hear? More delusional optimism? Does he know I love him? Is that what he has tried to tell me all along in those charged silences? If I let him, what will he say? That he loves me? Or has he been trying to find a way to turn me down gently? I can't stand the thought of losing him . . . having to mourn a maybe . . . something I almost had and lost.

It broke Jörg.

And it might break me too.

I wanted to have Cameron for two years, no matter how false our relationship might've been. But at first, I never wanted this to happen—to let love meddle. I always avoided getting to know Cameron precisely to avoid falling in love with him, because how could I force a man to love me back? The promise of money lured him into the deal. I could handle a business transaction. I couldn't bear opening my heart and risking him not wanting it. Now, nobody mentioned the *other* possibility—the possibility he might want it.

I want him to want me. But Cameron *cannot* love me. I can't *let* him love me. Though unintentionally, I've already put him in so much danger. I cannot claim him and condemn him into a permanent hide-and-seek with intelligence services. He would have my heart, but he would ruin his life, and I . . . I love him too much for that.

My whole body feels as if it's been bruised, my ego, my soul, everything has been discarded, and only one thing remains. My determination. Cameron must be protected. At all costs. Even from myself.

I seize the handle of my cabin's door, yet Cameron gently grabs my elbow, stopping me. "Alexandra, will you listen to me? I want to tell you something about your par—"

"We should start planning what we'll do next," I clip dryly, ignoring him. "Once everything is solved, I'll give you the money and we can part ways."

"Do you still think I want your money?"

"It's what we agreed on."

Cameron sighs. "I'm tired of this."

"It's about to end, for better or for worse." I yank the door open, running away from him. From the feeling of having him so close to me.

"That's not what I meant. And you really need to listen to me for a second. I won't let anything happen to you. Your—"

"I know what you meant, Cameron." Helplessness breaks my voice. I shrug his jacket off and hurl it at the sofa. "But what can I do? I have nothing."

Cameron raises his eyebrows and shuts us in with a firm click of the door.

I stand still, my chin high, but on the inside I crumble like a house of cards.

"You have nothing?" Pain washes across his face, draining all the color from it, including his redness due to the blustery weather on deck. His eyebrows drop over the overcast blue in his eyes. He parts his lips, but for a long while, he doesn't speak. "I can't believe you're saying that."

"What do I have, Cameron? Enlighten me because, for all I know, I have no parents, I have no home, no career, no friends left, I have no prospects or family or future."

"Me," he shouts. "You have *me*. I am right here."

I draw back, a hysterical snicker coursing out of my lips. "Are you? Right when I come to enjoy the idea of you and me being together for two years, it turns out that I can't have that either. They're stealing you away from me—"

"They're not stealing me away from you," Cameron cuts off with a grunt so dark it shuts me up. He points at himself with a curt motion and takes a step toward me. "I'm *here*."

I stare at him, my throat aflame, and retreat, hiding my hands behind me. This is making me look utterly ridiculous, like a little girl who's stubbornly refusing to wear a ribbon because it's red and not pink. "I can't give you anything but danger and pain. With me, there won't be a perfect life."

He raises his arms and drops them. "That's not how life works, Alexandra. Most times, we don't have the picture-perfect life. We have the messy and unexpected. But sometimes the messy and unexpected are what we needed all along. And I need *you*."

I recoil farther away, biting my lip. He's aloof no more. His eyes are wild, swimming with emotion, desperate to make me understand. Only I could pick a man who is cool as ice and turn him into a wreck.

"Why are you so scared of admitting you love me?" Cameron asks.

"Money taints relationships. How can a relationship start off as a business deal?"

"I don't want your money. My priorities have changed." His voice is unwavering. "Give me your heart instead."

And that is a plea from the bottom of his soul. A man out of breath begging not to drown. He's offering himself to me. A man imploring my love. I hate myself for feeling so wanted, so coveted, so cherished, while I stand as lifeless as a statue.

"You're a fool," I whisper. "I'm dangerous to you."

"And it's still my choice to love you despite it all."

My mother's words wash through me. *It's a sensible type of love, but is it the kind of love I want?*

Maybe Cameron doesn't want to be safe. Maybe Cameron is addicted to danger. Perhaps growing up on the streets wired him that way. There's no other reason why he'd want me. But does it really matter why he wants me? My life is a big unknown from here on. I don't know if it'll end when we make landfall or in ninety years. Yet he's accepted me and everything that comes along for the ride. How can I shun such devotion? How can I stare at him and deny what I feel for him? Perfect life or not, I'd be happy to die with him.

I blink, coming back to the cabin, and stare into his blue eyes. Damned be the consequences. All my objections melt away, leaving only a heart that, once given a voice, is screaming for Cameron, for his arms, those lips, the release of the blinding passion in my veins.

"I think I'll let you claim that kiss I owe you now," I say.

"Thank God," he grunts, walking toward me. He grabs my face and pulls me to his mouth, stealing my breath away. Licks of delicious pleasure stir inside me, and beating the need to come up for air, I tilt my head and drown in a new kiss, his burning lips molding onto mine.

Cameron tastes of alcohol and strawberries. If freedom had a taste, that'd be its flavor. And his tongue—it plays with mine, brushing, searching, caressing. His hands, once done cupping my face, sprawl on my back, pulling me toward his body, hips against hips, closer than I've ever been to him or any other man.

Elation cuts through me, raw with need. Cameron's kiss in Central Park was repressed, all the passion he could hold buried underneath composure and decorum, but this one lets it all loose. It flips my world upside down. I've never been kissed like this, with lips so bold, with kisses so deep it's almost as if he were kissing my soul. Elijah's kisses made me float with butterflies, pecks shy and slow, but Cameron's melt me head to toe.

I sink my fingers into his hair, curling his perfectly slicked-back locks. "Do you regret coming all this way with me?"

A puff of air runs through his nose, something like a chuckle. With a thumb, he caresses my swollen lips, and he pecks at them, once, twice, three times. My pulse stutters, pleasure curling my toes inside my shoes.

"I didn't. I don't. And never will I regret it. *Never.*"

I rise on my tiptoes, my arms going around his neck. His mouth traces my jaw, the curve of my neck, making me gasp. A need like thirst takes control of me. I ache for him. Having Cameron kiss me isn't enough. I need to lose myself in his body, melt in this fire, in his soul. "Don't leave my cabin tonight."

Cameron freezes on my neck and slowly comes back up. "I can sleep with you if you need—"

I put my finger on his mouth and caress his swollen bottom lip, wiping the rouge from my kiss. "I don't want to sleep."

There's a shift in his eyes. "Alexandra." All of a sudden, he's out of breath. The way he says my name is reverent. "You needn't rush. I'll be with you until death do us part."

"And what if death does us part tomorrow?" I wonder. "What if it does us part next week? Would you let me go without knowing what it is like to be loved and desired? Will you leave in the morning if I give myself to you?"

His brief smile is tenderly beautiful. "Not in the morning, not in the dusk. Not in a million years."

"Then let me have you," I whisper, like a plea.

With a stare so deep it undresses my soul, all Cameron says is "I'm yours."

Chapter Twenty-Six

May 7, 1915—Day 7 of 7

A deep, mournful horn pries me from the cobwebs of a dreamless sleep. Blinking, I unbury my head from the crook of . . . Cameron's neck. The pale morning light streams through a curtain gap. I still retain the warmth from Cameron's body.

As I'm about to merrily curl in with him, the horn blares once more, and the contrast with the usual morning silence sets an empty weight in my stomach.

Cameron rubs his eyes. "What the . . . ?"

I caress his bare chest. It's perfectly smooth—lean, straight lines covered by faint blond hair. Lust consumes me from the inside out. This gorgeous man is all *mine.*

His blue eyes flick toward me. I stare at his serious expression, unsure whether I made a mistake. Yesterday it was far easier. This morning, things are different. He's no longer lost in desire. I've given myself to him, and no matter his promises, this is where the truth will come up. He either loves me more or has lost all respect for me.

A dreamy smile shows on his lips. "Good morning, my love."

"Good morning," I reply as my hand retreats. He catches it and presses his mouth against my knuckles.

"How are we this morning?"

My breath hitches, remembering last night's sweet but raw feverish kisses; Cameron's unhesitant touch on me; his hoarse voice whispering my name; his muted moans making my blood race; his breath and licks on my skin. "We're quite well."

He raises an eyebrow. "Are we? Not tired?"

Considering we were awake until the dead of night, I should be. I bite my lip to repress my smile. "No."

He harrumphs, taking a look down to where our chests meet. He's seen my body, my bare flesh, counted the moles on my skin, found a birthmark on my back. Yet . . . I'll never get used to his gaze gliding across me, the tight heat imploding from within me.

He rolls over, making me gasp, and imprisons me under him. Cameron's smile turns wolfish and tangles my body in knots of anticipation.

He lowers his head and kisses me. "I must not have done it right if you're not tired."

I brush our noses. "On the contrary, you've done all the right things." I've not lost his respect, but in me still shines a sliver of doubt. "I still can't fathom why you want me."

"Icy eyes on a beautiful sun-kissed face," he whispers, "full, kissable lips; a warm, smooth, lean body—yes, a total mystery."

I chuckle, heat spreading in my cheeks and my belly. "Come now, you knew what I meant, you scoundrel."

He kisses me, cupping my face as if he was revering me. He trails my bottom lip with his thumb. "I know what you meant. You're definitely an insufferable creature. You turn my life upside down, and you test my patience, without a shadow of a doubt. You're entitled, impatient, stubborn, and opinionated."

"And you think that's good?"

He smiles at my widening eyes and entwines our hands against the pillows. "I do. Because you make my life interesting, thrilling, and new every single day. You said you'd never get bored with me? I'm the one who'll never get bored."

"And what about this?" I seek out his lips.

He pulls away, snorting.

I wiggle my hands to free myself, but he pins me against the mattress. Instead, I tangle my legs around his waist. "I've given myself to you without walking down the aisle."

Cameron buries his nose in the crook of my neck, kissing me where my vein throbs. "Works for me. Consider us married. I'll never leave now. I'm addicted."

My eyes flutter shut. "Do we have to leave the bed?"

"That's the last thing I want," he mutters on my shoulder.

The mournful horn of the *Lusitania* goes off again. Cameron grunts and plops his head into the messy locks of my hair. "No way to concentrate with that goddamn horn blaring every other minute."

"Why are they sounding it?" I wonder aloud, reality's claws dragging me away from the lofty heights of Cameron's arms.

"I don't know, but you smell of lavender, and that makes it so hard for me to pull away." His lazy harrumph sends a flutter down my belly, but he gives me a kiss and rolls to the edge of the bed. I immediately miss him. I caress his back as he grabs his pants from where he dropped them last night. Working on sliding his legs into his trousers, he casts a sideways look at me and smirks.

The horn whines again, making his smile drop.

"Wretched horn," he mutters, pushing himself upward.

Outside the bed, temperatures have dipped overnight, and I'm too self-conscious to amble around my cabin naked. Cameron locked the doors last night, but I still fear someone with a key might walk in on me. I wrap the sheet around me and bounce out of my narrow bed, tiny goosebumps running along my arms.

Cameron draws the curtain open, and I join him by the window. A cloudy mist sifts into the promenade, the sea hidden under a cloak of brume.

"They're warning nearby ships because of the fog," he says.

"It'll also reveal our position to U-boats."

Cameron kisses my forehead. "If they can't see us, they can't strike."

"Do you think the authorities will be in Liverpool?"

"They will be," Cameron says against my forehead. "I promise you, Alexandra."

All of a sudden, my full name sounds too serious. "Alix. Call me Alix."

His smile turns tender, softening the angles of his face so much he looks like a boy. "Alix." He says it with reverence, lightheartedness, and so much purity it fills my chest with love. He inhales to say something but presses his lips shut.

"What?"

"Nothing." He caresses my cheek. "I love you, that's all."

I smile. "Go on, have the bathroom. I'll wait."

Cameron washes and gets dressed in a knitted jumper and his trousers. In the time he's away at the Barbershop, I step into the tub. After last night, I'm sore in places I didn't think possible. Cameron is a tender lover, but we made love twice last night and the second time was rougher than the first.

Sleep threatens to pull me beneath the warm water, so I turn my relaxing ablution into an economical wash. I dry myself with a soft towel and put on a blue nautical wool dress. It's one of the warmest outfits I own. After last night, I don't want to see anyone just yet if only to live in my memories with Cameron a bit longer, so I don't call for Ilse. I put half my hair up in a white ribbon on my own.

Pinching my cheeks, I can't sweep away an anxious feeling. I don't know if it's the horn, still blaring in the fog, fear of lurking U-boats, or that our arrival in Liverpool seems imminent. Will Mr. Becker and Ilse turn on us, or will they help us escape? Will the authorities arrest Jörg?

On the promenade beyond my porthole, fog, far from dwindling, has become denser, and the only passengers who brave the weather do it under the layers of their best coats and capes.

My fingertips brush the cover of the photo album, still on the desk. There were a few photographs left to browse through. I might as well stay busy so I don't go mad wondering what will happen once we dock.

I flick open the tome, and as the cover clacks against the wood, a photograph flies out. Rolling my eyes, I snatch it from the floor, but when I'm about to put it back, the image in it stops me in my tracks.

And my heart with it.

I've never seen this photograph. It wasn't among my parents' belongings, not among their documents, or in the photo albums. I'm sure of it.

It's a portrait of my parents and a boy. My parents were smiling at the camera. Behind them, a blurry Christmas tree, the glow from the candles like phantasmal halos. My father hugged the boy with one arm.

The boy with haunted eyes. The boy who I doubt ever cared that I existed. The boy who took me years to forget.

My father's assistant.

Cameron.

In the portrait, he's blurry, not looking directly at the camera, as if he'd had a moment of shyness and the lens had caught him as he moved, but he's got a small smile on his lips. A part of me laughs it off because it's impossible. This boy can't be *him*. I had never seen him so close. But now I do. And . . . after learning Cameron's eyes, his face, his mannerisms, I can safely say this boy looks like him, only younger.

My fingers numb, my blood buzzes in my head. Slowly, I turn over the photograph, and clear as day, in handwriting, there is his name. Cameron Asher.

And under his name, those numbers—coordinates.

Coordinates Cameron knew how to decipher.

"He lied to me," I whisper with numb lips. Fake Addie. All those silences and half-finished sentences, there they are. The pity, the dark shadows dancing in his stare. The fact he knew what a numbers station was. The way he just *knows* how to slink into places and his knack for the forbidden. The cold blood. The confidence. How dismissive he's been. What a good liar he is. How he's ready for violence. How assured he's been through this whole charade while assuring me I won't get hurt. Mr. Becker's comment about a mentor . . .

My father was his mentor.

A spy mentor.

Cameron is a *spy*.

A liar. Smoke and mirrors. A fraud.

Dread knots around my throat. A nervous twinge sets in my knees. My back dampens with cold sweat. My soul screams, but my astonishment won't let me find my voice.

How have I been so *blind*?

On the other side of the door, Cameron announces himself with a firm knock. The whine of the door should make me turn, but I don't.

"Ready for breakfast?" he asks.

I turn. And as my eyes fall on him, I can't recognize him anymore. He still looks like the man who held me in his arms last night, but for all intents and purposes, he's a complete stranger.

"Cameron, did you know my parents?" I ask, voice thin yet pulled tight as a violin string. "Were you my father's assistant years ago?"

When I lift the photograph, still pinched faintly between my fingers, his eyes cloud.

He sighs and falls silent for a full minute. The pressure builds up in the cabin, air thick with tension. The only sound is that of the *Lusitania*, humming across the sea in a constant singsong of swish-swash. My heart races, ready to hear the bad news, and apprehension skitters through me, making me fidget.

"I did. Your father trained me to be a spy. Your parents sent me to protect you."

Chapter Twenty-Seven

The photograph slips from my fingertips, and it flaps on the floor at the same time my blood drops to my feet. Head dizzy, all I can do is huff. "If this is your idea of a jest, you have such a twisted sense of humor."

"It's not a jest. You saw the photograph."

I take a step back. "I know what I've seen. But it's impossible. I can't. I don't believe it."

"I know you can't, but it's the truth. While we were out on deck last night, I was about to tell you. And I've been meaning to tell you, many times. I just . . . didn't know how. So, I slipped the photograph into the album, hoping that you'd find it out at last." He shakes his head, his conflicted smile curling up. "You didn't remember me from the time I worked for your father."

He chuckles and shakes his head ever so slightly. The softest movement, but it's as though he's *disappointed.*

I stop breathing until my lungs burn. Cold shivers run down my back. I want to ask him to stop lying, to stop *teasing* me, because this must be a cruel jest.

"Because I refused to think of you," I growl. "Once you vanished, you were gone for good."

He pulls a face but nods. "That's fair."

"Why did you have that photograph? How? Why wasn't it in the albums?"

"It was never in your or your parents' possession. One of your father's associates gave it to me."

"One of my father's *spies*," I spit between my teeth.

"That was the way your father's associate found me," he continues, almost as if he hadn't heard me. "He never knew what the list was, where your parents decided to hide it, or in what format they kept it. The team had scattered by then, your parents' orders. But he came to check in on you and make sure I was carrying out your parents' mission."

"One of my father's spies . . ." I repeat, but this time my voice is lighter as my mind tries to configure my parents conducting late-night secret meetings with their team while I was asleep two floors above. "Just like you. The list Jörg was looking for."

"The coordinates and names on the back are all the spies in their ring, yes. Thanks to the coordinates, I located the areas where they live, where their safe houses are. They're all people in high places, positions of power. It's not a surprise Germany wants it. The members of the ring are likely funneling American help to England."

"How did my parents send you?" For a moment, my heart leaps with the ridiculous possibility my parents are alive and that's what he's been hiding from me all this time. "Does that mean they are alive?"

His eyes look like crystalline waters, glass-looking honesty. "No. They're not."

The weight of the world crumbles on me again, like mourning them a second time. A few seconds believing miracles could happen, only for hope to set my grief free.

My eyes well, and my body recoils, as if I'd been slapped. A shock as strong as the cold waters of the Atlantic.

"I . . . remember my name in that telegram in your apartment," I whisper, then fall as silent as the dead. I'm not sure why I recall it, as vivid as daylight. Perhaps, because it was the first dead giveaway. The first hint that Cameron was hiding something. "Were you talking to my parents?"

He inhales through his nose. "It was the first telegram they sent me. I kept it."

Why did they never trust me? Why did they keep me oblivious and trust Cameron instead? The cabin skews, the edges fading like a dying flame. I grab the desk behind me. "That inkling I had the first time I saw you . . . I felt like I knew you."

Why did I not hear my inner instinct? Why? Just because he's handsome? Just because I'm in love with him?

Cameron strokes my cheek, and it's as if he scalded me. I slap his hand off, tumbling aside. "Do not touch me."

"I need you to listen to me."

I shake my head. "Why did you not tell me the truth when we met?" I spit, hating how weak and broken I sound.

"I couldn't tell you." His voice is stern, no justification wavering in it. Betrayal hurts like a blade tearing into my flesh. "I was honoring your parents."

I clamp my mouth shut to stop the stream of insults I want to yell. "Honoring them? They should've honored *me*. By being honest with me. Did they know that Jörg was going to kill them?"

"They knew Jörg was around, yes. But not that he would succeed. Obviously. None of us believed that."

I let out a sigh that brings no relief. "Lord."

He comes to me. "Alix."

Hearing my pet name, I grant him a dirty look. "Alexandra."

Cameron stops, a glint of guilt rushing through him. He nods, a muscle feathering in his jaw. "Alexandra."

"You've put on such a remarkable show of cold blood, acting as if everything was new to you," I mutter through my gritted jaw. So many things make sense, many reactions that, in hindsight, should've given Cameron away. I squeeze my eyes shut, a bitter smile tightening my face. "You're indeed such a good actor."

"I'm the person your father trained me to be."

I let out a shuddery breath and cross my arms tightly over my chest. My legs tremble. I don't count on them to support me for long. "So, you're a spy too?"

"I used to be one, yes. Not anymore. Remember I told you about my childhood—"

"I cannot care about your childhood now, Cameron."

He sighs. "The night we met—"

"The night you came into my life with lies," I hiss.

He walks away, brushing his face and his hair, and sits down on the edge of the couch, his knee slightly bouncing. "Remember my father, yes? The policeman? It turns out my father met your parents years ago—"

"That's a lie."

"They helped him settle as a private investigator. He was their middleman and kept them informed on what was happening around them." His voice has a mocking quality, as if he is greatly amused and displeased at once. "After my father learned I'd become a thief, he sent me to your father to set me back on track. My father was still getting on his feet, founding his agency, and didn't have time to deal with me. I became your father's protégé. He trained me as a spy, physically and emotionally, taught me the trade, and I started working for him."

My eyes brim with tears, my entire being freezing in dull ice. "And you did for five years. Why did you disappear without a trace?"

"Because your father . . . made a fatal mistake. One day, he sent me on a surveillance round. Routine questions. Nothing too hard or dangerous. I asked my father to let me go on my own. I was almost seventeen. I joked that I could take it. But my father, call it policeman intuition, refused to let me go alone.

"It turns out, the people your father had sent me to were not the ones he thought I'd be meeting. They were impersonators. Things took a dark turn. We pulled guns, had to run, hide, and find a way out under gunfire. I'll never forget, looking at my father across the room and seeing the fear in his eyes. That moment, I felt forsaken. Betrayed.

Humiliated. Your father had grown complacent, he'd lowered his guard, and we were going to die because of an oversight.

"My father was shot. I was about to die. They held me at gunpoint. Only your father's intervention at the last second saved me. But my father . . . he didn't make it." He squeezes his eyes shut. "He died in my arms."

Shame pools under my cheeks. Oh, Dad. "I'm sorry." A sliver of compassion breaks through my chest, even when he's openly lied to me about his father. He always spoke as though he were still alive.

"I was angry at your father for a long time, Alexandra. I disappeared because I needed to find something as far as possible from the darkness of your family. Something to soothe the desire for vengeance running through my veins. I traded guns for books. Enemies for children. Danger for peace. But I never forgave your father."

I stay silent for a long time, staring at the wall. "Then why did you come . . . *help* me, if you hated my father so much?"

Cameron sucks in his lips. "Your parents contacted me in late December last year. The tone in the telegram alone raised the hairs on my arms, so very reluctantly, I accepted to meet them. For old times' sake. They didn't share much, but they told me they'd been tipped off about a German spy ring trying to make their way into America. I'd never seen your parents in such distress before. That shake in their voices, the same fear I saw in my father's eyes flashing through *their* eyes . . . And do you know what they were terrified of losing? Not their lives. *You.* They were scared for you. It made me understand that the fear I saw in my father's eyes that day was fear for *me*, not himself."

"What did they ask you to do?"

"They asked me to protect you if anything happened to them. They ordered me not to intervene, even if their lives were in danger. They wanted you safe. And just like that, I was awarded access to you. Something they'd never allowed."

Nothing beats in my chest, as if I'd been hollowed out. One minute, there's a tick, and the next, it's gone. "I was only a mission to you."

"At first, yes. You were. And I won't lie. While they were still alive during those first weeks of January, I wanted to get back at your father. They'd given me addresses, places you frequented, so I could find you if anything happened. While they were busy, I planned to fully take advantage of their blessing to be close to you. I'd walk into your life and make you fall in love with me. I laughed at the way your parents would've hated seeing us betrothed. Me, becoming their son-in-law. Then, I fantasized about breaking your heart and ruining your reputation. So your father knew what loss felt like."

My mouth falls open, and my back bumps against the wall. Serendipity was never at play for us. He dug his way into my innermost circle of acquaintances. And what about last night? What comes next? "You're playing with me. All this time . . . you wanted to hurt me."

He's used me, made me fall in love, and he's going to break me next.

"No." Cameron closes his eyes. "I love you."

I let out a shaky guffaw, pressing against the wall, my nails sinking into the wool of my dress. "Don't resort to that. I don't believe you."

"It's true, I love you," he counters, scrambling to his feet. "That was my initial plan, but when . . . when your parents died, and I met you . . . and I saw your will to live and outsmart the lie? Your intuition? Your wit? That was *breathtaking*, Alexandra."

I cross my arms. "Spare me your lies."

"I'm not *lying*. It didn't happen overnight." He steps forward. "I was resentful for a long while. In the beginning, it was only revenge. And then it was a mission. And then you offered me money, and I found just another way to use you, if only for those children in Brooklyn. Remember them?"

"Oh, how *noble* of you."

"But you . . ." he hisses. "You awed me with your independence and tenacity. And you were so heartbroken . . . I couldn't think of using you anymore. You became someone I tolerated, then a friend. You slowly erased my grief and my resentment, and I found myself admiring you, then falling in love with you. With your beauty, with your thoughts, with your sadness. With your cleverness and stubbornness and courage. You didn't hide. You charged ahead at life. And in the short span of a few months, I became wholeheartedly yours."

"I can't believe you did this to me," I spit, biting every word. "How did you let me go about with all these histrionics and ridiculous plans?"

"They're not ridiculous. I was close to breaking your parents' wishes and telling you, so, *so* many times. But your parents were clear. They wanted you safe from the danger of the spying world and to never, *ever*, be involved in it. They never wanted you to know. They begged me not to tell you. In my book, those were orders to abide by. Especially in death."

He's speaking of duty and permission. He only accepted my offer because my parents asked him to. "So why did you do it? Why did you tell me all of this now?"

He shrugs, opening his arms. "Because seeing you so heartbroken broke me. Because I want you to feel better. To know you're safe. That you'll be all right. Because after everything that happened between you and me last night, I couldn't begin this relationship with lies. I couldn't stand it anymore, Alexandra."

I chuckle, clenching my jaw. "Right when I thought I could trust you . . . you were also a lie. Has anyone ever loved me? Good Lord, I am alone in the world."

In two strides, Cameron closes the distance between us, grabs my hands, and puts them on his chest.

I try to slide them away, but he presses them harder against him.

"You have me," he whispers. "I am yours. I want to marry you."

"What makes you think I will marry you after this?" I ask as pure revulsion moves through my chest. "I hate my parents. For not telling me. For not trusting me. For not saying goodbye. And I hate *you*."

A muscle twitches in his jaw, but other than that, my disgust seems not to faze him. He bores his gaze into me deeper than before, if anything. "It's your right to hate them. Hate me. Hate us all." His tone is linear, unforgiving.

All this time. . . I could've been reassured with the truth. I could've worked with my parents. And if we had died, we would've done so as family.

"I need to be alone."

"I understand you're angry now, but you can still trust me. I'm your friend, your lover—"

"My nothing," I hiss. "*Nothing*, Cameron. You're nothing to me. Go away."

Cameron's jaw twitches. It seems as if he wants to say something else, but he nods, taking a reluctant step back.

I grit my teeth while his footsteps retreat. The door closes with a too-loud click. This entire steamer is as silent as a tomb. No laughs, no cheerful voices, no music. Nothing but steam and the swash of water. And this morning . . . this morning has dawned, choking me with death, lies, and dread.

I knew it. I knew he was hiding something. I can't believe he's done this to me. Desperation dizzies me, and my chest heaves up and down. I'm a sad clown everyone mocks. Nobody respects me. Nobody loves me.

A scream passes my lips, echoing on the walls. I snatch a pen off the desk and hurl it at the door. It hits the jamb, sending a splash of ink away before it falls flat on the carpet.

I collapse on my knees, sobs breaking out from my very soul. My chest hurts as if it were tearing open. I crumple my dress in my fists, trying to keep myself in one piece.

How small I've always been. A child in a world of adults. How powerless. I allowed myself to love, to trust, while I was nothing but a game. A game for my parents. A game for my fake fiancé. A game for the spies around me.

I sob until I'm empty, until my crying gives in to weeping, then whimpers, and all my strength has vanished. As if hollowed out, my tears dry, and only a dull pain remains. My head is abuzz, swimming in darkness.

Tired. I'm tired.

Gathering my last shreds of pride, I help myself up by grabbing the edge of the desk.

Behind me, the door creaks open. "I said I wanted to be alone. Go away, Cameron."

But the door slams shut, making me turn.

It's not Cameron.

It's Jörg.

Chapter Twenty-Eight

"Uncle Nigel," I croak, after a moment to rescue the name from the depths of my memory. I blink to clear my wet eyelashes. "I was about to start packing my trunks. If you excuse me. Please send for Emily."

"I'm not sending for Emily."

I frown, taken aback by his inflexible reply, and head to the bedroom. "Very well. I'll pack myself."

"You don't need to pretend anymore."

I halt at the threshold. The air crystallizes around me, tipping down the temperature in the cabin. I've never known true fear until now. Something drums from within, wrenching my guts in a numbing embrace. A wild, frantic cry calls from afar, beckoning my basic survival instincts.

I glance at my hat atop a chest of drawers. The pins are my only weapon. I should've stolen a knife.

"I'm not sure I understand," I say, unaware how I found my voice, and pivot on my heel to him.

He's standing straight, both feet firmly planted on the floor, hands held behind him. Uncle Nigel isn't in this cabin with me; Jörg is.

His smile tilts with sweet disdain. "One of the pursers merrily asked me if the pen situation had been solved and requested I'd not be too hard on you."

I gulp a dry swallow. "Are you going to murder me?"

"God forbid." He chuckles.

"No," I say. "You need me to get into England, don't you?"

He stoops and snatches the photograph from the floor. "Where is the list, Alexandra?"

"There is no list," I say, panic freezing my muscles. I do my best not to look at the piece of photopaper in his hands.

His mouth curls downward. "Fine. Do you know whom I don't need?" He wags the photograph. "Mr. Asher. Maybe that will prompt you to speak."

That lunges me forward. If he's done anything to Cameron, I'll kill him. "What have you done to Cameron?"

"Nothing. Yet."

"Yet," I echo, halting inches from him.

Jörg doesn't move but flashes an empty smile. *Get away from this man,* my brain barks, yet my feet don't budge.

"You will be an obedient girl if you want to ensure he's safe. Do you think you'll be able to do that, Alexandra? Lest he does not mean anything to you, and in said case, I do not think you'll pose any problem if I throw him—"

"Do not even think about it."

"So, he means something to you after all." He points at me with the photograph. "I must admit, I was not sure."

"You're ridiculous if you think I'll do as you say."

He ambles around the cabin. "Not even for Mr. Asher?"

I have no reply for that, so he continues, "You will remain in this cabin. Don't try to cry for help. The crew has been alerted you are going through an episode of hysteria and won't entertain you."

I grit my teeth, a spark of fury igniting in my chest. The thought I'm in danger wouldn't even cross their minds. "Do you think you'll get away with this?"

He smiles, tosses the photograph onto my desk, and snatches my hairbrush instead. "Of course I do. Look at how the world works, sweet Niece. With the snap of two fingers I can put together or undo your life. You were very clever to find yourself a man to advocate for you, but people like me, we always win."

"It must've been hard for you to see me every day, a living image of my mother," I say.

"You're the living portrait of your mother indeed, but you're incurring a major error, and that's assuming I have feelings for das Straßenmädchen."

"I don't know what that means, but your tone alone makes it clear it's not a pretty word. Is it true you don't have feelings for her anymore if you need to insult her? She might be dead, but she still makes you *feel*."

He lowers the brush onto the desk, rage moving on his face. "Last chance to tell me, Where is the list?"

I recoil toward the bedroom, but Jörg snags at my arm.

"I told you there's no such thing as a list," I spit, stiffening with fear.

"I guess you don't love your Cameron as much as you claim," Jörg says with sufficiency. "Love is such a cheap feeling after all."

"Don't dare put a hand on him." I lash out and smack his jaw. Then, I worm out of his grasp like my father taught me and whirl on my heel, breaking into a run.

But two steps away, Jörg ensnares my waist and drags me back.

"Don't hurt Cameron," I scream, kicking the air.

"I doubt I'll need to do it myself; something sharper will do the job," he says with a matter-of-fact voice as he throws me on the couch.

I land hard against the back, my mind configuring a reflective blade sliding into Cameron's abdomen. My fear festers into rage. He stole my parents from me. I won't let him take Cameron away from me too.

I pounce toward Jörg. I'm going to gouge his eyes out and make him chew on them. But his hand meets my cheek, and it slaps me back onto the couch. I fall on the seat, the world dizzy on the edges, my skull on fire.

Jörg fishes a small bottle out of his pocket. "Hopefully, in a couple of hours you shall feel more cooperative."

He uncaps it with a twist and pushes it to my lips.

I lash out and hit his leg, making him reel with a grunt.

Silence snakes over the cabin. Our gazes meet, a challenge running between us.

He sighs, and with a scowl, he lunges forward again. "Damn girl."

I stomp my heel on his shin. "Go to hell."

Jörg flinches but captures my head in the coil of his arm and shoves the bottle to my lips, forcing them open.

The liquid pools on my tongue, bitterness producing a retch from within me.

I spit reddish droplets onto Jörg's spotless suit. "Is this laudanum? I've never had it before."

"There is always a first time, dear." Jörg gently taps me on the cheek. "I thought Mr. Asher's multiple visits to this cabin might have proven that by now."

"It could kill me," I say.

Jörg lets go of me, but as soon as I'm freed, a cloth parts my lips and muzzles me. Jörg harshly ties a knot on my nape, catching baby hairs in it.

I lift my hands, but he catches them.

"My, my, let's not be dramatic," he says, securing a rope around my wrists.

My eyelids grow heavy. My stifled scream for help drowns in the cloth. I'm small; my body is incapable of fighting the laudanum. For someone used to it, it might take some time to feel the effects, but in me, it's like claws dragging me down. My limbs grow heavy with tingles, and my stomach churns with nausea.

I kick, but my leg's strength fades as it swings upward. The world tumbles as Jörg snaps me up and drops me on the bed.

⁂

The light has changed when my eyes lazily blink open. Bright sunshine on the white walls blinds me. I cover my face with an arm, rolling on my back. A bitter aftertaste on my tongue and a balmy numbness remain from the laudanum.

Everything is silent, the engine roaring in the absence of human voices. Has Jörg killed all the passengers?

Atop the chiffonier rests a glass of water. I lick my lips only to discover I'm parched like dried-out mud. With a roll out of bed, my legs give, and I trip, painfully hitting the floor with a knee. My head spins, and the world frays at its edges. I brush my temple and wait until the floor is steady and safe enough for me.

With weak limbs, I scramble to the chest and reach for the glass. As the water passes my lips, it occurs to me it might be poisoned. I wait for any choking, burning, any sleep dragging me away, but my body only responds with gratitude. I empty the glass with greedy gulps and set it down, faintly holding onto the edge of the chest.

Jörg has ungagged me and untied me at some point. I open my mouth, but I repress the scream. Jörg can't know I'm awake. He might be outside the doors, which are most likely locked. And yelling for help won't do me any favors if it's true the crew believes I'm going through a hysteria episode.

I'm on my own, and time is running against me.

Cameron. His name washes through me with spine-chilling terror. What has Jörg done while I was asleep? The album is no longer on the desk. The photograph is gone. My trunk is open, rummaged through, things out of place. Where is Mr. Becker? And Ilse? Have they betrayed us?

I look around with head jerks, searching for a way out of this cabin. Fog lifted a long time ago. Sun sifts into my cabin with noon brightness.

"The portholes," I whisper. I can open them and climb outside. Maneuvering with my weak limbs might pose a problem, but I can't risk staying here.

I rush to the porthole and latch it open. The salty breeze hits my face, clearing my thoughts. I take a ravenous gulp of air and look back, worried the wind might snake below the cabin door.

I need to be swift.

Nailing my boot onto the bed frame, I haul myself up. It falters, the sole rattling on the frame, but it holds. It shall suffice.

I push myself outward and—

A hand appears in front of me.

"Need some assistance?" Mr. Becker asks.

I shoot him a dead look, balancing on the porthole. "Are you helping me?"

"You still don't trust me all that much, don't you?"

"Not quite, but I guess I have to," I mutter, snagging at his arm. He's smiling. A lurch of violence flips in my stomach. "Where is Cameron?"

"That's our next stop." Mr. Becker hoists me out by grabbing me under my arms. My boots land with a thud on the deck, my hazy body slumping in his hold.

"You all right?"

"Of course not," I grump, staring into his green eyes with dead disdain. "I've been drugged with laudanum."

"Moving will help you overcome the stupor," he says, straightening me.

A man and a woman saunter out on deck. Mr. Becker entwines our arms and steers me down the promenade, as if we were taking a pleasant stroll.

"Good afternoon," he greets in passing.

The promenade wobbles. I lay my head on his shoulder. "How long have I been out?"

"Four hours."

"Where is Ilse?" I whisper in a pang of nausea.

The wind moves Mr. Becker's hair over his forehead. "Retrieving all the documents and things Jörg took from you, including your mother's diaries. They'll be returned to your trunk. We imagined you'd like to keep them."

I clear my throat and nod. Oh, what an *imp* he is. I'm starting to take a liking to these two spies, much to my dismay. "I'd appreciate that." The sea breeze ruffles my hair, bringing minty roasted lamb scent. "What time is it?"

"One. Most people are having lunch, including, guess who?"

"Jörg."

"There you go. Cameron is belowdecks. I don't know the exact cabin, but I know he's in second class somewhere aft on E-Deck."

E-Deck. How did Jörg move him across decks and corridors without anyone noticing? Grief and fear shove me to the railings. The gates on the Shelter Deck between first and second class are open. We scurry in unnoticed as the few passengers flock to portside to watch a smudge of land gliding on the horizon for the first time this week. Ireland.

Inside the second-class entrance, chatter and clinks waltz through the well above the dining room. We rush down the robust cascading staircase, stupor lifting off me with each step I take. With it gone, I shrink the more I wonder what they've done to Cameron.

Finally, taking a staircase aft, we reach E-Deck.

"Where?" I ask Mr. Becker, going down the narrow steps into the hall.

Mr. Becker trots through the passageways, taking his time to browse every number.

"We don't have all day," I sneer, following him.

He lifts a finger. "I'm trying to think what cabin he'd choose." He ambles through the central corridor, the finger he's lifted at me now pressed against his lips. "Let's see," he mutters, opening a door. A loud shriek. "My apologies. Wrong cabin."

He closes the door and moves on to the next, making my eyes roll.

"This must be the one." A sturdy door sandwiched between two other cabins portside. Nothing gives away that it's more special than the others. He tries the doorknob, but it's locked.

"Perfect," he mutters, producing a shiny key from his pocket.

"I take it Jörg still believes you're on his side," I say as he inserts the key into the lock.

"He might guess any moment I'm not." The door clicks open. Inside, Cameron is on the floor, sprawled against the wall.

"Cameron," I say, rushing inside. Kneeling, I stroke his chin, his cheek, his nose. He doesn't respond. He's cold to the touch, his lips white. I grab his shoulders and shake him, perhaps a bit more roughly than I intended.

Cameron's head sways and bonks downward.

"What has he done to him?"

Cameron sighs and stirs.

Mr. Becker feels his neck. "Laudanum. I'll bring water. Try to wake him up."

I shake Cameron, his back thumping on the wall. "Cam. I need you awake and moving."

His brow furrows.

I slap his cheek lightly. "I was too hard on you today, but I love you and I need you to wake up, Cameron."

Cameron's frown deepens, his eyelids fluttering.

"He's waking up," I yell.

Mr. Becker returns, kneels next to me, and pats Cameron on the cheek.

"Rise and shine, Fake Cousin-in-Law," he says, pushing Cam's head back. He puts a tumbler to his lips and slants the glass.

Water drifts into Cameron's mouth, overflowing from its corners.

"No, he'll choke," I hiss.

"He needs to move and make his body cooperate," Mr. Becker counters.

Cameron opens his eyes and spits the water. He falls sideways on my arm, coughing.

"There we go. He's awake now."

"What the . . . ?" Cameron gasps.

"That was unnecessary." I caress Cameron's back as a new fit of coughing rattles him.

He wrinkles my sleeve in a fistful.

"Breathe, it's all right."

Mr. Becker stands. "I'll go outside to keep watch. You have less than ten minutes. I'm being generous. Keep giving him water."

Chapter Twenty-Nine

Cameron's throat bobs as he gulps his second glass of water. His arm shakes, jouncing the liquid down his chin.

"How are you feeling?"

He puts the glass on the floor, nodding as vigorously as he can, which is better than a couple of minutes ago. "I'm good."

"Mr. Becker is outside, but we must hurry."

Cameron tries to rise, but his arm falters. His dose of laudanum must've been larger.

I hold him by the shoulder and assist him upward.

Cameron tumbles to the wall.

"Be honest, how are you?" I ask.

"As if I'd drunk ten glasses of rum," he admits. "But regaining my wits. Where am I?"

"A cabin in second class."

Shadows cross his face. "Did he hurt you?"

"No, he drugged me with laudanum and locked me in my cabin. Mr. Becker has helped me out, and Ilse is securing the documents and returning them to my trunk. Did he hurt you?"

"Not that I remember." He squints. A tinge of color is creeping into his skin again. "I was having a coffee in the Smoking Room. It had a bad aftertaste, and I felt dizzy. That must've been the laudanum. I remember I fought Jörg in my cabin, but that's as far as I can recall. Alexandra, I'm sorry about—"

Mr. Becker opens the door. "We must go."

I shake my head, as if to say *Later.* I barely remember the turns we took, but Mr. Becker does, striding ahead of us. Apparently, the only exit is through the same narrow staircase we used before.

As it comes into sight, Mr. Becker slows down and extends an arm to stop us.

My head shoots up to the top of the staircase and the shiny tanned boots slowly descending step by step. Jörg's features come into view, assessing the three of us with wary flicks. He's pressing his open jacket. He must have a gun on him.

I do my best not to retreat as he stops at the landing.

"Jörg," Mr. Becker says. "Ich bringe sie in ein anderes Zimmer."

My heart is in my throat, blocking my breath.

"Nein, bist du nicht," Jörg retorts. "Verräter."

Left and right, passageways lead into cabins. The sun creeps through the portholes, the waves outstretching in hazy mist and golden swells.

"When I tell you, run," Mr. Becker whispers. "Go to the bridge. I'll join you later."

"You're going nowhere," Jörg replies, sneaking his hand into his jacket.

"But—"

"No but, Alexandra. Run." Mr. Becker pounces toward Jörg and tackles him around the corner with a hard thud.

Cameron sprints for the staircase, towing me along, but I keep my neck craned toward the two men. Brutally lashing out at one another, Jörg slams Mr. Becker's head against the wall a couple of times. But Mr. Becker lunges forth. The last thing I see before I reach the upper deck is Mr. Becker falling atop Jörg, his fist connecting with his face.

On the D-Deck landing, Cameron halts in his tracks with a dead jerk and looks around.

I bump into him, taking in the smell of food and the clinks of silverware running across the corridor.

Cameron opens his mouth. "We should head—"

A shot reverberates from belowdecks, making Cameron and me wince down the corridor. Who was that? Who did we lose? An ally or an enemy?

The doors to the second-class dining room are thrown open, rows of long tables hosting guests across an elegant room filled with white columns. People and stewards stream outside, lured by the rumpus.

"Benson, Asher," Jörg shouts as we dash up the second-class grand staircase.

With a wrench of my heart, I look back as Cameron and I storm out on the portside promenade. Has he killed Mr. Becker?

Far away, rolling green hills and high cliffs glide by, a cool sunshine glimmering on the decks.

Cameron and I speed through the Shelter Deck among passengers suppressing gasps and murmurs.

I glance over my shoulder. Jörg slides outward on deck and almost tumbles to the floor. We fly by the windows of the medical quarters and the dining room. The doors of the Saloon's grand staircase creep nearer with every stride.

Amidships, Cameron swings on his free hand to swiftly leap over the fence delimiting third class and saloon.

Hitting the iron beams with my legs, I come to a painful halt. White dots fill my vision.

Cameron hastily grabs my waist and sweeps me over the handrail, and we both race down the promenade.

Jörg clears the fence with a leap, barking words in German. He's barely out of breath. Jörg is a highly trained soldier, more than his manicured looks give away.

Cameron takes me into the third-class entrance.

Glancing to my right, I locate the door to the stewardesses' quarters we used the first time we snuck into third class. "Where are we going?"

"We need to throw some dust in his eyes," Cameron says.

We jump down the stairs two steps at a time, winding through the encased D-Deck into the open hall on E-Deck.

Jörg's relentless footfalls resonate through the staircase. Just like last time, the E-Deck lobby spans into corridors left and right. Narrow stairs etch into F-Deck, and watertight doors behind us lead to the forward section.

I choose the latter, remembering the multiple pathways.

"No," Cameron mutters, pushing me to the narrow stairs to F-Deck. "This way."

He almost knocks a third-class man out of the way. The man grumbles in a Slavic language, swaying his wool flat cap.

Belowdecks, the engines are loud and the passageways narrow.

"There must be another staircase somewhere," Cameron whispers.

We take a couple of turns through a winding corridor with faint pools of light on linoleum floors, running into a porthole. The sea sloshes against the glass, turning sunshine into soggy streaks.

"Damn it, the other way around," Cameron mutters darkly.

I retrace our steps, Cameron trailing at my heels. My breath hitches as tanned boots take the first step of the staircase.

Cameron and I scuttle forward, hungrily sweeping for a staircase. One of the corridors ends at another porthole. Cameron and I run around the corner and into the next corridor, skidding to a stop at a dead end with three doors.

We're trapped.

"Fuck," Cameron says, drawing back.

We turn at the same time Jörg walks around the corner, hemming us in. A black revolver aimed at us catches the glint of the dim lights overhead.

"It seems you've got nowhere to run anymore," Jörg says, gloating and annoyance dragging in his voice. How dare we escape? How dare we make things difficult? We should've been easier to kill, clearly.

Jörg keeps his revolver trained on us, and time comes to a standstill.

This is it: He's going to shoot us in cold blood.

This is where it ends.

Cameron squeezes my hand, as if he were asking me not to let go of him, not even in death.

"I'm sorry," he whispers.

I look up, locking our gaze, hoping my eyes speak louder than words. No, I am. I'm sorry that he's going to die in the bowels of this ship. If Cameron had said no to my proposal, he'd be sleeping peacefully in his Greenwich Village apartment.

Sometimes I've wondered what I'd feel in the face of death. Fear? Grief? Ire? I'm surprised because I feel everything, and every feeling leads me to one specific point—Cameron, as though he were a point of convergence.

I can't accept this. I can't accept death before I can tell him I love him.

But if I can't tell him, I can show him.

And I would save him. Stop the bullet before it reaches him.

Something flashes in his eyes, and Cameron pulls me into his arms, shielding me with his body—to take the bullet for me. He's either seen my decision or decided the same as I did. This is true love. This is what pushed my parents together. This is what leads people to die for others.

A detonation bursts out across the walls, rippling through them like a wave, and the force shoves us to the floor with a violent jostle.

The world is sucked into silence, but my ears blare with high-pitched rings. Cameron's unmoving weight presses over me. I crack an eye open to the whirring lights on the ceiling and crane my neck to the corner. Jörg, several feet from me, stirs on the floor. His revolver lies abandoned, far from him.

All my thoughts vanish into thin air. I don't care what happened. If the Germans have struck, if the *Lusitania* has collided with a U-boat, if sabotage has happened aboard, if Jörg has already wounded me or Cameron.

I need to reach that gun.

Shoot Jörg in the head.

Kill him.

I crawl out from underneath Cameron and reach forward. Cameron seizes my skirt, but I have no time to celebrate that he's alive. My fingers tiptoe toward the barrel, inching excruciatingly slowly, until they meet the cold material.

I stand on shaky knees, pointing at Jörg, but a new blast rips through the walls. This time, the ear-piercing explosion seems to come from within the ship, and more powerful, it tears the *Lusitania* open like paper, cracks bursting across metal, the floor warping upward.

Cameron hooks his fingers around my sash and hurls me back, curling over me as black soot covers the fixtures overhead.

Chapter Thirty

The acid in the air burns my eyes and my throat. Choking on my own breath, I can only convulse until a hint of fresh air finds my nostrils.

My ears are ringing; underneath their din, a hiss growls like a hurt feline. The fixtures above shed an eerie red hue among undulating swirls of soot. Something cold swashes beneath me.

I reach out, my limbs splashing and plunging underneath ankle-deep water, and sit up, head spinning. At least five inches of water lap around me.

"Cameron," I scream and cough.

"I'm here," he shouts in my ear, straightening. "Let's move."

I roll on my knees and skew to my left, hitting the wall with a thud. Have I been wounded in the head, and my balance is affected? I rake my fingers through my hair, but I feel nothing as sticky as blood. Blinking, as Cameron also hits the wall with a thump, I feel the wall with my palm and realize there's nothing wrong with our balance. The *Lusitania* is listing forward.

We're sinking.

"We need to escape this hell," I whisper. Soot slinks into my breath, sending me into a coughing fit again.

Cameron helps me upward. Where's the exit? I wade through the flooded corridor, patting the wall, too busy to entertain the idea that Jörg stood in the corner before the explosions and now I don't know where he is.

Under the red light, I find the contour of the corner. And there are the stairs at the end of the narrow corridor, solid lines gleaming in red. The heavenly sight makes me plod ahead with leaps, but something latches around my ankle. Shrieking, I plunge flat on the water with a loud splash.

Jörg's claws, I assume, seize my calf, nails biting into my skin.

I scream underwater and desperately kick, paddling to spin upward and emerge, but I'm kept down, nailed to the floor.

Panic wins over me, and I swallow coppery water down my throat. Astonishment paralyzes me, liquid squeezing my lungs. I scream, but bubbles float upward. I must breathe. I *need* to. My nails scratch the floor as I try to break the surface.

A yank sets me free, and I surface to reddish darkness, gasping for a gust of unwelcome, suffocating air. I vomit warm torrents of smoky liquid. My throat is aflame with polluted salt, scorching wherever it reached. A cough rattles me, forcing me to bend forward.

Someone straightens me.

"Run," Cameron yells in my ear.

I push my heavy legs as if they were wading across mud, hurting from my hampered gait, every breath as sharp as the fine cut of a knife across my exhausted lungs. The air is thick and dark, leaving a revolting taste on my tongue.

I cover my face with my sleeve, unable to discern where I am anymore as my hand fumbles on the wall. My only solace is in knowing that Jörg cannot see us; the worst thing is knowing we all might die here.

My fingers finally graze the cold railings of the stairwell, soot shoving tears to my eyes.

"Thank God," I say under my breath.

Following up the steps is surprisingly easier, the tilt helping us. Water sloshes with us, invading the hall on E-Deck. It's pouring fast, grazing our calves by the time we set foot on the deck. Here, the lights are only a bit brighter than below, and people bump my shoulders as I slow down to inhale and cough.

Screams weave from afar, drowned out by the hissing coming from belowdecks. The portholes on the starboard side are dark, burning soot whirling into the hall through the hodgepodge of ripped metal from the staircase.

A torpedo must've struck us, or bombs must've gone off from within the ship. God, if there was anyone in those cabins. If we had chosen starboard instead of portside.

I take a handful of water to wash the soot off my eyes and mouth.

Cameron stays on the landing, gasping for air.

I look back, worried he might be hurt, but all he seems is out of breath, like me.

"Where's this soot coming from?" I shout.

"I think the boiler hatch had to be ripped—"

A shadow bursts from the water. Jörg, snatching Cameron's jumper, pulls and drags him into the rising flood.

"No," I scream as they both disappear.

I plunge back into the stairwell. They surface the next second, a mangle of arms and throwing fists.

I must do something. Remembering what my parents taught me, I balance myself on the handrail and haul up one of my legs, waiting until Cameron swings around and Jörg is in line with my heel.

I pitch it at the base of his neck, hitting him with a direct blow. It weakens him enough to release Cameron. With a powerful jab, Cameron throws Jörg into the water and tumbles upstairs with me.

"Are you well?" I shout over the noise.

Cameron nods, cupping my cheek; at the same time, he nudges me to the staircase. Other soaked passengers run with their life jackets to the upper decks with us. The space on D-Deck narrows among pressed bodies and hurried steps. My short breath races in and out through my weak throat. My head spins in the red lights, the world blurring and thrumming out, and my boots slip on the linoleum as we take the last turn in the staircase. My body throbs with the effort, itchy heat sticking my fully soaked wool dress to my skin.

People press, push, and crush me. I empty my mind in order to survive the tumbles, swallowed by tall walls closing in on me. I'm not here; I'm on a meadow near the openness of the sea, unfurling into grand horizons. I'm not suffocating, not being hurled in a moving tide of bodies.

Don't lose your footing, don't lose Cameron.

Tears blur my vision as Cameron and I reach the landing of C-Deck, my fingers barely curled around his jumper. The crowd spreads out, letting me breathe, and as ease loosens my chest, the red lights flicker and suddenly go out.

For a second, nobody moves, but all it takes is one scream for people to join the panic and stumble toward the faint sunshine filtering through the portholes of Shelter Deck.

Fright seeps into me, sending my feet clumsily among the passengers until I'm shoved out, spinning onto the promenade.

Cameron grabs my waist and pulls me into the cover of his arm. The world, so elegantly composed when Cameron and I ducked into third class, now skirmishes with fear and shouts.

The wide promenade quickly overcrowds with people holding onto whatever they can to avoid slipping down. Many hold onto others, dragging them down and knocking those who clamber behind.

Fingers claw toward Cameron's sleeve.

"Cameron," I shout. "Watch out."

The man holds onto him, pulling with a jerk. I grasp the railings, stopping Cameron from being dragged back.

Cameron grunts and kicks the man, who slips down and gets sucked into the swarm, trampled under two people. Deck chairs have gathered against the railings delimiting the promenade, but people have torn the gate open.

Near the first-class doors, a man is throwing fisticuffs for another man's lifebelt.

Cameron huddles with me and ushers me into the saloon hall.

"We need to gather my documents." Dread pitches my voice an octave higher. "They should be in my trunk."

Cameron halts dead, his eyes widening.

I look around. Water hasn't yet reached this part of the ship. Every piece of furniture that wasn't bolted to the floor has slipped—exotic potted plants and chairs mounted near the staircase—but I doubt some clutter is horrifying Cameron to such lengths.

"Where's Ilse? Do you think Jörg killed Mr.—"

Cameron shushes. "Listen."

My ears no longer ring, but they still buzz, and screams permeate the promenade, making me unable to hear anything beyond . . . the shouts coming from within the ship. People are yelling for help.

"Oh," I say.

Cameron and I whirl, trying to decipher where those desperate shrieks are coming from. With a shiver of intuition, I look up to the wrought iron cases surrounding the elevator shaft. A car is stuck, suspended in the air between decks.

"Oh, dear God," I mumble.

"Help us," a woman cries.

"We'll drown like animals," a man shouts. "Someone help us."

"We can't leave them there," I say over the din of shattering glass from the dining room.

Cameron's forehead fills with wrinkles, a dilemma flashing on his face.

"We need to help them," I insist.

People enter the hall but stalk aft through the corridors, not minding the people in the elevator. Except for one. Professor Brodrick, pale and disheveled, his hair windswept and his eyes wide.

"Cameron, Miss Benson," he says, out of breath. "How happy I am to find you both."

Cameron throws an arm around him. "Carlton. A relief."

"What happened to you both?"

I cough, my voice still weak. "We were belowdecks when the explosions went off. Please, you must help us take these people out of the elevator."

"We can't." Cameron's voice breaks, blue eyes glistering in his soot-stained features. "We'll never reach them before the ship sinks."

Professor Brodrick looks up, grabbing the wrought iron of the elevator case. "No."

"Cameron," I plead. "These people are imploring for their lives, knowing they'll drown in a box. We can't abandon them."

The tilt is steeper now, and iron groans in agonizing rales. The *Lusitania* might end up underwater in less than thirty minutes.

"Come." Cameron ushers me upstairs with an astonishing strength he's never used on me before. As I last glimpse onto C-Deck, water pours in through the promenade doors.

A ray of hope fills my chest when Cameron stops on A-Deck.

"Any ideas?" he asks, to both Professor Brodrick and me.

The car pokes a couple of inches over the edge of the floor, allowing me a peek inside—into the frantic, crazed eyes pleading for help, those dislocated jaws open in a terrified rictus. Gasping, I recoil as if the elevator were going up in flames, those expressions imprinted in my memory.

Cameron grips the wrought iron and tries to shake it, but it stands, unmovable, rigid.

"It's jammed," Professor Brodrick says, trying the upper part of the cage.

"Damn it," Cameron mutters.

They're too high to reach them from B-Deck; they're too low to help them from A-Deck.

"We need to help them, some way," I whisper.

Professor Brodrick and Cameron share a look. Carlton shakes his head.

"Right." Cameron seizes my wrist and pries me from the elevator.

"Cameron, no, please. We must save them."

I jerk, but Cameron relentlessly drags me down the stairs and the B-Deck corridor, pulling at my waist, taking me away by force. The elevator disappears behind a corner.

"No, Cameron. Professor Brodrick."

My cabin door is ajar. Cam pushes us both inside, ignoring my plea. Brodrick follows right in. Tears trickle down my cheeks, a cold hard stone setting into my bones. I'm on a sinking ship. All of this will lie on the ocean floor. Just like the *Titanic*—the orchestra bravely playing until the end, the cold water taking the lives of too many passengers. The horror stories are too close. Just three years ago.

"Cameron, we can't act like cowards," I beg. "Professor, please speak sense into him."

"Alexandra. Look at me." Cameron cups my face, tipping my head up. Desperation burns me like a wildfire, but determination is set in his pressed lips.

"You don't understand," I say. "If I survive this, their shrieks and terrified faces will haunt me. It's all I'll hear and see in the dead of the night."

"I know." He kisses me. "And I love you for being so selfless. But the ship's going down, and my duty is to protect you. Take a deep breath. Let's retrieve the documents."

I nod, taking a deep breath. I block out the distant screams, but a bitter lump rises in my chest nonetheless. Rubbing my sleeve all over my eyes, wiping fresh tears away, I venture into my bedroom, following Cameron and Professor Brodrick.

I open my trunk while they rummage in my wardrobe. There they are, the documents, the diaries, the photo albums. My eyes well again, and I'm unsure if it's the soot or my emotions. I must choose. What to save. What to lose.

I can't carry my mother's diaries. They're too bulky, too heavy. I kiss them goodbye.

I grab the testament, my locket, some photographs of my parents and myself, and the documents that prove that Jörg is a spy.

"Our life jackets are gone," Cameron says.

"Same in my cabin when I checked," Carlton says.

"It doesn't matter," Cameron mutters and points at me. "I'll put you into a lifeboat."

"First we need to snatch the information my parents kept, from their spy ring." Especially if we lost both Ilse and Mr. Becker.

"Excuse me, did you say spy ring?" Professor Brodrick says, still rummaging through the cabin for life jackets.

"A very long story." Cameron smiles, grabbing my jewelry box. From the bottom drawer, he digs out a rolled paper. "It's all here."

I take it into my arms. "How do we keep this from the water?"

Cameron rakes his fingers through his hair, letting out a sigh.

"Oh." Professor Brodrick steps in, waving. "My art pad. It's made of oilskin. It might not salvage the documents completely, but it will help."

Cameron grabs the professor's shoulders. "Absolutely, Carlton. Thank you. Where is your cabin?"

He points up. "On Boat Deck. If we rush, we might make it before the water reaches us."

Professor Brodrick and Cameron climb with me to the door, and we lumber one deck up among other passengers. Carlton's cabin is on the forward section of Boat Deck, numbered A-9. A spacious room with two beds and all the amenities.

Flipping the pad open, Carlton throws his charcoal pencils out, shoves my documents and photographs inside over some of his drawings, and hands it to Cameron.

Cameron squeezes his arm. "Thank you, Carlton."

"Likewise, Professor," I say.

"A pleasure," he says. "Now let's run."

Outside, the corridors are dark, the list a steep climb. The *Lusitania* is whirring, screeching, groaning, hissing. Panting and grunting,

Cameron, Professor Brodrick, and I trudge upward, following the strip of light up the hall.

As we enter the hall, a rattan chair tumbles in clumsy jerks, followed by other small objects. We manage to dodge the chair, but something hits my boot, round and shiny.

A thermos.

An idea skitters through me. Gasping, I stoop and grab it and unscrew the lid.

"Cameron, stick the art pad in here." The pad is soft. It can be folded.

"Brilliant thinking, Miss Benson," Professor Brodrick says.

Leaning on the wall, Cameron rolls and folds the pad and shoves it inside. "All right." He wrenches the lid into place again, sealing the thermos. "Carlton, my good friend. Go save yourself now. Thank you for everything you've done for us."

"We're in this together," Carlton says. "We'll be all right."

I place a hand on his arm. "A dangerous man is following us. A spy. You heard it yourself. He's hell-bent on murdering us. For your sake, it's better if you stay away from us now. You'll have better chances at survival."

Professor Brodrick looks at Cameron with quizzical eyes. "She jests."

"I wish she did," Cameron says, pulling him in for a hug with one arm. "Go save yourself."

"I see." He steps back. "Good luck to you, my friends. I hope we can see each other again soon."

I give Carlton a hug, too, my eyes welling. "Good luck to you."

Cameron and I watch him run out on the promenade. We stay still, looking through the open doorway, people blurring past it, the chaos, all trapped in a few split seconds.

Cameron sighs and grabs my arm. "Let's put you into a lifeboat."

"What about you?" I ask, trying not to pay heed to the terrified shouts in the elevator, hungry for life, begging for salvation.

"You don't have to worry about me."

"But I do," I say, my legs shaking. He's determined to bring me to a lifeboat, and in his reckless resolve he's jerking me to the portside promenade, but I can't keep walking without telling him I love him, that I won't leave him.

"No, Cameron, stop. Cameron, *stop at once*!"

I yank him back as he steps out on the Boat Deck. Inches away, a shadow hurtles down the promenade.

Cameron jumps into my arms as a whiff of the shadow caresses us. People scream, and a crash, wood against iron, bangs in the air.

Cameron locks crazed eyes with mine and huffs, clearly in disbelief that a lifeboat has nearly trampled him. Timidly, he steps out and peeks down the deck with me.

Half a lifeboat lies broken under the officers' bridge. Rivers of red run down the floor, following a trail of broken body parts from the poor souls who couldn't dodge the speeding projectile.

Reality clicks back in. The crew and men desperately try to swing the remaining lifeboats outward, shouting for more hands to push. People skitter up and down the deck. A man is shedding tears from bloodshot eyes. Near a skewed lifeboat, a man throws a punch at another one. A young couple hauls teak chairs overboard to help those who've jumped. A mother comforts her children while they wait. Several passengers, rushing in panic up the deck, slipping on the blood and sliding down the same as on a helter-skelter lighthouse at an amusement park.

The sea's maw is gobbling down the *Lusitania*, the tilt to starboard so pronounced we cannot even glimpse the line of the horizon from the port side.

"We need to move," I mutter, the mayhem kicking me into action.

Cameron nods, switching the thermos between his hands. "Starboard. You'll never get into a lifeboat portside."

Voices mention a German U-boat has torpedoed us. As I browse the promenade one more time, among the panicked crowd, my eyes find Jörg.

Chapter Thirty-One

Rage and hell shine in Jörg's eyes, bloodied streaks running down his face.

I seize Cameron's sleeve and bolt up the deck, elbowing people away. My boots slip on the blood, and I trip, but a rooted, wild instinct has taken over me and pushes me up.

Tumbling among other passengers and Cameron, I help myself on the handrail of the walkway between the superstructure and the second-class island. Over us, clouds of dark smoke freckled with embers fume to the open blue sky. The slate gray sea glides by, the ship plunging onward as if the crew had lost control over the rudder.

A bang blows specks of wood at my feet. The shot is drowned out by the releasing steam and the screams of the panicked crowd.

Jörg stands on the promenade corner, holding a gun.

"Fuck," Cameron shouts, covering me with his body. "Run."

Jörg shoots again.

Cameron and I jump behind a covered bench on the deck. Where's Mr. Becker?

A song of gunshots blares in the air, but the bullets don't shatter the bench, or the deck, and it's not only Jörg's revolver. As Cameron shoves me to the second-class deckhouse, my gaze falls on the first-class promenade. Jörg is aiming upward. At Ilse on the Navigation Deck. The glint of the sun catches on the revolver in her hand.

My heart leaps. Ilse is still alive. I'm almost happy.

A whirl down the second-class staircase, and I storm down two decks below onto the promenade on C-Deck, but the tilt is too steep. Cameron slips and falls on his side, dragging me down with him. The flip is quick, and it sends my stomach to my throat in the freefall.

I reach out to the floor.

"No," Cameron barks, capturing me with his free hand as we fall endlessly, uncontrollably, far from ledges or help. People jump away before we can knock them down. Soon, I understand why Cameron stopped me from touching the wood. With a slight graze of the floor, friction sears my exposed calf, a scorching pain opening my skin.

I scream, my voice reaching an octave higher when the end of the first-class promenade nears at breakneck speed. We meet the freezing, bubbly waters with a splash, my feet hitting the deck chairs with a loud crack from the wood. The blow stabs at my spine, and the salt burns my calf.

"Swim," Cameron shouts, paddling for the first-class doors.

From the upper part of the deck, a bullet dives into the water inches from me, a loud splash sputtering to the ceiling. Jörg stands atop the deck while people shriek and run away from him.

"Go," I yell at Cameron, treading desperately.

Jörg throws himself down the deck, sliding more gracefully than Cameron and me. Childish contempt wrinkles my nose; his cold-blooded elegance is insulting.

I wade after Cameron into the flooded hall, our waterlogged clothes dragging us down. The screams still come from the elevators, this time louder and more desperate. Water sloshes around the upper landing of the staircase.

"Stop," Jörg screams.

A bullet blows the water close to me, making me shriek. All my muscles scream in pain, exhaustion dragging every sluggish underwater step.

"Dive," Cameron screams. Then he submerges.

I follow him, breaking through the surface into the dark. Here, the world seems more peaceful. The engines, steam, and screams reach me from afar, and for a second I float idly, my hair and clothes ebbing weightlessly.

Shots go off, breaking the spell.

I paddle ahead, my elbow rubbing Cameron's every few strokes. How many bullets are in a revolver?

Something snatches at my dress.

I whirl, arms and legs slapping away, hitting objects underwater. My mouth opens in a bubbly scream to the face in front of me. Jörg.

His revolver goes off, a bang so loud it deafens me.

I must be alive, for my heart thumps like a hammer against heated metal, but it's hard to believe. My eyes creep open to the revolver. Now it's aimed at me. Jörg has missed the first time, but he won't again.

I slap the barrel away from me, then kick to the surface and emerge with a gasp, my lungs burning.

The hall is close to pitch dark; only slivers of light seep through the windows.

"Alexandra, thank God." Not far, Cameron plunges up and down out of the water.

"Don't come near me. Swim."

Jörg resurfaces with a splash, turning around as he searches for me, waving the revolver in every direction.

I lunge and grasp at the gun.

Cameron screams my name.

Jörg's eyes are vacant, his expression as lifeless, as though he were far away and his muscles were following an automated order. He jerks his arms, shoves me, shakes me, but I hold onto the gun. Jörg raises a fist, but I avert my cheek just in time, and his hand dips into the water.

Cameron lunges over him, dragging Jörg underwater. With the push, I'm also hurled beneath. It's swift, a glide down and up. I hit Jörg's chin with my shoulder as I emerge.

"Give me that gun, Valeria," he shouts and punches the water next to me, missing me by inches.

I swim back and kick his knee. He's seeing my *mother*. Not me. Is this his ultimate revenge? One thing is his mission for his country, but knowing what happened between him and my mother, I don't believe for one minute this isn't a personal matter. And I know . . . my death in Germany would've been slow. He would've made me beg for release.

Blood trickles from Jörg's hairline, washed-out stains running down his forehead. As he comes for me, I throw my knuckles onto the rawest part of the gash, landing with a solid thump.

Cameron grabs his head.

With a grunt, Jörg flinches and eases his grip on the gun. But before I can aim it his way, his elbow hits me squarely on the mouth and sends me into the water.

It's a contradiction, but fire can indeed survive water. Flames burn my skull, light flashing behind my shut eyes. In my stunned condition, my fingers weaken around the gun, and Jörg regains control of the handle.

I swallow water, my body trying to take air, and the unwelcome gulp of liquid down my gullet awakens me. My eyes shoot open. Jörg's dark profile blurs overhead, but the barrel is clearly aimed at me.

I don't want that to be the last thing I see. God, please. I want to close my eyes again, picture Cameron's smile.

I furrow my brow as a shadow drops on Jörg's head. He tumbles to the side and falls flat with a splatter next to me.

Cameron yanks at the tie of my blue dress and straightens me. I break out of the water with a gasp and vomit, salty nausea roiling through me.

The piece of wood Cameron used to knock out Jörg bobs away.

"Alix," Cameron says. "Are you all right?"

Jörg idles in the water, face beneath the surface.

I blink, my gaze fixed on him, how he moves, up and down. The water is tinting with dark crimson, swipes of blood staining the white ceiling.

The ceiling. The water is reaching the ceiling. And so are we.

I gasp, grabbing Cameron's hands. "We must get out of here. Where is the thermos?"

"In the staircase. I threw it one deck up."

In the murky hall, I wade with Cameron toward the staircase and dive to avoid the chairs bobbing together. I feel the tilted floor and follow the hard edges of each step.

For a second it's as though I've lost my way. The stairs seem to stretch out forever.

Oxygen in my lungs burns like a candle, but the water mercifully gives, revealing the dry parts of this sinking vessel. Unbolted objects tumble down and roll. But there it is, our thermos, resting against the wall. The water just inches from swallowing it.

Cameron snatches it while I clamber up the stairs with sodden clothes and hair plastered on my face, clawing onto the ornate railings.

The ship groans, and the water roars almost as if it were angry we've escaped its jaws. Outside, people keep shouting. And so do they from within the elevator.

A shiver lodges in my throat. But I can't scream.

We rush into the portside corridor. I trip over the linoleum and land flat on my stomach. The *Lusitania* is a funhouse of jagged edges that bite into my flesh and bones. Cameron helps me up, and nailing one foot on the wall and the other one on the floor, I advance with him in front of me.

I jump to save the gap between the corridors that cross to starboard. Hissing water waits below if I happened to plummet. What once were convenient passageways are now dark wells to a certain death.

"There's a door to the promenade," I wheeze, stopping Cameron.

"We're safer here." He pants. "It might be easier to reach the stern on the outside, but people might drag us down with them."

My chest is tight, and cramps knot my legs with every push upward. Behind, the gurgle of water reminds me that I can't stop to gasp for air. Exertion overwhelms me, and I find myself crying as we mercifully reach the end of the corridor. From there, we should turn left. Starboard and port converge into a passageway in the middle of the corridor. The problem is that said corridor has a steep fall of about eighteen feet.

"We must jump," Cameron says.

"We might break a bone," I counter. "We might even die. It's too great a fall."

He purses his lips, looking down. An idea strikes me. Water is rising faster on the starboard; we could wait until it reaches the corner.

I look back to measure where the water might be, and I scream, ramming into Cameron.

With the rising dark waters comes Jörg, slowly crawling to us with dark eyes and blood running down his temple.

"Jump when I tell you to," Cameron says, shoving the thermos into my hands.

He leaves my side without a warning.

I whip my head around. "Cameron, no."

With an arc, he plummets down the corridor. He lands arms first with a loud smack on the edge of the corner.

My hands clutch the flasket. "Cameron, are you all right?"

His feet seem to lose their grip. Cameron jerks down, and a scream dies in my throat. But at the last second, he secures the tip of his boots onto a molding and pushes himself across the archway and into the passageway.

He kneels, an arm tight around his abdomen.

"Are you hurt?" I cry out.

"It's just the blow," he yelps. All color has drained from his face. He stretches his arms out. "Throw the thermos, then jump to the aft wall and slide down. I'll catch you."

I look behind, and my blood drops to my feet. One swoop over the last corridor and Jörg will reach my spot.

With a jerk, I perch on the edge of the wall and throw the flasket in Cameron's direction.

Jörg tuts, moving a finger from side to side. "Do not even think about it, Alexandra."

"Watch me." I jump to the aft wall, and the blow bangs through my body. With a whimper, I slip down the molded walls, hitting myself at all the wrong angles, all the wrong places. My way down is a painful trip.

My nails scratch the white walls, leaving gray grooves along the surface as I attempt to slow down, and yell as I drop down the corridor.

But, mercifully, Cameron's arms catch me.

I land against his body with a thud, and we plunge flat into the passageway.

Cameron hits the wall with his back. With a grunt, he squeezes his eyes shut.

"Cameron," I utter.

"I'm all right," he groans, scrambling to a sitting position. Face still ashen, one of his eyes twitches. He says he's fine, but I know he's not. He's nursing his ribs with an arm while he slips the thermos under his shirt. My own body screams in stabbing pain, as though I were about to fall apart in tiny pieces. I can only imagine his pain, considering he's taken the brunt of our falls.

Jörg lands on the corner with a smack, making us jump and recoil. I gasp as he grabs a molding, but his fingers slip and he vanishes down the edge with a cry.

With shock-stricken eyes, Cameron and I stare after the empty archway. There goes Jörg. My parents died in fire and metal, and he dies in water and metal. It's almost poetic, how just it seems. The opposites, so strikingly different yet how mirroring they are.

"Go to hell," I grit through my teeth.

The tilt is almost impossible to sort, but I scramble to the open door aft, to the light of day. Under me, the ship shifts, slithers downward.

"She's plunging fast," I scream.

"Don't look back," Cameron bites with a murderous shout. "Onward."

I keep moving, looking at the light until it's blades in my eyes, blurring Cameron's skulking silhouette above me. The ship groans, breaks with strong blows; furniture bumps the walls, and glassware crashes against the floor. I can hear the wreck, the path of destruction grazing my heels.

On the promenade, people are holding onto the railings, both in second and first class. Under their life jackets, some of their clothes are ragged, faces bloodied and speckled by soot, and fear, it shines in every gaze I catch.

Following Cameron, I push myself around the corner, plopping with a groan onto the wall. We've made it out of those deadly corridors. The breeze cleansing my soot-filled lungs is a relief I never appreciated until today.

The bodies of those who jump overboard flicker as they drop to the water.

"What are we going to do?" I ask Cameron.

"We need to jump off the ship," he says, feral, *hoarse*. "If we stay aboard until the end, the suction will kill us."

He turns to portside.

I snag at his soggy sleeve. "It'll be easier for us to jump from starboard."

"No," he wheezes, a hand around his torso. "If she sinks too fast, she might crush us."

With a final lunge across the promenade on portside, Cameron and I grab the cold handrail. My boot slips, and my ankle twists at a strange angle. I straighten, ignoring everything but the sea, and climb the railings, swinging my legs outboard.

My chest shrinks at the unfurling sea in front of me. Not far to my left, the propellers protrude several stories in the air, a whirring blur going in endless circles.

"On three," Cameron says, holding my hand. "Don't let go. Landing will hurt. Try to enter the water with your feet first. When we're in, *kick*, kick as hard as you can against the current."

I nod. "One," I begin, my fingers squeezing Cameron's.

"Two." He tightens the grip. His eyes soften.

I love you, I want to say, but it's too late.

He casts a faint smile at me.

"Three," I say.

Cameron and I spring outward. Time stands still, the beautiful blue sky and calm slate gray waters making it difficult to believe I'm jumping off the *Lusitania*, yet the flip of my stomach draws me back into reality.

The drop is sudden, and I plunge into the sea with a splash. Pain shoots right up my spine, and cold shakes my body, stiffening my muscles.

I scream. Water slugs into my mouth.

The suction draws me to the ship, the enormous mass of the vessel going down fast behind us.

I kick, but my clothes are heavy and I'm tired. I kick as strongly as I can, as swiftly as I can, but I don't know where I'm heading, and beside me, Cameron's hand tugs mine in different directions, making us spin uncontrollably.

I've wasted too much oxygen with my scream underwater. My lungs are burning. I squint and find the streams of sunlight. Then I kick upward, thrashing away from the ship in a crazed race, nearly losing Cameron's hold.

Finally, my head breaks through the surface, and paddling against the waves, I take greedy gulps of air, the afternoon wind warm and sweet in contrast with the sea temperature.

Cameron embraces me and twirls us to the ship. The second-class deck-island of the *Lusitania* is disappearing under the sea, iron groaning like a mythical creature.

Cameron and I swim back, far from the ship, as she founders, gliding into her submarine tomb.

The aft mast and the Poop Deck vanish beneath the gray, swallowed under a circle of gurgling waters.

Chapter Thirty-Two

Soon after the *Lusitania* disappears under the waves, the ocean spits back the wreckage—oars, rafts, rope, chairs, bodies, and all kinds of panels. I stare after the water in shock until the foam dies down, as if nothing had been cruising across the sea just shy of an hour ago.

All around us, shouts rise to the sky.

When Cameron peels a strand of hair off my cheek, I crane my head around, my gaze studying him from hairline to chin. A small pool of blood stains one of his nostrils, and a trickle of crimson is smudged along his bruised cheek, the long gash still raw.

He puts a thumb to my lip, rousing a searing sting. "You're bleeding."

"Jörg elbowed me."

My lip trembles under his finger.

"We need to find the lifeboats," he says, paddling. "Let's swim—it'll keep us warm."

As my dazed state washes away, the immensity of the sea surrounds me. The waves are high, ebbing and flowing, closing in on me; the dark depths broaden under my feet, and I feel small. Too small.

As Cameron lets go of me to swim, I paddle, trying to keep my head above the water. Far away, the quiet green Irish lands have witnessed the tragedy. A rocky headland protrudes high and almighty, the hazy structure of a white lighthouse resting atop. Still, land, though visible to the naked eye, seems an unreachable dream.

Cameron and I whirl around every few seconds, but lifeboats are nowhere to be found. Oh, how ironic. All the fears the passengers had throughout the crossing have become real. The *Lusitania* now lies under the sea.

I can still imagine the submarine that has torpedoed us, gliding under our shoes like a hungry shark, its cold body caressing my calf like a feather.

I stop stroking. Did I imagine that? I turn to a dead body, lying face down in a uniform. *God.*

"I can't be here," I yell, kicking as hard as I can, getting away from the body.

The cool stabs me, and chills run through my body, making my lungs falter as though cracks were opening through them.

I flop underwater, but Cameron snatches me. "Hey, the ship's gone. But don't you dare follow her."

My teeth chatter, bewilderment shutting down my body. My head tilts back. The sky above stretches in blue, hollow, distant, and cold.

"Alix." Cameron shakes me. "Come, wrap your legs around my waist."

"No," I whisper.

"Nothing you didn't do last night."

I chuckle. I have no idea how he can make me laugh at a time like this. Last night seems so far, wrecked and spread in the wind.

"You'll drown," I say. He's been drugged, hit repeatedly, and by the way he winces and has nursed his lower chest, he's likely hurt his ribs. He must be more dazed than me.

He cups my cheek. "I won't."

"I can't. I'm too cold. My legs are numb."

"Then swim with me."

"The sea is too big, Cameron." And I'm too small.

The world frazzles at the edges, my arms and legs faltering, and I plunge underwater again, but Cameron brings me back to the surface.

"Alix, swim with me. One."

He drags me, pulling at my sleeve.

I move my legs in the ghost of a kick.

"Two."

Another kick.

"I can't," I moan, water slinking into my nose.

"You can," he barks. "And you will. Three."

One more kick. The cold numbs my body, but the exercise keeps me afloat and not dead from the neck down. Cameron counts to fifty. Fifty excruciating kicks that make my muscles scream.

At once, he comes to a dead halt. Afraid he's hurting, I open my eyes to his profile swimming away.

"Cameron," I say.

"Keep kicking!"

He swims to a teak chair and drags it back, mouth flattened into a line. I grab it with numb fingers. Near us, debris bobs by—wood, chairs, all kinds of wreckage, and *bodies*. Torn bodies of all shapes and sizes. The air is filled with hundreds of frantic, panicky yowls. Waving arms rise in agonizing efforts to keep afloat, gaping mouths plunging up and down in the water.

I sob and close my eyes. "Where are the lifeboats?"

"They must be somewhere."

The current brings a group of survivors fighting each other. In the distance, under the abrasive white sun, Ireland remains silent, indifferent to the cries for mercy. Has not anyone seen us? Have they not heard the explosions? My ears still buzz. I'm grateful I've not gone deaf.

I squint at the horizon. It seems as if I could distinguish the shape of lifeboats, but soon enough the image gets swept away by the rolling sparkling waves. Instead, the brawl drifts near us.

A man strokes toward us, his eyes fixated on the teak chair.

I gasp.

"Swim," Cameron hisses.

With faltering tingly limbs, I shove our teak chair, the sea lapping against me as though an invisible force were cruising among us, swelling the waters in its wake.

Cameron stops, clutching the teak chair with red fingers. "We're good here."

The man is no longer in sight, and the shouts have weakened. The only sound is the caws of gulls overhead.

"Do you think Ilse, Mr. Becker, or Carlton made it?" I blurt and freeze, my eyes widening. Not even my heart dares to beat. I didn't foresee the way losing any of them would punch me in the gut, cutting my breath short.

Cameron's voice shakes, "I don't know."

"Do you still have the flask under your clothes?"

He nods. "It's still there."

I keep kicking, but my fingers are too cold to cleave onto the chair. They shake, and my shoulders give. Cameron puts his hands over mine and holds tight. Under the remains of soot, Cameron's trembling lips are whitening. He's trying to be the strongest party here, but I can't let him carry that weight alone.

"Tell me something," I whisper so my teeth don't chatter.

"Whatever you want."

"Did you leave the note and the photograph of the real testament in my parents' townhouse?"

He shakes his head. "It was a spy on their team. The one who gave me that photograph of your parents and me. You saw his name in the other photographs. Joseph Wright. He contacted me but refused to give me any more information. I didn't know what he wanted to give you until I saw it."

I kick, rolling myself up onto the chair until I'm resting on it. "I'm sorry for this morning."

"No. I should've told you from the very beginning. We should've trusted you with that information." He brushes my cheek with a numb caress. "I promise I'll make up for every lie."

"You better," I tease, and he bites back a smile.

Cameron and I ward off the hypothermia by swimming around the wreckage, switching spots on the deckchair, no longer bothering to hide our chattering teeth.

"Where's the help?" I clatter. My mouth is parched, and the sun burns my skin, colored lights dancing on the edges of my vision. If the icy waters don't kill us, exposure will. "The *Lusitania* must've sent out distress signals before going down."

Cameron huffs, squinting at the empty horizon. "They must be somewhere. Let's switch again."

Underwater, my feet must be still in my boots, my skirt tangling around my legs, my stockings rolled around my ankles, but I can only feel ice, seeping into my bones.

"Alix," Cameron rasps.

I turn to him, sinking an elbow in the frame of the deckchair. "Yes?"

"They'll come back for us."

It sounds like a promise, but a shadow crosses him, a crack of doubt in his disguise of confidence.

I press my teeth together, a sliver of fear hollowing me out of hope. Still, I nod, because we must *lie* to each other. "They'll come back. They won't repeat the same mistakes from the *Titanic*."

"Right on," Cameron stutters. The ghost of a smile lifts his cheek.

We know they will come back at some point, but the sea might kill us sooner. In our faces, we both see it—this might be the end.

As if fate wanted to prove us right, the wails begin to die out, first in intermittent breaks; then a sudden silence washes over us. Laying my head on the chair, I track the numerous bodies floating by. Most of them are dead, eyes open to the sky. Some are still alive but mentally gone, nattering incoherently like thread and needle trying to stitch threadbare fabric together.

We wait and abandon our attempts at conversation. Cameron rests his head next to mine, his nose buried in my hair. He gives me a slight, tender brush; then . . . he doesn't move again. And my eyes . . . they start blinking too often, until they don't open again.

I know what it means, but I am too far gone to feel anything. No fear, no sadness . . . only surrender. Acceptance.

Help won't come. Humanity doesn't exist in wartime.

"I can't do this anymore, Cam," I mumble. My stubborn rigid fingers clutch onto the grooves of the chair, but my arms ache, my veins becoming chilly needles.

"Just a bit longer," he replies, but his voice is as sleepy as mine.

"I love you," I whisper, but Cameron only harrumphs.

Elijah and Lindsay flash through my mind, my parents. Smiles, hands wrapping mine, music, laughter, my parents' voices coming from the kitchen early in the morning . . . Without any more fight in me, I slip from Cameron. My nose goes beneath the surface, the waters closing over me forever.

A very remote part of me finds solace in death.

I'll see my parents again.

An upward tug shoots my eyes open.

"Not today," Mr. Becker says.

A man in uniform is grabbing Cameron on the other side, hoisting him up by the shoulders into a lifeboat.

I crane my neck up.

Mr. Becker winces as he sits me next to him. His clothes are drenched, his blond locks wavy behind his ears. "Alexandra, say something. Are you with me?"

"You're alive," I whisper, my head lolling on his shoulder.

"Of course," he says, all nonchalance. "I'm hard to kill."

Someone gives him a dry blanket, and awkwardly, Mr. Becker wraps me in it. Between hazy blinks, I take in his jacket's red-stained sleeve, the fresh wound on his forehead, and the growing bruising on his jaw and around his eye. The outcome of his fight with Jörg.

"Where's Cam?"

"He's in front of us," Mr. Becker says, turning my head.

If my muscles could spasm, I would flinch.

Cameron looks a pale hue of blue, and I'm sure I do as well. An officer is propping him up, putting a blanket on his shoulders, trying to make him talk. He mumbles, seems coherent enough to function.

"Let me go with him," I whisper.

Nobody says anything. Mr. Becker moves to Cameron's spot, and the officers sit Cameron with me. Once I'm curled against him, I doze off.

In shivering waking moments, my eyes blink open, only to quickly snap shut once more, the world losing all sense of time, stretching out in the endless ticks of a clock. At some point, I wake up in Cameron's arms, my legs hanging over his lap. His fingers are pressed on the side of my neck.

"See anything, Officer Jones?" Mr. Becker asks, not far away.

"Not yet." I know the inflection in the officer's voice, despair.

"When are those momes coming?"

"They might fear the U-boats."

"You're here," I whisper into the crook of Cameron's neck, emotions tumbling in my chest. I was a second away from letting myself stay under the gray surface, losing him forever.

He squeezes me.

I blink and grab his blanket, my heart leaping. I thought he was sleeping.

"I am," he whispers. "Keep sleeping; help will be here any moment now."

"Liar."

He chuckles just enough to move his chest.

I curl with Cameron the rest of the afternoon, too astonished to talk, too cold to move, listening to the wooden groans of our lifeboat. The watery sun doesn't warm our clothes, which stick to me in a chilly embrace. I choke up when I try to say anything. Too tired, I'm only able to obsessively spin around what I've gone through since January. My mind replays the sinking, Jörg, Professor Brodrick, Ilse. The crossing. Mrs. Bartlett. Professor

Holbourn. Captain Turner. Staff Captain Anderson. Mr. Vanderbilt. Miss Avis. Wondering who survived. Wondering who perished. I envision the photographs, the books, the clothes. All entombed within the walls of the *Lusitania* in the depths of this dark sea.

I've lost it all.

Except Cameron.

Except my unconditional right to my fortune and my father's respect. The two trapped in a thermos at our feet.

Seagulls caw over us, and waves lap at the hull of the lifeboat. The headland, which I've come to learn is the Old Head of Kinsale, stands passively behind our bobbing little lifeboat. My gaze studies the horizon blankly, expecting the faraway murmur of ships approaching us . . . yet finding nothing.

The officer and the two able seamen accompanying us and the other survivors—five women, two children, seven men—pull two more people from the water alive, but they have to let more corpses drift away than they rescue survivors, and every time they pull up a dead person, they square their jaws while tracing a cross on their foreheads. Then, they release them into the sea. Some of them let a tear or two roll down their cheeks, which they quickly tick away.

The sun moves through the sky, and by the time it starts diving behind the rolling lands of Ireland, bleeding over the green hills, the first signs of smoke billow on the horizon.

Cheers and hoots erupt from the lifeboats at the first spark of life in hours around the shipwreck. The officer ignites a hand flare and waves it in the air, standing tall on the lifeboat bow. As I swing myself straight, the waters around us open up, gray and ebbing, full of wreckage, bodies, and sprinkled lifeboats, illuminated by the twilight and flickering red flares.

A series of fishing boats arrive and circle the area. My chest shrinks for a long while, fearing an explosion might strike our salvation, but a faint smile moves on my lips as a trawler, the *Julia*, comes into sight next to us.

Chapter Thirty-Three

The scent on the *Julia* is pungent—fish, vinegar, and coal, and the floor is aseptically cold. But the crew finds us a spot in the main room around the stove, and nobody quirks a judgmental eyebrow as Cameron and I strip off our wet clothes, lay them down with others in front of the stove, and curl around each other in our underthings beneath the pools of four blankets.

Cameron strokes my back reassuringly for an hour, but still all the things I want to say die on the tip of my tongue. Swallowing a lump, I prop my chin on Cameron's shoulder and stay still as the crew of the *Julia* toils around us, the trawler's loud engines rumbling beneath us, taking us back to land.

A woman loses her cool, screaming and punching the floor. Her husband, I catch in a conversation, is lying dead on the deck. Tears should come to my unmoving eyes, but I'm paralyzed, trapped in the nothingness. I blink and flick over to two silent children standing like tiny statues next to the stove, blankets falling off their shoulders like cloaks.

A man coughs, curling around his blanket in a corner, and closes his eyes. I doubt I'll ever be able to rest again. Will he? Those horrified faces from the elevator; Jörg's maddened features; the dead bodies, hopelessly drifting away; the ship's groans—they'll never leave me.

A cup appears in front of me.

"Drink, you two," Mr. Becker says.

I force my muscles away from Cameron, my knee hitting the flask lying next to us. At least a hint of warmth has crept inside my numb body, and I don't want to leave his arms.

"What's that?" I croak, my airways hoarse.

"Lemonade," he says. "And I've also nabbed some biscuits."

"Thank you," Cameron whispers. He untangles our limbs, a smidge of pain flickering in a jaw twitch.

I shiver as I curl by myself under the blankets, sipping the lemonade sheepishly.

"What happened to you?" Cameron asks Adam. "We thought you'd been shot."

"I'm not that easy to kill. Thank you for the vote of confidence, you two. Long story short, Jörg and I fought. *I* stole one of his guns and shot. I ran to the bridge. I didn't find you there, so I searched for you among the chaos, but the sea washed me away. I was picked up by a lifeboat. Is Jörg . . . ?"

"Dead." I nod. "I think he is."

"He went down with the ship," Cameron says.

Mr. Becker frowns. "Did you see Ilse?"

I tell him about the last time I saw her, shooting from the Navigation Deck. "We never saw her again. I'm sorry, Mr. Becker."

"All right. Fine." He clears his throat, lowering his head. "You'd better call me Adam if we want to pass for cousins. Let's set some matters straight. This is not over. I'll call my contact at the Admiralty to let them know we've all survived. The Admiralty will procure us transportation to Liverpool. It'll be shorter than whatever other contacts you two have."

"I'll also tip off the others back home," Cameron says.

They start chattering over plans, two spies at play. It's hard to understand how they can get along this well, as if they weren't standing on different ends of this war a week ago, but it's probably my own distrust distorting my judgment.

Clenching my teeth, I grab the thermos and screw it open with a twist of my wrist.

My breath hitches when water leaks through the grooves of the art pad. I pry it out of the flask, the oilskin slowly uncoiling in my hand. It's wet, trickles pooling on the tanned surface.

"Oh no, what if it's ruined?" I whisper, tugging it open. But inside, the photographs, the list, the documents, and Professor Brodrick's drawings beneath it all are intact. The air returns to my lungs. My exhausted, aching lungs.

But just as relief fills my chest, tears also brim in my eyes. And it dawns on me that I'll never be ready. Not to admit that my parents are irrevocably dead. That my life has changed forever. That now I'm a target in a war I never wanted to partake in.

Cameron soothes circles on my back over my blanket. I don't find the strength to keep myself together anymore. When Cameron curls an arm around my waist and nudges me in for a hug, I close my eyes and sob.

It's almost midnight when we approach Queenstown Harbor. The lights flicker calmly on the water while gaslit streets run through the hills. On the quayside, a tumultuous crowd awaits the rescue ships.

Mr. Becker—*Adam*—Cameron, and I thank the crew of the *Julia* and disembark, Cameron helping me walk while nursing his torso with his free arm. I remember I twisted my ankle during the sinking, and now a muted pain builds up in my foot whenever I stand.

It's barely been a week since I left New York, but it feels an eternity away, as if I closed my eyes upon boarding the *Lusitania* and now I opened them to a new, numb world.

We're led to the Cunard building among a pressing swarm of Irish journalists and locals to give our names and report any deceased family members. My lips tremble as I try to say Jörg Müller, but Adam states it with uncomplicated resolution next to me.

But when it comes to saying his name to the officer, he locks eyes with me. As though he's asking me for permission. One last time. Before we jump into yet another dangerous lie.

I nod, too tired to even mind. Now, all I can play is this inheritance of lies. We had a deal. And when push came to shove, he fought Jörg.

He's chosen a side. And it's mine and Cameron's.

"Adam Benson." The name rolls off his tongue, like the good liar he is. "I'd like to send a telegram to Liverpool."

"Another one to New York," Cameron says.

"And another one to Paris," Ilse says.

I turn with a gasp, my hands closing over the thermos.

Ilse stands next to me, long brunette curls falling over her shoulders. Ashen and shivery, she's wrapped in a blanket she holds shut in one hand over her neck. Her left arm peeks out through the gap in the blanket, bandaged and in a fabric sling.

"Ilse, you're alive," I whisper, wondering if I should hug her, if I should stay away.

But my fake cousin makes the decision for me. Adam's arms fall around her as he whispers, "Gott sei Dank" way too low for anyone else to hear but me.

Relief settles through my body in ways that feel off, like a murmur. Then, my heart stutters, whispering that I'm betraying my parents. That I'm stunned. That my feelings are wrong. That once the shock of the sinking eases, I'll hate these two spies again.

I recoil, my ankle screaming in pain, and ram into Cameron while he states our names for the survivor records.

He slides a hand over my shoulders and ushers me between the pressed bodies. "Are you all right?" he asks, sitting me down on a crate.

I shake my head.

As we wait for the doctors to call our names, my stare wanders through the crowded building, looking for more faces to recognize. Miss Avis ambles past me, ushered forward by an officer. I smile, happy a familiar face has made it. I search for Professor Holbourn, Professor

Brodrick, Mrs. Bartlett, or Mr. Vanderbilt, but the room is a moving crowd of empty, unfamiliar faces.

Sobs and happy screams fight to stand out in the murmurs. At the gates, people hug, joyful grins appearing on sad faces.

The longer we wait, the more the glimmer of hope in Cameron's eyes fades.

I know who he expects to see. Carlton.

But Carlton doesn't show up.

And with that, I feel as though that spark of hope dies in me as well.

I drag Cameron into a hug.

"People are still being picked up," I say in his ear, if only to make him feel better. I shouldn't stoke his hope. Hope is as dangerous as love. But after what we've gone through, I need to protect his heart.

He nods on my shoulder, his arms pulling me closer. "Yes, he's probably fine. He's a clever man." He breathes in and out, and grunts at the back of his throat.

"Does your chest hurt?"

"Every single breath."

I pull away enough to cup his face, rub my thumbs on his cheeks. Cameron's gaze roves my face, a clouded ocean blue, like the depths of the sea, as if he were left with the *Lusitania.* I know what he must be seeing, what I caught in a mirror before we left our trawler behind. A shipwreck survivor. My soot-stained features, my frizzy curled hair, my wounded lip. My dress is wrinkled and dirty, and the stench of vinegar and fish has followed me just the way it's followed him.

But that's not where I want him to be. Not with the depth of the ocean. "Stay with me, Cameron."

Despite it all, despite the grief and darkness in his eyes, Cameron smiles. A small, soft tilt.

"What is it?" I wonder.

"I think you might be in love with me, Miss Benson."

I squeeze his face. "I thought that was already settled."

Cracking a faint smile, he steals a quick peck from my lips and rests his forehead against mine. "I wonder whether your parents are up in the heavens shaking their heads in disbelief or smiling."

"Why?"

He chuckles. The sound is low and solemn, almost a breath, but it's there. "They never wanted me to be with you. I'm sure they were scared I'd ruin you. Your father was quite categorical when he noticed you were catching my eye. *She's off limits, kiddo.* Literal words. A smack on my nape included. And here we are, you and I, engaged to be married."

Soft laughter escapes through my nose. That matches my father. My memories of him. "He'd find humor in the irony and laugh and bring you in for a hug to welcome you into the family." I pull Cameron away, look into his eyes. He will now be the only connection I have with my parents. "Will you do me a favor?"

"Anything you want," he says. "Name it, and it's yours."

"Tell me about my parents. The version of my parents that you knew. You'll always be the only thing I have left of them. Let me marry your memories and my memories. So I can fully know who they were."

A glimmer of love and a shadow of compassion flash in his eyes. Cameron leans forward, but when I think he'll kiss me, he rubs the tip of my nose with his, and whispers, "What do you want to know first?"

Chapter Thirty-Four

July 2, 1915
Southport, England

Swans glide by in the calm waters of Marine Lake as a soft summer breeze ruffles the leaves of nearby aquatic bushes. Across from me, Southport stretches with the lush King's Gardens and the town's intricate rooftops.

I take a deep breath. The Admiralty insisted Southport was just what I needed—a fun, breezy seaside resort city, full of life and long days on the beach, but sometimes all I can hear are screams where there's laughter and shots where only champagne is being popped open. It's hard to conceive of the warm sunlight caressing my skin, giving it a shade of light cinnamon, health slowly coming back to me.

I close my eyes, caressing the diamond ring Cameron bought for me straight out of his own savings.

"Is the spot beside you available?" Cameron asks, imitating a crossover between a scouse accent and Received Pronunciation.

I crane my neck up. He stands in a white summer jacket and shirt and light-brown trousers, and smiles at me under the brim of his white hat, his handsome face already healed from all his wounds.

Pleasureland, Southport's amusement park, brims with laughter and music behind us. One of the few that have remained open during the war.

"That accent was atrocious," I say.

"I'm learning," he says, grinning. "Don't be mean."

I wince, because the reason I don't like overdone accents isn't Cameron's adorable attempts but rather Jörg's fault. "Sit by my side, please."

Cameron takes a seat on the rocks next to me.

"But don't dare splash water at me," I warn him, lifting a finger.

"I would never," he says with a hint of pretended indignation. "But now I can do this without worrying."

He cups my cheeks, tilting my head, and ducks under the brim of my wide hat to melt his lips against mine. His tongue caresses mine, sending a swarm of butterflies down my belly, and keeps kissing my lips until I'm out of breath.

"Hello, Wife," he whispers.

I smile. "Hello, Husband."

His wedding band catches the sunlight. I've still not settled into Cameron being my husband. Two months ago, as I boarded the *Lusitania*, I didn't expect to marry him for love. I didn't expect him to stay. Yet he waited for me at the altar only two weeks ago. Cameron promised in front of God that he'll never leave me.

For the entire month of May, I had to heal from dehydration, sunburn, a ravaging pneumonia that had me bedridden for two weeks with high fevers, a sprained ankle, and the trauma. Cameron had to overcome flu, sunburn, a broken rib, and his own set of dark memories, which he's still battling. He often wakes up in the middle of the night, welling eyes and sharp breaths, feeling he'll drown.

Memories from the shipwreck barge into me. The ghostly, terrified faces of those I let drown in the elevator on the *Lusitania* and the plunging feeling of the sinking ship. I squeeze my eyes shut and shake my head, trying to shoo the images away.

Cameron shushes with a sweet tone and grazes my lips with his. "It's all right. Breathe. Here, I am here."

He plays strong, but he's still haunted by Carlton's death aboard the *Lusitania*. I often catch him staring at his friend's drawings, the ones we saved from the sinking. I'm still haunted by Carlton's and Alfred Vanderbilt's passing. Some things, we'll never forget, will always haunt us.

"Did Ilse tell you where to find me?" I ask. I left Cameron sleeping in after yet another bad night. Ilse stayed back, guarding the hotel. And Adam trailed after me.

"I know this seems like her doing, but I found you on my own," Cameron murmurs on my forehead, which he kisses. "Remember I am also a spy."

I tap at his chest. "How can I forget?" Now, living with Cameron is where I see all his quirks in full display. The way he seems to read my mind or have eyes in the walls. Does something fall? Cameron is already there, stopping it an inch before it touches the ground. He knows his way even in places he's never been before. Just like my parents, he doesn't know what leisure is. Even when he seems busy or deep in thought, I know he's got ears and eyes everywhere, his attention divided, reading me as much as he reads his surroundings. "I'm not sure how much I like the idea of keeping Adam and Ilse around during our honeymoon. I'll be safe with you."

London, the White Cliffs of Dover, Whitby, the Isle of Wight, Plymouth, Cornwall and Devon, Manchester, Wales, Edinburgh, and many quaint towns along the way . . . we're touring the entire island. We call it our honeymoon, but in reality, it's the Admiralty's orders. We can't stay for long in the same place until the war ends.

Cameron grabs my hand and kisses its back. "You'll always be safe with me. But keeping them around lets me give you all of me. Lets me give you my vulnerability. The real me. Not only the spy."

I smile. "And it turns out I really like the real you."

"You do, hmm?" He kisses me once again; then he lets out a sigh. "Look at it this way, we know them. If they weren't there, we'd still have the odd officer revolving around us." He winks. "I thought you were growing fond of them?"

I crane my neck to Adam. He's been reading his boring newspapers and a bit from *The Phantom of the Opera* on a bench not too far from me. Once they healed, he and Ilse rapidly grew used to their work at the Admiralty—protecting us, like they promised. Sometimes, I still wonder if they're human enough. If they're also as haunted as I am. Or if it's only that they've had more time to make friends with their demons.

If I will make friends with my own, in due time.

"And I am. But Adam still makes me feel as though I kept a predator as a pet."

"Fair. And knowing him, he would agree." Cameron chuckles and jerks his chin forward. "What about Ilse over there?"

My gaze browses the park. It takes me a moment to locate her across the lake, twirling a parasol on her shoulder as she walks down the promenade in a lacy white dress. To an outward eye, she looks like a young woman having a pleasant stroll, but I've come to know her and Adam all too well these weeks. They're aware of their surroundings, as much as Cameron is.

"Ilse feels like a mermaid," I say. "Beautiful but lethal. But she's a good kind of danger to keep around."

I won't admit it, but she's slowly becoming the sister I never had. These months, I've prayed much—in shame, in guilt, in anger. I've talked to my parents and God. I've asked for guidance. I've asked for forgiveness. I've reproached myself. I've begged to find peace. I've asked to feel hatred. And guilt. And sadness. But my parents, wherever they are, must be determined to keep me happy. I know they'd say there's a reason these two madcaps are in my life, even if I can't see why. That they're happy Cameron is taking care of me in their absence. Giving me the love I deserve. He's working relentlessly to provide me with a joyful life and make up for the lies, and he is showing he'll fight for my forgiveness and my love until his dying breath.

And so, no matter how relentlessly I seek the darkness, the darkness is always faster than me. Out of reach.

Cameron looks at the sky. "We'll probably keep them and the Admiralty around for as long as the war lasts. But let's forget about them for a moment. The war will end one day. And this is our life. How do you want to live it? What are your dreams, Alix?"

I bite my lip, tracing all the plans and pathways ahead. No one can bring my parents back, no one can change the wrongdoings of the past, but things are righting themselves. In New York, Mr. Tannenbaum has been jailed. My father's will has been contested, and Mr. Miller, my lawyer now, has been working overnight for weeks with the Admiralty. My parents' townhouse and the belongings Jörg sold have been rightfully returned to me and are patiently waiting all boxed up in trunks for the moment I come back. Elijah and Lindsay fully know what happened and have already told me they'll travel this autumn to meet me, wherever Cameron and I wind up. I have memories, photographs. And my husband.

He's right. Our lives are just beginning. And they're all ours. No matter the circumstances. We'll be moving often. But it'll be an opportunity to create something. Travel and see the world. Meet people. Decide where our destiny is. What we make of fate.

"For now," I say, "I think life is hell-bent on making me fall in love with England."

"I have the feeling England will charm you faster than I did, Fake Addie." Cameron winks, pulling a wrapper out of his pocket. When he opens his hand, the wrapper falls away, unveiling glistening iced bonbons, already soft in the summer heat.

I take one of them and let it melt on my tongue. There's a certain melancholy in the air of this island that I've come to enjoy—it's as if it told me my pain is valid and I'm allowed to feel it, that it will hold my hand in the silence. But I couldn't dislike this place even if I wanted to. I'm not morally allowed to disregard any form of home now, when so many on the *Lusitania* cannot experience life anymore. When so many are dying in the war.

And I shouldn't forget—this was my parents' home. Where their lives began. Where their love story blossomed. Here, I feel closer to them. Thanks to Cameron, I've been learning new things. Meeting their souls through him.

"That's hard to beat," I admit. "You charmed me quite quickly."

Cameron pops a bonbon into his mouth, a gloating smirk tugging at his cheek. "Let's go to the park. I want to ride the rollercoaster." He jumps to his feet. "Then we'll have a long walk on the beach and dinner, the two of us alone."

He stretches out his hand for me.

With a smile, I take it and leap to my feet.

"I'll never get bored with you, will I?" I say, sticking the last bonbon in his mouth.

He smiles at me. "Never, love."

Cameron spins me around, toward the amusement park and the rest of our lives.

Acknowledgments

For a long year as I wrote and edited this book, Alexandra and Cameron were all I could think about. They were with me through high and low and thick and thin. So, they're the first ones I should thank. Thank you, Alix and Cameron, for choosing me to tell your story. I'm honored to know you.

Thank you to Christine Goss. Thank you for your hard work selling this story, giving it its beautiful title, and making my dream come true.

Thank you to Elizabeth Agyemang, my wonderful acquisitions editor, who loves this book, understood it through and through, and was always there every step of the way. I could never have done this without you.

Thank you to Jon Reyes, my great developmental editor. Your hard work and notes were amazing. Thank you for the sharp insight you brought into this story.

Thank you to my copyeditor, Alicia Lea, for your exquisite attention to detail and saving me from several historical inaccuracies. Same for my proofreader, Cortni Merritt. You've both saved me big time.

Thank you to my lovely team at Lake Union—my production manager Angela Elson, my art director Tree Abraham, my cover artist Spencer Fuller, my marketing manager Brittany Morris, and cold reader, Will Fairless, and so many others behind the scenes. All great professionals who made this book better and made this journey to publication smooth sailing.

Thank you for helping me make this story a reality. Thank you to the amazing contributors from the Lusitania Resource (especially the sections headed "Passengers & Crew" and "Facts & History"), Vintage Dancer, and Oceanliner Designs for their wonderful job of bringing the sinking of the *Lusitania* and other historical events as well as clothing and places to life. You've been of great help in my endless hours of research.

I can't forget about my writing friends.

K.L. Brandt, my dear friend. We've been reading each other forever, and we've seen each other grow. Your talent and friendship have helped me evolve as a writer and as a person.

Jean-Maré Gagliardi. What to say? Your friendship is invaluable. Your talent is beyond this world. And I love that I can call you my friend. See you on our future book tours, and let's hang out in NYC! I'm manifesting.

Megan Shunmugan, bestie! We have been together through the querying trenches and got agents almost at the same time, and we're debuting the same year! Looking forward to sharing many more eight-minute voice notes with you.

Thank you to the first readers who helped me get this book in shape: Kiara Mars, Holly Riddle, and Lumen.

I can't forget other friends who, while not involved in this book, also helped me get here.

Sebastian D. P. Hidalgo, a soul friend if I ever met one. I'm so glad you're on this path with me. Always ready to listen and always ready to support.

Many, many other friends! Laetitia Beck, Sophia Vahdati. Taylor Grothe, Danai Christopolous, Maria Tureaud, Rebecca F. Kenney, Sarah Amalima. Taylor Epperson, Grace Morrow, Grace Viall, Sarah L. Hawthorne, and Amalie Frederiksen. Jaimie Hunter, Sarah Dorko, Belinda Grant, Susan Waters, Maia Strong, Laura Kohler, and Debbie Exton. Karla Gaudier, Avery Hart, Dabbie at Occult Hours, and Montse Madariaga.

The talented authors in the 2026 Debut Discord! Thanks for being there and for your support.

Thank you, reader. For being part of my journey. Hopefully you enjoyed this book as much as I enjoyed writing it.

I want to thank myself, for never giving up, for being stubborn, and for believing in myself and the beauty of my dreams even when no one else did. For seeing the vision and never ever stopping walking toward it.

Thank you to my spiritual guides and my soul family.

Thank you, Mom and Dad, for giving me life. Dad, thank you for teaching me your love for the written word. Mom, thank you for supporting me.

Thank you, God and the universe, for this blessing. For this life. For my dream career.

And last but not least, John. The love of my existence. I'll never get tired of exploring every facet of you in my books. Every man I write is a small fraction of you, including Cameron. To be loved is to be seen, and hopefully my books show you how much I love you. You were the first person I ever told I wanted to write, and you supported me with all your heart and all your open curiosity and playful, childlike wonder. Wherever existence takes us, know that you'll forever be my muse and you'll always be my greatest blessing. Thank you for loving me and always being on my side.

About the Author

Rebecca A. Carter is an author, editor, singer, and actress currently living in Madrid, Spain. A bilingual speaker of English and Spanish, she writes spellbinding fiction for young adults and adults. Her work ranges from historical, dystopian, and speculative fiction to fantasy, romance, and mystery, as well as lyrical prose. When she's not writing or editing, you can usually find Rebecca singing or working on a film. In her free time, she loves to dance, twirl the baton, and play guitar. She dreams of moving to London or Paris one day.